ALSO BY A. J. HARTLEY:

Beyond the Mirror Series
Monsters in the Mirror
The Mirroculist Mission
The Mirrors Shattered *(Coming 2020)*

FOR OLDER READERS

The Ghostly Chronicles of Preston Oldcorn
Cold Bath Street
Written Stone Lane

The Steeplejack Saga
Steeplejack
Firebrand
Guardian

The Hawthorne Saga
Act of Will
Will Power
The Cerulean Stone *(short story)*
The Slave Trader's Wedding *(short story)*
Cathedrals of Glass: A Planet of Blood and Ice

Co-authored with Tom DeLonge:
Sekret Machines: Chasing Shadows
Sekret Machines: A Fire Within

FOR ADULTS

What Time Devours
Lies that Bind Us
Tears of the Jaguar
On the Fifth Day
The Mask of Atreus
Macbeth: A Novel
The Woman in Our House

A. J. HARTLEY

The MIRROCULIST MISSION

Illustrated by Manuel Šumberac

uclanpublishing

The Mirroculist Mission is a uclanpublishing book

First published in Great Britain in 2019 by
uclanpublishing
University of Central Lancashire
Preston, PR1 2HE, UK

First published in the USA in 2012 by Razorbill an imprint of
Penguin Group (USA) Inc. as *Darwen Arkwright and the Insidious Bleck*

978-1-9129790-2-8

1 3 5 7 9 10 8 6 4 2

Set in 10/16pt Kingfisher

A CIP catalogue record for this book is available from the British Library.

Printed and bound in Great Britain by Clays Ltd, Elcograf S.p.A.

For Finie and Sebastian

Cast of Characters

DARWEN

ALEX

RIK

MR PEREGRINE

NATHAN, CHIP & BARRY

AUNT HONORIA

MOTH

WEAZEN

SCARLETT
OPERTUNE

JORGE

GABRIEL

Contents

The Mirroculist Mission

One
TAKEN

Darwen Sebastian Arkwright looked around, delighted by his first glimpse of Silbrica in weeks. He walked away from the portal, past a rainbow-coloured waterfall – which strobed first turquoise, then emerald green, then a yellow bright as liquid gold – and onto the over-grown track. He forced himself to look for signs of gnashers and listen for the roar of distant scrobbler engines, but he doubted either would be found here. It felt safe.

As Darwen pressed further into the forest, strange lemon-coloured plants with stems like columns and slick, funnel-like tops grew up close around him. A startled animal, no larger than a field mouse but with a snout almost as long as its body and fur that was tiger-striped green and yellow like grass, looked up from drinking at the funnel flowers, then slid effortlessly down the stalk and off along the path. The track wound right, then left, then right again, so that even when he turned to look back the way he had come, Darwen could see nothing but a thicket of the bizarre vase-like plants shifting fractionally in the breeze. Above these towered trees with smooth black bark and blue, fringed leaves long as coffee tables which reduced the world below to twilight. Somewhere in the distance he heard a bird or animal call, a strange, wild sound unlike anything he had ever heard before.

I should go back, he thought, knowing he wouldn't, not after weeks without access to a mirror through which he could cross into Silbrica.

Following the greenish mouse-creature, he took another few steps, and just as it looked like the track would peter out entirely,

he saw something ahead. A gate, made of crystalline rock, but not
built from pieces fastened together or even carved. It looked like
it had somehow grown out of the forest floor, eroded out of the
surrounding rock by centuries of wind or rushing water. It had to
be a portal to another part of Silbrica, what they called a locus.
The gate was hung with twining vines, one of which held a bright
white flower like an open hand, palm uppermost. Darwen peered
at it and saw, just beneath, a button set into the sparkling stone.
His hand reached, then hesitated.

Probably doesn't work, he thought.

It looked disused and forgotten. The stone was beautiful,
veined like marble but translucent as heavy, hand blown glass. He
could see his hand through it when he reached behind – without
really thinking about it, and pushed the button once.

Nothing happened.

Darwen waited, but there was no sound, no rush of steam.

I knew it, he thought. *Broken.*

His sense of imminent adventure faded and the forest felt
strangely dark and brooding. He turned and began cautiously
retracing his steps, suddenly keen to get back into the open,
alarming the tiny striped animal so that it scampered into the
undergrowth and vanished. And then the plants ahead of him
seemed to flicker. A yellowish light was playing softly over the
strange leaves and on his own coffee-coloured skin.

Darwen turned.

The portal had come to life. It wasn't the silvery light he had
seen in other Silbrican portals, but a pale gold, amber at the centre.

Darwen ran an unsteady hand through the tight curl of his hair. The gate would only stay open for a moment . . .

He ran towards it, leaping in without so much as a pause.

Everything happened very fast.

He found himself sprawled in a darkness so complete that for a second he thought he had been swallowed up by the Shade monster which surrounded its victims in empty blackness. Then there was a bright, flickering light and Darwen could see. The ground was dirt and strewn with leaves but there was a massive contraption that looked like it had been frozen in the act of emerging from the ground. It appeared to be an armoured bulldozer covered with clumsy pipes and boilers. The light came from behind it, but the machine itself was black, silent and clearly inoperable. The air felt humid as the jungle he had just left, and the smells were similar. But it was night, and that wasn't the only difference.

There was also the screaming.

He got to his feet, looking wildly around, trying to make sense of the flickering light which streamed around the dead bulldozer, bright as lightning in the darkness. For an instant the world became a shifting pattern of silver leaves and coal-dark shadows, and then he saw the boy.

He was the source of the screaming. He was young, about Darwen's age, wearing a T-shirt and shorts with trainers. His dark eyes were wide with horror and his mouth was open. Words were coming out, and though Darwen couldn't understand them, he felt the boy's terror.

The boy's legs were still, but he seemed to be moving anyway, pulling back towards the source of the light. He reached desperately out to Darwen, still screaming, and Darwen took an urgent step towards him. And that was when he saw it.

The light came from a brilliant circle on the ground behind the boy: a portal from which the bulldozer had been unable to emerge. It was shifting because something was blocking it out, something long and heavy that writhed snakelike as it reached up and through from the other side. It pulled the boy towards the gate, and Darwen saw the thick and fibrous tentacle wound around the child's middle.

Darwen hesitated, catching the boy's terror, then he reached down to the forest floor, desperately searching for anything that could be used as a weapon. He found a ball-like stone and flung it hard as he could at the pulsing tentacle. The stone bounced off, but the undulating movement of the snake-like arm paused for a second. Darwen stooped for another stone, but by the time he had straightened up with three more, the boy was being sucked down into the portal again, only now there were two tentacles coming through, reaching hungrily for whatever had attacked them.

The boy shrieked again, and Darwen flung another stone, missing. In almost the same instant the boy was pulled down and into the pool of light. Another pair of tentacles came creeping out, each one studded with suckers and ending in a set of tooth-like claws. They whipped forward with horrible speed, and any thoughts of trying to rescue the boy went out of Darwen's head.

He turned back towards the amber portal he had come through, praying it would stay open a moment longer. One of the tentacles reached for him, but brushed against a branch instead, seizing it for a moment, and tearing the limb free with impossible strength. Darwen surged forward, avoiding another tentacle which was snaking towards him. He risked one look back to the boy, but he was already gone and, blind with horror, Darwen leapt through the portal.

He didn't stop to look back, but he heard the tentacle follow him into the locus of the rainbow falls, heard the splintering of the crystalline rock as it tore the gateway apart from the inside. And still he kept running.

Two

THE WORLD STUDIES TEACHER

COSTA RICA

The following day marked the end of Darwen's first term at Hillside Academy in Atlanta and there was an air of excitement that even the school's strictness couldn't quite stifle. One more day and they would be free on holiday for two whole weeks. With a bit of luck, it might even snow.

But Darwen's mind was elsewhere. One thought burned bright and urgent in his mind as he stared at the stone sphere he had accidentally brought back from Silbrica: he had to find that boy. He had to save him.

Kahala Konkani – a wild-haired girl who once caused a power outage when the kitchens couldn't produce her vegetarian meal – asked him what he was going to do over the holidays and he didn't respond till she flicked him hard on his earlobe. The sixth graders filed into class where the science teacher, Mr. Iverson, stood owlish at his desk in his oversized glasses and patched lab coat.

"Our last day before the winter vacation," he said, smiling. "But that doesn't mean we don't work."

A tall white boy with blond hair and perfect teeth who was draped in his chair like he owned the entire room, and a slim black boy who was lounging like a bored cat, rolled their eyes at each other: Nathan Cloten and Chip Whittley, two of the popular kids who had never taken to Darwen. Nathan yawned.

"Today you have a special challenge," said Mr. Iverson, "at the request of our new world studies teacher. Class, I would like to introduce . . . Mr. Octavius Peregrine."

"Chuffing 'eck!" Darwen exclaimed, using one of his favourite phrases from his native Lancashire, in northern England.

"No way!" Darwen's friend, Alexandra O'Connor, exclaimed. "I mean . . . no way! Mr. P. is a teacher? Here?" Alex's mouth dropped open. She was washer thin and wore her hair in pigtails (jauntily fastened with with green glow-in-the-dark plastic skulls which in no way went with her Hillside uniform). Her eyes were wide with astonishment.

"Maybe it's a different Octavius Peregrine," said Darwen's other closest friend, Richard Haggerty, his face pink as usual. Rik seemed too big for every chair he sat in and looked slightly sweaty and uncomfortable indoors, as if he should be sitting astride a tractor somewhere chewing on a grass stalk. He had a rich southern accent and spoke slowly, but everyone knew that he was the smartest kid in the grade, particularly when it came to science.

"Because Octavius Peregrine is such a common name, you mean?" said Alex, deadpan.

And, as if on cue, the man they had known as a shopkeeper and one of the gate keepers of the world beyond the mirrors entered. Darwen was so dumbfounded that he barely heard a word of Mr. Iverson's speech about their new teacher's impressive independent research into the "archaeology and anthropology of ritual spaces and the ancient peoples who used them." Rik, meanwhile, was gazing at the old shopkeeper with new respect.

Darwen had last seen Mr. Peregrine three days ago, but their history went back far longer than that. It was Mr. Peregrine who, while masquerading as a shopkeeper, had given Darwen the portal-mirror that had led him to the magical world of Silbrica, the magical world on the other side. It was because of Mr. Peregrine that Darwen had discovered that he was a Squint, properly called a Mirroculist, that rarest of people who alone can climb through certain darkling mirrors, and even bring along others who are touching them – humans and Silbrican creatures alike.

With his friends Rik and Alex – the Peregrine Pact – Darwen had discovered a threat to the school from a former member of Silbrica's Guardian Council. The council member, Greyling, had assembled an army of hulking, green-skinned monsters called scrobblers, creatures with huge tusk-like teeth and red eyes behind brass goggles, armed with terrible energy weapons. At Halloween, those monsters had broken into the human world to take children to fuel their awful power generators. Darwen and his friends had stopped them, but the mirror Mr. Peregrine had given him hadn't survived the battle. Without that mirror, Darwen couldn't travel to Silbrica – couldn't visit its enchanting creatures or see its magnificent machinery. And so Darwen was left stranded in Atlanta, an ordinary but unfamiliar mundane city that Darwen had only come to a few months ago after his parents' deaths.

But then three days ago, Mr. Peregrine had produced another mirror. It had been damaged, presumably during the Scrobblers' earlier attack on his shop, and the old man had warned Darwen that this one was "one use only." Once entered, it would give Darwen a few hours in Silbrica before shutting down forever. This was the mirror Darwen had used last night. And thank goodness he had or he would not have seen the boy and the monster which had taken him.

And now, amazingly – since he had said nothing of it when Darwen had last seen him – Mr. Peregrine was their world studies teacher!

It was as if the world beyond the mirrors – a world in which Darwen had taken refuge, at least till it had been darkened by Greyling's war machine – had moved a little closer. Darwen might have no new mirror but with Mr. Peregrine now a part of his daily life, it was only a matter of time before he could go back to Silbrica and find the missing boy.

Mr. Peregrine, an elderly white man, was dressed as if he had researched the part in movies from half a century ago: a tweed suit with leather patches on the elbows, his usual gold-rimmed half-moon spectacles, and a flat-topped mortarboard cap like students wear for graduation. He was carrying a clipboard, and between his lips he held a huge and absurd looking pipe.

"Er . . ." said Mr. Iverson. "You know you can't smoke in here, Mr. Peregrine?"

"Really?" said Mr. Peregrine, as if this was most remarkable. "Thank goodness."

He knocked the contents of the pipe into one of the steel sinks and ran water on the burning tobacco so that for a moment the room was full of aromatic steam.

Baffled and intrigued, the students stared.

"Filthy habit," said Mr. Peregrine, smiling. "And quite horrible in the mouth. But I do like the smell. Oh," he said, turning to the class and beaming at them as if only just noticing they were there. "Good morning!"

The class responded in their usual drone – "good morning, Mr. Peregrine" – but the chorus was ragged and uncertain. Chip and Nathan were leaning forward, their eyes narrow with attention, scouring the new teacher for every bit of information – and any possible weaknesses – they could get. Darwen realised he was holding his breath, hoping the old shopkeeper would give him a private grin or a wink.

"Have you been discussing my little test?" asked Mr. Peregrine, nodding at Mr. Iverson's desk.

While everyone had been goggling at Mr. Peregrine, Mr. Iverson had set something beside his notebook: a small stone ball. Darwen's hand flashed to his pocket where he felt the cool and smooth surface of an identical sphere. He stared at the one on the desk.

What was he playing at? This stuff was secret!

"Your task," said Mr. Iverson, "is to determine where this object came from. At the end of the allocated time you will present two possible answers. I want good science here, people. Not guesswork."

"Immediately after the winter break," said Mr. Peregrine, "I will be leading you all on a world studies field trip overseas."

The class muttered excitedly.

"Where to, sir?" asked Rik.

Mr. Peregrine gave a saintly smile. "You tell me, Mr ... er ..."

"Haggerty," said Rik, playing along. Mr. Peregrine obviously didn't want the other students suspecting he already knew Darwen and his friends. "But I don't understand, sir," Rik pressed. "How should I know where we are going?"

"I mean," said Mr. Peregrine, "that you will decide where we are going by guessing where this object came from."

"What if we're wrong?" asked Jennifer Taylor-Berry in her refined, southern drawl.

"When the class has determined its best guess," said Mr. Peregrine, "that's where we'll go, right or wrong."

There was a stunned silence. A couple of people laughed and even Mr. Iverson smiled widely as if he thought this might be a rather odd joke, but as Mr. Peregrine continued to beam serenely, the science teacher's smile became rather fixed.

"You're not serious," Mr. Iverson said at last.

"I am most assuredly," said Mr. Peregrine. "It seems as good a system for choosing our destination as any."

"*Choosing* . . . ?" began Mr. Iverson. "But . . . won't we be . . . ?"

"Leaving in three weeks?" Alexandra O'Connor contributed, helpfully.

"Precisely so," said Mr. Peregrine, "so better get a move on."

And with another broad smile, he turned and made for the door. For a moment, Mr. Iverson seemed rooted to the spot, then he said quickly, "OK. Get into your groups. I just want to have to have a word with . . . I won't be long." And he followed Mr. Peregrine out into the hall.

The silence lasted less than a second before the class burst into a babble of chatter.

"He's got to be kidding!" exclaimed Naia Petrakis, an olive skinned girl with jet-black hair and large dark eyes.

The two paler girls beside her huffed delightedly.

"It's outrageous!" said Melissa Young to her best friend, Genevieve Reddock, though she couldn't help smiling as she said it.

"I think it's kind of cool," said Carlos Garcia, and because Carlos so rarely said anything, everyone but Chip and Nathan nodded seriously.

Bobby Park, the Korean boy who Alex thought cut his own hair, gazed at the door through which the teachers had gone and muttered, "who *is* that guy?" in an awed voice.

"He is different," said Princess Clarkson, a blond girl whose mother was a famous movie star and who was thus assumed to be an authority on style of all kinds, "classy."

Darwen and Rik exchanged looks. It was hard to believe, but the students – some of them at least – thought Mr. Peregrine was cool.

"Oh come on. He's already booked the trip," Nathan drawled loudly. "He just wants us to think we have a hand in making the choice. Typical Hillside trying to *'empower the leaders of the future'*. I for one won't play along. We should say the ball is from Disneyland. Call his bluff."

He pulled a comic book from his bag and started to read.

Barry Fails had left his seat and pressed his ear to the classroom door. "Shhh," he hissed. "I think they're arguing."

Half the class immediately thundered to their feet and joined him, straining to hear through the door. Darwen didn't move. Instead he turned quickly to Rik and Alex and said, "look." Holding his hand very close to his stomach so that no one else could see, he took the stone sphere from his pocket and showed them.

"He already gave you one?" whispered Rik. "The other kids won't like it if they think he's giving you preferential treatment."

"And they'll want to know why," said Alex. "I don't think we should let on we already know him."

"He didn't give it to me," Darwen hissed back. "*I* gave the other one to *him*! I found them last night *in Silbrica*. And that's not all. I saw him try to save a boy . . ."

He told them everything, and when he had finished there was a long wide-eyed silence.

"Dang," said Rik, quietly.

"A giant octopus thing with claws," Alex mused. "Doesn't Silbrica have any rabbits? Anyway, you shouldn't have gone in without us," she scolded. "We made the Peregrine Pact, remember?"

"The boy still would have been taken," said Darwen. "And if there had been three of us for it to choose from, maybe the creature would have got one of us too."

"You like to live on the edge, I'll give you that," said Alex, shrugging off her discontent. "'course, it's only a matter of time before you fall *over* the edge and die horribly. You might want to keep that in mind."

"I didn't do it on purpose," said Darwen.

"Which part?" asked Alex. "Going in without us, activating the weird gate or going through it? Only I'd think those things were pretty hard to do by accident. I mean, what? You hit the button by mistake and then, sort of, fell through . . .?"

"Of course not," Darwen retorted.

"OK," said Alex. "So when you said you didn't do it on purpose what you mean is you *did* do it all on purpose but you didn't intend to nearly get killed. Uh huh. Just so we're clear."

"The point," he said, "is that a kid was taken and I want to know what we're going to do about it."

"You know," said Rik, "you might not have been in Silbrica."

"Of course I was," said Darwen, "I went in through a mirror, remember? And there was a scrobbler machine of some kind."

"Yeah, but you went through a second portal, right?" said Rik. "Maybe it didn't move you to another part of Silbrica. Maybe it moved you to another part of *our* world."

"Wait, what?!?" Alex yelled gasped, slamming her fist on the desk.

Rik promptly shot her an impatient look.

"I suppose," said Darwen.

"The waterfall place was still light, right?" said Rik. "But the place where you saw the kid being taken was dark, so it must have been somewhere different. It could have been in Silbrica but it could have been in our world, and in a similar time zone to ours. Western Europe is only five or six hours different, so it might still have been dark there, but the place you describe sounds tropical. Africa or Asia would have been light at that time, so I'd say you were in central or south America."

"That's pretty smart," said Alex. "He doesn't look it, but sometimes he's positively bright."

Darwen shook his head. "It couldn't have been our world!"

"Think," said Rik. "The waterfall area was full of things you could only see in Silbrica. What about the place on the other side of the crystal portal? Was anything there unusual?"

"Other than the massive tentacled monster, you mean?" asked Alex.

"Other than the massive tentacled monster," Rik agreed.

Darwen sighed.

"I'm not sure," he said. "It were really dark. There were a lot of plants and trees, but I suppose they looked fairly ordinary. More like house plants than wild ones, you know? My aunt has one of those umbrella plant things. I'm pretty sure I saw a plant kind of like that."

"Tropical, then," said Rik. "And it was hot and humid, right?"

"Yes."

"What language was the kid shouting in?" asked Alex.

"Not sure," said Darwen. "But now that you mention it, I think it sounded familiar."

"Like Spanish?" Alex suggested.

"Could have been," said Darwen.

"One of the many languages you don't speak," mused Alex. "Too bad I wasn't there to translate. This kid, could he have been Latino?" asked Alex.

Darwen shrugged. "I suppose," he said. "I didn't really get a good look at him, and as I said . . ."

"*It were dark*. Yeah, we got that," Alex concluded.

"And the stone balls?" asked Rik. "You said you threw a few at the monster?"

"Yeah, I found them on the jungle floor. There were at least five of them. Different sizes. I still had two in my hand when I ran for it."

"And Mr. Peregrine clearly thinks a bunch of random kids

can figure out where they came from," Rik whispered. "There's no question: you were in our world, Darwen. And if we can find where the stone spheres originate . . ."

"We find where the boy came from," Darwen concluded.

"He's coming back!" yelled Barry Fails. The students scattered like cockroaches caught in a flashlight beam. They fought for their seats, pretending they'd been sitting quietly the whole time, as Mr. Iverson – who wasn't fooled for a second – returned.

"Well?" he said. "Have you formed your groups?"

There was a grumbling negative murmur throughout the room, but Rik nodded vigorously, indicating Darwen and Alex with his big pale hands.

"First come, first served," said Mr. Iverson, snatching up the rock and setting it on the desk in front of Rik. "Have a good look, Mr. Haggerty. In five minutes, I'll be passing it on to the next group. Everyone," he said, raising his voice, "gets the same access to microscopes and chemicals so you can try to identify what it is. Do not damage the object in the process of your analysis!"

"Where's Mr . . . . *Peregrine*, sir?" asked Darwen, trying to sound like he was unsure of the name.

"He went to speak to the principal about his trip," said Mr. Iverson, his voice carefully neutral. "I expect he may be there a while."

Rik lowered his face to the rock. Alex nudged it and it rolled to the edge of the desk so that Rik had to catch it. Darwen, clutching the other sphere carefully under the desk, scowled.

"It's a ball," Alex said. "So someone made it, right?"

"Probably," said Rik. "But hail stones are round and no one makes them."

"Really?" said Alex. "I thought hailstones were individually shaped by the great sky god Xanthor and his magic colander."

"Maybe if it started really high up in a molten state," said Rik, ignoring her, "like if it was shot from a volcano, it would cool evenly as it fell and come down perfectly round?"

He looked at Darwen, as if he might have an answer.

"Don't look at me," said Darwen. "You're the science guy. You want to know about British birds, I'm your man. Otherwise . . ."

"He's got nothing," said Alex.

"Which looks about the same as what you've got," said Darwen.

"Yeah?" said Alex, cocking her head. "How about this? It looks like a miniature version of Stone Mountain. Only darker."

"Stone Mountain?" parroted Darwen.

"Huge granite outcrop just outside the 285 loop road," said Rik, absently. "East side of the city. You're right, Alex. Granite contains quartz, feldspar, microline and muscovite, and this looks basically the same, but is darker."

Darwen gazed at Rik, impressed. Rik was the president of Hillside's archaeology club, and sixth grade's most enthusiastic amateur scientist, but he got a lot of his knowledge of Georgia rock from pottering about on his dad's tiny farm.

"Wait," Rik said suddenly. "*Darker than granite.* I know this. It's Granodiorite. It's like granite but has more plagioclase feldspar than orthoclase feldspar."

"Great," said Alex. "I'm really glad it's got more plagioclase feldspar as opposed to, I don't know, *arcansparklebargle*. Anytime you feel like speaking English, you let us know."

"It's the same stuff that the Rosetta stone is made of," said Rik. "You know, the tablet they used to figure out ancient Egyptian hieroglyphs."

"We're going to Egypt?" said Alex. "Cool."

"Not so fast," said Rik. "Granodiorite is found all over the world, so this could come from anywhere. We'll need something else to nail down its origin, like maybe a mass spectrometer."

"Let me check my bag," said Alex, staring fixedly at him. "Oh dear. I seem to have left all my multimillion dollar science equipment at home."

Rik's scowl deepened over the next five minutes, and when Mr. Iverson swooped in and took the stone ball from him, he exclaimed, "It's not fair! How are we supposed to figure out where it comes from? If it had unusual plant matter stuck to it maybe . . ."

"Sorry, Mr. Haggerty," said the science teacher. "You've had your look."

Rik sulked as the rest of the class got their turn.

Eventually, Mr. Peregrine returned.

Mr. Iverson was quick to meet him at the door, and Darwen sat up, straining to hear.

"So?" he said the science teacher, under his breath.

"So . . . what?" asked Mr. Peregrine, smiling his most serene smile.

"How did your chat with the principal go?" asked Mr. Iverson, glancing over his shoulder at the class so that Darwen had to look down quickly. "About the trip, I mean?"

"Oh!" said Mr. Peregrine, as if this hadn't been mentioned for weeks. "Oh that. Yes, he seemed most enthusiastic. *Cutting edge*, he called it, though I'm not entirely sure what that means."

"Cutting edge?"

"Yes, my idea of letting my scholarly investigation drive the student trip so that they are, as it were, on the ground doing first-hand research. Seemed most gratified. Charming man, the principal. Charming."

"Indeed," said Mr. Iverson, with a slightly fixed smile. "Well, wonderful. That sounds . . . wonderful." He turned quickly to the class and raised his voice. "OK, which group wants to make the first argument as to the stone sphere's origins?"

Darwen shifted, trying to attract Mr. Peregrine's attention, but the old man ignored him.

"Costa Rica," said Barry.

Darwen and Rik stared at him. Barry Fails – known, not terribly kindly, as Barry "Usually" Fails to his friends – had never answered a question in Mr. Iverson's class before.

"Specifically," said Nathan. "A small area close to the border with Panama on the Pacific coast. Possibly a tiny island just offshore called Caño."

"And your second guess?" said Mr. Iverson.

"We don't have one," said Chip with supreme confidence, "and it's not a guess. "It's from Costa Rica."

"And how did you reach your conclusion?" asked Mr. Iverson, a skeptical expression on his face.

"Googled *stone ball*," said Barry, brandishing an expensive-looking smart phone and grinning.

Darwen and Alex exchanged outraged looks.

"Can I see that?" said Mr. Peregrine. He was peering at the phone, fascinated. Barry handed it to him and he turned it over in his hands, gazing at the screen and smiling, rapt.

"What an extraordinary thing!" he whispered.

"It's just a phone," said Barry.

"And I think we should talk about scientific process," inserted Mr. Iverson. "Looking something up on Wikipedia hardly constitutes rigorous analytical . . ."

"So are they right?" Rik cut in.

"What?" said Mr. Peregrine. "Oh, I see. Well, let me think. Costa Rica . . ."

Everyone looked at Mr. Peregrine who seemed to hesitate before suddenly clapping his hands together.

"Is correct!" he exclaimed, apparently writing it down on his clipboard before returning the phone to Barry. "And that's where we will be going. We'll begin classes on . . . er . . ." he checked the clipboard, "*Costa Rica* after the holidays."

Nathan and his friends punched the air in victory and Barry did a little dance directed at Rik who was red-faced with fury.

"That's totally unfair," he muttered through gritted teeth.

"Look on the bright side," Alex cut in. "Nobody cares."

Rik couldn't argue with that. The students were too thrilled by the idea of visiting a country about which none of them knew anything to worry how the location had been selected. Darwen couldn't share Rik's gloom either. The stone balls had come from Costa Rica, and that meant the boy who had been taken by the monster had been there too. Knowing that meant they were one step closer to saving him. The thought almost made up for Mr. Peregrine behaving as if Darwen was just another nameless student.

Three
CHRISTMAS PRESENTS

D arwen hadn't expected snow in Atlanta. He had assumed the south was always hot, as it had been when he first arrived in September, but December proved as cold as he had ever known in northern England. Even so, the snow had been a surprise and for a moment, a brief but shining moment, it had almost been like home.

At school they had studied Hanukah and Kwanza – his teachers constantly looking hopefully for insight from Darwen, whose mother had been black, but he had never heard of it, and the details had to be offered by Alex and Chip Whittley. The teachers had called the upcoming break "winter holidays" but to Darwen it would always be Christmas. Except that it wasn't, not without his parents, not in this still strange and vast city so different from the little Lancashire town where he had been raised.

Darwen had not lived there since the summer when his parents had died in a car accident, and he had been transported to Atlanta to live with his slightly stiff but well-meaning aunt, Honoria Vanderstay. Four months later, they were still getting to know each other and she was fighting to get Darwen through his lowest point since arriving in the States, a low point that began long before the frustration of not being able to find the captured boy took hold.

Two weeks earlier, a series of boxes had arrived. Things belonging to his parents which had been sent on. Darwen and his aunt had avoided them for a few days, but in the end she had gone ahead and opened them, always watching to see how he was reacting to what was inside. It wasn't easy. Even the most ordinary of things were charged with memories. There was a china rabbit his mother had glued back together after Darwen had knocked it off the mantelpiece, and a cookbook whose stained pages were covered in scrawled notes added by his father.

"Dad's hotpot recipe," said Darwen, staring at the book so as to avoid his aunt's watchful gaze. "You're supposed to use lamb and kidney and stuff, but dad had this really great way of making it with just stewing beef and potatoes and onions. Mum put the crust on. We had it with piccalilli and red cabbage on Saturdays in front of the telly. Could we try and make it?"

But Honoria didn't cook.

"I'm sorry, Darwen," she said. "Every time I turn on the stove there's a good chance I'll smoke the building out. Maybe we can get it at a restaurant."

They tried but, unsurprisingly, couldn't find it.

Cooking aside, his aunt had tried almost painfully hard as the holidays approached. She bought and wrapped a mountain of presents, got a real Christmas tree delivered to their spotless apartment and swept up its fallen needles only when he wasn't looking. She made a list of everything Darwen wanted for Christmas dinner, including chipolata sausages – which he couldn't describe properly – and the paper crackers with novelty gifts inside, which she hadn't been able to find till Christmas Eve. She had revealed them with a delighted "Ta-da!" when she got home, and Darwen hadn't the heart to say that they looked much smaller and fancier than the ones he was used to. He had thanked her for her efforts and returned to his bedroom while she paid Eileen, the dreaded babysitter, singing along with manic determination to the endlessly repeated songs on a twenty-four hour, Christmas music station.

Darwen closed the door behind him and slumped onto the bed. On his bedside cabinet was a photo album: the blurred and random pictures he had gotten together before leaving England. He had spent more time in the last few days going through them, staring at the images of his parents than ever before, but the warm feelings he had from them when he needed them at Halloween were gone, and they merely left him feeling lost and alone. Two nights before, his aunt had taken him to a place called Calloway Gardens to see a huge display of Christmas lights, and though they had been beautiful – magical, even – he had found himself thinking back to when his parents had driven him to the Blackpool sea front to look at what they called The Illuminations. The lights at that brassy Lancashire resort town were, he knew, pretty tasteless compared to Calloway's elegantly lit trees, but he would have given anything to see them again, to be there in the back seat, laughing and pointing as his dad drove and his mum glanced back at him, smiling.

But that was all in the past. That portion of his life was over and Darwen found that all he really wanted right now was to escape the apartment and his aunt's frenetically perfect Christmas into Silbrica. He gazed at the replacement mirror through which he had crossed over into that strange jungle locus, but Mr. Peregrine had been right. It had worked once, and now was just a cracked and battered mirror. He couldn't get inside, couldn't even see anything more than his own frustrated and miserable reflection. He pictured

31

the nameless boy he had seen pulled from his Costa Rican home by a monster, torn away from his family and everything he knew, isolated and thrust into a new and terrifying reality.

Darwen had to find him. That meant talking to Mr. Peregrine, whose planned trip to Costa Rica clearly meant that he was working on the problem, though in ways Darwen didn't fully understand. They hadn't seen each other since school finished, and Darwen – if he was honest – felt badly out of the loop.

He had Christmas dinner with his aunt, 'Jingle Bell Rock' playing incessantly as she processed course after course, all supplied by a local restaurant and kept warm in her sleek, stainless steel oven. They pulled their crackers with their absurdly expensive trinkets – including real pieces of silver and gold jewellery – and Darwen listened as his aunt sang the praises of the turkey "which is usually so dry." He said nothing about his father's famously perfect roast turkey or his mother's sherry trifle, though he could almost taste them in his mind, and his heart bled silent tears when he thought he would never taste them again. His aunt gave him a half glass of wine with water in it "since it's Christmas" while he played conspicuously with everything she had bought him; and when he did cry, which was only for a moment, he managed to slip into the bathroom before she noticed.

As soon as Darwen heard the door buzzer and saw Aunt Honoria's pretended surprise at who could *possibly* be visiting today, he knew she had one more desperate trick up her sleeve. For a moment he was terrified that it would be some department store Santa come to pay him a special visit, but it wasn't.

It was Rik and Alex, and – knowing that his aunt had arranged it because nothing she could do alone would be enough – he sidled up to her whispering "thank you" into her shirt.

They were clearly conscious of Aunt Honoria's watchful presence and all they couldn't discuss with her around, so they babbled happily about the weather, their faces flushed, stomping their feet as they slipped out of their snow-spotted coats. Darwen announced that he was "right chuffed" to see them, which Alex translated as "very pleased." Rik had bought Darwen a guide to American birds, and Alex a framed photograph of the three of them on a school trip to the zoo. But they had one more package and it took both of them to lug it into the apartment.

"Did you bring that with you?" asked Aunt Honoria.

"It was in the hallway," said Alex. "But it's addressed to Darwen."

She indicated a faded slip of paper tied with twine to the brown paper package, on which were written words in spidery and unsteady cursive: *For Darwen. OP.*

Rik mouthed the initials and Alex rolled her eyes.

"Mr. Peregrine," she said. "I wouldn't advertise that our new world studies teacher is sending you a Christmas present, Darwen. Favouritism. Conflict of interests. Bad for both of you."

Unable to contain his excitement Darwen pulled at the string, feeling the weight of the thing and its curious shape. It was much too heavy to be a mirror, and he had to lay it on the floor and peel the wrapping paper away. He did so, and they all stared.

"It's an oven door," said Rik, bewildered.

"From a junk yard," added Alex.

It had once been white with a chrome handle and a heavy glass window in the centre, but it was now faded, chipped, rusted, stained and dented.

"Just what you always wanted, right Darwen?" said Alex.

"How . . . interesting," said Aunt Honoria, with slow caution, "only our oven already has a door. See?" She pointed into the kitchen with its matching stainless steel appliances.

"You could drill through the corners and bolt this one right on top of yours," Rik suggested.

Aunt Honoria's mouth opened and her head cocked slowly as if she couldn't find the right words.

"The window in the middle is nice and shiny though, huh, Darwen?" said Alex with a significant look. "Reflective, almost."

She was right. Darwen shifted in his seat, watching his face in the clouded glass of the door. It was a portal. It had to be. And it meant that Mr. Peregrine hadn't forgotten him, however much he pretended not to know him in class.

"And this Mr. Peregrine is your new world studies teacher," Aunt Honoria mused.

"Tough to believe, huh?" said Alex. "And leading a trip to Costa Rica as soon as we go back to school. Our survival chances don't look good, do they?"

"He's actually a sort of anthropologist," Rik inserted, leaping to the former shopkeeper's defence. "He's published and everything."

"He's a what?" asked Darwen.

"An Anthropologist," said Alex, ever the wordsmith. "Someone who studies people, their origins, culture, social structure," she said.

"In his case, he has sort of an outsider's perspective."

"Outsider?" said Aunt Honoria. "In what sense?"

"Oh, she just means that he's not from round here, right Alex?" Darwen inserted.

"And he's leading us overseas," Rik mused.

"Why do you keep saying that?" said Alex.

Rik was pink – pinker than usual – and he looked unnerved.

"What's the big deal?" asked Darwen, feeling a rush of loyalty for the former shopkeeper. "Mr. P will get it together."

Rik nodded, but he looked quickly away.

"You've never been out of the country before, have you?" said Alex, peering at him.

Rik sighed and shook his head. "I went to Chattanooga once," he muttered.

"That's in Tennessee," said Alex.

"I was six," Rik explained.

"And that's the only time you've been out of the *state*?" said Alex.

"I like Georgia," said Rik, weakly.

"And I like spaghetti-ohs," said Alex, "but I don't eat them at every meal."

As soon as his aunt went back to the kitchen to clean up Rik nodded at the oven door.

"You know what that is, right?" asked Rik.

"I hope so," said Darwen, wishing he could test the idea right there and then.

"When can we try it?" asked Alex. "We should see if we can get close to the place the boy was taken from."

"Might be good reconnaissance for our rescue mission," said Rik.

"Our *mission*?" Alex repeated. "What are you now, GI Joe?"

"That's what it is," said Darwen, "a rescue mission."

"Does it have to be the whole grade?" said Alex. "Does everyone have to come? I mean, this was *our* thing. We're the ones who stopped Greyling's invasion. Us! Not Naia or Barry, or Chip Whittley . . ."

"It's the only way we can get there while school was in session," Rik said, shrugging his broad shoulders.

"Costa Rica," Darwen mused. "You think it will be expensive?"

"You can bet on it," said Alex.

Darwen's face fell. His family in England had never had much money, and though his aunt seemed to be doing quite well for herself, he hated costing her more than was really necessary.

"I'm hoping my scholarship will cover it," said Rik. "If not, that's me out. There's no way my dad could get the money together with the way his work has been lately. What about you, Alex?"

"I'll be OK," she said. "A present from Dad."

"That's nice of him," said Darwen.

"Oh, he doesn't know about it yet," said Alex. "But Mom says that if he hesitates for a second when I call him about it, I'm allowed to ask how much he spent on his girlfriend's Christmas gifts."

Darwen wasn't sure how to react to this, but Alex gave an expansive shrug and grinned brightly.

Aunt Honoria returned, and Darwen quickly started to talk about what great Christmas gifts she had given him.

"I got a puppy!" Alex inserted delightedly. "I got to go down to the pound and pick her out myself. She's half-husky, half-shepherd, and half-something-else with floppy ears ..."

"You got one and a half dogs?" asked Rik.

Alex gave him a blank look.

"Three halves," said Rik, "husky, shepherd, floppy-eared thing. That's one and a half dogs."

"I also got a dictionary," said Alex, "and I'll be learning a new word every day. Here's one I already got down. *Pedantic*. It means nit-picky and too smart by half. And when you look it up, there's a picture of Rik Haggerty."

Rik rolled his eyes at Darwen.

"Anyway," said Alex, "she's called Sasha – which is like a Russian version of my name – and she's gorgeous, and loyal, and huge, and fierce, and someone gave her away, if you can believe that. She's not even a year old and some old lady said, 'I'm bored with you now, so you can go to the pound.' And you know what they do with dogs if no one adopts them there?" Alex's eyes grew wide.

Fearing Alex was about to rant at them for other people's bad behaviour, Darwen tried to redirect the conversation. "Well, you brought her home, so that's good. She'll like that."

"Yeah," said Rik. "A year or so with you and she'll probably learn to talk."

"I wish she *could* talk," said Alex. "Coz then she could tell me the name of the lady who abandoned her. I've got some things I'd like to say to her. When I grow up I'm going to set up an animal shelter where pets that don't get adopted can live forever."

"I thought you were going to be a singer," said Rik, grinning.

"Or a dancer," added Darwen.

"I can be those things as well," said Alex. "Oh, yeah, I'm going to be an actor too. Strictly theatre: no movies, unless they pay me so much that I'd be crazy not to do it."

"Four careers is a lot for one person," Aunt Honoria observed. "How will you find time for cooking and cleaning?"

"I'll pay people to do that for me, like you do," she said. Aunt Honoria flushed and looked out of the window, but Alex just kept talking. "My mom used to do that. When I was a baby, we had a nanny called Consuela. Why do you think my Spanish is so awesome? 'Course, we don't have a nanny now. Mom insists on looking after Kaitlin all by herself. But yeah, when we had more money – before my dad left – we had maids and gardeners and who knows what else. That's how I'm gonna live, with *staff*."

She paused to consider this, and a new idea dawned.

"Heck, I could pay you two," she exclaimed. "Rik, do the yard. Darwen, make me supper. Something with a bit of spice: some blackened catfish maybe, with a bowl of gumbo on the side. Or some Brunswick stew. The good kind, not that dog-food-in-water mess they serve at school with leaves sprinkled on it, like *that* will make it good. *Garnish*, they call it. Serve up any old slop with a few corriander leaves on top and they think it's high-class. Hockey puck steak cooked for about four hours till you can carve glass with it? No problem, we'll put a sprig of parsley on it and everyone will think they're in some restaurant in Paris, France. Oh look, there's the Eiffel tower, and I can hear the bells of Notre Dame, and how delicious this piece of blow-torched concrete on my plate is because of the *garnish* . . ."

Darwen grinned at Rik. Same old Alex.

"I thought the meals at Hillside were good," said Aunt Honoria, a familiar note of anxiety creeping into her voice.

"They are," replied Darwen quickly. "Kind of fancy, but good. Right, Rik?"

Rik, who would probably eat pulled pork and chicken wings at every meal given the chance, met Darwen's eyes and got the message. "Sure," he said. "They're great."

Alex rolled her eyes. "You just don't have my delicate palate," she said. "I have very sensitive taste buds."

"Sensitive as a battering ram," muttered Rik.

"I heard that," she said, unoffended. She gazed around the apartment. "Nice tree," she said to Aunt Honoria. "Could use more lights though."

"Oh yeah," said Rik. "Real sensitive."

When they had gone, Darwen sat beside his aunt on the couch in front of the gas fire, watching the snow falling on Atlanta's towers of offices and apartments.

"Good Christmas, Darwen?" she asked.

"Good Christmas," he said.

Clearly relieved, his aunt patted him on the head awkwardly and then got ready for bed. It had been a long day. Darwen said good night, then spent a minute gazing into the fire, listening to the sounds of his aunt getting ready for bed. The moment things went quiet, he dragged the battered old oven door into his room, careful not to make too much noise. He was propping it up, against the back wall of his closet when his fingers found something taped to the back: a scrap of paper. On it were numbers inked in Mr. Peregrine's untidy hand and a thumbprint, not in ink but in a dark, brownish red . . .

Blood?

Darwen frowned, but then he noticed the image that had appeared in the glass pane of the oven door. He had known that it would have become a portal by now, since the sun had been down for hours, but this wasn't at all what he had expected.

Four
THE GREAT APPARATUS

It was dark inside the oven-door portal, a tight, square tunnel made of metal. In fact it looked a lot like the inside of an oven except that it kept going back as far as Darwen could see. Darwen reached in tentatively, and the surface rippled where the glass should be, just as his old mirror had. Still, this wasn't the beautiful forest he had been looking forward to, and he wasn't sure he wanted to get into that cramped passage, no matter where it might lead him.

Come on, he thought. *Don't chicken out now. Mr. Peregrine sent the portal for a reason, probably something to do with the missing boy. and if the blood was anything to go by, it had cost him something in the process . . .*

With that, Darwen lay down on the carpet, pushed his arms in, and then crawled through the oven door, head first.

It was no better inside. Darwen could smell the metal in the air and his hands and knees were quickly coated with dust. The only light came from Darwen's bedroom, and his body was blocking most of that out. Darwen tried to adjust his position but only succeeded in whacking his head on the side, which rang like a gong. He considered climbing back out, but he pushed the thought away and started to crawl forward, half on his hands and knees, half-slithering on his belly.

The darkness thickened, and after a few yards Darwen could see nothing in front of him at all. He glanced backwards through his legs and saw the little square of light which was his bedroom glowing like a distant television in the night. He went on, slower now, feeling in front of him, his heart beginning to pound.

He wasn't sure how much more of this he could take.

And then, without warning, the floor of the passage sloped steeply down like a slide, the square angles rounding out so that the passage became a tube. Darwen could feel it with his hands, but it was absolutely dark down there, and how far it went or what was at the bottom, he couldn't begin to guess. He took a long breath and thought. Mr. Peregrine had given him the oven door. That was all he needed to know. Sure, the shopkeeper could be a little disorganised sometimes, and he didn't always have a firm grasp on the details of a situation, but he was absolutely trustworthy. Of that Darwen had no doubt.

He pulled himself over the lip of the passage and he began to slide down. For a second he tried to stop himself, but it was no good, and he was soon hurtling down through the tube.

Faster and faster he went. The chute banked suddenly to the right, then to the left. It levelled out for a moment and then dropped steeper than ever, so that Darwen cried out as he careened through the pipe. He rolled, felt the metal wall burn his elbow and tucked his arms in tight, shutting his eyes. Twice more the tube switched direction, turned him over, and gave one last burst of head-spinning speed. Then the roof was gone, and he could feel light and air as he shot across a polished metal platform on his back, slowed, rotating, and stopped.

Darwen opened his eyes and looked up.

Above him was a sparkling dome of brass inlaid with copper, and braced with polished chestnut-coloured wood. From the centre of the dome ran a glass tube filled with pulsing golden light, flecked with amber and pinpricks of white-like stars or diamonds. The tube came down into the heart of a vast and elegant machine and, recalling things Mr. Peregrine had told him before, Darwen knew where he was: inside The Great Apparatus.

Above him the tube ran up to the heart of the Hall where Silbrica's Guardians sat in perpetual council. It had been dying the last time Darwen had seen it – the energy purplish with spots of crimson, whole areas burned black like spent embers. But this was how it should be: bright like sunrise, but soft and full of life.

Despite the discomfort of his journey, Darwen found himself basking in the glow from above and smiling. It was like being inside a thousand clocks. All around the chamber were brass cogs and dials, some small as watch parts, some big as houses. Some spun freely, others seemed quite still, all were linked so that however different they were, they were clearly parts of a whole. There were flywheels and sprockets, levels and ratchets, levers, switches, springs, cranks and a hundred other machine parts for which he had no name. Everything shone, and the air was full of a soft but steady ticking, under which was a distant hum, like wordless notes sung in harmony.

The room was circular with the golden energy from above flowing down into the machine at its centre. From there, a hundred pipes ran like the spokes of a great wheel, to a rim composed entirely and unmistakably of portals, all framed in varnished wood and set with controls like those Darwen had first seen on the wooded hill where the fairy-like dellfey, Moth, lived. They had the same elegance, but were all slightly different in shape and the pattern in the wood grain, and as Darwen studied their bases, which were swollen and fluted like something between a column and a tree, an idea struck him.

They're growing, he thought.

Their roots spread beneath his feet. The machine fuelled the gates but they were also alive, drawing sustenance from Silbrica itself.

They were numbered simply from one to a hundred. Darwen checked the paper in his pocket – the one given to him by Mr. Peregrine – and walked around the outside till he came to number sixty-four. Then, just to be sure he would be able to get back out, he revisited the chute. He discovered that the entire pipe rotated and that the top side had steps built into it. Satisfied, he returned to the portal and began the process of opening the gate. First, he pulled a lever, then he turned a dial, and finally he pushed a button and waited as, with a great pneumatic hiss, the empty frame of the gateway shimmered into pearly brilliance.

Darwen paused, enjoying the moment. Then he stepped in.

On the other side of the gate, Darwen stood and stared. He had expected that Mr. Peregrine's instructions would have brought him back to the crystal waterfall near where he had seen that monstrous, tentacled creature grab the boy, but this was somewhere entirely different. Why had Mr. Peregrine brought him here? He was in a forest of what he thought was a kind of bamboo, though it was taller than any he had ever seen, its stems thick as tree trunks, its tops reaching forty, fifty feet into the night sky. Each trunk was smooth and slender, like tall, grey columns, and overhead they sprouted slim, silvery leaves that rustled like foil in the breeze. The gate he had come through was fashioned out of the same bamboo, and all around him were more of the same. There was a clearing which housed a familiar, ornate fountain with what looked like tiny bird houses, where greenish lights glowed and flickered. One of the lights was coming towards him.

"Moth!" exclaimed Darwen.

And so it was.

If the dellfey hadn't been so small, he would have hugged her. She looked healthy, her mechanical wings immaculately reforged showing no trace of the scorching and oil stains that had been there when he saw her last. Her face was a mask of delight.

"You found me!" she exclaimed. "The dellfeys feared we would not see you again after all the terrible things that Greyling did. We thought you would never return to Silbrica!"

"I was always going to come back," said Darwen. "I just couldn't find a way."

"Do you like my new home?" she said.

"It's beautiful," Darwen said, "yes. You won't go back to the old forest?"

"That locus has to grow," she said, shaking her head.

"So?"

"If we went there," she said, "we would grow too."

"You mean we'd get taller?"

"No," she said, her face a mixture of exasperation and dread, "we would get old."

"What?" said Darwen. "Why?"

"Remember the damage the scrobblers did, the trees they killed? A new forest has to grow."

"I don't understand," said Darwen. "So it's growing. Why would that make us get older?"

"Because that locus has been reset," Moth exclaimed. "The Great Apparatus has been adjusted so the forest can regrow."

"That was the machine with all the gates that I just came through?" said Darwen. "It can control the passage of time?"

Moth frowned and tipped her head onto one side.

"In a way," she said. "They can make it run faster in some locuses. Time is passing quickly in the forest now so that the trees can reclaim the locus." Moth made a bobbing motion in the air and her wings flickered with coppery light. "There was something you needed to ask me?" she asked.

"Yes," said Darwen. "I was in another locus. But then I found a way back into my world and there was a boy, and then . . . I don't know, something took him, right in front of me. I was just standing there and this huge tentacle thing had a hold of him and it dragged him through a portal and I threw stones but there was nothing I could do to stop it, and then it came after me and all I could do was run and . . . I left him."

As Darwen spoke he felt his skin prickle. His eyes were wide and his heart was racing.

"I just left him," he said again, horrified. "He was alone but I couldn't do anything." He blinked and cleared his throat. "So now I have to find him."

"No," she said, and she had become quite still. "You must leave."

"What do you think it was?" Darwen asked. There was something about the dellfey's manner which spoke of things she didn't want to say.

"I don't know," she said. "There are many strange beasts in Silbrica's wilder places."

"Yeah, you said. Scrobblers and flittercrakes and shades and gnashers. I know. This wasn't like any of them. It was huge and..."

"There are Hobstrils, Darwen Arkwright," said Moth, "and Drifters, and other monsters whose names I have told you before, some so terrible that we do not speak of them."

"Come on, Moth," said begged Darwen. "You know something..." He had seen something a look of horrified recognition in her face when he had said "tentacles," a flicker of terror in her eyes clear and desperate as a scream, which she had then banished completely.

"I cannot talk about that which you wish to know," the dellfey insisted, and her tiny hands shook. "You must go. Now."

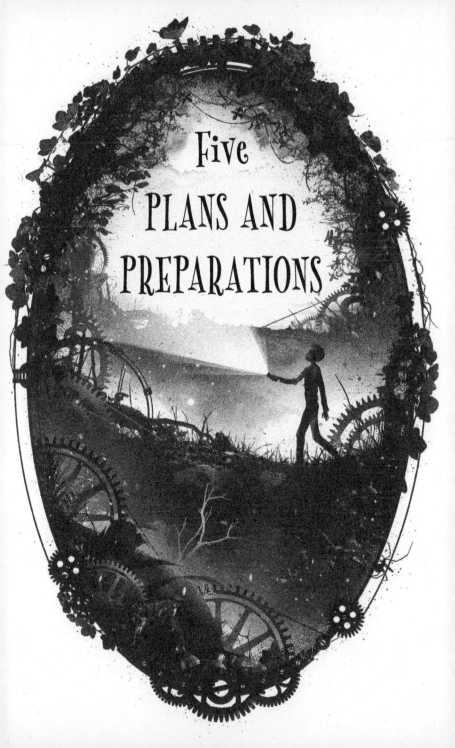

Five
PLANS AND
PREPARATIONS

With Moth being so pointedly unhelpful, Darwen felt an even greater need to get Mr. Peregrine, Alex and Rik all in the same room together. But Christmas was a tough time to get people to drop their plans, and it wasn't till the following Saturday that they were able to meet at a local bowling alley which, to Darwen, was almost as odd as Silbrican bamboo forests.

"We have to rent shoes?" he asked, pulling a sour face.

"Hey, when you have a puppy eating her way through your wardrobe, renting shoes looks like a pretty good option," Alex shrugged. "Anyway, it was your idea."

"I wanted somewhere where we could get away from my aunt and meet with Mr. Peregrine," said Darwen. "She thinks it's odd that he's friends with us."

"Ohhhh," said Alex, wisely, watching Mr. Peregrine as he inspected a selection of bowling balls a few lanes away. "Gotcha. Still, at least he's a teacher now, and not just some guy who sent you an oven door."

"Are you sure these are right?" Mr. Peregrine demanded of one of the attendants. "They seem very heavy."

Alex met Darwen's anxious eyes and smirked.

Rik was a superb bowler, throwing strike after strike, much to Alex's irritation. Having never done it in England, Darwen was hopeless but Mr. Peregrine was worse, cheerfully throwing one gutter ball after another and then watching keenly as if they might just pop out at the last second and hit all the pins. After a couple of games in which Rik systematically wiped the floor with them, Darwen gave up.

"So, Mr. Peregrine," he said, grinning. "You're a teacher."

"Astonishing, isn't it?" said Mr. Peregrine, beaming. "I have always rather liked the idea of being a teacher, but having to actually *know things* is proving more of a challenge than I had anticipated. And that school! So strange that some of the teachers seem determined to crush the spirits of those placed in their charge, don't you think?"

Darwen thought of Mr. Sumners, the maths teacher, and nodded his agreement. For a silent moment he stood next to Mr. Peregrine, watching Alex abandon the bowling with a shout of frustration, and he couldn't help smiling. Whatever difficulties lay ahead, he would be with his friends and with Mr. Peregrine. It was going to be a good term.

"So we're going to Costa Rica to find the boy I saw kidnapped," Darwen said, as Rik and Alex joined them. "Somehow, and it looks like we'll be doing this without Moth's help, we need to find where he was taken from, then we can cross over to Silbrica after him using whatever portal that thing pulled him through."

"And into its tentacled embrace," said Alex, dropping her bowling ball so heavily onto the floor that a big man with tattoos shot her an accusatory look. Alex turned to him and said "Hey, how ya doing?" holding his gaze until he flushed, shrugged and looked away.

"We may not need to actually *follow* the boy to the other side," said Mr. Peregrine delicately. "Our primary goal is not so much to bring him back as to identify his point of entry."

"What do you mean?" asked Darwen.

"There are ancient creatures in Silbrica and there are points, as you know," said Mr. Peregrine, "where the fabric separating their world from ours is fragile. Sometimes hunting beasts stray through the barrier. I was able to pass along what you saw, so the Guardians are now aware of the breach. They want us to find it and close it. That is our mission."

"But we have to get him back!" said Darwen.

"If the creature which you saw is, as I suspect, merely an animal," said Mr. Peregrine, "albeit a large and powerful one, I'm afraid it will be too late to save the boy. The incident took place two weeks ago. If a child was taken by a bear or a lion you would not expect to find the child alive after that time. In all likelihood . . ."

"No," said Darwen, cutting him off. "That's not good enough. I'll go through the oven door tonight and see if I can find Moth again. I might be able to persuade her to . . ."

"Oven door?" Mr. Peregrine echoed, vaguely.

"The portal you sent me. Thanks for that by the way. Too bad it's too big to take with us."

"Ah," said Mr. Peregrine. His face was blank, as if he had forgotten what they were talking about. Then he cleared his throat and said, "yes, of course. You are most welcome."

"So," said Rik, "you know a lot about Costa Rica, do you, Mr. Peregrine?"

"Oh," said Mr. Peregrine, his twinkle returning, "I thought it would be more fun if we went somewhere I knew nothing about. That way we all learn together."

"Or we all die together," said Alex brightly. "Sounds like a blast. Glad I ordered my passport."

"Passports?" said Mr. Peregrine. "Will we need passports?"

"Oh, yeah," said Alex, deadpan. "This is going to be awesome."

"I don't doubt it," said Mr. Peregrine, missing her sarcasm. "Now . . . Where are we going again?"

"Costa Rica," said Rik, flashing Darwen a pained look.

"Quite," said Mr. Peregrine. "I keep wanting to say Ecuador or Paraguay, but I think that's just because I like the sound of the names." He patted Darwen on the shoulder. "Well," he concluded, "it is time I should be going. Classes to prepare!"

He winked. When the old man had left them, Darwen turned to the others, frowning.

"Is it just me, or does it sound like the Guardians aren't completely grasping the situation?"

"Enter the Peregrine Pact," said Rik.

"Right," said Darwen. "Alex, you should poke around online. See if you can find anything about kids going missing in Costa Rica on the day I was there, December 14th."

"Why me?"

"Your Spanish is better than mine," he said.

"There are molluscs whose Spanish is better than yours," she said.

"And Rik?" said Darwen.

"Boss?"

"Go into research mode," said Darwen. "The more we know about the stone spheres and about plants and animals that live in Costa Rica, the better chance we have of tracking things that don't belong."

"And what are you going to be doing, oh great commander?" asked Alex.

"I'm going to see what I can find out from the other side," he said. "Moth knows something, and even if she won't tell me I can use the Great Apparatus to get me to every corner of Silbrica. If that kid is being held somewhere, I'll find him."

" When do we get to visit Silbrica again?", said Rik.

"Soon," said Darwen. "I promise."

"Your job sounds a lot cooler than ours," Rik grumbled.

"That's coz he's the Mirroculist," said Alex.

Darwen gave her a quick look, but she just shrugged.

"OK," she said, standing and gathering together four heavily loaded carrier bags. "I'm outta here. Got some gifts to return. I can't decide if my mother doesn't know me at all or if she does and wishes I was someone else."

For the next three nights, Darwen returned to Silbrica through the oven door and traced his way back to the rainbow falls, but found only the shattered remains of the crystal gate. Worse, the gate which connected him to Moth's bamboo grove wasn't working. He pulled the lever, turned the dial, and pushed the button repeatedly, but nothing happened. It worried him.

Feeling slightly guilty about not bringing Rik and Alex along, Darwen sampled portal after portal looking for anything that might link to the missing boy. He appeared among palm tree hedges in deserts of curiously red sand. He explored meadows of pink flowers which closed up, as if embarrassed, as he came near them. He trekked across great, green ice flows that sparkled like emeralds and watched a shaggy yak-like beast using its spiral horn to forage for roots. Only once did he find a locus resembling a jungle, a place the tentacled monster might call home, but it was so dark there, the air so thick with strange scents and noises that he made it only a few yards from the portal before deciding that unless he returned home he was going to wind up lost or eaten.

There were, of course, things other than Silbrica to worry about. The holidays were ending and school was around the corner. From time to time the weather threatened to delay the start of classes, and while there was no more snow they did get a significant ice storm, something Darwen had never seen before. Trees and power lines looked encased in glass, everything straining under the weight of all that frozen water. They were without power for an afternoon, but then – just when it seemed that the first school day would have to be cancelled – the sun came out, and Atlanta's beleaguered road crews and utility workers got a break.

"I've checked all the hot lines," said Honoria brightly, "and we're all systems go for school tomorrow. Make sure you get a good night's sleep."

"Great," said Darwen, meaning it. He wasn't looking forward to classes or dealing with the likes of Nathan Cloten, but delaying the start of school could jeopardise the trip and that just couldn't happen. Darwen had a mission.

That night he crawled through the oven door and shot down the chute to the Great Apparatus. Mr. Peregrine hadn't had an answer for him about how they would get into Silbrica from Costa Rica. What if they never found a working portal? This might be one of the last chances he had to explore the problem of the kidnapped boy from the Silbrican side. Steeling himself, Darwen returned to the only jungle locus he had been able to find.

It was extremely dark, the canopy of leaves overhead shutting out all but the softest starlight. Darwen took a small flashlight from his pocket and shone it around so that the colours leapt into sudden focus. The beam was narrow and seemed to emphasise the darkness around it. He moved cautiously away from the portal – its glass fronted dials and brass controls hung with the twining vines that grew up from the jungle floor – and found what looked to be a path. The air was thick with a warm, sweet-smelling fog that hugged the ground and pooled wherever the earth sank away. Darwen took two careful steps, imagining the missing boy calling for help, fighting back the certainty that this method of investigation was hopelessly random and probably dangerous. Who knew what lived in such a place?

The thought had just registered, when something moved a little way off the track. He stared into the shadows of a plant whose leaves were as big as rhubarb but flickered with a bluish glow like the tiny sea creatures Darwen had seen in nature documentaries. As he tried to catch the creature – if that was what it was – in the flashlight's beam, it flicked out of sight, leaving only an eddying swirl in the ground mist.

Darwen became very still, his light trained on the spot where he had seen – or half-seen – the movement under the huge and softly pulsing leaves, certain that something – or someone – was watching him.

It surfaced on the other side of the path like a warrior stepping out of cover to make his attack. Darwen swung the light towards it and its eyes tightened in the glare. It looked a little like an otter or a mongoose, but stood on its hind legs, its fierce little eyes and whiskery snout only inches above the undulating fog.

Darwen laughed – it was just a harmless rodent! "You scared me!" he remarked at the little animal. "You want to be more careful where you pop up."

"The same could be said of you," snapped the creature, waving a paw at the flashlight.

Darwen jumped and nearly lost his footing on the soft ground. "You can talk!" he said.

The animal's eyes hardened.

"Did you think only you could talk?" it said. Its voice was rough – a snarl with words in it – and would have been funny in one so small, except that the black eyes promised a nasty bite if you so much as sniggered.

"Sorry," said Darwen. "I'm not used to talking animals."

This too, it seemed, was the wrong thing to say.

"Talking *what*?" rasped the otter-like creature. As it spoke, one tiny claw rose above the mist, and Darwen could see that it cradled a brass implement with a long barrel and a broad, slotted muzzle. The animal pointed it menacingly in Darwen's direction.

"Is that some kind of . . .?" Darwen began.

Zap!

The little brass weapon kicked in the animal's paws and a bolt of orange flashed inches from Darwen's head and exploded against a tree like a firecracker.

"Oy!" Darwen shouted, angry. "Watch what you're doing with that thing!"

He swung for the animal as he spoke, fingers reaching to grab the creature by the scruff of its neck. It ducked and weaved with remarkable speed, vanishing again into the ground fog. As Darwen pounced on the spot where the creature had been, it popped up again like a gopher from a hole three feet away, its gun – or whatever it was – aimed squarely at the side of Darwen's head.

"I told you to watch where you were pointing that!" Darwen whispered, keeping very still.

For a long moment the animal did nothing but watch him shrewdly, then it lowered the weapon.

Darwen turned very slowly and then snatched like lightning, catching the animal around the midriff with one hand while he twisted the little gun away with the other. It sank its claws into Darwen's wrist and leaned in towards his face, tiny, pointed teeth bared so that Darwen had to hold the thrashing beast at arms' length.

"Put me down!" it rasped.

"When you put down that gun," said Darwen.

"Put me down first, and I will," said the otter-thing, suddenly sly and still.

"Oh, right," said Darwen. He tried to wrench the weapon from its grasp and it yelped with genuine distress.

"You'll break it!" it said.

"I won't break it," said Darwen. "But you have to turn it off, or I won't put you down."

The creature hissed like a cat, then its features sank into a comical sulk.

"Fine," it spat. "Fine. Look, see? I turned it off."

The creature took its free paw from the mechanism of the weapon and Darwen saw that a tiny bulb that had been glowing with amber light faded out. Very carefully, Darwen turned and set the now limp body of the animal on a tree stump which rose out of the mist.

"There," he said.

The animal did not respond.

"Come on," said Darwen. "I put you down. There's nothing wrong with you."

The otter-thing opened a baleful eye and glared sorrowfully at Darwen.

"What?" demanded Darwen again.

"I let you do that," said the creature. "If I'd really wanted to fight you . . ." The animal considered Darwen carefully and something registered in its head. Its body flexed so that what had looked like someone's discarded fur hat became lithe and supple again, rippling with life and strength, and it sat up, its eyes focused and hard.

"You," it said, thoughtfully, "are a child. A human child. And you are here alone which means . . . Which can *only* mean, that you are . . . the Mirroculist!"

As it said this last word a transformation came over the creature. All trace of brooding or irritation vanished. It became alert, excited, and as Darwen watched, it began to skip on the spot, the brass muzzle of its weapon waggling about, forgotten.

"You," it announced, with a thrill of delight that rippled through its fur from head to foot, "are Darwen Arkwright!"

And it bowed.

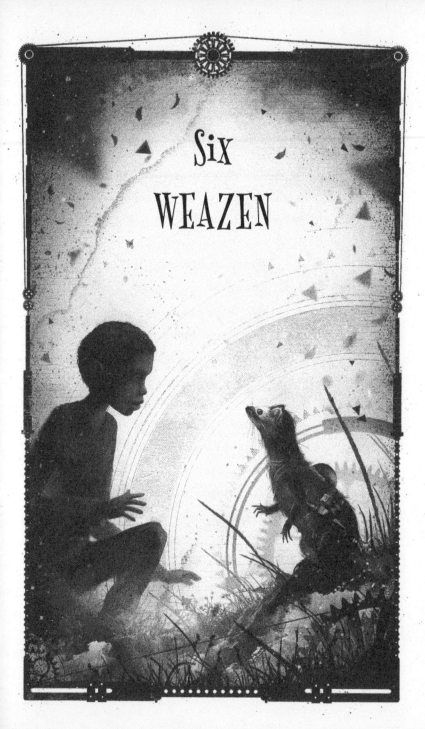

Six

WEAZEN

Now that he could see it properly, Darwen thought the creature which had ambushed him looked as much like a weasel as much as it did an otter, though its fur was slick and dark as a mink's, except around the eyes, so that it looked to be wearing a pale mask. Its paws, however, belonged to no animal he had ever seen, because though they ended in serious-looking claws, the digits were long, like fingers so that the paws finally looked less like paws and more like hands. Around its waist, it wore a belt that housed a holster for the weapon, a power pack, and a series of loops from which hung a helmet like a soup bowl with a chin strap, a long knife in a scabbard and a tiny buttoned satchel.

"What kind of . . .?" Darwen began, but decided that *animal* was sure to cause offence.

"What is your name?" he tried.

This seemed to work. The little animal puffed up its chest and performed a species of salute.

"Call me Weazen," it announced, "Peace Hunter."

"Is that your surname or your job, Peace Hunter?"

"Both," said the creature called Weazen. "I keep the Silbrican peace by hunting out those who threaten it, don't I?"

"Like a police man," said Darwen. "Or something," he added less certainly. It was hard to imagine Weazen, who was no more than two feet tall from snout to tail being much of a law enforcer, even with that little brass blaster of his, but he supposed that were he a dellfey or something of similar size, he might feel differently.

"Some'at like that, yeah," said Weazen with a smirk and a

sideways look. He picked at his teeth with one long claw. "Only I'm an independent contractor, aren't I?"

He started to absently groom his ears, watching Darwen.

"So," said Darwen. "How do you know who I am?"

At first Darwen thought the little creature was having a coughing fit, but he realised that Weazen was laughing.

"How do I know who he is, he asks!" Weazen chuckled. "The Mirroculist thinks his actions are a secret in the land he saved! That's most amusing," he added, wiping his eyes, and forcing himself to calm down.

"Word gets about, does it?" Darwen said.

"That it does, Darwen Arkwright. That it does."

"OK," said Darwen, who was beginning to see an upside to the chance encounter. "Well then, I'm sure you – as Peace Hunter, and what have you – will have heard that a human child was taken from my world – a place like this – by a Silbrican monster."

Weazen stopped laughing abruptly and his face got that shrewd look again, his head tipped slightly to one side, his bright eyes narrow.

"Hmmm," he mused. "Out of my league is that. But yeah, I've heard of it. Not the same as last time, mind," he said, as if thinking the matter through, and Darwen was struck by the idea that Weazen might not be absurd as a kind of policeman after all. "Last time it was the big gates and the machines all over the place, but this time . . ." he shrugged thoughtfully. "They tried it again," he said. "But it didn't work. I saw the wreckage. Burned-out scrobbler equipment half in and half out of Silbrica, like they couldn't get it through the portal. Then things go quiet for a while . . ."

"And then?" Darwen prompted.

"Rumours," said Weazen. "Whispers of something different, something alive and very old that no one has seen for years, centuries even."

"A thing with tentacles," said Darwen with certainty.

"Hmmm," Weazen echoed, nodding and smiling a strange, mirthless smile which showed his sharp little teeth. "Too big for the likes of Weazen," he added, "but yeah. The Guardians say nothing, but I know its name. So do the dellfeys. It's been in and out of their bedtime stories since before the Guardians came and they call it . . ." Weazen hesitated and did a half-check over his shoulder, as if anxious no one would overhear him. "They call it the Insidious Bleck."

Darwen suppressed a shiver. Moth had told him that name one of the first times they met. He still remembered her fear, guessed that was why she didn't want to talk abut it. "What is it?" he asked.

"No one knows for sure," said Weazen darkly, "because those who see it don't tend to stick around, if you catch my drift."

"Where can I find it?"

At this the little creature looked at Darwen, its face wry.

"Find it?" it said. "You don't find the Insidious Bleck. It finds you, and then you run. Very fast and as far away as possible."

"But how do you fight it?" Darwen pressed. "Surely you as a Peace Hunter know . . ."

"I know which battles can be won," said Weazen seriously, "and which give you the choice of retreat or, if you like . . . total destruction. Take it from Weazen, who has seen sights told only in songs: you can't win against the Bleck. If that is what is taking children, Darwen Arkwright, you will have to let them go."

"Never," said Darwen. "I won't."

"You're a tough one," Weazen said, nodding in a grandfatherly way. "But you've got to have a bit of *nouse*," he said, tapping the side of his head. "Sometimes, my lad, you have to know when to walk away. This is one of those times."

"No," said Darwen. "We could fight it together. You could come with me . . ."

But the little creature was shaking its head sadly, and suddenly it looked old.

"You should go back to your world, Darwen Arkwright," he said. "There may be a way to fight this thing from there. Here in Silbrica, you are up the proverbial creek with nary a paddle in sight."

Darwen tried to unravel this remark.

"You can't win," said Weazen, to be clear. "Most creatures that hunt are themselves hunted by something larger or more terrible. Very few have no natural enemies, Darwen Arkwright."

"You are saying this Insidious Bleck is one of the apex predators?" asked Darwen, borrowing a term he had learned from Rik. " The thing that lives at the top of the food chain that everything else tries to stay away from, like tigers or great white sharks?"

"Right, and correct," said Weazen. "In the forests of Silbrica, the apex predator is the Insidious Bleck and I'm pretty sure it would eat your tigers and sharks – whatever they are – for breakfast. So I'll say it one more time. Go home."

And so saying, he bowed once more, adjusted the settings of his weapon, and dived neatly into the carpet of fog, leaving Darwen alone.

"Wait!" Darwen called after him, but Weazen did not surface again, and after a few minutes, Darwen gave up waiting. He had already been in Silbrica too long and couldn't risk being trapped inside the oven door after the sun rose. It was time he got back.

He returned to the Great Apparatus and rotated the chute so he could use the built-in steps up to his bedroom, then he crawled in and started to climb. It was a long, exhausting ascent. At last he could see the bright hatchway of the oven door up ahead, but then he saw something which stopped him cold.

Legs.

Long, slim legs in black slacks. Aunt Honoria was in his room.

Seven

UNDER

A CLOUD

Darwen panicked. How was he going to get out without her seeing him?

He had frozen in the shaft so she wouldn't hear the metal echoing as he moved, but then decided that she wouldn't be able to hear him for the same reason she wouldn't see him behind the oven door. He slithered as close to the end of the square shaft as he could without poking his head out into the room.

The duvet had been torn from his bed and the floor was strewn with clothes from his wardrobe. Honoria had obviously gone nuts searching the room. How long had she been there fretting over his absence? She was sitting on the edge of the bed now, her phone clutched tightly in one hand and a hanky in the other. He could hear her sobbing.

Great, thought Darwen. *Now what?*

He had, he figured, two choices. Stay where he was until she moved far enough away that he could get out and come up with some plausible explanation about where he had been, or come right out of the oven door in front of her very eyes. Then, if she didn't have a heart attack on the spot, he would have to tell her everything.

Boy, he thought, *do I not want to do that.*

In the last few months he had grown more comfortable with his aunt, but she was a practical, no-nonsense woman. Darwen didn't think there was room in her head for Silbrica and its various monsters. At best, she'd have him seeing a psychiatrist twenty-four hours a day. At worst, she might believe him and spend the rest of her life in terror of what might be lurking behind the bathroom mirror.

No, he decided. *He could not tell her.*

Which meant he had to wait till she left but not too long, because once the sun came up, he was trapped. He sighed, shifting to find a more comfortable position in the confines of the shaft, but it wasn't possible. He lay on his back, staring at the metal inches from his face, and when he had exhausted the interest value of that, he closed his eyes.

He woke with a start, banging his forehead on the metal. For a moment he had no idea where he was, but then he was rolling, straining against his cramped and aching muscles to peer out into his room. He heard voices but they were distant and he couldn't see his aunt no matter how much he twisted and turned. He thought he heard the crackle of a radio like on cop shows. She was probably sitting up in the living room with the TV on. Now was as good a time as ever.

He worked his arms through the oven door, grabbed it by the rim and pulled himself out in one smooth motion. He got to his feet hurriedly, and without thinking of what he was going to say, walked quickly into the living room.

Honoria wasn't watching a cop show. She was sitting on the couch looking teary, and with her were two police officers, one male, one female. Darwen stared at them, and as they turned to gape at him, he said the only thing he could think of:

"Hi."

It was a disaster. It was dangerously close to dawn, which meant he had been missing for at least six hours. The police had been searching the building, waking their neighbors in the process, calling his friends and teachers, and scouring the surrounding streets. Worse, Darwen could think of nothing that would explain his absence. He suggested he had fallen asleep under the bed, which sounded so deeply stupid even in his own ears that he couldn't believe he was saying it.

"But I looked there!" his Aunt exclaimed.

It was awful. The cops were annoyed with both of them, uncertain who to blame. No one was convinced by Darwen's story that he had never left his bedroom – though he was able to argue this point convincingly since it was, in a manner of speaking, true – but they couldn't figure out how he had got in and out of the building unseen. The female cop insisted on going back over his room in search of a rope ladder, but since they lived on the seventeenth floor, nobody thought that plausible either.

Worst of all, of course, was Aunt Honoria. Darwen braced himself to be yelled at, but she just cried, and said, between sobs, that she was glad he was back. It didn't make him feel like he had gotten away with anything though. She looked more than humiliated that the police thought her incompetent, more than scared that he had been missing. She looked crushed, as if Darwen's acting out just proved what a failure she was as a parent, all her careful Christmas planning exposed as an empty shell, an idea of family that wasn't real.

"I thought you were doing so well," she said, suddenly exhausted. "I thought *we* were doing well. I'm so sorry, Darwen."

Darwen had hoped that going to school would take his mind off the previous night's fiasco, but it was only when he reached Hillside that the full scale of the disaster became clear. In her panic, Honoria had given the police the names of every kid in his class, and their midnight calls generated a lot of hostile looks. His classmates watched him everywhere he went, scowling and muttering. Darwen, tired beyond anything he had felt before, tried to avoid their eyes, but it was impossible.

"Bet you thought that was funny, huh Arkwright?" remarked Chip Whittley as they filed into the assembly hall. "Waking my mother at two in the morning? Like you might be with *me*? Like we're *friends*?"

"I never told anyone you were my friend," Darwen shot back.

"Yeah, right," said Chip. "Maybe if you had friends who weren't total losers you wouldn't have to lie about it, and maybe you wouldn't be out in the streets in the middle of the night breaking shop windows and selling drugs."

"What?" Darwen gasped.

Chip sauntered away.

"Ignore him," said Rik. "Nobody thinks that."

"They will now," grumbled Darwen watching Chip saunter away. Chip was high fiving Nathan Cloten.

"I'm going to tell him . . ." said Darwen, elbowing his way out of the line and toward Chip.

"You'll tell him what, Darwen?" said Rik, laying a heavy hand on his shoulder.

Darwen stood there feeling furious and powerless.

"Ahhhh Mr. Arkwright," said a sardonic voice behind him. It could only belong to Mr. Sumners, the maths teacher who took delight in pointing out Darwen's failings as a student.

"I suggest you get back in line," said the teacher with a nasty smile. "Wouldn't want to have to call your ahhhh aunt on the first day, would I? Even if it would make me feel a little better about losing an hour's sleep last night."

"They called you?" Darwen blurted, his face flushing.

"I'm sure you think that hilarious."

"No," Darwen protested, adding at the last moment, "*sir.* I don't. It was a . . . a misunderstanding."

"They seem to follow you around, don't they Mr. Arkwright," said Sumners coolly. "I think we'll need to establish some ahhhh very clear rules, you and I, just so we don't *misunderstand* each other."

The teacher walked away and Darwen took his place as the principal, Mr. Thompson, walked out onto the stage. Darwen noticed with a stab of guilt that even the Principal looked tired, as if he might have been dragged from his bed in the small hours by a police phone call.

A perfect start to the New Year, he thought heavily.

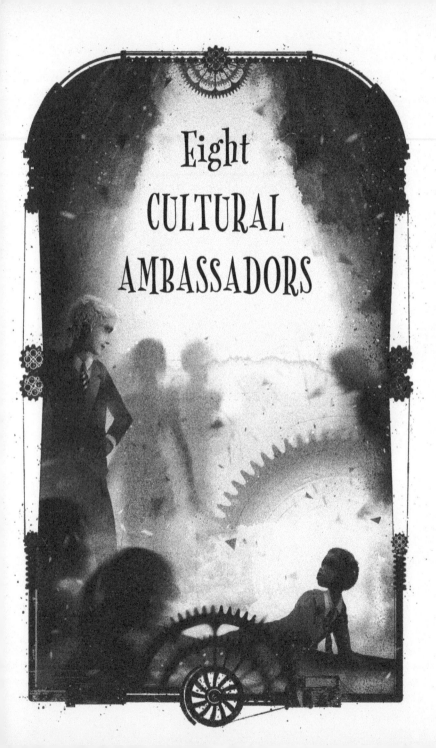

Eight
CULTURAL
AMBASSADORS

The principal's announcements went through Darwen's head without engaging his brain. All, that is, but one, the reminder of the sixth grade trip organised by the new world studies teacher, Mr. Octavius Peregrine, who they welcomed with the obligatory three second burst of applause. Details of the trip, said the principal, a little uncertainly, had been mailed, though some were still being resolved. Darwen saw Alex grin at that. One of the details as yet unresolved seemed to be where exactly the trip would go.

"It's definitely Costa Rica," said the principal, looking far from definite, "though the precise . . . er . . . *vicinity* . . . is still being finalised so as to benefit from our new world studies teacher's on-going research. Hillside's involvement in such investigation will, I am sure, be another feather in our collective cap. College admission boards are surprisingly impressed by such things. I am also sure that the trip will be an innovative learning experience, and that you will serve as our little school's finest cultural ambassadors. Now, let us conclude with the Hillside Academy Principles of Learning."

As the rest of the students boomed them out – "memorisation, organisation, and logic" – Darwen glanced over at Mr. Peregrine who was smiling, blinking contentedly, unaware of the slightly dubious looks he was getting from some of the other faculty. Darwen wished he was closer. He had to talk to him, tell him what he had learned from Weazen about the name of the tentacled monster. But he couldn't get to him now, and besides, Mr. Peregrine was talking to an olive-skinned, skinny boy with quick, uneasy eyes who Darwen had never seen before.

"Who's that?" he asked Rik as they marched out.

"The new kid," said Rik, eyebrows raised. "Gabriel something. They just introduced him. Weren't you paying attention?"

Darwen shrugged.

"So," said Rik. "Do I need to ask where you were when the cops were calling my Dad in the middle of the night?"

"No," said Darwen, lowering his voice. "I was on my way back and my aunt was in my bedroom. I waited behind the oven door, but fell asleep . . ."

"You fell *asleep*?" echoed Alex who had just joined them, her face like thunder. "How nice, getting a little shut-eye while the rest of the school searched for you. You must have been *right chuffed*."

"Don't you start," said Darwen.

"That means happy, yeah? *Right chuffed*?" Alex continued, testing the phrase in her mouth in what was supposed to be a version of Darwen's accent. "*I got an oven door for Christmas. I were right chuffed.*"

They entered the homeroom classroom and moved to their desks, Darwen frowning.

"You need to put a lock on your door, man," said Rik.

"I don't think my aunt will go for that right now. She thinks I'm . . . I don't know."

"Insane?" suggested Alex. "Bonkers? Mental?"

"Sad," said Darwen. "She thinks I'm not adjusting well to being here, I suppose."

He looked down, flushing. Rik patted his shoulder awkwardly.

"I'm fine!" Darwen protested. "She's got it wrong, that's all. I just couldn't think up a good enough excuse. I'm fine."

"Fine," said Alex, with her trademark skepticism. "I'm totally convinced. You hide your feelings about as well as my dog. Hey Darwen!" she exclaimed with ridiculous enthusiasm, "wanna treat? Wanna go on the trip? Good boy, Darwen!"

"Funny," said Darwen.

"You wanna know the truth, Darwen Arkwright?" said Alex, leaning in close. "You wouldn't have gotten into this mess if you had taken us with you – you know, me and Rik, the people who stood by you every step of the way when the school was about to go down in a blaze of scrobbler glory – instead of going into Silbrica by yourself. So don't expect sympathy from us."

Darwen turned to Rik for understanding, but Rik looked down, his face glowing like a stop light. His friends had clearly had this conversation before without him.

Darwen nodded once, eyes downcast.

"OK then," said Alex, as if that closed the matter.

"Stand behind your chairs, class," said Miss Harvey. "Some of you seem to have forgotten how to conduct yourselves over the vacation. I realise this is your first day back but I will make no further allowances. Now, single file to your first class which is, I believe . . ."

"Science, Maam," Rik supplied, happily.

"Quite so, Mr. Haggerty. Lead the way."

Rik marched down the hall so quickly that everyone had to jog a little to keep up.

"It's not a race, Mr. Haggerty!" called Miss Harvey.

"He's another with Sasha's gift for self-restraint," said Alex.

"Sasha?" said Miss Harvey.

"My dog," said Alex. "She's half-husky, half-shepherd and half-floppy-eared-something-else while still only being one dog, not, you know, one and a half. She's very talented."

"To class, Miss O'Connor," said Miss Harvey. "In silence."

They slowed a fraction and Darwen felt a foot come down hard on the back of his ankle. He stumbled and fell headlong on the floor, knocking Genevieve Reddock down with him. As Melissa Young shrieked unnecessarily, the class's neat line broke apart giggling and several more people managed to fall over in the confusion, including Gabriel, the new boy. Miss Harvey came marching down the corridor shouting about discipline and "all this fooling about." Darwen rolled over and found himself gazing up into the tanned, handsome face of Nathan Cloten.

"Have a good trip, Arkwright?" he asked, grinning maliciously. Then, as the new boy accidentally bumped him in the ribs, he snapped, "Watch yourself, amigo."

Gabriel blushed and shuffled away.

Darwen got to his feet and brushed himself off, averting his eyes.

"Darwen, I'm surprised at you!" exclaimed Miss Harvey as she swooped in and started dragging people to their feet.

"It weren't me, Miss," Darwen sputtered, his Lancashire accent kicking up a gear as it always did when he was flustered. "It were Nathan, right? 'e stood on ma foot and . . ."

"I am not interested in excuses, Mr. Arkwright," said Miss Harvey in a chill voice. "Hillside Students take responsibility for their mistakes, misjudgments, and misdemeanours."

Another line from the school brochure, Darwen guessed.

"Now," said Miss Harvey, "do you think you can make it to science class without treating the other students like pins in a bowling alley?"

"Bowling would be better, Miss," said Alex. "We'd still be standing and he'd be in the gutter. Trust me. I've seen him bowl."

"That's enough, Miss O'Connor," said Miss Harvey. "Off you go. Left, right, left, right."

And so they did, though the moment they were out of the teacher's earshot Darwen could hear Nathan behind him, whining in what he thought was a comical imitation of Darwen's accent: "*It weren't me, Miss. It were Nathan, Miss. Miss, will someone teach me to speak English? Please, Miss. Only, I'm a complete moron, Miss.*"

Darwen stared fixedly at the back of Genevieve Reddock's head. "The sooner I can get on that plane, the better," he muttered.

"You're still allowed to go?" said Genevieve, turning, eyebrows raised.

"Of course," said Darwen, with a rush of panic. "Why wouldn't I be?"

Genevieve raised her eyebrows, but she said nothing and turned away. Alex leaned in.

"Well the teachers – not to mention your aunt – think you've been climbing out of skyscraper windows," she said. "They might not all think you're a juvenile delinquent who breaks shop windows and sells drugs, but I'm not sure they see you as a cultural ambassador right now."

Darwen's heart sank. It wasn't just a trip. It was a mission. Not going was not – could not – be an option.

The rest of the week was completely dominated by the upcoming trip. Science classes focused on the Central American rainforest, Mr. Peregrine's world studies classes had turned – albeit vaguely – to Costa Rican history and culture, and Spanish classes were swamped with what Nathan derisively called "tourist phrase book stuff": *"I would like some red beans and rice, please," "How many pesos does that cost?",* and *"Why is my luggage in Nigeria?"* Everywhere Darwen turned, people seemed to be talking about the trip in excited and panicky terms. Genevieve and Melissa seemed to have been clothes shopping all through the holidays, and were keen to break down their travel wardrobes for whomever would listen.

"Of course, we won't be able to make the final choices," said Genevieve, "until we know what kind of hotel we'll be in. If we're spending most of our time by the pool, that's going to change the way I accessorise."

Darwen caught Alex's eye and they exchanged a knowing look. If Mr. Peregrine was involved, it was unlikely they would be spending much time lounging by a hotel pool. Of course, if everyone assumed Darwen was a juvenile delinquent, not liking what kind of accommodation Mr. Peregrine had planned would be the least of Darwen's problems. Conversely, not being there to save the boy would, naturally, rank at the top.

As if reading his mind, Alex leant over and whispered.

"I have news, by the way," she said. "I've been reading Costa Rican newspapers online."

"And?"

"The boy you saw taken was called Luis Vasquez," she said.

"He was the second to go missing."

Luis, thought Darwen. Finally he had a name.

"And that's not all," said Alex. "His brother, Eduardo, kept going into the jungle, searching for him. A week later whatever took his brother, took him too."

That evening over dinner – pasta with a green, strong tasting sauce his aunt told him was a "simply divine" pesto – Darwen finally raised the question.

"So, about the sixth grade trip," he said, trying to sound casual.

"I got a letter," said his aunt, palms down on the table top, face unreadable.

Darwen knew she had. He had recognised the envelope with its embossed HA emblem, and had seen enough to make sure it wasn't another summons to a parent/teacher meeting about his behaviour.

"It's only a week away," he said. "I should probably be packing. If I'm going, like."

He looked at his plate. His aunt wasn't speaking but he could feel her eyes on him.

"You want to go," she said finally.

"Is it too expensive?" he asked, looking up.

"No," she said, waving the question away. "I can find the money. I may have to work longer hours while you're gone . . ."

"So I can go!?" Darwen exclaimed. "I mean, I'm sorry you'll have to work extra hours. I didn't know you could work longer hours than you already do. I don't mean you're not around enough or anything," he blundered on, knowing he was making it worse but unable to stop, "I just mean that you work really hard and I really appreciate it and everything . . ."

"Darwen . . ." she said.

Darwen stopped speaking abruptly and looked into her shrewd dark eyes.

"Where did you go?"

Darwen didn't need to ask what she meant.

"I never left the apartment," he said. "I swear I didn't. I'm fine. I'm happy. I'm not homesick . . . well, not too much. Not usually. And I'm not shoplifting or dealing drugs . . ."

"Who said you were dealing drugs?" Honoria gasped.

"Just some kids at school," said Darwen, wishing he hadn't said it, "trying to get me in trouble."

"Do you have enemies at school, Darwen?"

Darwen's brow furrowed. He really wasn't sure. There were kids like Nathan and Chip who didn't like him much, but enemies? No. He met her concerned, watchful gaze and shook his head.

"Just, you know: kid stuff," he said. "Nothing bad. Nothing I can't handle."

"And you really want to go on this trip?"

"Yeah! Rik and Alex are going, and there'll be loads of teachers there too. They're basically shutting down a bunch of classes for the older kids so enough faculty can go."

"They do say they have a very high student-to-teacher ratio," said Honoria, approvingly.

"There you go then," said Darwen. "That's good isn't it? And it's *innovative and experiential learning*."

Honoria nodded sagely, as if she thought this – whatever it was – was a good thing.

"And," Darwen concluded, "Mr. Peregrine is leading the whole thing so . . ."

"So?"

"Well," Darwen finished lamely, wishing he hadn't brought the ex-shopkeeper into it at all. "He's nice, isn't he?"

"Darwen," said Honoria very seriously, "he gave you an oven door for Christmas."

"Right," said Darwen. "Yes. He's got a . . . you know . . . quirky sense of humour."

He tried to smile in an upbeat kind of way. His aunt laid down her knife and fork and sat back, blowing out her breath in a long rush which took her eyes up to the ceiling. At last, she shrugged.

"OK," she said. "The books say I'm supposed to let you find yourself so . . . OK."

"I can go?"

"You can go," she breathed, swallowing back what Darwen felt sure was a sob. "But keep your nose clean or I'll cancel, and if I hear so much as a rumour of you wandering off while you are there, you'll be on the next flight home, you hear me?"

"Yes, ma'am," said Darwen, gripping the stone sphere in his pocket.

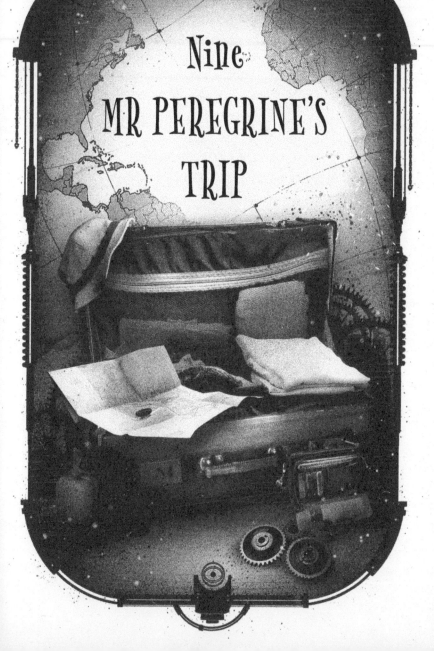

Nine

MR PEREGRINE'S TRIP

Darwen had been trying to catch Mr. Peregrine alone for days, but he always seemed to be dashing off, his arms laden with maps and travel documents. At last he found him behind a stack of books in the world studies classroom.

"What's the Insidious Bleck?" Darwen asked. He had wanted to ask Moth the same question last night but, once more, had not been able to enter her locus.

"Nothing," said Mr. Peregrine, without looking up from his book. "A fairy tale monster. Where did you . . .?"

"Didn't you say that about the Shade?" said Darwen.

"Hmm?" said Mr. Peregrine. "Oh, yes. You saw one, didn't you? Well done!"

"I think the Insidious Bleck is the thing I saw," Darwen persisted.

"Really? Well, you have been right before. And besides, whatever we call it, it's still just a lost and hungry animal."

"All the more reason to find Luis as quickly as possible," countered Darwen.

"Who?" said Mr. Peregrine.

"Luis Vasquez," said Darwen. "The boy who was taken."

"You know his name?" asked Mr. Peregrine.

"Alex found it online," said Darwen.

"Online?" Mr. Peregrine echoed.

"It doesn't matter," said Darwen, grinning. "How are we going to find him?"

"Well," said the teacher. "I suppose we'll have to figure that out when we get there. Our first priority is plugging the breach between worlds . . ."

"We still need some way of getting to Silbrica while we're there . . ."

"Darwen," said Mr. Peregrine, rubbing his temples like he was developing a headache. "I'm sorry, but I really must get on."

Darwen turned to go but caught himself.

"Mr. Peregrine," he said.

"Yes Darwen?"

"You do believe me about Luis, don't you?" Darwen said. "About the monster pulling him into a portal, I mean."

"My dear boy," said Mr. Peregrine, "of course I believe you. Did you doubt that?"

Darwen blushed and looked down, but he felt better.

"Now, I'm sorry," said Mr. Peregrine, "but . . . these little countries in the middle," he said, peering at a map of Central America, "are very confusing. I keep forgetting which one we're going to. Wait, I think I have the map upside down . . ."

"Right," said Darwen, with another twinge of anxiety. "I'll leave you to it."

Darwen had assumed that the air of mystery and strangeness which hung around Mr. Peregrine would go away once the students started having classes with him. He even feared that the former shopkeeper would turn out to be incompetent in the classroom and would become a bit of a joke. He couldn't have been more wrong.

For one thing, there were rumours about him. Several of the students thought they recognised Mr. Peregrine, and one of them,

Carlos Garcia, remembered that he had seen him three months before on that most famous night in Hillside's history, Halloween. There had been a party at school, a fancy dress 'Hop,' which had ended with power outages and explosions and policemen running about trying to establish order. People saw strange things that night, and though most of it was chalked down to costumes and fireworks, the students still talked about it in hushed and excited tones. Now they remembered that this strange new teacher had been on campus that night, that he had somehow taken charge, consulting with the police and EMTs, and telling the teachers what to do. Parents had been overheard saying they thought he had saved student lives.

"He just took over," Carlos murmured to Gabriel and a rapt audience of twelve-year-olds, "ordering people about and everything, but he wasn't even a teacher! So who was he? And what happened to him afterwards? At the end of that night he just walks away and no one sees him till the last day of term when he's suddenly the world studies teacher?"

Darwen, Alex, and Rik avoided each others' eyes, and Darwen found himself irritated that Carlos – who was usually so quiet – should pick this moment to come out of his shell.

"I heard he's a kind of shadow principal," said Jennifer Taylor-Berry in her rich southern drawl. "That he comes in when the school is in trouble."

"I heard he works for the government," said Simon Agu, whose father was a diplomat at the Nigerian consulate on Roswell Road. "Some kind of secret agency connected to paranormal activity.

I mean, there was stuff that happened at the Halloween Hop that no one has ever explained properly."

"Yeah," said Alex. "Because what's going on in an Atlanta middle school is a matter of national security. And you say *I* have a vivid imagination!"

"Nice one," said Darwen, as soon as the others had traipsed off looking shame-faced.

"Maybe, but these kids aren't utterly stupid," said Alex. "Mr. P is going to have to watch himself or even Barry Fails will start putting two and two together."

Barry "Usually" Fails was, as Darwen sometimes said, as thick as two short planks.

"Anyway, the Peregrine Pact is supposed to be us," Alex concluded, "you, me, and Rik, not the entire school."

Mr. Peregrine's demeanour in class didn't help the situation. He did a lot of smiling, as if he had secret knowledge which amused him, and taught by asking questions, waiting sometimes for minutes at a time until someone came up with the right answer. Darwen suspected that the teacher didn't actually know a lot of what he was teaching, but the others took these long silences as a clever strategy to make them learn for themselves.

"Best teacher we've had," said Bobby Park, "at least for this subject."

"I wonder who he is, though," said Melissa Young to Genevieve Reddock, conspiratorially. "I mean who he *really* is. He's obviously not from round here and has lived in all sorts of places. You can hear it in his voice, see it in his eyes. He knows things the other teachers don't."

Darwen, Rik and Alex made eye contact again, then – as they seemed to be doing a lot lately – looked hurriedly away.

The night before they left, Darwen went over his luggage with his aunt twice. It seemed that the only thing he wasn't packing was the stone sphere, and that was only because Aunt Honoria had yet to learn of its existence. "Are you sure you won't need warmer clothing?" she said, considering a T -shirt skeptically.

Darwen consulted the list which had been sent from the school again.

"Says warm weather clothes," he said. "Costa Rica is in the northern hemisphere but only just and it's actually summer there now."

"But wait, it also says long pants and sturdy walking shoes," replied Aunt Honoria, horror dawning. "You'll be burning up!"

"I'll be fine," said Darwen, smiling and patting her hand. She returned his smile with an effort and her eyes welled up.

"Oh, insect repellant!"

"What?" exclaimed Aunt Honoria, the shock of their having possibly forgotten something nearly causing her to swoon.

"The list says I need insect repellant for mosquitoes and stuff," said Darwen.

"There's a pharmacy on the corner," she said, quickly composing herself. "Get your coat on and we'll walk down together."

By the time they were back, weighed down by the medical supplies with which Aunt Honoria planned to pack his suitcase, it was after sundown. Darwen waited patiently, trying to look appreciative as his aunt doubled the weight of his luggage with boxes of pills and bottles of sprays and ointments.

"That's to keep the bugs off," she said. "That's to put on the bites if they get you. This is if you can't go to the bathroom, and this one is if you're going too much. Don't mix them up or it could get ugly . . ."

"I get it," said Darwen. "Thanks."

She paused and took a breath, as if resigned that there was nothing more she could do. "OK," she said. "Let's get some rest. I'm sorry I can't come to the airport with you. I have to . . ."

"Work," said Darwen smiling. "I know. It's fine."

She hesitated at the bedroom door, then turned meaningfully back to Darwen. "I'll miss you, you know.," she said.

"I'll miss you too," Darwen answered, surprised that it was true.

"And please, Darwen . . ." she said.

"What?"

"Be careful."

His aunt had no idea just how careful Darwen *wasn't* being. That night, he travelled through the oven door one last time in the hopes of finding any information that could help in their search for Luis and his brother. Anything that would make their mission in Costa Rica easier. But the gateway to Moth's bamboo grove remained troublingly sealed, and though Darwen retraced his steps to the crystal waterfall he found nothing helpful. He had hoped for another glimpse of Weazen the Peace Hunter or some clue that would make his mission clearer but he found nothing; no new evidence revealed itself.

At last, Darwen returned to his room. He put on his pyjamas and snuck into bed. And though he remained frustrated by his lack of progress, he stared up at his featureless ceiling safe in the knowledge that for once, the morning would bring something almost as exciting as Silbrica. The prospect of being away from home with his friends for a whole week thrilled him, but when he finally fell asleep he dreamed he was searching for a boy called Luis among jungle vines which turned into tentacles . . .

Ten
INTO THE WILD

The Atlanta airport was vast and crowded, and though Darwen had been through it once before, he found it all very intimidating. Mr. Peregrine bustled about looking dazed, so it was Miss Harvey and Mr. Sumners who had to ultimately engineer the logistics of gathering the students and marching them en masse to the departure gate.

"What's Sumners coming for?" asked Darwen, wearily. "He's a maths teacher."

"High faculty to student ratio, remember?" said Rik.

"Maybe we can push him out half-way there," said Alex. "He can swim to Miami. It would be a shame if the sharks got him, though. I hate sharks, but they *are* endangered, and eating maths teachers can't be good for them."

Besides Mr. Peregrine, Miss Harvey and Mr. Sumners, the sixteen sixth graders were accompanied by Mr. Iverson, and the foreign language teacher, Miss Martinez.

"We need to make sure we're always with Mr. P," said Alex.

"Or Mr. Iverson," said Rik.

"So long as we stay away from Sumners, I don't care," said Darwen.

Their flight would take them south over Florida and out into the Atlantic, then between Cuba and the coast of Mexico, before dropping further south past Belize, Guatemala, Honduras and Nicaragua. They were to land in San Jose, Costa Rica, and then get a local connection further south still to Drake Bay which sat on the Pacific side almost on the border with Panama. The names meant almost nothing to Darwen, far away places as strange as anything in Silbrica, and he sympathised with Mr. Peregrine who was as unfamiliar with them as he was. At least Darwen didn't have to pretend he was an expert on world studies.

Once they had waved off their families and trundled through security, the excitement started to mount, and by the time they were on the plane it was like someone had turned a volume control up on the students. They were laughing and gossiping, flicking excitedly through Rik's brand new *Field Guide to Costa Rican Wildlife*, planning and speculating, squabbling and – in the case of Alex – singing very loudly.

"We are not the only people on this aircraft," said Miss Harvey. "Miss O'Connor? Miss . . .? Will someone please tell her to take those earbuds out?"

Alex continued to croon at the top of her lungs, her eyes shut. She didn't respond when Rik, who was getting fidgety, tapped her on the shoulder, so Darwen leaned over and pulled the earbud right out of her ears.

"Hey!" she roared. "You could just ask, you know."

"That is what we have been trying to do," said Miss Harvey, icily.

The group quieted but a few moments later produced a great cheer as they felt the aircraft tip up and away from the runway. Mr. Peregrine, who seemed to be having the time of his life, cheered loudest of all, so that Mr. Sumners shot him the kind of look he normally reserved for Darwen's homework. Darwen found himself grinning widely at Rik, unexpectedly delighted that they were in the air at last and a huge step closer to starting their mission. In the next row, Gabriel, the new boy, was sitting looking blank-faced beside Melissa Young who was ignoring him and leaning over to whisper to Genevieve Reddock.

"First flight?" asked Darwen, turning all the way round.

"Second," said Gabriel.

"Mine too," said Darwen. "I think it's brilliant."

"Hey, Darwen," said Genevieve. "Is this Mr. Peregrine the weirdest teacher you've ever had or what?"

It wasn't a criticism. Darwen peered over to where Mr. P was sitting, collecting all the tiny bags of mini pretzels no one wanted and piling them up in front of him gleefully like they were treasure.

"Pretty weird," agreed Darwen, grinning.

They landed in San Jose and emerged from the plane pointing at the mountains which surrounded the town. The warm, muggy air hit them so everyone shrugged themselves out of their winter jackets.

"Northern hemisphere geography, southern hemisphere seasons," Rik muttered.

Darwen and Alex exchanged knowing looks. They had been told this a dozen times so that they wouldn't stuff their luggage with winter clothes.

"You OK?" asked Darwen.

"Fine," said Rik. "Why wouldn't I be? It's just a regular town, right?"

Except that it wasn't a regular town, not by Georgian standards at least, and not only because all the signs were in Spanish. It was bustling with pedestrians for one thing, and though there were cars, traffic lights and shops which might just have passed unnoticed in parts of Atlanta, the whole still felt different, if only because of the wooded mountains that loomed in every direction. They made everything feel just a little strange and unfamiliar.

"I like it," Alex pronounced, as they took the shuttle bus across town to another, smaller airport. "It's like Silbrica without the monsters."

"Let's hope so," muttered Darwen.

The students were glued to the bus windows, all except Nathan and his friends who played cards at the back, but even they took notice of the rush of mingled concern and excitement when everyone saw the planes they were to board next. There were two, each one built to carry no more than a dozen.

"We're flying in those?" gasped Barry Fails.

"Propeller planes are perfectly reliable," said Mr. Iverson, considering the slightly battered aircraft. "Even . . . er . . . older models like this."

Rik who had stopped dead to stare wide-eyed at the small, dodgy-looking planes, had to be virtually shoved into the tiny airport. Darwen gave him an encouraging smile as they checked in but it didn't seem to help.

"Isn't this a treat!" exclaimed Mr. Peregrine as he gazed at the antique planes.

"Everyone stand on the scales with your luggage," called Miss Harvey, who seemed rather less enthusiastic. "Ladies first, single file and with dignity."

An official from the airline checked the weight of each student and their bags, and told Princess Clarkson she was nine kilograms overweight. Princess looked scandalised, then brandished a credit card and announced she would just pay the overage.

"I'm afraid not," said the official, shaking his head and smiling. "Each passenger is allowed eleven kilograms of luggage. No more."

"Then I'll just buy another seat," said Princess.

Darwen and Rik gaped at her.

"No," said the official, still smiling as if he was used to this. "The plane is full. If you need the bag, we can fly it down tomorrow, for a charge. If you can manage without it, you should leave it here and collect it on your way back."

Princess sighed theatrically.

"Fine," she snapped. "Bring it tomorrow."

She waggled the credit card.

"What is in the bag," said Mr. Peregrine, "which you cannot manage without, Miss . . .?"

"Clarkson," prompted Miss. Harvey.

"Stuff," said Princess. A huddle of students had gathered around and more were pricking up their ears.

"Of what kind?" pressed Mr. Peregrine.

"Personal stuff," said Princess with a haughty glare.

"Could you be more specific?"

"Er, Mr. Peregrine?" inserted Miss Harvey, "I don't think we need to know precisely what Miss Clarkson is carrying, in fact I'm not sure we are allowed to ask . . ."

"Getting another bag to us tomorrow is going to be extremely inconvenient for whomever has to actually bring it," said Mr.

Peregrine. "I want to be sure we are not wasting anyone's time, as well as this young lady's money."

Miss Harvey frowned, but before she could say anything, Princess muttered *"fine"* and unzipped her bag with a flourish.

"Happy?" she said.

"This," said Mr. Peregrine peering into the pink suitcase, "is a device for drying hair? And this entire container is full of make up. These," he said holding up a dress of shimmering, lustrous fabric studded with sequins, "are evening gowns . . .?"

"Gotta have something to wear for dinner, don't I?" said Princess, as if she had made her point.

"Where we are going, these," said Mr. Peregrine, searching for the right words. "aren't going to work."

Princess opened her mouth to protest, then closed it just as quickly. Mr. Peregrine's kindly face spoke volumes about where they were going.

As Princess, dumbstruck, watched her pink suitcase carted into storage, and Genevieve Reddock put a supportive arm around her shoulder, Alex turned to Darwen. "That," she said, "was pretty cool. Did you see the designer label on that dress? Sell a case full of those and you could probably buy Rik's house."

"Thanks," snapped Rik.

"What?" said Alex. "I'm just saying."

They squabbled as they walked across the runway and up the narrow metal stairs into the plane. Inside they had to bend over, squeezing into their tight little plastic seats and strapping themselves in with considerably more care than they had on the jet from Atlanta. Darwen's tiny window gave him an unnervingly good view of one wing and an engine, and if he looked ahead he could see right into the cockpit, where the two pilots were flicking instruments to make sure they were working.

The engines were loud, starting deep and low like the revving of a scrobbler motorbike, then growing higher and more nasal as they approached take-off. The students who had been so excited before were now edgy and quiet, avoiding each other's eyes. Instead of the long, slow taxi the jet had made, the tiny plane reached its bumpy, rattling take-off speed alarmingly quickly, and in seconds they were up and banking hard as they climbed.

Darwen waited for the engines to stall and for the plane to drop out of the sky like a rock, but when time passed and nothing of the kind happened, he began to relax. The plane stayed below the cloud level so he could see the city fall quickly behind them, instantly replaced by densely forested hills where, it seemed, no one lived. He thought wooded, because that was what the proper name – rainforest – suggested, but the word which insisted itself into his mind was one which had popped out of *Treasure Island*; the word was *jungle*.

The land below was a thick green carpet, but these were not fields, they were treetops, the canopy of a rich ecosystem positively throbbing with life. Darwen stole a look at Rik and was pleased to see he sensed it too. Rik's anxiety had melted away once they got airborne, and there was a hungry excitement as he gazed at the jungle below.

And somewhere down there, thought Darwen, *is a creature that doesn't belong, and it's taking kids* . . .

"Good thing Princess dumped her evening gowns, huh?" said Alex.

They landed less than an hour later on a grassy strip of land cleared of trees with what looked like a bus shelter next to it. It was so hot when Darwen climbed out that he thought he was too close to the plane's engine but as he walked away and the temperature didn't change, he tugged at his tie and unfastened his collar button. Then someone screamed.

Darwen spun around and saw Barry Fails, one hand clasped over his mouth, the other pointing at something long and green in the grass: it was four feet from head to tail, and covered with spines like something out of one of Darwen's old dinosaur books. Several people jumped and took hurried steps away.

"Chuffin' 'eck!" Darwen gasped.

"It's a dragon!" Barry exclaimed.

"Probably," said Rik, taking a step towards it. "Or, since dragons don't actually exist, it's an iguana."

He said it casually, but he shot Darwen a look and there was a flicker of uncertainty in his eyes that Darwen immediately understood. They had, after all, seen plenty of things that shouldn't exist: flittercrakes, and scrobblers, gnashers, shades and other things for which they had no name. They had come here searching for a monster called the Insidious Bleck. Were there dragons in Silbrica? Darwen had no idea, but if there were, it was at least possible that they might be here too . . .

Rik got a little closer to the iguana and squatted beside it. The massive lizard took a few slow, lumbering steps away, then settled again, watching him. Rik was sweating heavily but looked as happy as Darwen had ever seen him.

"Man," Rik muttered, almost to himself, "this is going to be a great trip."

The other students didn't look so sure.

They were loaded into dirty jeeps and pick-up trucks with their luggage and driven along a narrow winding road through the jungle, occasionally passing clusters of ramshackle houses. At one point they forded a swollen river and the water rose alarmingly, well above the wheels, though the drivers seemed unconcerned, laughing and calling to each other in Spanish as if nothing could have been more normal.

Alex, who was riding up front, leaned towards their driver, a small man with a deep tan and a faded baseball cap, and said something in Spanish. When the driver nodded and muttered a few words, Alex began looking around at the river with new urgency.

"What did you ask him?" said Darwen.

"If there were crocodiles in this river," said Alex, without taking her eyes from the brown, sluggish water.

"And?" Darwen pressed, staring.

"There are," said Alex. "Lots. And sharks."

"Sharks?" said Rik. "But sharks don't live in rivers. They live in the ocean."

"You'd think," said Alex, still scanning the water uneasily.

Darwen wanted to think the driver was pulling her leg, but he wasn't so sure, and it took the edge off his enthusiasm. In his mind he saw the slobbering shark-mouths of the gnashers from

Silbrica and, imagining them swimming up and down the river, he gripped the arm rest a little tighter.

They disembarked on a stony beach lined with coconut palm trees, where a single vulture sat tearing at a stinking fish the size of a sheep.

"Gross," said Genevieve Reddock, stepping hurriedly away as if she might throw up.

Though it was hot, it was also overcast and the sky promised rain. Darwen moved down towards the shore, picking his way between the hundreds of tiny hermit crabs which seemed to be everywhere. Mr. Peregrine came waddling down the beach, looking like some kind of robot penguin: he had changed into the kind of rubber overalls that fishermen use for deep wading. Barry Fails pointed and laughed, but the other students took this to be an ominous development.

"Why is he dressed like that?" asked Rik, looking alarmed. After all the talk of sharks and crocodiles, Darwen couldn't blame him.

Moments later, Rik got his answer. The students were loaded onto motorboats, which meant having to wade knee-deep into the ocean and clamber on board, assisted by a pair of strong local men.

"My shoes are ruined!" exclaimed Princess Clarkson, sitting miserably on the side of the tossing boat.

No one said anything. Even the teachers were silent and watchful. It was becoming clear that Mr. Peregrine's idea of a school trip was not what they had had in mind, and some of them were starting to worry about far more than their shoes.

"We take the boats around the coast," Mr. Peregrine announced happily. "Just twenty minutes or so. The camp can only be reached by water."

"Camp?" Mr. Sumners repeated in a stony voice.

"That's right," said Mr. Peregrine, apparently oblivious to the fact that everyone except Rik was starting to look genuinely panicked. "You can't experience the jungle from outside, can you? Got to get right into it. Live in it. Sleep in it."

There was a rumble of thunder and the first steady pattering of rain. Somewhere from the tree-lined shore something started to call, a wild, whooping shout that might have been a bird or something else Darwen couldn't begin to name. Maybe it was the call of whatever had taken Luis. It was a sound that would have been quite at home in the strange and unpredictable world beyond the mirror, but this time, Darwen thought with an unsettled feeling in the pit of his stomach, he couldn't just climb back into a safer and more familiar reality. Here, weirdness and danger were everywhere.

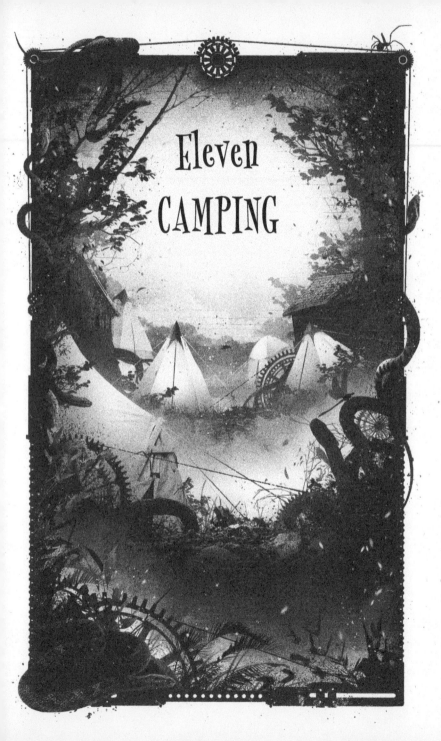

Eleven

CAMPING

The tent camp redefined the term "basic." There was a long, tin -roofed shelter open on one side where meals would be served at wooden tables with benches. There was a makeshift building which constituted office, kitchen and storage unit. At the back, at the end of a path which wound through heavy vegetation, there was a complex of toilets, washrooms and showers made of concrete blocks. Darwen peered in and saw, squatting beside one of the toilets, a brown toad the size of a volleyball. There was no hot water, and the electricity was powered by a generator which ran for only two hours each evening. Darwen eyed it warily, half-expecting to find little seats with wires running to great Silbrican batteries, but the generator looked quite harmless. There was no computer, no fridge, no phone, and the students who had brought mobile phones quickly discovered that they were miles from any service. Accommodation was in a series of yellow tents on wooden platforms, each tent just big enough for three students and their luggage. The tents, they were told, should be kept zipped up at all times to keep the snakes out, and no one was to move around at night without a torch.

"Can I share with you?" asked Gabriel.

Darwen gave Rik a shrug and said, "Sure. Come on in."

Alex was sharing with Naia and Kahala.

"Thanks," said Gabriel, half-apologetically.

He was olive-skinned and dark haired and his voice – on the rare occasions that Darwen had heard him speak – had a lilt to it that sounded like Carlos's.

"So . . . where are you from?" asked Darwen.

"Florida," said the new boy, his eyes down.

"This is gonna be way more fun than anything in Florida," said Rik, slapping Gabriel heartily on the back so that he almost fell over. "A bit, you know, *exotic*, but fun nonetheless."

"Tell Alex," said Darwen, rummaging through his backpack. "She didn't sound too thrilled about the crocodiles and sharks."

"Alex is a city girl," said Rik sagely. "Me, I'm a country boy at heart. Living in the rainforest for a week . . . ?"

"Jungle," said Darwen.

"Rainforest," said Rik. "Surrounded by the kind of nature most people never get to see? Trust me, this is going to be a blast. I read there are jaguars around here."

Gabriel looked like he was going to say something skeptical, but he caught Darwen rolling his eyes at Rik's enthusiasm, and just grinned.

"Come on," said Rik, checking his watch. "We have a meeting."

"Do I have to go?" asked Gabriel. "I would prefer to stay here and read."

"Wouldn't risk it if I were you," said Darwen. "I'm sure Sumners is looking for an opportunity to remind everyone that Hillside rules still apply."

They crawled out and put their shoes back on.

"Don't forget to zip the tent," said Rik. "All the way. There's a bit still open."

"Nothing could get through . . ." began Darwen, but Rik pushed him aside and carefully zipped up the last half inch. "Better to be safe," he said, breezily, as if he didn't really care one way or the other.

The camp was only yards from the ocean, and the sandy dirt swarmed with even more hermit crabs than before. The three boys followed the path up to the dining shelter. It was late-afternoon and the light was already softening. Halfway up, Rik paused, gazing through the heavy branches towards one of the other tents where an old man in shorts and a screamingly loud Hawaiian shirt was snoozing in a hammock tied between two palm trees.

"Is that . . .?" he said. "It can't be . . . Mr. Peregrine?"

It could and it was. The former shopkeeper clambered awkwardly from the hammock as they watched, and checked the gold pocket watch on its chain which he had fastened to the belt of his shorts.

"Oh, that's just wrong," said Alex, who had appeared behind them and was gazing at the spindly old man in his shorts and sandals. "That man needs a suit. I don't care if we're in the jungle. He needs a suit."

Mr. Peregrine beamed at them as he sauntered over, gazing up at the once again threatening sky. A vivid, green bird – some form of parakeet, Darwen guessed in amazement – soared overhead, and Mr. Peregrine pointed at it, smiling proudly, as if he had arranged for it to be there.

"What a delightful place," he said. "Quite remarkable."

The students made uncertain noises in response, so Rik swooped in with "it's fantastic," as if he was their elected representative. Alex raised her eyebrow.

"And it's just starting!" said Mr. Peregrine.

"I'll bet," said Alex darkly.

"First, dinner," said Mr. Peregrine, unabashed, "and then we meet our guide. You're going to like him. He's a real expert on the area."

"Pretty cool, huh Darwen?" said Rik.

"What?" Darwen replied, vaguely. He had been gazing off into the trees which marked the beginning of the jungle proper.

"You OK?" asked Alex.

"Just, you know," said Darwen. "Keen to get started. The mission, I mean."

"Cut yourself a little slack," said Alex. "We just got here."

"We don't even know where to start looking for the boy, man," said Rik.

"Luis," Darwen shot back. "His name is Luis. And if we don't know where to look then we had better get on that, don't you think?"

"We will," said Alex, her tone rising to match his. "But we just got off the plane, Darwen, and we can't just wander off into the jungle without any idea where we're going! Sheesh."

"Someone needs to be looking for him *now*!" Darwen returned. "Don't you get it? His parents have been taken from him and he's been alone for weeks now."

"You mean he's been taken away from his parents," said Alex.

Darwen blinked.

"What did I say?" he said.

"That his parents have been taken away from him."

"Oh," said Darwen, flushing. "Same difference."

Dinner was served at the uneven wooden tables of the long shelter. From their seats there, the students of Hillside Academy could look out over the camp's gardens to the Pacific beyond where the sunset was painting the clouds with a blaze of colour. They ate red beans and rice on tin plates, followed by a selection of extraordinary local fruit – mango, banana and pineapple – all of which tasted so like it had been picked only minutes ago. The students' mood improved significantly.

"That wasn't bad," said Alex. "Could use some hot sauce, but yeah, not bad. Tasty. Scrumptious, even. Healthy too. And fresh. A hearty meal . . ."

"OK, Alex," said Rik, shooting Darwen and Gabriel a knowing look. "You liked the food."

Not everyone did. Princess Clarkson had refused to touch anything but a few pieces of fruit, and Barry Fails had complained loudly that there was no meat.

"I could have brought some if I'd known we were coming to, like, the Third World," he said.

"And stored it where?" asked Nathan Cloten lazily. "There's no fridge."

"If I'd brought some, you'd want to share it," Barry persisted.

"Oh yes," said Nathan. "Rancid hamburger á la Usually. Sounds delicious."

Chip Whittley gave his woodpecker laugh, and Miss Harvey told him to be quiet.

"We are still to behave like young ladies and gentlemen," she said, "even if the surroundings are a little . . ."

"Rustic?" Alex offered. "Rural? Woodsy?"

"Oh, I'm so glad," said Nathan, "that despite all the luggage restrictions we were able to find room for O'Connor, the Incredible Talking Thesaurus."

"Thesaurus?" said Barry. "Right. 'Cause she looks like a dinosaur."

"Thank you, Barry," said Miss Harvey with tired finality. "Always helpful. Now, simmer down, Hillside. It's time to meet our guide and I want you to make a good impression. Remember, 'Manners maketh man' and 'learning is the path to self-improvement.'"

Alex rolled her eyes, but a hush had descended on the students who were craning to see who was striding up the path from the camp below.

The man who was coming toward them through the gardens might have stepped out of a movie screen. He was perhaps thirty, tanned, athletic, with jet-black wavy hair and large dark eyes. He wore a short-sleeved safari shirt and rugged looking shorts with hiking boots. He also had a sizeable snake draped over his shoulders, and judging by the way he was holding its head, it was alive and irritated.

"This," said Miss Harvey, her voice carefully neutral, "must be Jorge."

There was an uneven attempt at the typical Hillside greeting – "good afternoon, Jorge," but too many of the girls were nudging each other and giggling, while the rest were trying to get either as close to, or as far from, the snake as possible. One in the latter group was Rik.

"I thought you liked animals?" said Darwen.

"I do," said Rik through tight lips. "Just not . . . those."

"Hi," said Jorge simply, smiling to show white, even teeth,

a gesture that was met with even more giggling from the girls. "My name is Jorge and I will be your guide."

"What's the snake called?" asked Carlos.

"He is not a pet," said the guide. "I found him in the kitchens and thought I would show him to you before I released him back into the forest. Normally I would not handle him, but today I make an exception, so you can see one of the beautiful creatures who is sharing the camp with us."

This last remark did not get quite the response Jorge seemed to want.

"Do not be scared," he said. "He is a boa constrictor. Not poisonous."

"Couldn't he, you know, squeeze you to death?" said Bobby Park, looking alarmed.

"No!" Jorge laughed. "He is only a baby. It will be many years before he could kill you." He paused. "I am joking, of course. He will probably only reach about ten feet long. Here in Costa Rica, it is the venomous snakes that we need to watch out for."

Bobby didn't look entirely comforted.

"And are there poisonous snakes here?" asked Darwen.

"Oh yes," said Jorge cheerfully. "I saw an eyelash viper on the flowers by the showers . . ." he considered, "four days ago. It is not there now. When you walk past the bushes, even here in the camp, you should always keep your arms close to your body. Snakes sometimes coil around branches with flowers," he said, curling one hand around the other, "and wait for birds or other prey. Some of them are very aggressive and quite dangerous, so please be very careful. Also, pay attention to the ground, especially where there are a lot of fallen leaves, and never put your hands where you cannot see. Two weeks ago . . . No, one week ago . . . Wait. What day is it?"

"Monday," said Mr. Sumners. He was watching Jorge carefully, apparently unsure whether the man was stupid, dangerous or both.

"Really?" said Jorge. "Huh. In the jungle, all days are the same. So, one week ago I saw a bushmaster on the trail we will be walking tomorrow."

Rik went pale. Jorge noticed.

"Yes, this is a very dangerous snake. That and the fer-de-lance. We have both here." He sounded quite proud. "So it is very important that you are always on the alert."

"Do you have anti-venom?" asked Nathan, shifting in his seat.

"We do," said Jorge. "But it will take a long time to reach a hospital from here and *antivenom* is . . ." he waggled his hand: shaky, unreliable. "It will be much better if you do not get bitten."

The students exchanged wary looks and Jorge started to speak again with more urgency.

"You need to understand that this is a very wild place," he said. "People are used to thinking of the land around them as theirs, the places where they live and work and sleep. Animals in such places are pets or have strayed in from outside. But here in the jungle it is the other way around. It is people who do not belong here. You are in the world of the animals, and some of them can be quite . . . what is the word . . . *lethal*. Yes. So please pay attention."

The students had gone quiet again, some of them looking thrilled, others clearly terrified. The teachers were quiet too.

"It's because of stuff like this," whispered Kahala to Naia, "that my parents left India."

Darwen, who had grown up in a little town where there were no dangerous animals of any kind, tried to give her an encouraging smile, but his heart wasn't in it.

"Tomorrow we will go on our first hike in the jungle," said Jorge. "We will not disturb the forest. Take only pictures and leave only footprints. It is very important that you dress appropriately and do exactly as I say."

No one said a word, and for a moment there was no sound but the noise of the distant surf on the beach.

"I have posted a list of what you should wear tomorrow on the notice board, and you should study that before you go to bed. There is a battery-operated lantern for each tent. Turn it on by twisting this part," he said, demonstrating on a small hand-held lamp which produced a bluish glow. "We recharge them during the day. Breakfast is at 5:30 am. We leave at 6 am, without you if you are not ready. Get a good night's sleep. Tomorrow will be . . . quite strenuous."

Barry Fails turned, muttering to Chip.

"It means hard, Usually," said Chip. "He's saying tomorrow is going to suck."

"No," said Jorge, beaming. "Tomorrow will be glorious: a day to remember for the rest of your lives. I can't promise we will see any wildlife because this is a jungle, not a zoo, but I think it will be a very special day for you all."

And with that he bade them good night. The students broke into huddling groups, some of whom went immediately to consult the notice board. There was an air of quiet panic, touched here and there with excitement.

"No flip-flops!" wailed Melissa Young, studying the notice in disbelief. "What am I going to wear?!"

"Time for bed, I guess," said Rik.

"In a moment," said Mr. Peregrine, who had appeared beside them with a mug of what looked like tea. "I'd like a quick word."

"Good," said Darwen, who wasn't remotely sleepy, "I wanted to ask where . . ."

"I'll check the notice," said Rik. "Come on, Gabriel," he added, giving Darwen a significant look. Darwen nodded gratefully, then turned to the teacher.

"So," he said. "Where do I start?"

"Tonight," said Mr. Peregrine, "you don't. You rest. Tomorrow . . ."

"Tomorrow!?" Darwen exclaimed. "I've come all this way. Luis was taken weeks ago . . ."

"Darwen," said Mr. Peregrine, his voice gentle, "your mission is to find the tear in the barrier between worlds so that we can mend it. If we chance to find the missing child in the process, of course we will try to rescue him but we have only one week, much of it taken up with school work and excursions. You need to make progress quickly."

"But how?" asked Darwen. "How am I supposed to find a patch of jungle I saw for a few seconds weeks ago?"

"The Guardians trust your gifts as a Mirroculist," said Mr. Peregrine, lowering his voice as he turned to face him. "Tomorrow's hike will take you through part of the region where we think breaches have opened."

"Portals," Darwen said.

"Portals suggests someone is controlling them," said Mr. Peregrine. "This is just a tear in the fabric separating us from Silbrica. Tomorrow during the day you can do little more than observe, but in the evening you will cross over."

Darwen's heart leapt.

"You know where there's a portal!?" he exclaimed.

"Let's just say that I think I can get you in," he said, winking. "Come to my tent first thing in the morning. I have something for you."

"What is it?" said Darwen.

"Patience, my boy, patience," said Mr. Peregrine with a chuckle. "Trust me: you are going to like it."

Darwen nodded, then asked the question that had been nagging on his mind ever since he and classmates had begun trudging through the jungle, "So we really are all here because of me – the whole class, I mean --so that I can wander around the jungle looking for holes in the fabric of reality?"

"And," said Mr. Peregrine with a twinkle in his eye, "for the excellent pineapple."

With that he left Darwen to his thoughts, but as he rose Darwen's gaze flashed across the dining shelter and settled on Nathan Cloten, who was watching him with a suspicious look on his face. Darwen turned hurriedly away. He had felt responsible for saving Luis and his brother before, but as he scanned the dark ground for venomous snakes and who-knew-what else, that feeling swelled as if all of Princess Clarkson's excess luggage had been strapped to his back.

We're here because of me, he thought. *So anything that happens from here on is . . .*

My fault.

"Ready to head back?" said Rik, interrupting Darwen's realisation. He nodded in Gabriel's direction to indicate that they weren't yet alone. The skinny boy was loitering behind Rik looking lost.

"Uh, sure," Darwen muttered.

"Not sure about these lanterns," said Rik, peering at the one in his hand. "We'll have to stick pretty close together."

"What does the list say?"

"Pretty much what you would expect," said Rik. "Strong shoes or boots which you don't mind getting wet and muddy. Actually the main gist is that you should expect everything you wear to get wet and muddy."

"Perfect," said Darwen. "How's Gabriel?"

"OK, I guess," said Rik. "Doesn't say much. Probably a bit freaked out by all this."

"Imagine that," said Darwen, dryly.

The three boys wandered down towards the tents, got their toiletries and came back up past the dining shelter to the washrooms. The toad which Darwen had seen earlier was still there, squatting fat and watchful by one of the toilets, his presence ensuring that his stall stayed off limits to the students from Hillside.

Darwen was brushing his teeth when, an immense and shiny brown cockroach scurried across the floor. One of the students screamed.

"Just like back home," said Rik. "Outside, I mean. Not in the house. Not usually."

Darwen grinned and went back to cleaning his teeth, but as he did so he caught a flash of colour in the mirror, a face over his shoulder, and a strange one at that. He spun round.

There was no one there.

"What?" said Rik.

"Nothing," said Darwen instinctively. He had imagined it. Still, it was a strange thing to have imagined.

The face had been pink and shiny, like a mask or a doll. It was tipped at an odd angle, like the person was leaning back and to the side. Its eyes were round and bulging, glassy, and the mouth was wide open and dark inside, as if frozen midway through a wild and maniacal laugh. Darwen wasn't sure why he thought the laugh would be terrible, but he was, as if he had heard it before.

He shuddered, staring at his expression in the mirror.

"You look like you've seen a ghost," Rik remarked, toothbrush held perfectly still in one hand.

"Thought something was behind me," said Darwen, checking again. "Must have been a trick of the light."

"But . . ." Rik looked around and then whispered. "The sun has just gone down. Maybe the mirror is . . ."

"I don't think so," said Darwen, studying it. "It's just a regular mirror. Or it is now."

By the time they were done it was truly dark, the kind of darkness Darwen had rarely experienced, having spent his life in cities and densely populated towns. It reminded him of being inside the Shade: a thick almost liquid blackness that obliterated everything outside the meager glow of the lantern. Darwen, Rik and Gabriel squeezed inside the tiny circle of bluish light and inched their way back along the path towards their tent. Rik kept his arms rigidly at his side so he couldn't accidentally brush against any of the vegetation which seemed to breathe musky perfumes at them from the hot night. All around them insects chirped and frogs called with strange, unearthly voices.

The boys took their shoes off on the little platform outside the tent proper, and then crawled into bed, saying nothing, oppressed by the darkness and the sounds of the jungle. Darwen lay there, eyes open, listening for whatever might be moving close by, wondering if he would dare to go back out into the darkness if he needed to pee. He thought of the washrooms and the mirror: the laughing face. He rolled over, trying to push the idea away and focus instead on getting some rest so he would be ready to begin their mission. It was hours before he got to sleep.

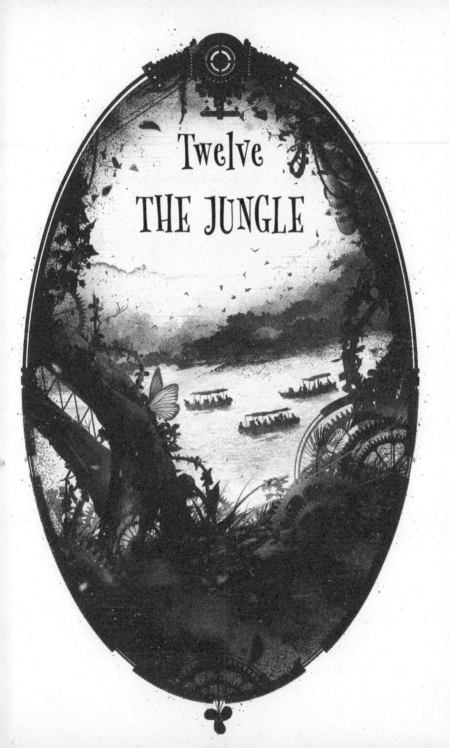

Twelve
THE JUNGLE

The sound that woke him could only come from Silbrica: a repeated roaring bark, deep and potent as a lion, and so terrifyingly loud that it sounded like it was right next to the tent. Darwen sat up, but it was still dark and he could see nothing.

"What the chuff is that?" he hissed.

The sound paused for a second, then rolled up again, swelling in volume.

URRRR . . . RAGH! AGH! AGH! AGH!

"We gotta get out of here!" muttered Rik. "Whatever it is, it's right outside."

"So you wanna go out there and meet it?" Darwen shot back. "Where's the lantern?"

"Here, but all that will do is give it light to eat by," said Rik. "Try this."

Darwen felt something digging him in the ribs. He took it. It was a heavy flashlight – at least eighteen inches long.

"What are you giving it to me for?" hissed Darwen.

"So you can see what it is when you go outside!"

"You're the one who wanted to go out!"

"Shh," said Gabriel suddenly. "I think it's gone."

The three boys grew very still, listening hard. Darwen thought he could hear sobbing from one of the other tents. Then, just as the night seemed to have quieted at last, it began again.

URRRR . . . RAGH! AGH! AGH! AGH!

And this time there were more answering cries from all over the camp. Whatever was making the noise, there were several of them. Darwen's eyes were wide, though he could see nothing, and suddenly, he had to know. He threw off the single sheet he was lying under and blundered out into the night, snapping on the flashlight as he slipped into his shoes. The deafening cry came again. He shone the beam of the flashlight around the tree until he located the source.

Something was crouching in the branches, a squat, heavy body and long powerful limbs covered with hair. He adjusted the beam and found a small black face with deep brown eyes, and a heavy pouch-like wattle around its neck. He remembered the pictures in Rik's wildlife field guide and found himself laughing, first with relief, then with a kind of delighted joy.

It was a howler monkey. The trees above the dining shelter were full of them, and their great booming chorus rang out like an artillery bombardment.

Well, thought Darwen, *fat chance of going back to sleep now.*

He yawned and stretched, then stuck his head back into the tent to grab his toiletries.

"Is it a jaguar?" whispered Rik.

"Three of them," said Darwen. "And they look really hungry."

As Darwen walked away he heard Rik sigh "hilarious," through the tent. Amazingly, Gabriel was already snoring.

The darkness had softened fractionally, and out over the ocean Darwen could see the pink of dawn, but he still couldn't follow the path up to the washrooms without the flashlight. Bugs scattered as the beam advanced, some of them huge, not just roaches, but grasshoppers and mantises and centipedes with six-inch, segmented bodies that shone hard in the flashlight. Twice Darwen stopped to give the insects chance to get out of the way, and he started to wonder if he should have stayed in the tent till sunup.

The howler monkeys had gone quiet, but from time to time Darwen heard a soft *thunk*. Scanning the trees with his flashlight, he saw that the monkeys were nibbling on small round fruit and dropping the cores onto the shelter's tin roof as they finished eating. The dropping sound he had heard. He grinned to himself as he watched them, fastening the beam of his flashlight on one of them and watching as it ate, nonchalantly, looking around like a man finishing breakfast and considering what kind of weather the day would bring. And then, quite suddenly, there was something else up there in the tree, a large cat-like face that flashed into view, fangs bared.

The monkey dropped from its perch, swinging and barking at the top of its considerable voice, setting the other howlers off so that in a second the entire camp area was alive with their booming calls. But this was no monkey dawn chorus. It was full of fear and panic. If these were cattle or horses, thought Darwen, they would be stampeding.

Something was after them, something Darwen had caught in his flashlight just before it could pounce. He swept the torch beam over the tree and caught a flash of movement, something larger than the howlers, almost as big as Darwen, but moving as the monkeys did, loping from branch to branch on long arms. He tried to follow it, but it was too agile, too fast, and in a moment it had gone completely.

What on earth . . .?

He thought of the face he had seen, which he had thought was dark and cat-like, but that couldn't be right, not considering the way it had moved. He stood quite still as the howlers fled inland into the forest, their cries fading with them, and he realised he didn't want to go up to the dark washrooms alone. He turned and headed back to the tent.

"Rik," said Darwen as he stuck his head inside. "Wake up."

"Wha'?" groaned Rik, rubbing his eyes. "Dude, it's still dark."

"It's dawn," said Darwen. "We have to go see Mr. Peregrine."

Rik grumbled, but he came out onto the platform, peering carefully into his shoes before putting them on.

"You know what time I got to sleep?" he said, gruffly.

"No," said Darwen.

"Neither do I, but it was late. I kept thinking there was something alive in the tent with me."

"There was," said Darwen. "Me and Gabriel."

"I mean bugs or . . ." he faltered.

"Snakes?"

Rik shrugged and looked away.

Darwen told him everything he had seen, about the monkeys' terrified flight and the curious creature stalking them in the trees. Rik was impressed, but not in the way Darwen had hoped.

"Man, you are so lucky!" said Rik. "I wonder what it was. A jaguarondi, maybe or a margay. There are six different cat species in Costa Rica, you know. I am *so* jealous. First day and you've already seen a wild cat . . ."

"But it moved like a monkey."

"That must have been something different. Probably one of the howlers."

"It was bigger than the howlers," said Darwen. "I'm sure."

"Well," said Rik, shrugging. "You'll have to ask Jorge on the walk. He probably sees them all the time." Then he added, wistfully, "I hope the howlers come every morning. I'd love to get a good look at them."

"I might prefer an extra hour's sleep," said Darwen, rubbing his eyes. "I'm barely awake enough to stand. I hope this hike isn't hard work."

"Well, way to jinx it," said Rik as they reached Mr. Peregrine's tent.

"Sleep well?" asked Mr. Peregrine brightly.

"Not really," said Darwen, sniffing the air. The tent smelled slightly sour, like spilled vinegar.

"Oh dear," said Mr. Peregrine without a trace of remorse. "I slept like a top. Good morning, Richard. Now, it goes without saying that what I am about to give you must remain strictly secret."

"What about Alex?" said Darwen.

Mr. Peregrine blinked, then smoothed his hair with the back of his wrist like a cat grooming itself.

"Of course, you can take Miss O'Connor into your confidence," said Mr. Peregrine, as if this was a given, "but no one else, yes?"

He produced a tubular leather case about two feet long and fastened with buckled straps. Smiling, he presented it to Darwen and inclined his head as if he was bowing.

"What is it?" asked Darwen.

"Open the holdercarrier and see."

Darwen undid the straps, popped the cap off the tube and slid out four telescopic brass rods, like the parts of a tripod or the poles of a tent. They were designed to snap together to form a square, and pressed into soft ground so it would stand upright. Two small devices were clamped to the uprights. One was a contraption of cogs and sprockets not unlike the screen device Darwen had used to protect himself from the eyes of the gnashers and scrobblers until it had got broken during their attempted invasion on Halloween. The other was a glass-fronted gauge displaying five numbers and with brass wheels on the side by which those numbers might be adjusted.

"It's already been set," said Mr. Peregrine, "so don't alter the dial."

"It's a gate," said Rik.

"Precisely so, Mr. Haggerty," said Mr. Peregrine, clapping his hands with boyish delight. "A portable portal, and one which can be set to connect with a number of different Silbrican locuses. Very rare, and very expensive. You must be careful with it."

"And it will get me to Luis?" gasped Darwen, not bothering to conceal his excitement.

"Ah, the missing boy," he said. "Well, it will get you to Silbrica, indubitably. But it must be used in secret, and that means where no one will stumble on it while you are inside, not just when you are coming and going. If the gate were interfered with while you were in Silbrica, you may not be able to use it to return. And, of course," Mr. Peregrine concluded, "it can only be used after sundown."

"And what do I do when I'm in?" asked Darwen.

"We," Rik prompted.

"What?" said Darwen. "Oh. Right. What do we do when we're in?"

"Investigate!" said Mr. Peregrine airily. "Ask around. Put your ear to the ground. Play the gumshoe, the detective. Find out where the weak points are in the barrier between Silbrica and this place."

Moments later, as the two boys walked away, Rik grumbled, "Not very specific is he? Investigate? How? I mean, where do we start once we're through?"

Darwen glanced down at his shoes, then shrugged, his eyes lighting up. "We look for Luis."

Ten minutes later they were eating breakfast with the rest of the students: yoghurt, cereal and fruit with juice and coffee. Half the students had had a lousy night's sleep, and Jennifer Taylor-Berry swore that she had seen a bat the size of a chicken flying around the washrooms. This, of course, made Darwen think of the strange cat-faced creature he had seen in the trees, while prompting everyone else into an animated discussion of the howlers.

"I thought it was a tiger!" yammered Barry Fails to anyone who would listen.

"Which had swum over from Asia," said Rik.

Barry didn't get it.

"I thought we were dead, man," he said. "Totally."

He wasn't the only one who felt they had had near death experiences over the last few hours, but the mood was generally upbeat, and whatever had terrified the students at night seemed quite exciting now that they could actually see where they were going.

"I hope we see something cool today," Barry added, and with this even Rik couldn't disagree.

The only people who didn't seem caught up in it all were Chip and Nathan, both of whom seemed quiet and a little surly, as if resenting how much everyone else was enjoying the prospect of their first hike. Princess didn't seem too pleased either, but that was because, as Alex was quick to point out, she had brought absolutely nothing suitable to wear. Jorge took one look at the spangled sandals she wore to the beach and sent her slouching back to her tent.

"We have some boots you can borrow," he said.

Princess wrinkled her nose as he produced them, though whether that was because of what the boots looked like – knee-high rubbery plastic of the type Darwen called Wellingtons – or because they had been worn by other people, she didn't say.

Darwen was delighted to see that Mr. Sumners looked absurd in wide, flapping shorts and a cowboy hat shading his pink face. Their tight-laced home room teacher, Miss Harvey, was wearing carefully ironed pants, long boots and a blousy shirt tucked meticulously in at her waist, but her normally well coiffed hair looked wild and frizzy no matter how much she fiddled with it. The boys stared at her, blinking, as if unsure who she was, and she gave them a hard look, practically daring them to speak.

"All aboard!" called Jorge, striding down the shingle with a backpack and water bottle slung over his shoulder.

There were three small power boats which had to be maneuvered into position with their sterns towards the beach. The students squealed and shrieked as they waded out into the surf and were hoisted into the boats by the shirtless local boys who doubled as drivers. The teachers divided themselves and clambered awkwardly into the boats one at a time. They all looked very self-conscious, though Darwen thought that Miss Martinez was having more fun than she wanted to let on. Mr. Peregrine, clad once more in his rubbery deep waders, just smiled and gazed out over the open water as everyone got into their life jackets. The oddest looking of the group was Gabriel who had rigged an Atlanta Braves baseball cap with a kind of veil made out of fishing net.

"Keep the bugs off," he said.

Darwen, who couldn't see his face properly, just shrugged and grinned in a way he hoped was encouraging.

It was going to be a hot and humid day. Beyond the thin line of beach, the world was the green of the jungle on one side and the blues of ocean and sky on the other, and if the boat would stop tossing long enough for him to enjoy it, Darwen thought it would look like paradise. But the boat did not stop, and as it hit full speed Darwen's stomach started to squirm with each slap of the boat's keel. After half an hour, he was feeling queasy, and after an hour he was miserably nauseous. The boat bounced from side to side sending Darwen's head flopping as if he were a rag doll. He gripped his knees and stared at the boat's wet plastic floor.

"How much further?" he called over the engine noise, without looking up.

"One more hour," said Jorge, brightly.

Another hour?

Ten minutes later the roar of the boat's engine cut out and they drifted to an uneasy, sloshing stop. Darwen looked up, praying they were at the shore, but the boats were still out in open water, and all the students were gazing in the direction Jorge was pointing. Holding his stomach, Darwen peered out and saw something large and dark surface briefly, its sides flashing in the sun. Then another close by, and a moment later, another which puffed a cloud of water only feet from the boat.

For a split second he thought, "it's the Insidious Bleck!" but then the students oohed and ahhed as Jorge proclaimed the shapes in the water pilot whales. The cloud they had blown out dispersed around the boat and several students groaned and winced. Darwen got a lungful of the rancid-fish-and-ancient-garbage stinking substance, so that for a second he had to hold on to the side of the boat, certain he was going to throw up. As he did so, he realised he was not alone. Someone else was staring green-faced into the water. It was Sumners. For a moment their eyes met and a kind of desperate understanding passed between them. But then the maths teacher vomited for real into the ocean, and Darwen turned quickly away as the boat restarted.

They were heading roughly south along the pacific coast, always in sight of the shore a mile or so off to their left. To their right, a strangely flat-topped island loomed.

"That is Caño Island," said Jorge. "Some of the best snorkelling in Costa Rica. We will do that tomorrow."

"In the boat again?" asked Darwen, a little desperate.

"There is no other way to get there," said Jorge, cheerily.

And then, at last, the boat was slowing and pulling in towards a stretch of beach not clearly different from what they had been passing for the past two hours.

Two hours, he thought. *And no way back but the same lousy boat ride . . .*

Amazingly, he and Sumners seemed to be the only ones stricken with seasickness. Rik was trying to be sympathetic, but he was clearly having a wonderful time and couldn't wait to start the hike. As the boat coasted through a placid and reedy river estuary, Darwen inched himself towards the back so he could be first off. As the pilot reversed the boat up to the shore, Jorge leapt out and manhandled the stern end in the sloshing waves before extending a strong brown hand to Darwen.

He didn't need to be told twice.

He leapt down, splashed his way up the shore and collapsed onto a fallen tree trunk, his eyes shut, revelling in the sudden stillness of the world. When he opened his eyes again he was surprised to find that he had been joined not by Rik but by Mr. Sumners.

"Boats," muttered the maths teacher. "I'll kill Peregrine."

Darwen laughed in spite of himself, but that made him feel worse, so he went back to sitting very still and quiet until everyone was ashore. Mr. Peregrine came well up the beach before climbing carefully out of his rubber waders and directing the students along a path.

"You don't look too chuffed," said Alex as the group began to walk inland. "Can you be *unchuffed*, or only *right chuffed*? I want to be able to use it correctly."

"I'm not too chuffed with you, right now," Darwen muttered.

"I see you were bonding with Sumners," said Alex, pretending to be offended. "You *must* be sick. I had no idea seasickness affected the mind."

"Hilarious as ever, Alex," said Rik. "Feeling better?"

"Yeah," said Darwen. "I'll be OK in a few minutes once the ground stops moving."

Rik grinned.

"What, no '*hilarious as ever*' for Darwen?" said Alex, punching Rik on the shoulder as they set off after the others.

"He's an invalid," said Rik. "Be nice."

"Let's hope it's nothing serious," muttered Alex. "If you need to go to hospital you can forget it. We are in the middle of nowhere."

She was right, of course, but Darwen knew that whatever the place looked like, it was exactly where he needed to be, and that thought focused his mind on something other than his seasickness. They had passed Caño Island and that meant they were in the region known for the strange stone spheres, the place from which Luis had been taken.

"*Nowhere*," Alex repeated. "Officially. Find Nowhere on a map and we are in the middle of it. Nowhereville, population: us."

"OK, Alex," said Rik.

"I'm just saying that if anything terrible happened and we needed serious medical attention," she went on, "you know like if we got bitten by a massive bushmaster snake like that one right there . . .!"

She screamed, pointing into the undergrowth beside Rik, who bolted to the other side, white faced, just as she started to roar with laughter. There was, of course, no snake.

"Man!" she exclaimed. "You *really* don't like snakes, huh? I mean, *really*. You bolted like a jack rabbit from a cougar."

"Dag gum it, Alex!" Rik shouted.

"What is the matter?" exclaimed Jorge, running back towards them.

"Nothing," said Rik, reclaiming his dignity as best he could. "Alex's sense of humour . . ."

Jorge glared at them. "We do *not* make false alarms here," the guide said fiercely, "and we do not make more noise than is necessary. Remember. Pay attention!" He tapped the side of his head, staring at each of them, and then marched away.

"Nice going," said Rik.

Alex raised her eyebrow. "Whatever, snake boy."

Thirteen
CLAWS

The vegetation tightened as soon as they left the beach, and soon they were following a narrow trail through hot, dense forest of the kinds of plants Darwen had only seen in greenhouses. From time to time, the group would stop and Jorge would talk about the trees, the ecosystem, or some particular creature, like the leaf-cutter ants whose parade lines crossed the path from time to time, each tiny orange insect bearing a piece of bright green leaf several times its own size so that the forest floor seemed to run in emerald rivers. They also paused at the actual rivers and Jorge scanned the water carefully before instructing everyone to wade across.

"Looking for crocodiles," said Alex to Rik. "And sharks."

"Sharks live in the ocean," said Rik, dismissively. "The driver was just trying to freak you out."

"Actually, she's right," said Jorge, who seemed to have gotten over his initial irritation with them. "These rivers are brackish – part fresh water, part salt. When the tide is high and the rivers rise, sharks swim up from the coast to hunt. Bull sharks, mainly. Much more dangerous than crocodiles. Sometimes tourists go missing and then, a few days later, we find their clothes beside one of the rivers where they decided to swim."

He shrugged and smiled at the silliness of the visitors, apparently not noticing that all the students – and Mr. Iverson – were now moving twice as quickly across the shallow river.

But, to the students' relief, they saw no sharks and only one small crocodile sunning itself on a sandbank. What they did see was a variety of monkeys, an ant eater, a motionless, greenish sloth, and a dozen exotic birds including a massive scarlet macaw that flew overhead, the sun flashing on its brilliant plumage. To Darwen's eyes it was nearly as exotic and remarkable as anything he had seen in Silbrica. It wasn't until they had paused for a packed lunch that they found the tapir.

In appearance, tapirs are somewhere between very large black pigs and small hornless rhinos. They are rare and endangered, and Rik had expressed a great deal of excitement about the possibility of seeing one. So when Jorge became very still and raised his hand in the air to silence the students, it was Rik who had craned to get a better look, Rik who had first whispered that he thought the great beast was sleeping, and Rik who had quickly amended that verdict when he saw the blood.

"It's dead," he said, his voice heavy with shock. "Something killed it."

He was right. Though Jorge and the teachers tried to shield the mutilated carcass from the students' eyes, they saw enough, and while some of them became subdued and even a little weepy, Barry led a gleeful discussion about what could have brought the big animal down.

"Got to be a jaguar," he said. "Look for tracks!"

There weren't any, but close to the tapir's body there were a lot of smaller paw prints, each about the size of Darwen's fist. Miss Martinez had pressed a handkerchief to her mouth at the sight of the dead creature. As she looked away, Darwen slipped past her to get a better look.

He was glad his stomach had had time to settle since the boat ride. The tapir had been half-eaten, though the sight was sadder than it was horrific, and Darwen was able to take it all in without flinching. The wounds on the body matched the odd little paw prints they had seen in the muddy earth: four short talon marks, one of which extended backwards like the claw of a bird, while one at the front was two or three times the length of the others. Darwen turned to find Rik at his shoulder and their eyes met.

"No cat would leave marks like that," Rik whispered.

"And the tracks don't extend onto the trail," said Darwen.

"So they attacked from the trees," Rik agreed.

"They're a lot smaller than the tapir, but there are several of them..."

"A pack, working together," Rik mused. "Each one bigger than a monkey..."

Darwen was watching Jorge. The guide was pacing round the carcass, studying the tracks and the wounds, then looking up into the forest canopy, his face baffled and concerned.

"Move back there," said Mr. Sumners, bustling over and spreading his arms like a cop on a TV show steering people away from a crime scene.

Darwen rejoined the group in silence, thinking of the strange creature that had spooked the howler monkeys that morning, the creature which did not show up in Rik's field guide.

"Still," said Rik, "it's not what you saw when you went into that jungle locus, is it? You saw a huge tentacle. These things are more like apes."

"So things are worse than we thought," said Darwen. "There's a breach in the barrier between worlds, and the Bleck is leading things through. Dangerous things."

"What's that?" called Barry.

He was pointing through the trees to where something dark and hulking leaned out of the ground. The students peered through the trees.

"It's just some old bulldozer," said Nathan Cloten. "Looks like it's been there a hundred years."

In fact, of course, it didn't. It looked part steam train, part tank. It was a massive, clumsy machine spouting pistons and fly-wheels and a pair of grotesque chimneys, and sticking out in front of its massive, tracked wheels was a huge plough-like blade, big enough to handle the oldest trees. It looked antiquated, but it had only just begun to rust and Darwen was prepared to bet that it had been there no more than a few months.

"Looks like it was burrowing up out of the ground when it stopped," said Barry.

"You are such an idiot, Usually," said Nathan, casually.

Darwen looked at Rik and Alex but they were watching Jorge who had suddenly started directing everyone's attention to another column of leaf-cutter ants that were marching across the trail.

"They do not eat the leaves," he was saying. "They are farmers, and use the leaves to fertilise a kind of mushroom which they eat."

Darwen wondered if it was his imagination or if the guide was deliberately distracting the group from the spectacle of the paralysed bulldozer, a device which had clearly originated in another world entirely.

It was mid-afternoon and Darwen was sitting on the damp edge of the tent platform he shared with Rik and Gabriel while he recovered from the return boat ride. It had rained twice already today, long heavy showers that began and finished abruptly, but which pounded the ground till it swam. The sky was clear again now, but the air felt thick and heavy. Alex swung lazily in a hammock fastened between two trees, watching as a pair of white-faced capuchin monkeys browsed in the branches only feet above her.

"In mourning for the dead pig, Arkwright?" called a jeering voice. It was Nathan, with Chip and Barry in tow.

"Yeah," Chip added, "Redneck Rik was crying his eyes out."

"Nobody cried," said Darwen, shielding his eyes with his hand.

"Yeah, right," said Nathan.

"Another devastating Cloten repost," said Alex. "You must be on the debate team."

"I can't believe they didn't let us bring it back and roast it up for dinner," said Chip. "A nice bit of steak. Way better than that slop they served yesterday."

"That was a very nutritious meal," said Alex, wiggling out of the hammock as if her family's honour had been called into question.

"Probably the best food you've ever had, right O'Connor?" said Nathan, putting on a rustic southern accent quite unlike his usual precise tone. "You head on over to Haggerty's for chitlins and gravy?"

"What's chitlins?" asked Barry.

"Cheap, nasty stuff," said Chip. "I'd rather eat that dead tapir right where it was."

"Yeah!" Barry agreed, stupidly.

"I told that guide . . ." began Nathan.

"Jorge," Alex inserted.

"Whatever," said Nathan. "I told him to cut a piece off that hadn't been damaged and we could barbecue it, but he was like *'we must pay attention to the world of the forest. We take only pictures and leave only footprints.'* And dead animals, apparently. I mean, what's the point of the stupid, useless tapir if we can't even eat the ugly thing when it's . . ."

Bonk.

"Hey!" said Nathan, grabbing the back of his head and ducking. "What the . . .?"

Chip stooped and picked up the object that was still rolling at their feet: it was a piece of fruit about the size and shape of a lime.

"Who threw that?" Nathan demanded spinning.

Standing a little way up the path to the dining shelter was Mr. Peregrine.

"Perhaps," said the teacher, "it was one of the monkeys, or another of the wonderful creatures which live in this place, offended by your heartless remarks about the tapir."

There was a shocked pause.

"*You* threw it?" said Nathan, aghast.

"You did not listen to what I said," said Mr. Peregrine, smiling benignly and waving at a fly that was buzzing round his head.

"You might consider using your ears as well as your mouth."

"Whoa!" said Alex.

The others just stared at the teacher, who had started to gaze up into the trees.

"There is no way that was a monkey," said Nathan, half to himself, as if not quite able to believe the alternative.

"I, alas, did not see the incident," said Mr. Peregrine. "But I would advise you to show a little respect to the creatures we encounter..."

"The stupid monkey couldn't understand what I said," sneered Nathan.

"Really?" said Mr. Peregrine. "Such certainty in one so young. I find that if I assume less about the world around me, I learn considerably more. Now," he said, producing a bag of shiny green and gold sports jerseys, "if you would put these on, I believe that Miss Martinez and Miss Harvey are organising a football match with some of the village children."

There was so much strange news in this seemingly casual remark that everyone forgot what Nathan was so upset about. There was a village? There was going to be a football match? Involving *Miss Harvey*?

For a moment Darwen thought that Mr. Peregrine was making the whole thing up to distract them from what Alex was soon calling the Mystery of the Flying Fruit, but it turned out – bizarrely – to be true. At the southern end of the beach was a horse trail which skirted the forest and, between a cluster of ramshackle, single-storey wooden buildings, was an area of cleared grass just large enough for a football field. A dozen local kids, some the children of people who worked at the tent camp, others who had come over from Drake Bay, were kicking a ball around. They wore faded and stained cotton T -shirts and shorts with either ratty trainers or nothing at all on their feet. By comparison, the Hillside kids looked like world champions in their official green and gold uniforms.

They just didn't play like them.

True, the Hillsiders hadn't brought their boots – though since the opposition was largely barefoot this wasn't much of an argument – and true, they weren't used to playing together as a team, and true, many of them didn't have much experience playing football, and true, Gabriel, who said he played a lot in Florida, didn't show up, but none of that could explain away how utterly they got crushed. After ten minutes the locals were leading by four goals to nothing, and after half an hour it was seven to one, the lone Hillsider goal coming when Darwen had run half the length of the field and slotted the ball into the centre where Nathan tapped it home. Their eyes met briefly but Nathan didn't thank him for what was, Darwen felt, a gift. Other than that one high point, the game was a disaster.

Rik, who was looking more than usually huge, lumbering and pink, was sweating heavily as the local kids zipped around him. Alex had been running madly round the field, but Darwen didn't think she had touched the ball once, and seemed more interested in practicing her Spanish on the opposition.

"Miss O'Connor," called Miss Harvey. "If you are not going to play, kindly leave the field."

Alex shrugged and walked off, and the local girl she was chatting to went with her to keep the sides even, at least numerically. They sat on the edge of the field where some of the adults – both teachers and a few of the men and women who worked at the camp – had gathered to watch.

When Miss Harvey blew the final whistle, Darwen, Carlos and Simon shook hands with the other team, while the rest of the Hillsiders skulked away looking exhausted and surly in their now soiled green and gold jerseys.

"You lot are really good," said Darwen to a boy who had scored a spectacular volley. Carlos translated, and the boy shrugged, smiling.

"Thanks, Carlos," Darwen said. Then he turned toward the field's edge. "Alex," he called. "Here a minute."

"What am I, your servant?" shouted Alex, stomping across the grass. "Your majesty called?"

"What is it?" asked Carlos. "What do you want to know that you need Alex O'Connor for?"

"It's nothing, Carlos," said Darwen. "Just . . . I was curious where he learned to play like that."

"I can ask him," said Carlos, pleased with the opportunity to be useful. "His name is Felippe, by the way."

"Hi," said Darwen.

The boy nodded. Carlos started speaking in rapid Spanish. Darwen glowered at Alex.

"Don't look at me," she whispered. "Anyway, I already know."

"What?"

"While you were kicking that ball around like the future of civilisation depended on it, I was making friends. And gathering news."

Darwen stared at her, but Carlos was already giving the other boy's answer about where he learned to play which amounted to "here." Darwen nodded and made impressed-sounding noises while trying to suggest that he now needed to be somewhere else.

"Wow," he said again. "That's great. Well, maybe we can play again . . . Bye!"

He waved vaguely and walked away, leaving Carlos and Felippe looking slightly confused.

"Well?" he said as soon he and Alex were out of earshot.

"I met this girl called Sarita. That one there." She waved, and a slim girl a year or two younger than them with shoulder length hair waved back. "I used my natural charm and started by telling her how much I missed my dog. Which is true, by the way. Anyway, we talked for a while and she said that very odd things have been going on."

"Luis," said Darwen. "He was from here?"

"Him and four others," said Alex. "Two more have disappeared since Luis and his brother."

Darwen stopped walking and stared at her.

"Five?" he said.

"Over the last six weeks."

"What do they think is happening?" he asked.

Alex shrugged.

"Some of them are saying it's a jaguar," she said. "But jaguars never hunt people."

"Why do they think it's a jaguar, then?"

"Well, I don't think the possibility of abduction from another world accessed only through mirrors has been seriously considered," said Alex. "There are some pieces of odd machinery which have appeared in the jungle – like that bulldozer thing we saw this morning – but they clearly don't work and look abandoned. No one is connecting a few old-fashioned engines to the missing kids."

"So what have they done about it?"

"Same as we would," said Alex. "They called the police."

Darwen was amazed that the idea had not occurred to him. They might be in a remote part of the jungle, but that didn't mean there was no law enforcement.

"So there's an investigation?"

"I guess, though they don't seem to be making much progress."

"If what is attacking them is taking them out of this world entirely," said Darwen, "that's hardly surprising is it? What did you learn about Luis?"

"Our age," she said, "smart, good football player. Ordinary, except that he and his brother were inseparable, closer than twins, though they didn't look alike. Sarita said that when Luis went missing, Eduardo searched the jungle for three days and nights by himself. His parents had to force him to go to bed because he collapsed miles away and had to be brought back by boat. The following night he was out again. They figure he stumbled on whatever took his brother a couple of nights after that. No one has seen him since."

Darwen stared at the ground suddenly overcome by a tide of anger and sadness. He had no brother, but he knew what it was like to lose your family, the people who knew and loved you best.

Alex had opened her mouth to say something else, but stopped. There was a distinctive thrumming sound getting louder each moment: a helicopter, approaching from inland and travelling very low. The kids who were still on the football field scattered to the edges, grinning expectantly. When the helicopter came into view and slowed, hovering briefly before descending, several of them clapped and waved. The grass flattened and the trees swayed in the wind of the rotor, and then the chopper was sitting in the middle of the field where they had been playing only minutes before, as out of place as a bulldozer in the jungle.

Fourteen
SCARLETT OPPERTUNE

D arwen's first thought was that it was a police helicopter, but then the door on the side of the cockpit opened, and he knew it wasn't the police.

A long, slender woman's leg reached down, a leg ending in a bright red shoe with a high pointed heel. The heel sunk into the grass, but the woman wrenched it free and stalked away from the chopper smiling.

She was, Darwen supposed, beautiful in the way that movie stars are beautiful: perfect, regular features, blue eyes, flowing blond hair and an air of polish about her which – in this rough and ready setting – made her seem unearthly, as if she had strode out of the pages of a magazine. She wore a crimson jacket and skirt which matched her shoes, and her long finger nails were the same vivid colour. She reached into a spangled handbag and pulled out what Darwen thought were sweets which she proceeded to distribute among the clamouring local children, walking among them like a princess. It took a moment for him to realise that they weren't sweets at all.

"She's giving out money!" Alex exclaimed.

Sure enough, she was handing out large yellow coins quite unlike anything Darwen had seen since arriving in Costa Rica.

"Maybe it's chocolate," he said, thinking of the foil-covered chocolate coins he used to get in his Christmas stocking in England.

"If it is," said Alex, "no one's eating it. It looks like gold. It can't be though right, coz that would be, you know, nuts . . ."

The kids danced around and shook the woman's hand and then scampered off, some to the little houses where their parents were emerging, others running to the camp. They looked more than happy. They looked delighted, like the answer to their prayers had just drifted down from the heavens.

Not everyone was pleased to see the woman and her helicopter. Jorge came running from the tent camp, shouting and exclaiming in a mixture of English and Spanish as the noise of the chopper's slowing blades finally died away.

"Who are you?" he demanded. "This is a protected environment. You cannot land here."

She turned and looked him up and down coolly, the tip of her tongue moving between her shining ruby lips.

"You must be the jungle guide," she said in a voice that was much lower than Darwen had expected but still reminded him of slowly dripping honey. She sounded pleased and one corner of her mouth twitched in a half smile. "Jorge," she said. "I seem to keep missing you. So glad we will finally have the chance to chat a little."

Jorge's eyes seemed to lose a little of their fire for a moment but, as the students began to gather silently around, he came back at her with a new surge of anger.

"I demand to know who you are and what you are doing here," he said.

"Demand?" she said with a throaty chuckle. "Let us not get above our station, Jorge. There is no need to demand what will be given to you freely. My name is Scarlett Oppertune, and I'm here to give the people who live here a chance at a real life."

"What are you talking about?" said Jorge. "They have real lives."

"Living in the woods?" she returned with amused condescension.

"Making a few pesos bringing milk and cheese in for the tourists? Miles from decent hospitals, schools and law enforcement? With no opportunity for advancement or profit and surrounded by dangerous animals?"

"This is their home!" exclaimed Jorge.

"For now," said Scarlett smoothly. "But everyone is free to make their own choices. Or they are where I come from."

"Which is where?" said Jorge.

"I represent Sunbelt Vacation Properties," she answered, flashing a brilliant, toothy smile. "We build hotel chains."

Jorge's eyes widened.

"You want to build a hotel! Here?" he said. "We're on the edge of a nature reserve! This is one of the most bio-diverse regions in the world."

"I know!" said Scarlett Oppertune, her blue eyes bright, "and think of how many tourists will want to see it if they don't have to sleep in tents! It's time all this 'nature' was shared with the world, don't you think, Jorge?"

The guide looked lost for words, like the air had been driven from his body, but Rik stepped up.

"If you develop the area," he said, "you wipe out the environment which makes it worth visiting!"

"Not at all," Scarlett said, smiling. "You know how big these woods are? We won't get rid of all of it. And if we make it smaller, that will make it so much easier for people to find the fuzzier, less dangerous birds and animals, now won't it? Once we've got the park boundaries redrawn so we can get some decent roads through here, an airport, a mall or two . . ."

"A mall?" gasped Jorge.

"Tourists have to shop," she said, winking and smiling. She seemed completely unaware of Jorge's outrage. "Maybe a hunting lodge ..."

"You'll never get the government to approve," said Rik, his face pinker than usual.

Scarlett's gaze lingered on him and her right eyebrow twitched with something like amusement.

"You don't think a government will give up a patch of land covered with trees which generates next to no income," she said, smiling at Rik, "for a sack full of cash up front and the promise of more once the tourist jets start landing? Please."

"But it's ..." Rik fumbled for a word.

"Illegal?" Alex cut in. "Immoral? Unethical? Exploitative?"

"All of those," said Rik, as red now as Scarlett's shoes.

"It seems that way to you," said Scarlett, "because you are ..." she settled on the last word with her sweetest smile yet, "a child."

She smiled again, this time in a pitying sort of way, and Rik glared at her, furious and embarrassed, as she took the brown hand of one of the smallest local kids and said, "Okey dokey. Let's have a chat with your mom and dad, shall we? I expect *they* might be interested in freedom and the pursuit of happiness."

She turned in the direction of the little cinder-block houses.

"I don't trust people who use words like that," said Alex.

"Like what?" said Darwen.

"Like they're flags that you wave to get people cheering."

They watched Scarlett walk away. Several of the local kids had flocked to her, touching her fancy suit and gazing happily up at her, though Sarita and Felippe kept their distance, muttering to each other. Scarlett moved slowly, beaming down at the smaller kids who were holding her hands, and Darwen was reminded of an old science fiction movie he had seen on TV with his dad, where a man moved up a ramp into a spaceship surrounded by fascinated little aliens.

Jorge watched her go, speechless, then turned and stomped back towards the tent camp. Rik was muttering furiously.

"Come on," said Darwen, bracingly. "Nearly time for dinner and then we get to try out Mr. Peregrine's portable portal."

"Did you hear what she said?" Rik demanded, rounding on him.

"Yes," said Darwen, "but . . ."

"Doesn't it matter to you?" Rik said. "That we've come all this way to see this amazing place and the things that live here and she's going to tear it down to make a few bucks!"

"Well," said Darwen, who had never seen Rik so angry, "not *all* of it."

"Oh, not all of it?" repeated Rik, his voice loud and heavy with sarcasm. "That's all right then. I was worried they were going to bulldoze all the region's endangered species into the sea, but so long as they're leaving a few trees for the tourists to look at over their TVs, that's OK. A coconut palm or two, yeah? Tourists like coconuts. Hang a plastic monkey on one of them and no one will know the difference, right Darwen?"

"Hey, don't blame me," said Darwen. "I'm just saying it might not be as bad as it sounds . . ."

"You know what, Darwen?" said Rik. "You're right. It won't be as bad as it sounds. It will be worse. Trust me: I've seen it back home. Because once the forest goes it doesn't come back and everything in it goes away. Forever."

Darwen, unable to think of anything to say, looked down and Rik began stalking off after Jorge.

For a long moment, no one said anything, then Darwen heard Alex's voice.

"Anyone ever told you that you're a huge comfort to your friends when they're upset?" she said, adding before he could respond, "Ever wonder why not?"

Dinner that night was tense. Rik didn't speak to anyone, but he glowered at Princess Clarkson when she made the mistake of saying that she thought a hotel would be an improvement on the tent camp. The other students were quiet, and though some of them were sympathetic to Rik, there were others who thought Princess had a point. The generator wasn't working properly so the water was cold and they had to go to bed as soon as the sun went down since they couldn't see their hands in front of their faces. To make matters worse, it began to rain again, a drenching downpour that turned the paths to streams and sent the students running for their tents, where they sat, steaming and damp, listening to the drumming of the rain on the nylon. The humidity was so high that even when the rain stopped, nothing dried out, and their wet clothes began to smell sourly of mildew.

"Well?" said Rik. It was the first word he had said all evening and Darwen and Alex just stared at him. They were sitting at the long tables in the shelter, watching the other kids as they filed back and forth from the washrooms and headed to bed.

"Well what?" said Darwen.

"Don't we have something to do?" said Rik in a low voice, his eyes loaded with meaning.

"You mean . . . where Mr. Peregrine said we should go?" said Darwen.

"Obviously," said Rik.

"We thought you . . ." Darwen couldn't think of how to end the sentence.

"He thought you were mad at everyone and wouldn't want to go," said Alex in a matter-of-fact voice.

"What?" said Rik. "Darwen, you aren't the only one who wants to save Luis, you know. I was upset about . . . It has nothing to do with this. So. Now?"

"Er . . . Great," said Darwen. "Yes. We can set the portal up in the trees behind the dining shelter. No one will see it there."

Rik nodded.

"You want me to get it from the tent?" he said.

"Sure," Darwen said. "Meet us by the sinks in ten minutes. We'll wait for everyone else to go to bed and then sneak round the back and into the woods. Bring your flashlight."

"OK," said Rik, and for a moment he looked cheerful again, but as he half-turned to leave he seemed to think better of it and stopped. "Were you two going to go without me?" he asked.

"No," they both said at once.

"We hadn't even talked about it," said Darwen, conscious that while that was true, he and Alex might well have gone to Silbrica by themselves had Rik not spoken up.

Rik nodded but looked unconvinced.

As he walked away, Alex shrugged.

"Come on," she said. "Sumners is giving us the stink eye."

It was true. They were the last students still sitting at the tables and the maths teacher was watching them suspiciously. They got up and made their way up to the bathrooms, Alex pausing to smile at Mr. Sumners and wish him "a very good night's sleep" along the way.

Sumners watched their backs as they walked away, but then said something which stopped them in their tracks. "What on earth, Mr. Haggerty, are you carrying?"

Darwen and Alex wheeled to see Rik carrying the long leather tube containing the portable portal. He was staring at the maths teacher, pale, his eyes wide open in what Alex called his "deer in the headlights" look. They were about to go back towards him when he spoke.

"Toiletries, sir," he said.

"In that thing?" said Sumners with undisguised disbelief.

"Special travel pouch, sir," said Rik, improvising. "Toothbrush, soap rod, vacuum packed towel, all in a handy space-saving container. My dad got it from a late-night TV ad."

"Did he indeed?" said Mr. Sumners, peering at the leather case. "There's a towel in there?"

"Not a hand towel," said Rik. "A bath towel. There's a plunger on the bottom that sucks all the air out."

"Huh," said Sumners, who looked like someone had sucked all the air out of him. "Well, get a move on, boy. Everyone else is already in bed."

"Yes, sir," said Rik. "Thank you, sir."

He came up the path grinning.

"Not bad," muttered Alex. "I'm not sure about 'soap rod' but the plunger-on-the-bottom thing was a nice touch."

"It's a good thing he didn't ask to see it," said Rik.

"Oh come on," said Alex. "If there's no risk, there's no fun. Meet me here in five minutes. Gotta pee."

Rik's eyes met Darwen's and they grinned at each other. Darwen found himself looking at one of the mirrors over the sink and, remembering the unsettling impression of the laughing face over his shoulder, looked quickly away.

"I wish Mr. Peregrine had some more specific plans," he muttered. "I mean whatever killed that tapir . . ."

"Hey guys, whatcha doin'?"

It was Gabriel, still in his cap with the veil.

"Oh," said Darwen. "Hi Gabriel. We're just . . . you know . . . getting ready for bed."

"Where are your toothbrushes?"

"Already cleaned our teeth," said Darwen, smiling awkwardly. "We're just . . ."

"Going to sneak out and see if we can see the stars," said Rik. "I'm a bit of an amateur astronomer."

"Oh," said Gabriel. "Cool. Is that your telescope?"

"Yeah," said Rik.

"Can I have a look?"

"Well, it's kind of . . . expensive and I don't really . . ."

"Please," said Gabriel. "I won't break it. Promise."

"Sorry," Darwen said. "Astronomy club rules. Members only."

"And the members are you two and Alex O'Connor, right?" said Gabriel, looking crestfallen.

"No . . ." said Rik.

But at that moment, Alex emerged and Gabriel's expression hardened.

"Oh, *Alex*," said Rik. "I thought you said, er, Melissa."

"If you don't want to be my friend," said Gabriel, "you could just say so. There's no need to lie."

"It's not that, Gabriel, really," Rik protested, but the skinny boy was already walking away.

"Nice save," said Alex. "*I thought you said Melissa.* Very convincing."

"Oh shut up," said Rik.

"Well," said Darwen, as Gabriel disappeared. "We'd better get on with it. Has Sumners gone?"

"Looks like," said Alex.

They set off around the back of the washrooms and into the trees behind the dining shelter, following Rik's flashlight.

"Do we really need that?" whispered Darwen. "Someone might see."

"I'll take getting caught over stepping on a bushmaster, thanks," said Rik.

They inched further into the woods.

"Gotta say," said Alex. "Not a fan of those washrooms. I don't know if it's the lizards and toads but I always feel like I'm being watched. Naia and Kahala think they're haunted."

"By what?" said Rik. "The ghost of a howler monkey?"

Darwen stopped walking.

"How about here?" he said.

Rik handed him the leather package and they set about snapping the brass frame together. Though the rods did extend some, the portal was still only about a yard square.

"We'll have to go through one at a time," said Darwen, as he snapped the dial with the locus number to one upright and pushed it into the soft earth.

"How?" asked Alex. "We won't even be able to see through if we're not touching you."

"I'll reach back through for you," said Darwen. He was winding the watch-like device on the other upright. "Ready?" he said. When they nodded, he pressed the button on the side.

There was a soft whoosh, a crackle, and the air framed by the portal flickered before stabilising into the tiny window of a brick building.

"Weird," said Darwen.

Fifteen
THE HOUSE
IN THE WOODS

"What's weird?" said Alex, who couldn't see. She snatched at his hand.

"Oh," said Darwen. "Sorry."

He took Rik's hand too and the three of them stared through the portal in amazement. It had to be one of the strangest things Darwen had ever seen: a cracked and dirty window frame with a brick surround sitting in a dark Costa Rican jungle.

"Maybe it connects to that central machine you told us about," said Alex.

"Only one way to find out," Darwen answered. "I'll have to let go of your hands while I get the window open, but I'll stick my hand back out for you, so don't go anywhere."

"And don't you go on without us," said Alex. "The Peregrine Pact, remember? It's not just you."

"I know," Darwen answered, irritable.

He released them, stepped up to the slender brass frame and reached in. The air buckled slightly, but then his fingertips found the hard surface of the window glass. He pushed, but nothing happened, so he reached for the wooden frame and lifted. The window slid up easily, though the opening was still only about a foot and a half wide.

Darwen grabbed the ledge and pulled himself in, realising as he did so that the window was several feet up. Below him was a cracked porcelain sink marked with brown water stains. He climbed down head first, bracing himself against a brass tap, crawling into the sink itself, and finally jumping onto an uneven tiled floor.

It was a bathroom. Old and badly in need of repair and redecoration, but a bathroom nonetheless.

"Weird," he said again.

He used a wooden laundry hamper to climb back onto the sink and from there he reached through. He felt Alex grab his hand and he pulled her part way, till her head was through and she could see what she was doing. Then he did the same for Rik.

"Hey," said Alex. "Our very own bathroom! And not a lizard in sight."

The house – if that was what it was – felt cool, and smelled musty. One thing was certain, they weren't in the jungle anymore.

"This is awesome," said Alex. "Before we went into Silbrica to see exotic, weird stuff, right? To get a break from boring old reality. Now we go to Silbrica to use a decent bathroom, maybe watch some television, and generally get away from the weird, exotic stuff all around us!"

Darwen opened the bathroom door and stepped out onto a narrow landing. It *was* a house, and a small one at that. There were wall-mounted gas lamps that glowed bluish, though several of them didn't work. What light there was showed peeling, textured wallpaper spotted with mould and a carpet grey with dust. Darwen doubted they'd be sneaking in here to watch television.

They were, apparently, upstairs. There were two scratched doors on one side of the hallway – bedrooms, presumably – and a narrow staircase to their left which went down in three angular turns.

"This place feels . . . I don't know," said Alex. "Familiar. Like I've been here before, or dreamed about it."

Darwen felt the same way, but he couldn't think of when he might have been here. It reminded Darwen of the old terraced houses in Lancashire, but one which had been derelict for years. There were no signs of portals or the elegant machinery he was used to in Silbrica.

He pushed open the closest door and saw what he had almost expected. A dim room with a bay window, a mouldy-looking bed and a wardrobe with its doors hanging open. He stepped inside and the floor creaked beneath him. He pulled the curtains open. Outside he saw trees, their branches brushing up against the house, and again he had that odd feeling that this wasn't the first time he had been there.

He rejoined the others.

"Downstairs, I suppose," he said, leading the way. There was something about the stair carpet that seemed familiar too, and the wallpaper at the bottom. He frowned and looked at Alex, who had the same expression on her face. Rik, by contrast, looked merely interested.

"What?" he said.

"This place doesn't ring any bells?" asked Alex.

"Nope," said Rik. "Never been anywhere like it in my life."

"Shhh," said Alex. "Listen."

They all became still, and Darwen could hear it too, a faint clicking and chittering that seemed to be coming from somewhere down the hall.

Machinery?

It was possible, he supposed, but it didn't sound quite right somehow, and he could feel the hairs on his arms and neck starting to stand up, like his body remembered something his brain didn't.

Alex pushed past him, down the hall and into a kitchen. Darwen followed, with Rik trailing behind him, but she became quite still, blocking the door. Darwen gave her a shove, and she turned. Her expression stopped the two boys cold.

"I know where we are!" she hissed.

Darwen had never seen her look so scared.

The chittering had grown louder. Darwen turned towards it and saw another half-open doorway into a tiny lounge with a fireplace and a table with the shattered remains of an old tea set . . .

And a floor littered with pale balloon-like objects which Darwen instantly knew were eggs. Maggots, three feet long, milky white but with black pincer mouths covered the rotting furniture, and over in the corner were five huge, shiny insects, all as big as he was.

The Jenkinses.

That was what they had been called when Darwen had last seen them: huge, horrible insect-creatures disguised as an elderly couple whose bodies they wore like flesh suits. But it couldn't be. At least one of the Jenkinses had been killed by the train months ago. But there they were, and now Darwen knew why the house had seemed both familiar and unfamiliar. He had, after all, not been upstairs last time.

They looked like giant mantises, though they were the hard and shiny black of beetles, and they had large, compound eyes like flies. They were, perhaps, a little smaller than the two that had disguised themselves as the Jenkineses, but that made them no less repulsive or dangerous.

Last time Darwen and his friends had only escaped because of the screen device he had broken at Halloween.

His first instinct was to make for the front door, but that wouldn't get them back to the jungle camp. "Back upstairs!" he gasped.

The insects responded as if they hadn't known he was there. Their whip-like antenna flicked towards him and their mouth parts opened, drooling. Then they moved, a sudden scuttling, one across the egg-strewn floor, one up and over the ceiling, a third diagonally across the wall.

They were fast. Much faster than the Jenkinses had been.

Rik cried out. Alex just stared, hands clasped over her mouth. Darwen pushed both of them back into the kitchen. As he did so, Rik slipped on some nameless slime on the tiles, knocking Alex onto her back. He slumped heavily against the wall, splitting the rotten plaster open, and out of the wall cavity fell two huge pale maggots, both at least a yard long, one landing wetly into Alex's lap.

She screamed, thrusting it wildly from her, eyes shut against the horror of it. Rik rolled to one side, as the other one arched its back and pulsed towards him, its black horny lips gaping.

Darwen looked wildly around for a weapon and, finding a heavy saucepan, he snatched it up and flung it at the maggot. The pan bounced off the creature's rubbery body, went straight up into the air and came down handle first. With a soft splosh, it impaled the maggot, and the creature began to whip back and forth, emitting a thin and awful scream.

For a moment Darwen was frozen with horror, aware that two of the mantis creatures were approaching fast but somehow unable to move. One of them glared at him, its mouthparts uncoiling, and then it sprang. It shot through the air with astonishing speed, its clawed feet splayed, and then something happened. There was a flash, and a pop like a firework and the insect fell heavily, smoking as it slid lifelessly across the floor. Darwen turned back towards the front of the house and there, silhouetted in the open doorway like an Old West gunfighter, was a tiny animal cradling a smoking weapon on which glowed a pinprick of amber light. It stepped into the light of the hallway and Darwen recognised the dark, stoat-like form.

Weazen!

"Evening," he growled, and fired again at the other mantis, which ducked and weaved as a cabinet of mouldy crockery exploded behind it. He spat to the side, then fired again. "Can't hold 'em off for long. I suggest you do a runner, mate."

Darwen dragged Alex to her feet as Rik ran back through to the staircase. Behind him, he could hear the click of insect feet, and the crack of Weazen's blaster. As they got into the hallway, Darwen glanced back through the kitchen door. At first there was nothing, and then the head of the first creature appeared, upside down on the door's lintel above him. He ran, and it came after him, scrabbling across the ceiling.

Rik and Alex pounded up the stairs. Darwen was momentarily sure that the steps would be rotten too, that they would fall through into some appalling maggoty nest, but they managed to successfully reach the top and bolt across the landing to the bathroom. Darwen gave chase, and was almost at the top of the stairs when he felt something snag in his hair.

His hand brushed at it automatically, but he felt the stick-like insect leg, and his revulsion gave him a new burst of speed, breaking the connection. He flew up the last three steps and down to the bathroom, slamming the door behind him on the first of the three insects.

"Lock it!" Alex screamed.

Darwen snapped the little brass bolt home but he knew that wouldn't hold them. Through the door, he could hear the sounds of their clicking beaks and scratching claws as they groped and fumbled, desperate to gain entry. "Curtain rod!" he yelled, putting his shoulder against the door as it shuddered under the weight of the insect assault Darwen could hear the clicking of their beaks and their scrabbling claws right up against the wood of the door.

Rik climbed onto the edge of the bath and lifted the brass shower rod down. Together they tried to brace it between the foot of the toilet and the handle of the door. The insects were pushing harder and one of the door's thin panels had started to bulge and crack around the edges. Darwen heard the distant zap and crack of Weazen's weapon, but knew there were too many of the insect monsters for the Peace Hunter to handle alone. For a moment he hesitated, wondering if he should head back.

"Help Alex!" shouted Rik, taking up position with Darwen at the door. "She can't get out without you. Now, Darwen!"

Darwen stepped away and the door quivered for a terrible second, until Rik could take his place. Darwen took Alex's hand, helped her onto the sink, and kept hold until she was up and through the window.

"Now you," he said to Rik.

"The door's not going to hold," Rik answered.

As if to punctuate the point, the loose panel in the top left-hand side, popped right out, and something long and clawed reached in.

There was a cabinet under the sink. Darwen dropped and opened it, hoping vaguely for bug spray. There wasn't any. What there was, was a glass bottle of bath salts. He grabbed it, swinging it hard at the insect leg that was reaching for Rik. The leg was snatched back, and in that instant, Rik made a run for it, Darwen seizing his hand as he clambered onto the sink.

Darwen vaulted up after him, pushing him through the window as the bathroom door flew open and crashed against the wall. One of the shiny bugs skittered in on the tiled floor, another on the ceiling.

Darwen shoved Rik through and leapt for the window frame, grabbing and pulling in one motion. Something grabbed at his feet and he kicked wildly, connecting with what he thought was a giant insect head, propelling himself the rest of the way through.

Rik and Alex grabbed his arms and pulled him through into the dark of the jungle. For a moment he felt the sudden warmth of the night, and then Alex was screaming, and he turned to see the first of the insects clambering through after him. Rik leapt backwards, but Alex picked up a rock and smacked the wind-up contraption on the side.

The first insect was half through when she hit the device the second time, and there was a shrill scream as the portal failed, and the mantis's head was lopped neatly off. Alex hit the gate once more for good measure, and the slim brass frame buckled and snapped.

She turned on Darwen and her face was wild, her breath coming in great surging gasps.

"Let's NEVER, go there again," she shouted. "OK?"

Darwen sank to the moist earth, panting.

"It may be the blind, screaming terror of the giant homicidal bugs, talking," said Rik, in a dazed voice, "but were our lives just saved by a ferret with a rocket launcher?"

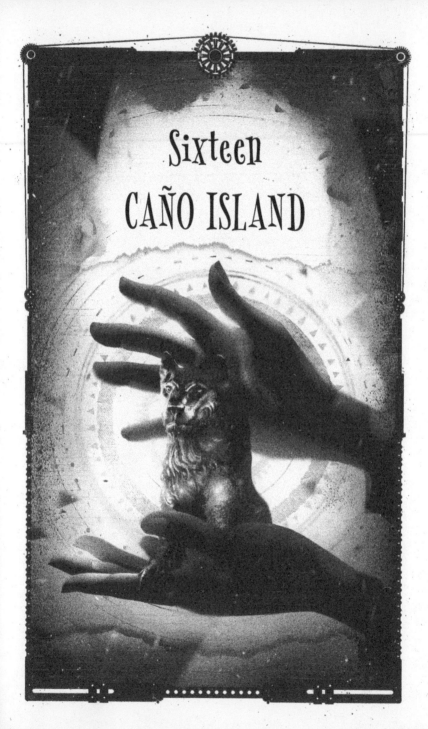

Sixteen

CAÑO ISLAND

Mr. Peregrine flexed the bent and ruined remains of the portable portal in the morning sun. Repair was, quite clearly, out of the question.

"Couldn't you have just dismantled it?" he asked, sounding forlorn.

"There wasn't time," said Alex.

Rik and Darwen eyed each other sheepishly. Taking the gate to pieces now seemed the obvious thing to have done.

"Right," said Mr. Peregrine, weighing the shattered remains like it had been a family heirloom. "Well, this presents a difficulty," he said. "Unless we can find the original breach, we have no way of getting into Silbrica from here."

"That's your concern?" said Alex. "Do I have to point out that this is the second time you've sent me to that house and its charming inhabitants?"

"Yes," said Mr. Peregrine, thoughtful. "Terribly sorry. You are sure these creatures were the same as the Jenkinses?"

"Er . . . yeah," said Alex. "Giant man-eating bugs in people suits tend to stick in your mind like they are tattooed on the back of your eyelids, so yeah, I'm pretty sure."

"Quite," said Mr. Peregrine, and for a moment he looked miles away, but not vague as he often was. His brain was working a mile a minute and his eyes had a narrow, fixed quality."

"Still here," said Alex.

"What?" said Mr. Peregrine, coming out of his reverie with a start. "Yes. Well, as I say, sorry about that. I suppose the equipment malfunctioned. Most unusual."

"Malfunctioned?" said Darwen. "It was tampered with. Someone changed the setting to send us there."

"No one has had access to it except us," said Mr. Peregrine.

"It was in the tent all day yesterday," said Rik. "Anyone could have gone in and messed with it."

"A person?" said Alex. "You know, Nathan Cloten and Chip Whittley act like they didn't see anything unusual back at Halloween, but what if they did? What if they are spying on us?"

"What about this Peace Hunter?" said Mr. Peregrine. "His arrival sounds most suspicious."

"Weazen helped us escape," said Darwen. He didn't know for sure that if the little creature had made it out alive, and the sense of responsibility weighed on him like cold, wet clothes.

"Or he came to catch you and found you already in a fight," the teacher mused.

"No way," said Alex. "I only got a glimpse of him but he's way too cute and fuzzy to be working for the Bleck. I hope he got out OK."

"No one," said Mr. Peregrine, "is working for the Bleck! It is an animal. Nothing more. You must not invent things to worry about. You have classes to focus on and the breaches . . ."

"But what about Luis?" Darwen sputtered.

"I don't see what you can do to help him," sighed Mr. Peregrine. "For now, keep your eyes open and do try to enjoy yourselves. This is a once-in-a-lifetime experience."

Darwen looked away, but Alex nodded for him.

And, as it turned out, they did enjoy the day.

For one thing, the boat ride was better, most of the way at least. They followed the same course as they had the previous day, but the water was calmer, and Darwen's nausea didn't kick in till they started veering out towards the flat-topped island. By then, Darwen, Alex and Rik had already agreed that their top priority now was finding another way back into Silbrica. Darwen didn't know how they were going to do it, but knowing his friends agreed with him made him feel better.

They pulled into a rocky bay, and Jorge talked about safety issues while the driver handed out snorkels, masks, fins and life vests.

"We stay in this area here," said Jorge, pointing. "The current will push you but if you drift too far, we will come get you in the boat. The rocks are sharp, so pay attention, and be alert. If you see a shark bigger than this," he held his hands about three feet apart, "shout."

"Are we likely to?" said Simon Agu, staring.

Jorge shrugged.

"Probably not, but if you do they will most likely be white-tip reef sharks. Not dangerous." He looked at the sky. "Not at this time of day."

Darwen watched the students exchanging the now familiar mixture of uneasy glances and thrills of excitement. Gabriel was first in, casting aside his cap with the absurd veil, and looking more at home than they had ever seen him. He dove straight down, blew out a fountain of sea water from his mouth and laughed out loud.

"Wow!" said Alex, climbing awkwardly over the side. "He's coming out of his shell."

Only Mr. Peregrine, still clad in his chest-high waders, showed no sign of actually getting ready to swim.

"You not going in?" Rik asked him.

Mr. Peregrine shook his head. "Not much of a swimmer," he said.

"You can just float about," said Rik. "See? We've got life jackets and everything. It's quite safe. I'll keep an eye on you."

Mr. Peregrine shook his head again. His usual pallor had developed a greenish tinge. "I don't like water," he whispered, wincing away from a few drops on the side of the boat like it was acid.

"I thought only Darwen and Mr. Sumners got seasick," Rik answered.

"I don't mind being *on* it," said Mr. Peregrine, regarding the water carefully. "I just don't like being *in* it." Then gathering some semblance of composure, he added, "wasn't exactly much opportunity to practice my swimming while I was running the shop, unfortunately."

"Oh," said Rik. He gave an apologetic shrug, put on his mask and tipped awkwardly backwards out of the boat. He hit the water with a loud, slapping splash, but came up grinning, both thumbs up. Darwen met Mr. Peregrine's anxious eyes. They were alone except for Jorge who had extended his hand towards Darwen.

"You sure you won't come?" said Darwen to Mr. Peregrine.

"You go ahead," said the teacher. "Maybe I'll come in later."

They both knew this wasn't true, but Darwen nodded anyway, then inched into position, arms outstretched for balance.

Jorge sat him on the edge of the boat, back to the water, and checked his mask. "Ready?" said the guide.

Darwen nodded and Jorge gave him a gentle nudge backwards.

Darwen hit the water with his shoulders but it didn't hurt, and though the life jacket felt hot and constraining, he was glad to get out of the bobbing boat. As the others started to swim about, he took a moment to float quietly by himself, fiddling with his mask, while his seasickness passed. He was still waiting when Rik burst from the surface.

"Hot dang!" he shouted. "I saw a parrot fish. Right in front of my face! I could have touched it. A real, wild parrot fish!"

Soon everyone but Darwen was popping up laughing and whooping with delight, swapping tales of what they were seeing under the bright blue water. Hating to feel so left out, Darwen bit down on the snorkel's mouthpiece, and dove.

His queasiness was forgotten the moment he went under. The world beneath the water was glorious. He was surrounded by schools of exotic fish, so brilliantly- coloured that it was like being inside an aquarium. The rocks below him gathered and thrust in strange, swollen formations like the landscape of an alien planet. Delicate corals of white and pink bloomed in shafts of bluish light.

And among it all moved the fish. Darwen saw dozens right away, perhaps hundreds, silver shoals moving as one, and bright, beautiful individuals for which he had no name. He gasped in wonder at it and found himself, like the others, laughing privately with delight as something, roughly the size and shape of an American football, idled past. A puffer fish, he thought it was called. For a moment he understood perfectly Rik's outrage at Scarlett and anything she might do to destroy the beauty of this place.

He broke the surface and found Jorge floating close by.

"Good?" said the guide.

"Chuffin' brilliant!" said Darwen, and went back under, taking a deep breath this time so he could dive. He swam deep into a rock crevice alive with orange fish, swimming down till the pressure in his ears began to hurt. He rolled easily onto his back and floated to the surface, past what he took to be an angel fish with a long dorsal fin which trailed after it like a ribbon of white and gold. At the surface, he blew the water from his snorkel and whooped with delight.

It was a perfect morning. Apart from Mr. Peregrine, who never made it into the water, the mood at the ranger station on the beach where they landed for lunch was exuberant. Even Nathan and Chip had forgotten to be sour about the "nature" for which they were generally so disdainful, and Princess Clarkson had stopped whining about the conditions of their accommodation. She ran her fingers through her golden hair, and blithely declared that it would dry in the sun "just fine."

They ate peanut butter sandwiches at wooden tables under the shade of the cliffs which lined the beach, and watched a huge and spiny black iguana scaling the rocks.

"It's like something out of *Jurassic Park*!" exclaimed Barry, and for once, Darwen thought he was right. It was odd, he thought, after all the strange things he had seen on the other side of the mirror, that a part of the real world could only be compared to movies.

The sandwiches were dry but no one complained, engrossed

as they were in swapping tales of what they had seen in the water. Simon and Carlos had seen a sea turtle, while Melissa and Genevieve had spotted a jellyfish, and Chip had seen what he claimed was a moray eel.

"It was green," he said, "with these little beady eyes, and it had its mouth open so you could see its teeth, like little knives in a row . . ."

Each story produced another rush of excitement and pleasure.

"So," said Mr. Peregrine, now out of his waders, as they packed their rubbish to take back in the boats, "how am I doing?"

"Great," said Darwen. "Best school trip ever."

"This afternoon I fancy you might learn something more directly connected to your mission," said the old man in a low voice. "I am confident that you and Mr. Haggerty will find it especially compelling."

Darwen felt his pulse quicken. It was about time.

"Students!" called Miss Harvey. "Everyone with their walking shoes on in single file. Stand in front of me in two minutes."

"We're not going back into the ocean?" called Naia with cartoon dismay.

"Not just yet. Mr. Peregrine and Mr. Iverson have something to show us before we do any more snorkelling."

Someone groaned.

"This is not a holiday," Miss Harvey reminded them. "It is a school outing. We are here to learn, to immerse ourselves in that which we do not know in order to emerge enriched by the experience. Now Hillside. Quick march."

And they began to trudge up the winding slope that climbed inland from the beach, winding their way through cactus scrub and heavy-leafed rainforest shrubs. Lizards skittered in the underbrush and Jorge gave another of his favourite warnings about *paying attention to the nature*, if only because some of it might kill them if they didn't.

The trail was easy to follow, and in ten minutes they had reached a partially open area in the woods where the leaves had been swept and a square of top soil carefully removed.

"It's a dig!" exclaimed Rik, picking up a trowel from a box of tools.

"The Caño Island archaeological site," agreed Mr. Iverson, beaming at Rik. "Right up your street, I think, Mr. Haggerty."

"Archaeology?" groaned Kahala. "I wanna go back and see the fish."

"Hey, check it out," called Barry. "Cannon balls."

For the briefest of moments, Darwen thought he was right. The forest floor and the area around the dig itself was scattered with stone balls of varying sizes, several of them as big as large pumpkins. Darwen's gaze moved from them to Rik, but his friend's eyes were fixed on Mr. Iverson who had crouched to consider one of the spheres. It was about the size of a tennis ball, and though it was greenish with lichen it was clearly identical to those Darwen had thrown at the monster which took Luis. The science teacher turned quickly and gave Mr. Peregrine a probing look.

"These are the famous stone spheres," said Miss Martinez.

"They are found only here and on the mainland close by. They are about a thousand years old, perhaps more, carved by the ancient people who lived here long before Columbus came. Their precise function is uncertain but they seem to have been used to mark special places and events in the ritual lives of the tribe. This is a graveyard."

"Cool," said Carlos.

And if this wasn't the exact spot from which Luis was taken, thought Darwen, then it was somewhere very like this and very close. There was a portal to Silbrica around here. There had to be.

"Since he has been assisting the archaeologists, Jorge will explain the excavation," continued Miss Martinez. "Afterward, he will answer questions, so start to think about what you'd like to know. Quietly, Mr. Fails."

As Chip and Barry elbowed each other, the guide began to talk. "The Caño Island site where you stand has been used by people for many centuries, though we do not believe they lived here," he said. "Perhaps they came here only to bury their dead."

"Is the island haunted?" asked Barry.

"Questions later, Mr. Fails," said Miss Martinez firmly.

"I am sure that the people who used to come here thought the place special," said Jorge, by way of an answer, "and yes, I'm sure they had all kinds of stories about the island's function as a cemetery. Recently a discovery was made here at Caño. In addition to the stone balls we found *metates* – a kind of stone slab for grinding corn – and several of these."

From his pocket he drew a clear, plastic box with something

yellow inside. It looked like a tiny figure, strangely-shaped, but roughly ape-like.

"Is that gold?" exclaimed Princess Clarkson.

"Yes," said Jorge, shifting as the students crowded in closer. "I will pass it around, but handle it carefully and do not open the box."

As the students cooed over the gold figurine, Darwen turned his attention back to Mr. Iverson who had moved quietly over to Mr. Peregrine and had started to speak in a low, urgent voice touched with something – accusation or suspicion – which Darwen had never heard from him before.

"That sphere is like the one you brought to class," he hissed. "No. Not *like*. It's the same. Identical. Where did you get it?"

"Oh, you know," said Mr. Peregrine airily. "You tend to acquire things in your travels."

"*You tend to acquire things*?" whispered Mr. Iverson, so that Darwen had to strain to hear over the babble of questions being directed at Jorge. "How do you acquire an ancient and valuable artifact like this and then toss it around at school like it's no more than a punctured football? Did you know what it was? Is there something about this trip that you haven't told the other staff?"

Before Mr. Peregrine could answer, Mr. Iverson caught sight of Darwen watching him. Listening. The science teacher gave Darwen a long, level stare. Flushing, Darwen turned quickly away. At the same moment, Rik nudged him. It was his turn to look at the gold figurine.

Darwen considered it carefully through the magnifying glass

which came with it, at first just so that he wouldn't have to look at Mr. Iverson who he sensed was still watching him, but then with real interest. The tiny statue was indeed ape-like, long limbed and hunched, but the head was that of a jaguar and the paws showed long, savage-looking claws. Though the figurine was only a couple of inches long, the feet were finely modelled and showed bird-like talons, one extending backwards, three more going forward, the middle one of which was considerably longer than the others.

"Do these things have a name?" Rik asked the archaeologist.

Jorge smiled and shook his head.

"The ancient people of this region made images of many animals and the gods or spirits associated with them," he said. "Sometimes they created hybrids: different animals combined. This is one of those. I call them *pouncels*," he added, shrugging and smiling apologetically, "but that is just me."

"You should call them, like, Killer Death Monkeys," said Barry.

"Pouncels," Alex echoed musingly. "Yeah. I like that."

"Or Jungle Monsters of Death," Barry continued.

"Or tapir killers?" whispered Darwen to Rik.

Their eyes met.

"The claws?" said Rik.

"Exactly like whatever left the tracks in the woods," said Darwen, as soon as the group spread out to consider the stone spheres around the site.

"But if these pouncel things are from Silbrica, then they didn't just start coming through recently," said Rik. "Those gold figurines are a thousand years old. If the people who made them knew what the pouncels looked like . . ."

"Then there has been a tear in the barrier between the two worlds for a long time," Darwen agreed. "It was probably sealed up years ago . . ."

"But has come open up again," Rik concluded.

"Come open," said Darwen, "or been ripped open on purpose."

"By what?"

"By the Insidious Bleck," said Darwen.

"But Mr. Peregine keeps saying the Bleck is just an animal," said Rik, sounding worried.

"Aye," said Darwen, half-turning to look at the former shopkeeper. "He does. But at least we know that one of the breaches or portals is on this island. And if the pouncels can get through from Silbrica, then we can go there from here. We just have to figure out how."

Seventeen

THE BLUE MORPHO

As soon as Darwen had recovered from the boat ride back to the tent camp, he joined the line of students progressing up to the dining shelter, as ordered by Mr. Sumners.

"It will be Jorge talking about animals," said Chip with a showy yawn. "Something seriously lame."

It wasn't, but the student response was unanimously unenthusiastic. The tables were spread with notepads, pens, books and charts.

"We're not having classes here?!" exclaimed Kahala.

"This is a field trip, Miss ahhh Konkani," said Mr. Sumners, "not a holiday. You are here to learn, and learning takes work. Take a seat, and I want at least ahhhh eighteen inches between each student. This place has enough distractions as it is."

The rest of the day was given over to forty-five-minute of science lectures (botany, zoology and marine biology) from Mr. Iverson, Spanish from Miss Martinez, history from Miss Harvey and world studies from Mr. Peregrine, each subject tailored to Costa Rica. As they worked, Mr. Sumners hovered, watched and listened.

"What's he even here for?" asked Darwen again.

"He's the senior faculty member," said Rik. "Genevieve overheard him saying he calls the principal from Drake Bay every evening to report on how the trip is going. Apparently Principal Thompson wouldn't have let Mr. Peregrine bring us otherwise. He has to take the boat," he added, grinning. "Not his favourite part of the day."

Mr. Peregrine ended the session talking about the hunting techniques of the people who lived in the forest before the

Europeans arrived. "Tomorrow," he announced, "we will be making bows and arrows in the traditional style, and Mr. Iverson will explain the physics of how they work."

Mr. Iverson sat up abruptly, and from the upward motion of his tufty eyebrows Darwen felt sure this was the first he had heard of Mr. Peregrine's lesson plan. He shrugged his acceptance, but watched the world studies teacher with his head slightly on one side.

"Sit down, Mr. ahhh Fails," roared Mr. Sumners.

Barry had leapt to his feet and started shooting imaginary arrows at everyone in sight.

Darwen turned to look and saw Carlos and Alex apparently arguing.

"He said so," said Alex. "You saying he's a liar?"

"You must have misunderstood," said Carlos.

"What?" asked Darwen.

"Oh, nothing," said Alex. "Our friend Carlos, here, is saying that our school-appointed guide is a liar, that's all."

"I didn't say that," said Carlos. "I just said that he's not from round here . . ."

"I asked him," said Alex, "and he said he was from San Jose."

"No way," said Carlos. "Ask Miss Martinez. Listen to him, Alex. He's not from anywhere in the Americas. He's a European, from Spain. He may have lived here a while, but you can hear it."

Alex opened her mouth to protest, but at that moment a great "ooh" went up from the students.

Darwen turned and saw, fluttering haphazardly through the shrubs of the gardens beside the dining shelter, a huge butterfly. It must have been six inches across, its wings flashing with turquoise and aqua and a deep, vibrant blue bright as the summer sky and gleaming like metal. It wove in and out of the bushes and then flew gracefully into the shelter itself, weaving, bobbing as if borne on an invisible breeze, and then, astonishingly, settling on one of the long, wooden tables.

"A blue morpho!" exclaimed Rik, fumbling for his camera.

The students flocked to the table to consider the massive and dazzling creature as it rested.

"Give it some room," said Mr. Iverson. "Butterflies are very fragile."

"It's gorgeous!" exclaimed Naia.

WHAM.

The heavy book slammed down onto the butterfly. The leg and fragment of wing which stuck out never even moved.

Chip Whittley looked at what he'd done and, in the momentary shocked silence, shrugged. "What?" he said, the hint of a smirk fluttering at the corner of his mouth. "It was only a bug."

There was an explosion of outrage from the other students and from it, Alex flew at him, fists balled.

Chip's composure evaporated, but he moved too slowly to dodge her first punch. He stumbled back against one of the tables and she was on him, arms flailing. Chip cried out in shock and within moments, Mr. Sumners was dragging Alex away, giving her a warning stare when she looked poised to attack again. For once, she didn't speak, but her eyes were bright with angry tears.

"Don't move," said Mr. Sumners, pointing squarely into her face, "or I'll have you on the next plane home."

"And him?" said Mr. Iverson.

The science teacher's face was white and hard, quite unlike his usual expression. He was furious.

"What about him?" asked Mr. Sumners.

"What do you propose to do with this boy?" said Mr. Iverson, his voice trembling with the effort of not shouting.

Chip looked hot in the face and he was watching Alex warily, but a hint of the smirk remained. He shot Nathan a glance.

"What Mr. Whittley did is no excuse for such an assault . . ."

"No excuse?" repeated Mr. Iverson, his voice colder than ever. "I think Miss O'Connor's anger is perfectly understandable. If I were not a man of considerable self-control . . ."

"You'd do what?" asked Mr. Sumners, pouncing on the remark.

There was a sudden, tense silence. Mr. Iverson lowered his eyes and said nothing. The students watched, riveted. Taking the silence for a kind of apology, Mr. Sumners nodded, smiling mirthlessly.

"I think what Mr. Iverson meant to say," said Mr. Peregrine, stepping forward suddenly, "is that people of violence, people who have no appreciation for life or beauty, people who think the destruction of what others value is a source of amusement, cannot be reasoned with. They can, perhaps, be taught, but they do not want to be. They are the worst kind of thugs and will grow up – if they show such tendencies as children – to be the worst kind of adults."

This extraordinary speech produced almost as much shock and bewilderment as Chip's destruction of the butterfly had done, but from the looks being levelled at Chip by the other students, there weren't many who disagreed with it, and Darwen felt a rush of pride in Mr. Peregrine.

"If Hillside stands for anything," he continued, "it is that such behaviour cannot be permitted. I recommend in the strongest possible terms that this matter be raised with Principal Thompson so that he may determine if Mr. Whittley should be allowed to remain on the trip."

For a moment Mr. Sumners said nothing, just looking from Mr. Iverson to Mr. Peregrine and back as if they had just started speaking double DutchSwahili, before curtly nodding and turning to Chip. "Clean it up," he said, nodding at the table.

Chip sighed and reached for the book, but Alex stepped forward again.

"No," she said.

Mr. Sumners tensed, poised to block her if she attacked again, but she just said, "I don't want him to touch it." Sumners hesitated, then nodded slowly. Chip shrugged and turned his back to them, shooting a grin at Nathan as he did so. Alex moved slowly forward, took the book in both hands, and lifted it carefully. She set it down and for a moment, and everyone but Chip looked at the broken remains of the once-magnificent butterfly. Naia turned quickly away, her face in her hands, and Genevieve Reddock muttered "oh no."

Saying nothing, Alex tentatively lifted the butterfly by its wings then, cradling it in her open hands, walked towards the bushes over which it had flown. She held it in front of her chest as if she was part of a ceremony and wordlessly, the students followed her.

She moved down into the tent camp, selected a sunny spot beneath a tall palm tree, and dropped to a crouch. She seemed uncertain where to lay the insect down and Darwen hurried forward.

He brushed some stones away from the surface of the ground and then dug his fingers in to the dirt as she sat quite still beside him, hands outstretched. Darwen scooped a shallow grave out of the soft earth and waited as Alex laid the butterfly inside it. Between them, they covered the vivid blue wings with the dirt and stood up.

The other students were clustered around them in silence still, but the spell broke almost immediately. They looked suddenly embarrassed and uncertain of what they were doing, and seconds later, they had dispersed. Chip, Nathan and Barry had not come down, but were watching, blank-faced, from the dining shelter where the teachers also stood, saying nothing.

"Come on," said Darwen.

Alex, who had been staring up at Chip, her face expressionless, nodded. Rik glowered at the ground and muttered as they walked down to the shore where they sat in silence, watching the sky soften as the afternoon turned to evening. Darwen wanted to talk about the gold figurine and its links to the creatures which he was sure had brought down the tapir, but the time didn't feel right.

At dinner they sat as far from Nathan, Chip and Barry as was possible and avoided their eyes. Once, Barry waggled his arms in what was clearly supposed to be an impression of a wounded butterfly, but no one laughed and Rik shot him such a murderous look that he abandoned the joke and went back to his food, grumbling.

As darkness fell and the students picked their way to the bathrooms in a trail of bobbing flashlights, Darwen, Rik and Alex sat alone in the dining shelter listening to the sounds of the waves below and looking at the stars. Rik was telling them about the constellations.

"But there's still a pole star, see?" he was saying, "because we're just north of the equator and . . ."

"I miss my dog," said Alex.

"Excuse me?" said Rik.

"I'm just saying," said Alex. "I miss Sasha."

Darwen reached over and put a hand on her shoulder and Rik, who had been about to say something, nodded sympathetically.

"How am I supposed to go after Luis if we can't find the portals?" said Darwen suddenly.

"I was talking about the stars," said Rik, miffed.

"I know," said Darwen, who had been watching a pair of hermit crabs scurry softly through the grass. "Sorry. But, I know the portals are here. I can almost feel them. There has to be one on the island, but where? But we've been to the dig site and we've trekked through the jungle . . ."

"Rainforest," corrected Rik.

"Rainforest," said Darwen, "and I thought we'd see a big, iron gateway like the one Greyling built at Hillside last year. Or we'd see something like that little stove in the janitor's basement, you know? The one that was a tiny portal that they used for passing all the stuff they stole from us. But we've seen nothing, and so far as we can tell, neither has anybody else."

"It's a big jungle," said Alex.

"Rainforest," said Rik.

"Whatever," said Alex and Darwen together.

"It can't be random," said Darwen, shaking his head. "If those gold figurines are the same as the things that are wandering the jungle ... *rainforest*," he corrected himself before Rik could get the word out, "then they've been coming here for centuries. But if it's just a tear in the barrier between worlds, why doesn't the Council know exactly where it is?"

He moved his foot towards a rock which hopped slowly into the darkness. It was another of the large, brownish toads that cropped up all over the camp. Darwen winced.

"I know that building a hotel here would be bad," he said, a little defensively, "destructive to the environment and, you know ..."

"Exploitative," suggested Alex.

"All that," said Darwen. "But it would be really nice to be able to go to bed for a night – just one night – without worrying what might already be in the tent when we get there."

Rik was about to respond when they heard the first shot.

Eighteen
DEMONIO

There was no question that the bang which had suddenly torn through the jungle night, sending the birds squawking and the monkeys howling, was anything other than a gunshot. There were no cars to backfire, no construction workers with heavy equipment, nothing that could create the hard, short crack, and the two others which followed.

Somebody was shooting.

Darwen had never heard a real gunshot before. It wasn't quite what he had expected – tighter, flatter than the booming cannons he had heard in movies, and without the electric fizz and roar of Weazen's blaster. Still, he ducked instinctively.

A fourth shot.

Then silence.

Moments later, the camp was a chaos of flashlights, whirling, stabbing into the night around the tents. The quiet was torn by a confusion of voices: teachers, guides and camp workers, but most of all, the Hillside students.

"What was that?" shouted Carlos.

"Is someone hurt?" faltered Genevieve.

"That was a shotgun!" called Barry, gleefully.

"No it wasn't," said Rik, quietly, almost to himself. "It was a rifle."

"You can tell the difference?" asked Darwen.

"I live on a farm." he replied absently, listening to the night, eyes closed as if he was trying to strain out the babbling excitement around him.

"Oh yeah." said Alex, appearing on the path beside them. "This

215

is exactly what my mom had in mind when she agreed to this trip. Snakes and toads and getting shot at. Awesome. But at least we'll be safe in our hotel rooms: oh wait, no, we're in tents, which means we're all gonna die horribly . . ."

"Hillside students!" bellowed a voice.

It was Mr. Sumners in striped pyjamas and a belted bathrobe with what looked like a shower cap on his head.

"Students make your way up to the dining shelter. Quickly and quietly, please. Don't run, Mr. Fails!"

"What do they want us up there for?" asked Darwen.

"To make sure we're all still alive," said Rik.

"Oh yeah," Alex mused. "When my mom gets my first postcard they're gonna need to sedate her till I get home. *Dear mom, didn't get eaten by sharks today, but did get shot at. Wish you were here. With a house. And a tank. Yours, Alex.*"

"Quiet, everyone," said Mr. Iverson, who was still dressed. "Sit at the tables so we can do a head count."

Miss Harvey bustled among them, pointing as she counted.

"Thirteen, fourteen," she muttered. "Fourteen. We're missing two."

Simon Agu emerged from under the table grinning broadly.

"Fifteen," she said. "Sit down properly Mr. Agu. This is no time for jokes. Who else is missing?"

The students looked around.

"No one, maam," said Rik. "You must have miscounted."

She started again but came to the same number. "Fifteen," she said. "Who is not here?"

"I think you counted me twice," said Barry Fails.

"No, Barry, I didn't," said Miss Harvey crisply, "and if I had, we'd be missing two people, wouldn't we?"

"Oh," said Barry. "Right."

"Where is Mr. Cabrera?" said Mr. Iverson, peering around the tables.

"Who?" said Barry.

"Gabriel!" Rik exclaimed, aghast, turning to Darwen. "He just . . . slipped my mind. We're sharing a tent with him and we completely forgot him."

The students shone their flashlights into the gardens below in the awkward silence.

"We should check the tent," said Darwen to Rik.

"Us?" said Rik, looking apprehensively into the darkness.

"Us," said Darwen with a finality he didn't really feel. "Miss Harvey, we'll be right back."

"What?" said Miss Harvey. "I would really prefer that you stayed . . ."

"I will go with them," said Mr. Peregrine, appearing from the kitchen end of the dining shelter in a bathrobe so long it looked like a cloak. He was holding one of the battery-powered lanterns above his head and his grey hair shone softly in the light so that he looked, for a moment, like a figure from a stained-glass window, saintly and powerful.

"Very well," said Miss Harvey.

Rik and Darwen set off at a run, not bothering to wait for Mr. Peregrine.

Darwen felt suddenly responsible for Gabriel, to whom he had been – it was suddenly clear – a lousy friend. The kid knew no one, had been tacked onto a group who had been together for one term already, a group which had proceeded to ignore him almost completely. Darwen and Rik had let him share a tent with them, and they had thought they were doing him a huge favour, but instead of keeping an eye on him, helping him make friends, they had neglected him entirely . . .

There was a flash of movement in front of them. Darwen shone his flashlight ahead and caught a streak of motion, then another, then several altogether.

He gasped and took a step backwards.

The cat-headed, monkey-like creatures Jorge had called pouncels: a pack of them. Maybe ten or fifteen, all about the size of German Shepherds. One of them stopped with uncanny control and turned to face him, snarling. The head was smaller than a jaguar's, but not by much, and the bared teeth were long and sharp. It had yellow, glassy eyes with black, vertical pupils. The creature spread its clawed paws, each with one overlarge and deadly-looking talon, and lowered its head as if about to spring. It put out its tongue and hissed, a long, slow rasping sound that raised the hair on the back of Darwen's neck.

And then, as Darwen stood rooted to the spot, it took off, racing after the others in a long bound that took it out of Darwen's flashlight beam and into the night. In no more than a second, they had gone.

"Whoa," said Rik. He looked pale in the lamplight and badly scared.

"Still think they're too small to bring down a tapir?" said Darwen.

Rik shook his head briskly, mouth closed and eyes staring. Mr. Peregrine was coming down the path behind them.

"Slow down," he said. "I'm supposed to be escorting you . . ."

"Did you see them?" Darwen demanded.

"See what?"

"The pouncels!" said Rik and Darwen at the same time.

"The what?"

"Pouncels," said Darwen. "Like the figurines Jorge showed us! There was a pack of them, right here in the camp. They must be working for the Bleck."

Mr. Peregrine shushed them, hurriedly looking over his shoulder.

"Show a little discretion," he said in a whisper. "We came looking for Mr. Cabrera . . . And here he is."

Dazed and bleary eyed, Gabriel was emerging from their tent. He looked tired but also embarrassed and alarmed. "What's going on?" he asked. "Where is everyone?"

"Didn't you hear the shot?" asked Darwen.

"Shot? What shot?" said Gabriel. "I was asleep, I think."

"In your clothes?" said Rik.

"I was tired," said Gabriel, he sounded weary and Darwen thought he was on the verge of tears. It all seemed quite clear to him now. The boy felt abandoned and alone. He'd probably been in the tent for ages, miserable and homesick. Getting to sleep would have been a relief.

"Come on," Darwen said as kindly as he could. "We'll get you up to the dining shelter. Let me get my pack of cards and we can play till they figure out what happened."

He put an arm around the boy's shoulders, but Gabriel flinched, and Darwen let him be. Darwen knew what it was like to feel different, an outsider, and he also knew that a sudden outpouring of pity wasn't the answer. Instead he stuck his head in the tent, grabbed the playing cards from his bag, and zipped the tent closed.

They moved up to the dining shelter and there was a rush of noise as the others saw them approach.

"Why didn't you come when you were called?" Miss Harvey wanted to know.

Alex looked ready to scold Gabriel but Darwen caught her eye and, for once, she thought better of it. Darwen fished his cards from his back pocket and prepared to deal.

"OK, Gabriel," he said. "What can you play? Blackjack? War? Whist?"

But Gabriel didn't answer. Jorge had appeared with two of the local men who worked at the camp, one of whom had been watching the football match the day before. It was him, a heavyset man with a thin, black moustache who was cradling the rifle. Jorge was talking quickly to Miss Martinez who was looking serious, and the man with the rifle was nodding and gesturing. Miss Martinez seemed doubtful. She leaned in and Darwen thought he caught a word repeated back to the man with the rifle: "*Demonio?*"

The man nodded emphatically. Jorge shook his head and waved the word away, but the man with the gun rattled off a stream of irritated Spanish. Darwen turned to ask Gabriel what they were talking about but the boy had slipped silently into a dark corner and was watching the debate closely.

"I don't care if he was attacked by a fire-breathing T-Rex," Mr. Sumners roared, "shooting those stone balls you are all so fond of out of its nose: he cannot discharge a firearm this close to a camp full of children! Tell him."

The squabble escalated. Miss Martinez shepherded the man with the gun away from the crimson-faced Mr. Sumners and spoke in soothing tones as Mr. Iverson tried to convince the students that the danger had been dealt with.

"But what did he shoot at?" Kahala wanted to know.

"Probably a margay or an ocelot," said Jorge. "He was protecting his livestock, but he should not shoot such creatures. I am sure the sound scared them off and they will not return."

"Them?" said Rik. "You said a margay or an ocelot."

"He thinks he saw more than one," said Jorge, gesturing hopelessly.

"Both of those are solitary hunters," said Rik. "They wouldn't attack in a group."

"I think he was mistaken," said Jorge.

"What does *demonio* mean?" asked Darwen.

"What?" said Jorge, clearly dodging. "I don't think that's what he meant."

"It means demon," said Carlos. Everyone went quiet. "Mr. Delgado – the man with the gun – said a pack of demons came out of the jungle and attacked his chickens. He shot at them, but they escaped."

"Rainforest," said Rik, grudgingly. "A pack of demons came out of the *rainforest*."

"Thanks," said Nathan. "That makes much more sense."

"All right, that's enough," said Miss Harvey. "Time for bed."

There was a general sputter of exasperation, but several voices rang out louder than the rest.

"You think that Scarlett woman has already built any hotels around here?" said Princess Clarkson, "'cause I've about had it with this place."

"No way am I going to bed after all this," called Melissa Young, who looked quite terrified.

"Bed!" shouted Bobby Park, "with demons on the loose?"

"Mr. Park," said Miss Harvey, very stern, "I personally give you my word that you will not be attacked by any mythical monsters overnight. You too Miss Young. Bed. Quick march."

Protests turned to groans, but several were genuinely frightened. Miss Harvey relented a little, and spent a few moments huddled with those who seemed least sure of returning to their tents. Only Darwen, Alex and Rik held back, keen to see what else they could overhear.

"Mr. Arkwright," said Mr. Sumners. "You are, ahhh, still here. Why is that?"

"Waiting to go to the bathroom," said Darwen.

"I can't be sure from here," said Mr. Sumners, smiling mirthlessly, up to where Carlos was coming back down the trail, towel and toothbrush in hand, "but they would seem to be vacant."

"Only the ones with the toads, sir," said Darwen, improvising. "I don't like toads."

"No," said Mr. Sumners, bending and peering into his face with careful emphasis. "Neither do I." He checked his watch. "Very well. I want you in bed in four minutes and not a second more. And walk!"

"Come on," said Darwen to Rik, trudging up towards the bathrooms, casting one last look back to where Miss Martinez, Jorge and the man with the rifle – now joined by Mr. Peregrine – continued to chatter in rapid Spanish.

"And you, Miss O'Connor," said Mr. Sumners. "Or are you afraid of toads as well?"

"I never said I was afraid of 'em," muttered Darwen, as Alex fell into step beside him.

"Just his lucky guess, then," said Alex.

"What happened to Gabriel?" said Rik, looking around. "One minute he was over there, the next . . .?"

"He likes to keep to himself," said Alex. "Didn't even join in the football match. You didn't notice?"

Darwen and Rik exchanged shame-faced looks.

Moments later they were brushing their teeth. Alex had been right. None of the students much liked the washrooms. They tended to go in groups and get out as quickly as they could. It was only a matter of time, Melissa Young had said, before someone peed in their bed because you'd have to be crazy to go up to the haunted washrooms alone at night. Darwen figured their fear had more to do with snakes than ghosts, but still . . . he understood their concern. He bent over the sink and spat. As he straightened up, it happened again.

It lasted only a second, but there, quite clearly, right over his shoulder, as if standing right behind him . . .

The laughing face.

As before, it didn't look real exactly. More like a model, and its eyes were glassy and dead. Its mouth gaping, showing white, even teeth.

Darwen spun around, and though there was nothing there, he was sure he could hear the wild laughter trailing away. And once more, in its wake, came the nudge of a memory that was just out of reach. That thing, whatever it was, he had seen it before, heard it's laughter before, long ago.

"What?" asked Rik. He was looking at Darwen closely and his voice was low.

"Nothing," Darwen shrugged. "Just . . . I don't know. Nothing."

"OK," said Rik. "Fine."

Rik thought he was keeping secrets. Remembering how put out they had been about him visiting Silbrica without them, Darwen relented.

"It's stupid," he said, putting his toothbrush away.

"Go on."

"Well, it was only there for a second," said Darwen. "Less. But it looked, sort of like . . . a clown."

"A what?" said Rik. "Like a circus clown? Red nose and all that?"

"No," Darwen answered, trying to fix on the details. "The face wasn't made up or anything. And it wasn't a real person. More like a model or a doll. Laughing."

"O . . . K . . ." said Rik, looking uneasily at the mirror.

"I told you it was nothing," said Darwen.

"A happy clown?" asked Rik, hopefully.

"Kind of," said Darwen apologetically. "More manic."

Rik frowned.

"That's gonna give me nightmares," he said. "Not a big fan of clowns."

"Me neither," said Darwen, shuddering. "Let's just . . . forget it, OK?"

"Fine by me," said Rik.

Darwen splashed water on his face, and, when he straightened up, managed not to look back into the mirror.

"What was all that about?" said Alex.

"Darwen thinks he saw . . ." Rik began.

"Nothing," said Darwen. "I didn't see anything."

"If you're keeping secrets from me . . ." Alex began.

Darwen turned to say something, but stopped. There was confused movement down in the tent camp: running people, some of them shouting. Even from here Darwen could sense their panic, their fear.

Something had happened. Something new.

"Quick!" said Darwen, snatching up his things and hurrying down towards the commotion.

"You've got to hand it to Mr. P," said Alex, as the three of them hurried back the way they had come to see what was going on. "His trips are never dull."

Nineteen
NIGHT
TERRORS

There were four of them: a young man, two teenage boys and a girl. Darwen recognised the kids from the football game. One of them was Felippe, the boy who had scored the spectacular volley. He looked quite different now: urgent and anxious, and he was looking around like something might attack him at any minute. The young man was carrying a small axe. They made for the man with the rifle – Mr. Delgado – who was with Jorge and the teachers in the yellowish light of the generator lamp, and began speaking all at once.

There was a moment's silence. Then the rifle slipped from Mr. Delgado's grasp. It clattered to the ground and for a moment he stood there, his hands clamped over his nose and mouth, frozen in some terrible rush of emotion.

They hadn't seen Darwen, who had stuttered to a halt in the shadows behind the dining shelter. He pulled Alex and Rik in beside him. "What are they saying?" he asked.

"I'm *trying* to listen," said Alex, shrugging out of Darwen's grasp and pressing her head to the wooden upright.

The young man picked up the fallen rifle and started moving back the way they had come. The boys and the girl dragged Mr. Delgado after them though he still seemed to be in a kind of daze.

"What's wrong with him?" asked Rik.

"Quiet," said Alex, her voice low, her face serious.

The teachers were muttering among themselves, then broke hurriedly apart. Jorge went after the locals. Miss Harvey, Miss Martinez and Mr. Iverson all went down to the tents. Mr. Sumners went into the makeshift office by the kitchen, and Mr. Peregrine sat at one of the tables, as if waiting.

"Well?" said Rik. "What's going on?"

"Another kid has been taken," said Alex. "A girl called Calida. Felippe's sister. Right from her bed. They're going there now."

For a long moment no one spoke.

"It can't be the pouncels," said Rik. "We saw what they did to the tapir. They attack. They feed. They leave. They don't kidnap."

"Nice," said Alex.

"Rik is right," whispered Darwen. "The pouncels behave like . . . well, like animals. The thing I saw in Silbrica was different. It thinks. Maybe the Bleck is just using them to wreak havoc or drum up fear."

"I don't like the sound of that," said Alex.

"We should go the village," said Darwen, ignoring her. "Look for tracks."

"We're supposed to be in bed," said Rik.

"Yeah, sneaking around tonight of all nights seems like a really bad idea," Alex agreed.

"Sumners has gone," said Darwen. "I say we follow. Quietly."

"No way," said Rik.

"Come on," said Darwen. "This is what we came for!"

"What is?" asked Alex.

"To learn what is happening here," Darwen replied. "Another kid has been taken. We have to follow while the trail is fresh."

"What trail?" asked Alex.

"We won't know unless we look, will we?" Darwen shot back.

"I don't know, Darwen . . ." Rik began.

"Look," said Darwen, taking charge. "I'm going to follow them. You can come with me, or I can go alone. Your choice. But we're supposed to be the Peregrine Pact, remember?"

Rik and Alex looked at each other, then shrugged their half-hearted agreement.

"OK," said Darwen. "And no lights."

"What?" hissed Rik. "Are you serious? There's snakes and God knows what else out here."

"And if we run around with flashlights they'll catch us and send us back to bed before we've seen anything," said Darwen. "Come on."

Darwen knew that Rik and Alex were looking at each other, trying to decide whether to protest, but he went anyway, slipping into the darkness of the grounds. He could see Mr. Sumners sitting inside the little office, tapping anxiously on a desk, but was sure they were invisible outside. He used the glow from the window to find the path, and padded cautiously along it. So long as they were out in the open, there was enough light from the moon and stars that they could just about make out the path, but once they were under the trees, traipsing toward the tiny villageany visibility that they had disappeared, they really were in the dark.

"This is a bad idea, Darwen," Rik muttered.

"OK," said Darwen. "One flashlight between us pointed straight down. Keep close together."

He snapped on the beam and aimed it at the leaf-strewn ground. Something skittered into the underbrush unseen.

"O . . . K . . ." said Alex. "Walk. Slowly."

They moved cautiously through the forest, the warm air humming with insect noises and the otherworldly calls of frogs. Somewhere far off, something shrieked, but whether the creature that made the sound was human, animal or bird, was from their world or that beyond the mirrors, Darwen could not say. Rik could correct him as many times as he liked, but to Darwen this was and always would be the jungle.

"Just keep the light steady," said Alex. "I saw something move over there."

She tucked in her arms and Darwen felt her shudder as a moth the size of his hand – so big he actually could hear the beating of its wings – fluttered inches past their heads, swooping at the flashlight. For a moment he thought of his dellfey friend, feeling a twinge of anxiety about why he had not been able to get back into her bamboo grove. He was considering this uneasily when he noticed horse hoof prints in the rain-softened earth of the trail. There was nothing else to suggest anyone ever came this way except for the creatures that called the place home. To their right, Darwen could hear the waves breaking on the rocky portion of the shore and see the glow of the moon through the trees, but to his left the jungle stretched for miles.

They heard voices. Darwen looked directly ahead and saw a space where the deep shade of the trees stopped. It was the football field and the cluster of tiny houses. He snapped the flashlight off, then closed his eyes tight to get them used to the dark. Alex and Rik both groaned but he shushed them.

"If I get eaten by something in these woods, Darwen Arkwright," hissed Alex, "I'm going to have something to say about it."

Darwen pressed on, feeling the ground with his feet with each step. The voices were getting louder. A woman was crying. A man was shouting angrily and someone else was responding in a placating tone which was not helping the situation at all: Jorge.

Darwen veered inland across the moonlit field, moving towards the lights of the houses, and nearly stepped on a large iguana which hissed at him. Under a great, spreading tree was a roughly-timbered shack with an open veranda hung with hammocks. There were people there. Darwen could make out Felippe sitting on the deck, his head in his hands. Jorge was standing, murmuring, continually lowering his palms as if urging calm, and then looking up into the branches which hung over the house.

Darwen, Rik and Alex hugged the treeline and moved slowly closer, certain they would not be seen unless someone shone a light right at them. It was Mr. Delgado who was doing the shouting. Darwen was glad to see that someone else had the gun now, because his fury was frightening. He kept pointing at Jorge and shouting, cursing, spitting at the ground, calling "Calida," and finally collapsing beside the hammocks, weeping uncontrollably.

"Her father," whispered Alex.

Darwen said nothing, but he suddenly felt embarrassed, even ashamed, that they had come skulking around these people's grief. What had he been thinking intruding like this, sniffing for clues while a family mourned their lost child? Shouldn't he of all people know that this wasn't the stuff of adventure? He turned around, pulling at the others wordlessly, determined to get out of there before they were caught spying.

Alex shot him a look, and as their eyes met, he stumbled on something at his feet, and fell sprawling to the ground with a dull splat. The next thing he knew he was lying on the forest floor, up to his elbows in a slippery and foul-smelling mud. Though the area around them was quite dry, Darwen had somehow managed to find a round, saucer-like depression which must have been holding rainwater for days. The brown goop was everywhere: all over his face, hands, and clothes. He had even managed to splash some of it onto the others, and they glared at him with disbelief and annoyance. Darwen tried to get to his feet, slipped in the forest slime, and landed on his back.

Alex gave him a look of withering contempt, as if he was being stupid on purpose, but she didn't get chance to say anything. A flashlight from where the adults were talking came lancing through the darkness towards them. Then another. Voices called, and Darwen heard the distinct and terrifying snap of a rifle being cocked to fire.

"Run!" he yelled. Darwen scrambled, sliding in the mud, gripping the stone over which he had tripped in the first place, realising even as he got to his feet and began to sprint, that it was perfectly round, and was not the only one on the ground there. There was a ring of them – about ten – circling the muddy depression in which he had just been lying.

He dashed blindly along the path after the others, feeling the light vanish as soon as they reached the treeline.

"I can't see!" sputtered Rik.

"Just keep moving," said Darwen, catching up with them.

"Do they think we might be the missing kid," asked Rik, "or the things which took her?"

"Well," said Alex, "there's three of us, and Darwen currently looks like the Creature from the Black Lagoon, so I don't think they're looking to take us home and feed us empanadas."

"Good point," said Rik. "Shine the light on the ground.

"And Darwen," Alex added, considering the mud on her shirt, "don't touch me, OK? This stuff stinks."

"Just *move!*" hissed Rik, exasperated.

They jogged along the trail, eyes glued to the shifting pool of light at their feet. From time to time they glanced backwards into the darkness, but if the villagers had seen enough of them to give chase, they were a long way back. They slowed, getting their breath back, but as soon they did, they heard something new above the constant hum of the jungle and the surf, a steady, rhythmic pounding.

Horses.

Darwen, Alex and Rik began to run again, harder now, all thinking the same thing: could they get back to the tent camp before the horsemen caught up, or did they have to hide in the jungle? If they waved the horsemen down, would they get chance to explain themselves before someone took a shot at what they assumed to be a pack of ravening pouncels?

Darwen turned to see how close the horsemen were, so he was the last to see the flashlight coming towards them from the tent camp, the last to realise that they had nowhere to go, the last to know they had already been seen, and the last to recognise that the man in front of them was the one person they wouldn't have wanted to catch them out of bed at night.

"What in the name of all that's holy are you doing out here at this time?"

Darwen spun around. Rik had raised the flashlight slightly and in its beam he saw the pink and furious face of Mr. Sumners, the maths teacher.

"Could have been worse," said Alex. "We could have been shot."

Darwen couldn't argue with that, but it didn't help. Sumners had flagged the horsemen down and sent them back to the huddle of forlorn little houses looking disappointed and angry, then marched Darwen, Rik and Alex back to the camp and bed, refusing Darwen permission to shower and wash his clothes.

"But I'm filthy," Darwen had protested. "The tent will stink."

"You should have thought of that before you ahhh, decided to poke your nose into other people's business," said Sumners, "risking death and dismemberment in the process for your friends. And you, Haggerty," he had said, glaring at Rik. "You're supposed to be smart. I would have thought you of all people would know the dangers of wandering around in a place like this at night."

They walked back to the tents in silence, Alex clearly peeved that she wasn't the one who Sumners recognised as the clever member of their little group. "That was a bad idea," she finally said, as if to recoup some faith in her own intelligence, "Following them to the village. Terrible idea."

"What are you looking at me for?" said Darwen.

"Because it was *your* bad idea," she said. "We told you."

"It was your choice," Darwen muttered.

"Yeah?" said Rik. "What about *we're supposed to be the Peregrine Pact, remember?*"

"Hey," said Darwen, defiant, "you didn't have to come."

"Next time," said Alex, "maybe we won't. You might be the Mirroculist, Darwen, but that doesn't mean you get to make all the decisions."

She stalked off.

"I just thought . . ." Darwen began.

"Save it," said Rik. "I'm beat."

They didn't speak as they walked the rest of the way. Darwen was annoyed so he just muttered a *good night* to Gabriel who had sat up as soon as they unzipped the front.

"A kid has gone missing?" Gabriel asked, his meek voice suggesting that he already knew the answer.

Darwen paused. "How did you know?"

"I heard them shouting," said Gabriel, his face unreadable in the dark. "Which one is it?"

"A girl called Calida," he said. "Felippe Delgado's sister. He was the one who . . . but you weren't at the game, were you?"

"No," said Gabriel. "I, uh . . . don't know them. I was just curious."

He didn't sound curious. He sounded upset, though he had spoken through gritted teeth as if trying to get a hold of himself. Darwen asked him if he was OK, but the boy didn't respond.

Darwen lay there in the dark, exhausted. Moments later, he was asleep. He dreamed of the jungle and of huge brightly coloured snakes which hung from the trees and slithered across the path in front of him. For some reason, they didn't bother him, but the further he moved into the trees, the more of them there were, and soon it was difficult to walk without stepping on them. They were also getting bigger, and some of them now were marked with a black zigzag pattern down their backs: these, Darwen knew, were very dangerous, and the dream quickly turned to nightmare as they multiplied, emerging from the underbrush on all sides and approaching him with implausible deliberation. As the largest one reached him, mouth gaping to reveal a swelling tentacle where its tongue should be, he heard wild, maniacal laughter. He turned and there between the trees was a seated figure, rocking back and forth with odd, jerky motions, its head tilted backwards and its mouth open. It had red curly hair and wore the garish, oversized clothes of a clown . . .

Darwen woke with a start.

It was hot and muggy in the dark tent, and Darwen felt himself sweating, even though he was only covered by a single cotton sheet. He pushed it back and then kept quite still, listening, waiting for his heart to slow as his memory of the dream faded. He could hear Rik snoring softly. And then, just as he was about to drift off again, he heard the unmistakable sound of the tent flap being slowly, carefully unzipped.

For a moment he lay quite still, staring into the blackness. The sound came again. Someone was coming in.

Darwen sat up, one hand reaching desperately for the flashlight under the bed. He groped along the plastic floor and found it, swinging it up and turning it on.

The tent entrance was half open, the zipper moving down, gripped by a spindly black claw. Another was pushing the flap wide, and through the gap the swinging beam of the flashlight found a cluster of black eyes, and hard, shiny mouthparts.

Darwen shrieked, scrambling backwards on his bed, the light lurching around the tent as the flashlight slipped from his hands. He had the impression of something large stepping quickly inside and he held his hands out in front of him, terrified that the thing would touch him. He could hear skittering movement inside the tent . . .

Rik grunted and woke. Darwen's fingers groped for the flashlight again, finding it and directing it once more on the tent door.

"What?" gasped Rik. "What is it?"

The flap was still unzipped, but there were only the three boys inside. Darwen swung the light around and Gabriel sat up, rubbing his eyes and looking scared.

"Something came in," Darwen gasped. "I heard it."

Rik snapped on the rechargeable lantern and held it up.

"Check under the beds," he said, grimly. "On three. One. Two. Three."

The three boys thrust their heads under the beds, turning from side to side but finding nothing more than half-open luggage and their own anxious faces.

"You must have dreamed it," said Rik.

"No way," said Darwen. "Someone opened the tent."

"Have you been out, Gabriel?" asked Rik. "To go to the bathroom or something?"

The skinny boy shook his head fervently but his eyes were cautious, watchful.

"There's nothing here, Darwen," said Rik. "Maybe someone got the wrong tent by mistake."

"Maybe someone was trying to go through our luggage while we slept," suggested Gabriel.

"Maybe it was nothing," Rik replied. He sounded irritable, as if he thought Darwen was being dramatic to attract attention to himself. "Can we *please* try to get some sleep?"

Darwen said nothing. He couldn't be sure what he had seen, not with only the lightning flicker of his erratic flashlight, and he *had* been having a nightmare . . . But he saw in his mind's eye the rail-thin leg with the little, black claw, the clustered hard, black eyes and the beak-like mouth with the pulsing, black feelers beside it.

A name came to mind: a stupid, ridiculous name that made the tropical night feel cold as November in Lancashire.

Mr. Jenkins.

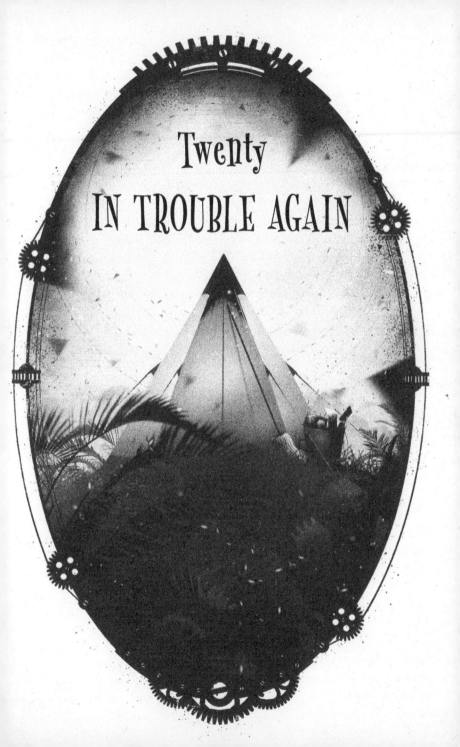

Twenty
IN TROUBLE AGAIN

The next morning Rik still looked crestfallen and surly. Sumners had taken the night to think of a suitable punishment, and had come up with something that hit Rik particularly hard. After breakfast, while the other students worked on their bows and arrows and then went on another jungle hike, Rik, Darwen and Alex were to stay behind with Miss Martinez and help the cleaning staff.

"What's the point of coming here if we're not allowed to look around?" he sputtered to the others. When they didn't respond, he added, with less anger and more sadness, "the hikes are the best part."

Rik didn't speak again until the rest of the students were in the motorboats, Nathan, Chip and Barry waving and laughing as they pulled away. He didn't even look up as a pair of white-faced capuchin monkeys started dropping half-eaten bits of fruit onto the roof of the tent.

"I hear you had a nocturnal visitor," said Alex as Rik stomped off to start work.

"Mr. Jenkins," said Darwen. "Or something like him."

"Can't have been," said Alex. "We smashed the gate that led to their charming cottage. How could one of them be here?"

"Same way I was here, or hereabouts, weeks before ever getting on the plane," said Darwen. "I came through a portal."

They were sitting on the platform outside Alex's tent.

"That *particular* monster finds a way through to this *particular* spot in the jungle and then finds your *particular* tent?" Alex replied. "It's too much of a coincidence."

"It's not a coincidence at all," said Darwen. "It's all connected. The thing which once called itself Mr. Jenkins was looking for me. I'm sure of it."

"I'm surprised it could fit in the tent with your giant ego."

"I'm not saying I'm special," said Darwen. "I'm just . . . I don't know. Involved. Central to this whole Silbrica thing . . ."

"So long as you're not saying you're special," said Alex, wryly.

"It's because of what I saw that we're here at all," said Darwen.

"So the rest of us are what? Your sidekicks? Your helpers?"

"You remember the Halloween Hop, Alex?" said Darwen, suddenly fierce. "I didn't want to go. I wanted to sit in my room. You made me go because you thought I was important. I was the Mirroculist. I still am. That makes me special. I didn't ask to be. I'm not even sure I want to be. But I am. That's all there is to it."

Alex considered him for a long moment, then nodded seriously. "OK," she said looking up towards the dining shelter. "Miss Martinez is coming. Better get your stuff together Captain Special, you've got some scrubbing to do. Too bad being a Mirroculist doesn't get you out of cleaning."

Darwen glowered at her, but she grinned and eventually he did too.

"There you are," said Miss Martinez. "Come on, there's work to be done. Mr. Haggerty is helping Señor Torres bring the supplies up from the beach to the kitchen. Miss O'Connor, you can help Juanita replace the bed linens in the tents. Mr. Arkwright, you have to go to the village and apologise for the confusion you caused last night. You will need to extend your sympathy to the Delgado family. And quick march."

Darwen's heart sank. "Can't Rik and Alex come with me?" he said.

"They are busy with other tasks," the Spanish teacher answered brusquely. "Tasks which will be assigned to you also when you return. And take a shower. *Rapido.*"

Darwen showered in the only stall without a lizard, toad or insect more than two inches long. He put on shorts and a T shirt, sprayed himself with mosquito repellent and set off to the village along the coastal track, wondering what on earth he was supposed to say in his idiot-Spanish. How was he supposed to convey his feelings about the loss of their daughter and his ridiculous behaviour which had made the situation worse, when his language skills hadn't gotten beyond "Is this a banana? No it is a pineapple."

Who dreams this stuff up? he wondered. *Is this a banana? No, it is a pineapple. Seriously? Who would ever say that? I mean, my Spanish might be rubbish but I'm not a complete moron. I can tell the difference between a banana and . . .*

The thought died as he spotted the muddy depression into which he had fallen. The stone spheres which had ringed the damp hole last night, were all gone. He stood, looking at the little hollow, wondering why it was the only piece of ground that still looked wet.

"Are you lost, little boy?"

Darwen looked up. It was a bit like looking at a picture of a shopping cart in the middle of the desert or a fussily-upholstered couch on the edge of a cliff, so clearly did Scarlett Oppertune not belong in this place. She was dressed today in an electric blue suit with padded shoulders, matching high heels, and an elegant little purse. Her watch, ring, and designer spectacles were all studded with diamonds. Her perfectly made-up lips were wide and smiling, her eyes bright, and her head cocked slightly to one side with an expression of welcoming interest, which Darwen did not trust for a second.

"No," said Darwen. "I'm going to the houses."

"*Houses*," she repeated, with a still broader smile that suggested he was stretching the definition of the word. "Get a good look," she said. "After what happened last night, I don't think they'll be here much longer."

She was still smiling, still looking perfectly cheerful, so Darwen was at a loss to explain why he felt cold and uneasy, as if he was alone with one of the pouncel creatures he had seen the night before.

Scarlett's eyes narrowed thoughtfully, but the smile didn't alter, as if it was held in place by wires. "So," she said. "What are you doing out here at this time? Shouldn't you be out looking at birds or something with your little friends?"

"I've come to talk to Mr. Delgado," said Darwen, wondering what business it was of hers. "What are *you* doing?"

"Talk to him about what?" she asked, ignoring his question, and it was there again, that watchful curiosity beneath the cat-like smile.

"I . . . I just need to find them," he said. It was going to be hard enough talking to the Delgado family. He saw no reason to explain himself to this woman first.

She looked at him, and for a moment Darwen thought she might try and stop him, but then she shrugged and the smile buckled at one side so that it looked more like a smirk. "Better hurry then," she said. "I'm not sure how much longer they'll be here."

"They're moving out?" asked Darwen, aghast.

"I paid them the first installment this morning," she answered. "I think Mr. Delgado will be hunting the jaguar that took his daughter first, which is understandable. But once that is dead, they'll be on the next boat out of here."

"To where?" Darwen demanded. "To do what? This is their home. Their life . . ."

"Not anymore," said Scarlett, still smiling that wide, bland smile. "They've suffered a deep and touching loss here. Hardly surprising they want to put it behind them. As for what they will do . . . Well Mr . . . whatever your name is, it's not good to look after people too much. Better that they make their own way in the world. If they don't have the knowledge or the skills to do that," she concluded, still smiling, "well that's what you environmentalist-types call natural selection, isn't it? The survival of the fittest. Well, run along. You might be able to catch them before they go shoot themselves a kitty."

She didn't actually clap in girlish delight, but it was a near thing. She beamed, like she was saying they were going to roast marshmallows or something, and Darwen felt the kind of revulsion he had experienced when he first saw the toad in the shower stall. He stepped deliberately round her and started to run towards the buildings at the edge of the football field.

Whatever else she was, Scarlett was telling the truth about the Delgado family. As Darwen got close to the house beneath the great tree he could see a woman – the woman he had seen crying the night before – loading cardboard boxes onto the porch outside. The door was wide open and the place looked deserted already. Darwen watched her work for a moment, feeling stupid and ashamed, then said "*hola*." She looked up, but did not seem to recognise him, and for a long moment Darwen just stood there, clasping and unclasping his hands.

"*Lo Siento*," he said.

Sorry.

And since he didn't know if that was the right word exactly, he added the only other word he could think of and the girl's name, "*Excusa. Por Calida.*"

He knew he wasn't making any real sense.

Mrs. Delgado was a strong-looking woman, but her face looked weary beyond measure. She considered him, smiling sadly, then took a few steps towards him and sat on the edge of the porch. Beside her as if forgotten was a bag spilling gold coins: Scarlett's pay off.

"Señor Delgado . . .?" Darwen asked.

Mrs. Delgado gave a long, slow shrug which somehow said that she didn't know where her husband was or what he was doing. Darwen tentatively raised his hands, miming someone shooting a rifle. She nodded and shrugged again, a gesture which was both knowing and hopeless, and then motioned for Darwen to approach her. Uneasily, he did so. She reached up and touched his face, looking into his eyes. The woman's hand was rough, but the touch held an almost painful tenderness and her shining eyes suddenly brimmed over so that tears flowed silently down her cheeks.

"I'm sorry," said Darwen, in English. "If there is anything I can do to bring your daughter back, I will. I promise."

Mrs. Delgado nodded once, though Darwen doubted she had understood what he had said, then reached absently into the bag of coins and pressed one into his hand.

"No!" he exclaimed. "This is yours. Please . . ."

But she waved his protests away, patted his hand, and then hauled herself laboriously to her feet. Without another glance, she returned to work. Darwen looked at the coin in his hand, felt its curiously-rough surface, and took a last look at the porch where the child's hammock had been hanging until a few hours ago. He scanned the wooden deck for anything that might resemble the tracks of a pouncel. The creatures' long claws would surely have left nicks and gouges in the soft wood . . .

There was nothing.

He looked up at the tree, but that seemed unmarked as well, though the act of looking up reminded him that Jorge had done the same. He gazed out towards the rest of what they called a village, though it was really only five little houses. The most distant looked the newest, a tidy log structure with a porch where one of the local girls was sweeping, a bucket of cleaning supplies at the foot of the steps. The girl's incongruous, pink jacket was hanging on a hook by the door, and even at this distance its brass buttons sparkled in the sun.

As he took one last look at the Delgado house, Darwen saw that it was not completely deserted after all. Felippe was standing at the window, watching him, his face blank. Darwen raised a hand in greeting, feeling foolish and awkward, and the boy inclined his head in acknowledgement.

He walked back to the camp, his mind full of questions. There was no sign of Scarlett, so he had been able to study the muddy depression in the earth and make sure that the stone spheres were indeed gone. Could that be why Scarlett was so keen to get her hands on this piece of land, that she planned to sell its archaeological treasures? The stone spheres must be worth a lot of money to collectors, but if she was able to take them so easily while the villagers were distracted by the hunt for a missing child, why bother buying the land? And who was Scarlett anyway? She had gone out of her way to talk to him. She had even called him "Mr . . . whatever your name is," as if she knew him, and had remembered at the last minute to pretend otherwise.

It made no sense. Neither did the coins. Why was an American developer paying for land with gold? He looked at the coin. It didn't have the smooth surfaces of worn metal and when he ran his fingertips lightly around the edge he could feel tiny points and angles, some of them quite sharp. He held it up to the light and saw that it had no visible design. It wasn't so much a coin as a gold disc, and the metal was oddly marbled and uneven.

Darwen trudged through the humming jungle, watching the trail for snakes, feeling hot and damp and exhausted. Two days ago it had all seemed so exciting, but he was tired of the smelly tent and of not knowing what was going on. He felt no closer to rescuing

Luis or his brother Eduardo, and with another child gone, who knew how long they would be allowed to stay?

Miss Martinez spotted him the moment he returned to the camp.

"Where do you think you're going, Mr. Arkwright?"

"To my tent, Miss," said Darwen.

"Go and help Mr. Haggerty in the kitchen."

"Yes, Miss."

Rik's mood hadn't improved, and it wasn't hard to see why. Lugging plastic boxes and crates of canned food and other supplies up from the beach was no picnic, and the camp's pantry was so small that everything had to be carefully stacked.

"What's this?" asked Darwen, hoisting two plastic bins full of white powder.

"Non-dairy creamer," said Rik. "There's no fridge, so everything has to survive at room temperature. Which would be fine if that didn't mean, like, a hundred degrees."

"One only," said the athletic-looking kitchen helper they called simply Torres. As usual, he was wearing jean shorts and no shirt. "One box for here, the other to go out to the ranger station on Caño Island."

"So I've got to take it back to the beach?" grumbled Rik.

"Not till the boat is ready," said Torres. "Tomorrow. Put it there."

As soon as the local went out, Darwen relayed the story of his trip and his encounter with Scarlett. He handed Rik the coin Mrs. Delgado had given him.

"Is this money?" said Rik. "It has no numbers on it. Can I show it to Mr. Iverson?"

"What for?"

"See if we can do some tests on it or something," said Rik, holding it up to the light and squinting at it. "Does that look like pure gold to you? If it's not, maybe the villagers aren't getting what they think they're getting. Not sure we could do much in the way of real tests out here, but it's worth a look."

"There's something about that Oppertune woman," said Darwen. "I don't know what it is, but I think she's connected to the missing kids."

"How?" asked Rik.

"No idea," Darwen answered. "It's just a hunch." He looked out of the window and saw Alex walking down from the trees behind the dining shelter. She was moving quickly and looking nervously about. Darwen called her name.

She jumped, thought for a moment, and then walked over to the kitchen. "What?" she said, poking her head around the door.

"Aren't you done cleaning the tents out yet?" asked Darwen.

"No, I'm not. That's it? You wanted to see how far behind I was while making me more behind?"

"Keep your hair on," said Darwen.

"I don't know what that even means," she rejoined, walking off and letting the door snap shut behind her.

"What's eating her?" asked Rik.

"Got me," said Darwen. "What was she doing up in the jungle back there if she's not done cleaning?"

"Rainforest," supplied Rik, automatically. "Probably just taking a break. Getting a little air. If the other tents smell as bad as ours, I couldn't blame her."

"It's not my fault," said Darwen. "If Sumners had let me take a shower last night ..."

"Yeah, yeah," muttered Rik, "it's Sumners' fault that our tent smells like a possum's armpit."

"All right," said Darwen, "It's my fault. Happy?"

"If I still have to sleep in there, then no, not particularly, but it's cool. What did you tell Gabriel?"

"Not much," said Darwen. "He didn't seem to mind."

Rik stared. "Did he still have a nose?"

"He spends so much time in there I expect he's forgotten what clean air smells like," he said. "He did care about Calida though. Have you seen him with the local kids at all?"

"No," said Rik. "I know he's shy and all, but he really won't talk to them. Sarita came into the camp yesterday and he bolted for the tent the moment he saw her. Kind of rude, I thought."

"Are we done?" asked Darwen.

"Just about. I guess we're supposed to help Alex now. If we're quick, maybe we can do some work on our bows and arrows."

Alex, it turned out, had made very little progress at all.

"How can you have only done one?" asked Rik. "You've had hours."

"One hour," said Alex. "And it's hard work. Let's see how fast you clean the next one and I'll go hang out in the kitchen with Torres."

"That's what you think I've been doing?" said Rik. "Hanging out?"

"Oh, I'm sorry," said Alex. "No doubt you've been scrubbing the beach or rescuing stranded whales or . . ."

"Will you two give it a rest?" said Darwen.

The three of them fell into a sulky silence which lasted until lunchtime, when the hikers returned full of tales of the birds and animals they had seen. Rik's mood darkened still further and when Darwen asked why the Hillside kids weren't all talking about Calida's disappearance, he gave a nasty laugh.

"She's not one of them, is she?" said Rik, eying Nathan across the dining shelter.

Darwen was shocked. "You think they don't care?" he said. "Even the worst of them aren't that bad, Rik."

"Yeah?" said Rik. "Nathan Cloten's a big fan of poor people, is he? Thinks we're all just the same whether we wear Hillside's glorious green and gold or not? I hope you're right. I'm going to get some more fruit."

Darwen thought of Scarlett with her little coins and her big plans, and he thought of Luis and Calida and Eduardo and the monster which had taken them; and he knew, just *knew*, there was a connection which he had to make if he was to do any good at all.

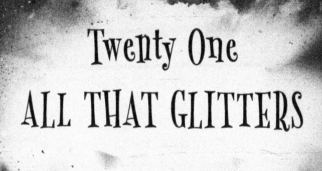

Twenty One
ALL THAT GLITTERS

The afternoon was to be spent in group study. Darwen, who couldn't face the prospect of working with Rik and Alex without something to distract them from their current moods, seized the opportunity to talk privately with Mr. Iverson as soon as the science teacher arrived. "Show him the coin, Rik," he said.

Rik's face brightened immediately.

"Wait," said Alex. "This is Peregrine Pact stuff. You shouldn't be telling a teacher."

But Rik already had his arm in the air. "Sir?" he said. "Could you help us try to figure out what this is made of?"

As Alex glared at him, Mr. Iverson considered the coin.

"Where did you get this?" he asked, his face hawkish.

"Found it," said Darwen, ignoring Alex's *told-you-so* stare. "That woman – Scarlett Oppertune – was giving them out to the kids on the football field. She says they're gold."

Mr. Iverson looked at him. "You found it?"

Darwen blushed. "Kind of," he said. "One of them gave it to me."

He didn't know why but he didn't want to discuss Mrs. Delgado or her missing daughter. Mr. Iverson returned his attention to the coin and nodded.

"I'm not sure we'll be able to do much," he said, "but there are some fairly simple tests used in archaeology to see if something is gold. Let me get everyone else started and I'll come find you."

"I'll go get my field guide," said Rik.

"The birds and animals thing?" said Alex vaguely. She was fidgeting and glancing around as if looking for an opportunity to sneak off.

"No," said Rik, as if she was being unusually dull-witted, "the archaeology one."

"That got destroyed last year," said Alex.

"I got a new one," said Rik. "You didn't think I'd come to a place like this without it, did you?"

"How silly of me," muttered Alex, as he headed down to the tent. "I know if I had a book about archaeology I'd take it just everywhere, to church, into the shower. Maybe he needs to feed it or it dies."

"What is it with you at the moment?" Darwen demanded.

"He shouldn't have told Iverson," she said. "We should be keeping this stuff to ourselves, not sharing it with the whole school."

"But there was something on your mind before that happened," Darwen pressed. "What?"

"Nothing," she said, looking away.

"Yes, there was," said Darwen. "You've been biting everyone's head off as soon as they speak to you and you're twitchy all the time."

"Twitchy?"

"Yeah, like you want to be somewhere else."

"Somewhere I can take a bath maybe, somewhere there isn't something lethal hiding under every bush?"

"No," said Darwen, "it's more than that. Ever since last night, you've been jumpy, impatient, like you're waiting to do something by yourself."

"A girl went missing last night, Darwen, or don't you remember? Taken right from her bed. And everything just goes on as normal, like nothing happened. Hikes and classes and stuff. I think Rik is right. It's not a Hillside kid, so no one cares."

"I don't think that's fair," said Darwen.

"And what about you, Darwen? All you're thinking about is your Silbrican mystery, like it's just an adventure."

"It's not an adventure; it's a *mission*."

"And while you're having fun with that people are dying."

"We don't know that," said Darwen. "She might be OK. Somewhere."

"Well, animals then."

"Animals are dying? What do you mean?"

Alex hesitated, and as she looked away, the colour rose in her cheeks. "Oh, you know, shrinking environments and Scarlett's plans for a hotel. And Chip Whittley killing that butterfly. And the entire village hunting a jaguar even though there were no paw prints anywhere near the house. It's stupid. And typical. If in doubt, kill something."

She sounded genuinely angry, but Darwen was sure there was something she was not saying, and when he continued to look skeptical, she turned back towards the tents.

"Here's Rik," she said. "Hi Rik. Let's hear about those tests Mr. Iverson was talking about."

Rik was surprised, but only for a moment. He was too pleased by the idea of sharing the wonders of his field archaeology book with them. Darwen continued to watch Alex, and as she avoided his eyes, he became more sure than ever that she was hiding something.

"OK," said Rik. "So there are three tests we can do without any special equipment and a fourth if we can get hold of some acid."

"Not sure I want to be handling acid even if we can find some," said Alex, all business now. "What are the other three?"

"We need an unglazed porcelain tile, a magnet, and a piece of glass," said Rik. "I have a magnet on the end of my flashlight so I brought that too. It's pretty powerful."

"I'll get a glass from the kitchen," said Alex brightly. "They might have some unglazed ceramic as well. I'll take a look."

"Thanks!" said Rik. "She cheered up," he observed as she walked away.

"Didn't she just."

"What?"

"Don't know," said Darwen. "As usual, I have no clue what is going on."

"You think she's hiding something? From us? You're imagining it."

Darwen watched Alex positively prancing back up the path towards them, a water glass in one hand and a ceramic jug in the other, grinning like the cat who got the non-dairy creamer.

"I hope you're right," he said.

Because if there was one thing he was sure about in the baffling haze which hung over this trip like the mist clinging to the jungle, it was that he needed his friends. Last night after they had squabbled he had tossed and turned for hours. Some of it was the mystery and their lack of progress toward finding Luis and his brother, but some of it was just the tension he felt with Rik and Alex, and knowing that they were right. It *had* been his fault. He had taken over, ignored their advice, and gotten them in trouble. He needed to be careful about that. Danger he could stand, but not loneliness. Not now.

"OK," said Rik. "Pass me the jug, will you? Right, now run the coin against it."

"Done," said Alex.

"Did it leave a black mark on the ceramic?" said Rik, head in his book.

"Nope," said Alex.

"OK, so it's not pyrite – fool's gold. Could be the real thing. Now try the magnet."

Darwen took Rik's heavy flashlight and put it up against the coin.

"Anything?" said Rik.

Darwen pulled the flashlight slowly away.

"No," said Alex. "Wait. Try that again."

Darwen repeated the action and this time it seemed like the coin stuck to the magnet for a moment.

"Maybe a tiny bit," said Alex.

"Hmmm," said Rik. "Pure gold should show no magnetic properties at all. Try the glass."

Alex took the glass. Gabriel was hovering at the edge of the table, watching closely, and a couple of the other students were craning to get a better look from their seats.

"Can you scratch the glass with the coin?" asked Rik.

Alex tried.

"Nothing," said Alex.

"Which means what?" said Darwen.

"All minerals have a measurement of hardness from one to

ten," said Rik. "It's called the Mohs scale. Glass has a hardness of 5.5, gold of 2.5 to 3. So true gold shouldn't scratch glass."

"And this didn't," said Alex. "So it's gold?"

"Not necessarily," said Rik. "It could be, or it could be made of something else with a similar hardness, like copper, say."

"So we don't know anything," said Darwen.

"If it's magnetic, then there's something other than pure gold mixed in at very least," said Rik. "Copper isn't magnetic either, so it can't be that, or not purely that."

Mr. Iverson returned with a box. "Oh, I see you found your book, Mr. Haggerty. Any progress?"

Rik repeated the results of the experiments so far and then summarised his instinct. "I'd say it is gold, but there are other minerals blended with the metal, so it's probably cheap."

"Which would suggest that the villagers are being ripped off," said Darwen.

"No surprises there," Alex remarked, shaking her head.

"Try this," said Mr. Iverson, setting the box on the table and opening it. Inside was a potent-looking microscope. "I hoped it might come in handy."

"Cool," said Rik.

As they set the microscope up, the crowd of students watching got larger despite Alex's advice that they should all mind their own business. Rik turned on a light at the instrument's base, positioned the coin and peered into the eyepiece. He adjusted the focus and magnification and, for a long moment, no one spoke. Rik eventually sat back, but his face was confused, even shocked.

Mr. Iverson looked in and his body suddenly became quite still and tense.

"What is it?" said Alex. "Here, let me see."

At last it was Darwen's turn, and at first he thought he'd made a mistake. The surface of the coin didn't look regular or solid at all. It was pocked with little holes and irregular shapes. He adjusted the focus and saw why the metal felt so uneven, even sharp to the touch. It looked like the surface of the little balls he sometimes made by combining the tinfoil, sweet wrappers. If this was a coin, it was one unlike any he had ever seen before.

But why?

"What am I looking at?" he asked, still staring into the eyepiece. He rotated the coin slightly. As he did so, a tiny feature of the metal caught his attention. It looked oddly familiar. He stared at it trying to remember where he had seen that precise shape before.

"I said the gold was probably very cheap," said Rik. "But that's not the only explanation. It could also be very old."

"How old?" asked Alex.

"Hundreds of years," said Rik. "Maybe more."

"It can't be," said Mr. Iverson.

"It would make sense," said Rik. "The impurities in the metal: copper, and other minerals including trace elements of iron that give it a slight magnetic quality."

"Are you suggesting . . .?" Mr. Iverson began.

"What?" asked Alex, exasperated. "What do you think it is?"

And then Darwen remembered. In the heart of the coin he

could make out a tiny hook which had not been completely flattened into the surface, and now he could also see the way that the metal's marbled surface laid out the outline of a strange leg: a leg with talons on the end.

He sat up and gaped at the others.

"It's a pouncel," he said. "These coins have been stamped from the figurines they found on Caño Island."

Twenty Two
DISCOVERIES

There was more red beans and rice for dinner, something even Alex couldn't get enthusiastic about. "Once or twice is fine," she exclaimed, exasperated. "Great, even. But every night? How about some jambalaya with jalapeño cornbread?"

"We eat what they eat," said Rik, nodding to the staff. "It's local stuff. That's why the fruit is so good. Anything else has to be imported, and that's expensive. In case you hadn't noticed, these people don't have a lot of money."

"Fair enough," said Alex, resolving to eat with greater enthusiasm. "And it is pretty good, really."

"What do they have," said Rik, putting his knife and fork down suddenly, "except their history, and their life in the rainforest? Nothing. And Scarlett is taking those things away from them, paying them off with gold which is nothing more than the mangled remains of their own past."

Darwen and Alex stared at him surprised as much by his passion as by his expression.

"The mangled remains of their own past," Alex echoed. "That's good. I'm gonna write that down. *Remnants* is better though. The mangled remnants of their noble history."

"Contempt, is what it is," said Rik, ignoring Alex's editing. "Scarlett is rubbing their noses in their own desperation. She comes in her helicopter and her fancy business suits and she tells them they're poor, and reminds them of how dangerous their life here is . . ."

"Kind of is," said Alex.

". . . and then – just to show how little she respects them and their culture – she buys them off with . . ."

"The mangled remnants of a once-noble past . . ."

Rik turned to yell at her, but changed his mind. "Yes," he said. "Exactly."

Alex nodded thoughtfully.

"You're right," she said at last. "It's terrible. We should stop her."

"Could Scarlett know anything about the pouncels?" asked Darwen. "The real pouncels, I mean, not just the figurines."

"I don't see how," said Rik. "Why?"

Darwen scowled. "I don't know," he shrugged. "It just feels . . . weird. An odd coincidence."

"That's what coincidences are," said Alex. "They feel weird."

"Scrobbler technology in the jungle," said Darwen. "Missing kids. Creatures crossing over from Silbrica. I feel like I'm missing something."

"Like what?" asked Rik.

Darwen just shook his head and shrugged again.

"And we still don't know how to get back into Silbrica," said Alex. "Fat lot of good having your own pet Mirroculist if there are no portals for him to open for you."

She was, annoyingly, maddeningly, right.

They cleared their dinner things away, played a casual game of darts in which everyone stood a long way from the board every time it was Alex's turn, and then went up to the washrooms to get ready for bed.

Darwen moved to turn on the tap, and it was there again in the mirror.

The laughing face.

He froze, looking at it from the corner of his eyes, terrified that if he moved a muscle, it would vanish. It was just as before, pink and shiny, the hard eyes with their manic glare, and the gaping mouth. Then he heard it, the laughter cycling round and round through his head, and this time he saw the head jerk back into blackness, then come back, as if yanked into place by a wire.

And suddenly he knew what it was.

The memory he had almost been able to taste came back to him clear and whole. He was, perhaps, seven. His family had taken a trip to the seaside in Blackpool, an old Lancashire resort town. They had gone to the funfair there, the theme park that they called The Pleasure Beach, which had been built for all those Victorian holiday makers who had started to come by train over a century ago.

Inside the park, over by one of the rides, there had been this glass case, containing a life-sized figure dressed as a clown, with a smaller clown on its lap. The sign above said it was Blackpool's "World-Famous Laughing Man." Darwen's dad had told him it hadn't always been dressed as it was now, but it had been there for decades, since before the war, he thought. It was mechanical. One minute, it was sitting still and dead-looking, and then it would start rocking backwards and forwards in its chair, its head thrown back, and this awful laughter coming from it. It never stopped. Just went on and on laughing and laughing all day. His mum had hated it, and it had given Darwen nightmares for weeks. Even now, the memory made him shiver.

But if he was right, and that's what the image in the mirror was, then what was that flash of Darwen's past doing in a Costa Rican jungle camp?

That night Darwen lay awake, listening to the sounds of the forest, trying to make sense of all he had learned, and trying just as hard to shut out the memory of the mechanical clown's hysterical laughter. Everything but the clown came back to Scarlett: her plans to get rid of the village, the money she used which wasn't real money at all but a kind of ancient echo of Silbrica. Even the disappearance of the children seemed to be helping her get rid of the village. Could she be working for the Bleck?

Rik and Gabriel were both asleep, or seemed to be. Rik snored like a donkey, but Gabriel never made a sound so that more than once, Darwen had shone his flashlight over to Gabriel's bed to make sure the boy was still there. Darwen felt sorry for him, had done since he arrived, though he knew he hadn't really helped make him feel welcome.

Maybe you should tell him why you're really here, he thought.

No, said Alex's voice in his head. *Bad idea. The kid is scared of his own shadow now; what would he be like knowing that the woods were full of monsters waiting to grab him?*

Darwen grinned in spite of himself. That was exactly what she would say, and he suspected she would be right. And then a word came to him, a word which didn't seem to belong in this set of ideas at all, but somehow slotted itself in perfectly. The word was: "helicopter."

He breathed it aloud, then sat up, shrugging off the sheet and reaching for the flashlight. "Rik," he whispered. "Rik!"

But Rik didn't wake and Darwen hesitated before poking him. He didn't want more bickering, he didn't want to get Rik into trouble again, and he certainly didn't want to wake Gabriel. For a moment his hand stayed where it was, index finger extended and ready to jab Rik in the shoulder.

But then he withdrew it and slid quietly out of bed. As he got dressed in the dark, he noted that the night was hot and heavy with the promise of more rain, so the tent felt clammy and oppressive. It wasn't much better outside, but there was a faint breeze coming in off the ocean. He shone his flashlight into his shoes to make sure nothing had crawled inside, then put them on, sitting on the edge of the platform and wondering how bad it would be if he was caught out of bed at night again.

The word hovered in his mind as it had when he had first glimpsed it coming in over the trees: helicopter.

That was how Scarlett had first arrived. It had been dramatic and, most importantly, it had been loud. But since that first day, he had not heard it again. Which meant one of two things. Either Scarlett had another way of getting to and from the village – though there was no way she was hopping out of the boat and wading up through the surf in those immaculate high heels of hers – or she hadn't left. She could have come and gone by helicopter while Darwen had been hiking or out at Caño Island, but he had not left the camp since seeing her this morning, and there was no way that helicopter could have come and gone without him noticing it.

So where was she? Not here in the camp, surely. So she must be staying in the village. But where? Someone like her would loathe the living conditions in this place.

The answer came immediately. In his mind's eye he saw the carefully maintained hut set back from the others, the pink jacket with the brass buttons. How could he have thought a jacket like that would be worn by one of the local girls? The one he had seen sweeping the porch had left a bucket of cleaning supplies at the foot of the stairs just the way the maids he saw in his aunt's building did when they were going from one apartment to the next. There was no doubt that this was Scarlett's place, and if she was spending whole nights in conditions she would surely despise, she must have a reason for it.

Maybe she knew where the tear in the barrier between worlds was. Maybe it wasn't just a tear. Maybe it was a portal after all, a way into Silbrica that could be opened and closed on command . . .

Darwen turned his flashlight to the path and set off along the coast and into the jungle. He moved quickly and quietly, keeping his eyes on the track and avoiding the leaf litter in which snakes might nestle. Once as he turned to look down to see the ocean he caught sight of what he first thought was a flittercrake – the strange, flying creature he had first glimpsed in an Atlanta mall – but as the animal flew back and forth, he realised it was some kind of large bat which was fishing from the air with its hind feet. He shuddered and started walking again. He didn't mind bats on television, but the thought of those long, drooping legs tangling in his hair gave him the screaming creeps.

He hurried on through the steamy darkness and at last, felt the relief of open sky as he got out from under the trees. There was the football field, and just beyond it, the huddle of buildings where the camp workers lived. There were no lights, no sign of movement, and the hammocks on the porches were all deserted. No one wanted to risk being outdoors at night.

Darwen turned off his flashlight, and moved carefully between the buildings along the closest thing to a street, though it was little more than a path from which the tiny houses were set back, looking at each other. He walked past the oldest four, two on each side, moving towards the new one which sat silent by itself, its back right against the treeline. As he got close he could smell its fresh-cut timber but that only made it feel out of place and a little sinister.

He had no idea what to do next.

He put one hand on the stair rail, then tested the first step with his foot. It creaked, and he adjusted, suddenly aware of his heart thudding in his chest. There was a window beside the door. It had mosquito netting tacked around it and curtains inside, but Darwen thought there was a gap between them. If he could get up there, he might be able to get a look in . . .

He tried the second step and, when it made no sound at all, the third. One more and he was up on the porch decking, only a few feet from the door. He lifted his right foot, spreading his arms for balance, and took another step, listening hard.

Nothing.

One more step and he was touching the wall. He shifted and the planking groaned loud beneath him.

He froze, breath held, eyes wide and staring at the wall, terrified that even looking around would make more noise.

Seconds passed. Ten? Thirty? He wasn't sure.

At last he took the final step to the window and peered in through the two-inch gap in the curtains. There was only darkness.

Now what?

He considered shining the light in through the crack, but knew that would just alert anyone inside to his presence. He had come this far. There was only one choice.

He took two, quick, quiet steps, avoiding the plank which had creaked, and put his trembling fingers on the door handle. He grasped it, feeling the sweat on his palm, listening for any sign of movement beyond the constant hum of the jungle, and then, with infinite care, he turned it.

There was a tiny snap, and Darwen felt the weight of the door in his hand as it swung free. He pushed it carefully, and it made no sound as it opened.

Several things struck Darwen at once. First, he sensed the darkness inside soften a little, though he could still barely make anything out beyond hulking black outlines. There was a scent too, sweet like perfume but with something a little sour under it, masked like the persistent edge of vomit after a bathroom has been disinfected. He knew that if someone was lying awake, they would see him standing there in the doorway, but he needed the light so he stayed where he was and waited.

Still, incredibly, nothing happened. No movement, no breathing. Nothing.

He took a step inside, hands outstretched in front of him, but he knew he would find nothing without light. His body was tense and he felt cold, though the sweat was running in his eyes. Carefully he turned and pushed the door silently so that it almost closed, then he dropped slowly to a crouch, put the flashlight down head first on the floor, and turned it on.

He paused and raised it just a crack off the floor. Thin, yellow light rippled around the room casting long, flat shadows all around. There was a wardrobe, a door to what was probably a tiny bathroom, a bedside table with a battery-operated lantern, another window looking down towards the sea, and . . . a bed. Darwen stared at it, trying to make sense of its lumps and creases. He raised the flashlight a fraction more and now he could see.

There was no one there.

He released his breath in a long sigh that contained a laugh. He put one hand to his chest as if to calm his racing heart, and then shone more light about the room.

There was no gate to Silbrica here. No mirror, no oven door, nothing that might provide a portal for the pouncels.

He considered the carefully made up bed. It hadn't been slept in. He shone the light underneath it, checked the bathroom – which also was mirrorless – and then opened the wardrobe. It was full of brightly coloured suits on hangers. Darwen pushed a garish, pink one aside and staggered back in horror.

Hanging on the rail, wearing the blue suit he had seen her in that morning, was Scarlett Oppertune.

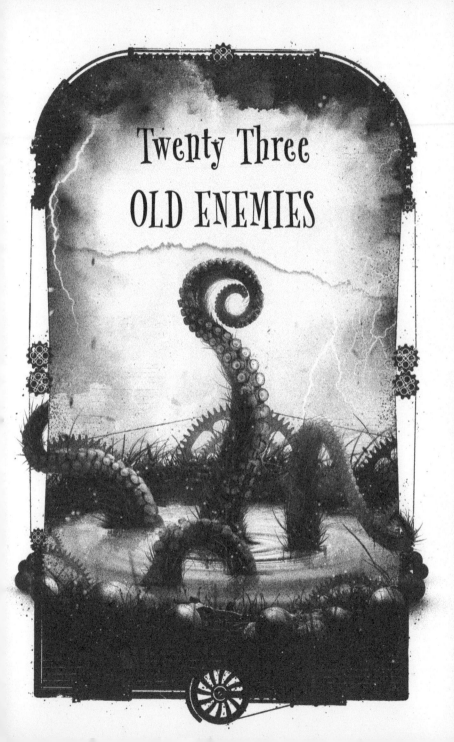

Twenty Three

OLD ENEMIES

It was Scarlett Oppertune, or something very like her. In fact it looked like a Scarlett Oppertune *suit*, a costume which went beyond clothes and had some kind of mask built in. And pinkish gloves. They hung there, limp and rubbery, but when Darwen plucked up the courage to touch them they felt horribly like flesh. He shone the light on the thing's face, and knew immediately that this was no mask. The detail was extraordinary, the tiny wrinkles, the eyelashes, the smear of makeup on the cheeks. He forced himself to touch the face, to lift one drooping eyelid, and was repulsed to find a staring, faded eye glaring back at him.

His first thought was that Scarlett was dead, drained somehow, her skeleton removed so that she just hung there, but then he remembered that awful night when he and Alex had encountered the people who had called themselves the Jenkinses. What had seemed to be a kindly, old grandmother and her husband, had turned out to be little more than suits like this one, the true inhabitants being the giant insect-like creatures he had seen again only a couple of nights ago.

Darwen closed the wardrobe door so he wouldn't have to look at it anymore. He turned towards the bed and, for the first time, his eyes strayed to the window and, feeling the air move fractionally, realised it was open. He snapped off the light. Something was moving outside.

It was too dark to see clearly but it seemed to Darwen that there was something like a gargantuan snake out there, yards long and thick as an anaconda. He dropped to a crouch, hands gripping the window ledge as he stared in fascinated horror.

The creature was moving. One end stayed almost still while the other – what Darwen thought was the head – rotated like the hand of a clock. As he watched, he saw it complete one cycle and then begin again. It traced one more circle, then started doing something else, pushing objects into place around the rim. In the dim light, Darwen thought that they rolled as the monster moved them.

The stone spheres, he thought. *And what the thing has just made is like the muddy hole I fell into . . .*

The thought was incomplete in his head, when he realised that the creature outside had stopped what it was doing and was moving quickly across the ground, towards the open window. Towards him.

Darwen gasped. He turned towards the door before realising that he was on the wrong side of the bed.

The monster was almost at the house. He had no choice. He dropped to the floor and rolled under the bed just as the snake-thing slid up the wall and in through the window. He felt the weight of it on the bed above him, saw the shadows leap as the lantern clicked on a soft, bluish glow, but it didn't pause, sliding over and down with a soft slap as it hit the floor, inches from his head.

He lay absolutely still, stiff with fear and revulsion. The creature slithered heavily to the wardrobe and Darwen couldn't help himself. He had to see. He angled his head back and watched as the creature reared up and wrenched the wardrobe open with its teeth. Its tail flexed, flicking a hair's breadth from Darwen's face, and then it slipped into the wardrobe among the hanging suits. Darwen gaped as the thing forced Scarlett Oppertune's slack jaws wide open and then eased itself nose first into her mouth. The long, slow body followed, yard by terrible yard, and it was like the Scarlett suit inflated unevenly, squirming, shuddering, filling. There was a series of metallic snaps, and with each one, a flabby limb became firm and straight like the fabric of an umbrella, tautening as it goes up. The new weight of the thing brought it down from the rack of hangers, but Scarlett Oppertune, high heels and all, stepped out of the wardrobe as if nothing could be more normal.

Darwen just stared, knowing that if she looked down, she would see him.

She didn't. She stalked back to the table and turned off the lantern, then climbed onto the bed and lay there. Darwen was motionless, wondering if she might hear his galloping heart no more than a foot away from hers, assuming the creature inhabiting her body had anything as ordinary as a heart.

He didn't know what the creature was, not really, but he had seen something very like it before. It had been the true shape of whatever lived inside Miss Murray, his former world studies teacher who Rik had called – with uncanny perception – Murray the Moray, like the eel with the razor-sharp teeth. She had led Greyling's attack on Hillside. Could that be why he had felt like Scarlett knew him, that she had almost called him by name? Could it really be Miss Murray? And if it was, what could that possibly mean beyond the fact that, if she got the chance, she would surely kill him?

He lay very still on his stomach, wondering how long it would take her to get to sleep, wondering if she would sleep at all, and what would happen if she suddenly got up and saw him lying there. He had to get out.

He had been able to get the front door open silently when he came in and he hadn't re-latched it behind him. If he could crawl quietly across the floor, he might be able to slink out. He spread his fingers on the wooden floor and felt his muscles tighten as he prepared to move. He eased himself out a fraction, then paused, waiting. He could see the faintest greying of the blackness around the edge of the door, and he focused on that as he inched his way out from under the bed.

Slowly, so slowly it felt like hours, he raised himself onto his hands and knees, one tiny motion at a time. Keeping the toes of his shoes and the barrel of his flashlight off the floor, he began to creep towards the door: hand, then knee, then the other knee, then the other hand: four movements, each one a risk, to advance eight inches.

Then something touched his left hand.

A cockroach the size of a cell phone.

Darwen forced himself to stay still and silent as it climbed up his left arm and over his back. He fought the impulse to cry out, and crawled another eight inches. The roach rattled across the floor, and Darwen froze, sure that Scarlett would put the lamp on to see what was making the sound. The noise changed, and Darwen risked a look back into the darkness.

He thought he could just make out the shape of the bug moving up the leg of the bed and onto the thin covers, black against the pale sheet. It wandered up towards the pillows, and then, without warning, the figure in the bed whose shape he had not been able to see properly, shifted suddenly. A pale hand snatched at the roach, grabbed it, and lifted it wriggling up towards the head.

Darwen turned away as he heard the unmistakable crunch of teeth.

Then he was moving again, reckless in his desire to get out. He didn't look back, but he heard the slow chewing, felt the presence of the creature in the bed behind him like a nightmare he couldn't shake.

One more hand-knee 'step' and he felt the door against his head. He moved, shifting the door fractionally, and before he could stop it, it closed with an audible click that sounded like a gunshot in the silent hut.

There was a noise like a breath from the bed, and Darwen got clumsily to his feet, fumbling for the door handle, as he turned to see if Scarlett was coming for him. From where he was he couldn't see anything, wouldn't see her till she was virtually on top of him. The latch clicked again as he worked the handle, and this time he couldn't wait, couldn't be careful or slow. He snatched the door open, and stepped hurriedly out, only just resisting the urge to sprint off the deck and down through the village.

He knew he was making noise, but fear drove the concern away. There was a flash of light, and he winced, sure it was Scarlett's lamp, sure that the creature inside her was coming after him, but then there was a crash of thunder overhead and he realised it had just been lightning. By the time he reached the stairs, it was raining. He risked a look back, and as another ripple of lightning creased the sky, he saw that the door had swung softly shut. There was no sign of pursuit.

He wanted to get as far from this place as possible, but there was one more thing he had to see. He ran silently through the rain around the side of the house, keeping a safe distance from that open window, to the spot where he had seen the thing like Miss Murray – or Scarlett, or whatever he was supposed to call her now – in her eel shape, scooping out the saucer-like depression in the ground.

He found it easily and without needing the flashlight. It was exactly as the other had been, and he had been right: she had circled the shallow hole with a dozen of the ancient stone spheres.

But why? She could easily have been seen doing it, so why take the risk?

Darwen crouched on the edge of the circle, looking back up to the isolated hut. The rain was getting heavier by the moment, and little rivulets were forming in the village and rushing down towards the beach at his back. The circle itself was starting to fill with water. It was time for Darwen to get back.

He got up to leave, and the shift in his perspective, coupled with a timely sheet of lightning overhead, revealed something new: his own reflection. As the shallow depression filled with water it was turning into a great mirror!

Darwen stared, his mind racing, oblivious to the driving, hammering rain. Then the pool was full to the rim of stone spheres, and something happened.

There was another flicker of energy, but it wasn't lightning. It was soft and greenish, and it ran around the mirror-pool, leaping from stone to stone as the circuit completed. And then the surface of the water was buckling and sloshing not because of the raindrops hurtling into it but because something was coming through, something far too big to be contained in that shallow puddle.

It was long, and thick and studded with suckers, purplish and black on the top, but pale beneath, and though it looked snake-like Darwen knew instantly what it was. The tentacle reached its pointed tip into the sky as if tasting the air, and then it surged through, yards at a time, and behind it, came more, filling the pool as the monster squeezed in through the portal.

Darwen's terror finally broke out. He gave first one cry, and then another, shouting to the village to wake up, to defend themselves before the thing in the pool took their children.

Lights came on, and he saw the pale face of Scarlett Oppertune in her window. But he did not run. Instead, he kicked at the stone spheres, pushing them away from the circle. The greenish light around the pool flickered and stalled. The great tentacles seemed to hesitate, hanging suspended in the air with a strange and sudden stillness, and then they and the Insidious Bleck to which they belonged were sucked back into the pool with a splash, and were gone.

Twenty Four
LIES

No one believed Darwen. He had no hope of persuading the adults what he had really seen, so he had made up some half-baked story about sleepwalking. He didn't care if the villagers thought him stupid, or blamed him for interrupting their night's sleep. It didn't matter to him whether or not they knew that he had probably just saved another of their children from the monster in the pool. He had just found himself out here, he said, woken by the thunder, and then he thought he had seen something, but it had turned out to be a trick of the light.

But if he thought that he would be allowed to get away with merely looking foolish, Darwen had another thing coming. One of the men sleeping in the village was Jorge and he was instantly suspicious. He insisted on personally escorting Darwen back to the camp, where he was handed over to the teachers to repeat his sleepwalking yarn.

"And you do this a lot, do you?" said a bleary-eyed Mr. Sumners. "I don't recall your aunt referring to your ahhhh somnambulant strolls on your medical form."

"My what?" said Darwen.

"Your sleepwalking," said Sumners, his patience strained to breaking point. "You'd think she would have mentioned something like that considering where we were going."

"Oh," said Darwen. "No, I've never done it before."

"Is that right?" said Sumners. "Next time, do us all a favour and sleepwalk into the ocean, Arkwright, OK?"

"Yes, sir," said Darwen.

"Looks like you're on tent cleaning duty again tomorrow," he said.

"But sir . . ."

"Good night, Mr. Arkwright. Try to make it back to your tent without dropping off. I'd hate for you to step on something deadly . . ."

"Yes, sir. Right, sir. Good night, sir."

Darwen trudged back towards his tent with his flashlight trained disconsolately on the ground so he didn't see Mr. Peregrine till he almost bumped into him.

"Want to tell me what really happened?" said the teacher.

They walked down to the beach where they wouldn't be overheard and sat on a fallen palm trunk facing the black ocean. The torrential rain had stopped as suddenly as it had started, and the sky was already clear enough to see stars.

Darwen told Mr. Peregrine everything: Scarlett's sinister transformation, the part played by the stone spheres in the creation of the portal, and the terrible thing which had started coming through it, a creature Darwen was now prepared to name aloud. "It was the Insidious Bleck," he said. "I'm sure of it."

"Well," said Mr. Peregrine, "Let's not get ahead of ourselves. I think you are right that the stone spheres are somehow connected to the portals – that would explain why the ancient peoples who lived here treated them with such reverence – but what you saw coming through could have been any number of Silbrican beasts. As to the nature of Miss Oppertune . . ."

He hesitated thoughtfully and Darwen felt his doubt.

"What?" said Darwen. "I saw the suit-thing the creature inside her used. I saw her out there making the portal."

"Well, it was very dark, Darwen," said Mr. Peregrine, "and you were – understandably – scared. There's no shame in admitting that. You need not invent . . ."

"I'm not *inventing* anything," said Darwen, his confusion turning to anger. "I know what I saw."

Mr. Peregrine held up his hands in surrender and smiled. "Darwen, you have done what you came here to do," he said, "and it is a remarkable achievement for which you should be very proud. You have solved the mystery of how Silbrican creatures are coming through and this will undoubtedly save lives. But your suspicion of Miss Oppertune, unpleasant though her plans may be, seems to me beside the point . . ."

"No," said Darwen, standing up, his face dark with fury. "The children haven't been taken by Silbrican animals hunting at random. It's the Insidious Bleck, and it's being brought through on purpose by the thing we used to call Miss Murray. I don't know why, but that is what's happening."

"If that were the case," said Mr. Peregrine reasonably, "why would Miss Oppertune be trying to drive the villagers away? She would want the children here."

"I don't know," said Darwen. "You tell me. You're supposed to be the one who helps me figure this stuff out, aren't you?"

"Yes," said Mr. Peregrine, "I am. And I am telling you that your work is done, and well done. I will pass the information about the stone spheres along to the council and they will seal the breaches by their own means. You have completed the task assigned to you and can now concentrate on enjoying the rest of the trip with your friends."

"What about Luis?" said Darwen, his voice a little high.

"It's over, Darwen," said Mr. Peregrine. "You have a busy and fun-filled day tomorrow. You'll need your strength to enjoy it. Bedtime."

He spoke with such finality that Darwen didn't bother protesting. He turned, leaving the old man sitting in the dark, and made for the tent camp, dazed and struck by the special pain that comes from feeling totally powerless.

"Been out for a stroll?"

It was Rik. He was sitting in the dark in his pyjamas on the platform outside the tent. He snapped his flashlight on and shone it in Darwen's face.

"Not now, Rik," said Darwen. "I'll tell you all about it in the morning."

"Why bother?" said Rik. "You obviously didn't think I was worth taking along wherever you've been."

"What?" said Darwen. "Rik, seriously, this isn't the time."

"Sure," said Rik, whose face was pink with anger, "why tell me? It's your business, right? Private Mirroculist work?"

"Shh . . ." said Darwen glancing at the tent. "Gabriel might hear."

"Yeah," said Rik, getting up and turning back towards the tent. "Wouldn't want anyone to know what's going on. You're big on secrets, aren't you, Darwen?"

"It's not like that!" Darwen hissed.

"Really?" said Rik, bitter and unconvinced. "How many times have you been through to Silbrica since Halloween by yourself, when you knew Alex and me were dying to go in with you?"

"You weren't there!" Darwen exclaimed. "It was Christmas. You were at home . . ."

"You could have invited us over for a sleepover," said Rik, even redder now as he revealed a hurt he knew sounded petty and stupid.

"A sleepover?" Darwen exclaimed, who couldn't believe he was having this conversation now after everything that had happened over the last couple of hours.

"A sleepover," Rik snapped. "It's something friends do."

"Silbrica is dangerous, Rik! Don't you get it? It's not a holiday resort where you can go to look at cool animals like they're in a zoo. Half of those animals will take your head off as soon as look at you."

"So you're protecting us?" Rik shot back. "Is that it?"

"Yes!" said Darwen, realising this was true for the first time. "You know how many times I've gone over what happened at Halloween and thought about how badly it might have ended? If something had happened to you or Alex? You know how I would have felt about that?"

"Because it's all about how you feel, right Darwen?"

"That's not what I meant."

"You didn't even tell us about Weazen till after we saw him," said Rik, furious now. "How is that protecting us?"

"I just didn't think you needed to know!" Darwen roared back Immediately, he wished he hadn't said it.

"And there it is," Rik said, quieter now. "You thought you knew best. Again. OK. Well now we know. Well, Darwen, thanks for your protection, but for future reference, we don't need it. We don't want it."

"Fine!" yelled Darwen.

"Fine!" shouted Rik.

"Wait," said Darwen but Rik was already unzipping the tent and crawling in.

Darwen sat outside in the dark for another five minutes before following him. He didn't think Rik was asleep, but when Darwen whispered his name, he didn't respond. It was some time before Darwen climbed into bed, longer still before he fell asleep, and his dreams were full of the mechanical clown lurching in its chair, roaring with laughter, while great snakes with Scarlett Oppertune's face coiled around it.

Darwen got up when the howler monkeys started calling. He took a cold shower, dressed and ate alone as soon as Mr. Torres had laid out the breakfast buffet. He reported to the kitchens and told the staff he was to help with cleaning again. As the other students came up to breakfast, he went from tent to tent with a bucket of cleaning supplies. He waited to be sure Mr. Peregrine wasn't inside before going in to clean. The vinegary scent was stronger now, but Darwen didn't try that hard to get rid of it. Serve the old man right for betraying him.

He knew he was overreacting but that was what it felt like to Darwen. Mr. Peregrine had not believed him about Scarlett and had ordered him to abandon his search for Luis and the others. Either on his own authority or on the Guardians' orders, the old shopkeeper had betrayed him.

When Darwen emerged, Alex was waiting for him, eating fruit from a bowl.

"This cleaning thing wasn't supposed to be a career choice," she said. "The word is that you decided to wake the entire village in the middle of the night. Sleepwalking, supposedly, which is about the dumbest excuse I ever heard. Rik doesn't know any different and 'would prefer not to discuss it, if you don't mind' so I'm assuming you two had one of those 'he broke my toy tractor' fights that boys have. Wanna give me your version?"

Darwen sighed and sat on the edge of the platform beside his bucket. He told the same story he had told to Mr. Peregrine, this time including an account of that conversation and the one he had had with Rik.

"Wow," she said. "You are making yourself popular. Thought about running for class president?"

"We don't have a class president," said Darwen.

"Sure we do, Darwen. You're the very first. And it's all because we love you."

"Were you planning on saying anything helpful, or are you just here to take the mickey?"

"See, why couldn't you have fallen back on a colourful British expression like that last night? No one would have understood a word you said, which would have been better than that sleepwalking hogwash. Honestly, that's the best you could come up with? That's just sad."

"You believe me?"

"About Scarlett the snake woman and the Insidious child-nabbing tentacled whosit?" she said. "Sure. You're dumb, but I can always tell when you're lying."

"Thanks a lot," said Darwen.

"You're welcome. Anyway, you need to finish up. We're going zip-lining, whatever that is. Meet on the beach in . . ." she checked her watch, "half an hour. Get your bug repellant, camera, strong shoes, blah, blah, blah. The usual surviving-in-the-wilderness stuff."

"I'm ready," said Darwen. "Why don't you hang out with me for a while? I've been trying to think through why Scarlett might want the land the village is on if it's not just about building a hotel . . ."

"Not now," said Alex. "I've got to get ready."

"I'll come with you," said Darwen.

Alex hesitated. "I have to . . . do private stuff," she said. "Pee and what have you."

Darwen considered her. She was being evasive. Maybe she was going to report back to Rik. "Come on, Alex . . ." he began, but she cut him off.

"It's not just Rik who's mad at you, Darwen, OK?" she said. "You did it again, going off by yourself, figuring you'd just report your adventures to us afterwards. We're not your fans, Darwen. We're supposed to be friends. More than that. We're the Peregrine Pact."

"I'm not sure I want to have much to do with Mr. Peregrine, if you want to know the truth," said Darwen.

"So you really are alone," she said. "I hope that makes you happy."

And with that, she stalked off.

With nothing better to do, Darwen went down to the beach early and sat on the same palm trunk where he had talked to Mr. Peregrine the night before. Gabriel was already there, alone and wearing the ridiculous cap with the veil again.

"Cleaned our tent out," said Darwen.

"Good," said Gabriel, adjusting the veil so that Darwen could see his face.

"You should get out more," said Darwen. "Get some air and sunshine. Maybe we could organise another football game with the kids from the village."

Gabriel's eyes flickered, and Darwen thought he looked pained.

"Tough here, isn't it?" said Darwen. "I mean, exciting and full of neat stuff, of course, but still . . . tough. And then these kids going missing . . ."

Gabriel looked down, but Darwen caught that flash of anguish in his face again.

"Listen," he said. "If you need someone to chat to, you know, since you're new and all, me and Rik are . . ."

"What?" said Gabriel, looking up again, his face now blank.

"Sounded like you were yelling at each other last night."

Darwen said nothing, relieved to see Genevieve Reddock leading a gaggle of girls down from the camp looking excited and – as always seemed to be the case on this trip – a little uneasy.

"What's zip-lining?" said Darwen, changing the subject, as the girls splashed noisily passed them and climbed into the first boat.

Gabriel shrugged. "I guess we have to get in," he said.

"Always," said Darwen, miserably.

They waded out and climbed aboard the first of the three boats next to Genevieve, Naia and Kahala. Mr. Peregrine was already onboard clad again in those ridiculous rubber waders. Darwen said nothing and avoided his eyes. There was no sign of Rik. They were pulling away from shore before Darwen saw him, walking down to one of the other boats with Alex.

"How long will we be in the boat?" he asked Jorge.

"Ten minutes," said the guide. "We're just going round to Drake Bay."

Darwen breathed a sigh of relief.

"Is it true you sleepwalk?" asked Naia Petrakis.

"Not usually," said Darwen.

"Rough place to start," supplied Kahala.

"Yeah," said Darwen, turning away in the hope they would drop the subject. He seemed to be doing a lot of that lately. The thought made him feel more alone than he had since coming to Hillside. He thought of Lancashire which felt so very far away now, and a wish rose in his mind, clear and sharp and fully-formed, an image of him returning to his parents and telling them about all the amazing things he had seen in Costa Rica. They would sit with plates of steaming hotpot and talk about everything that had happened since he left England, since they had died. He stared at the water as the boat bounced over its surface, turning away so that no one could see his face.

Since he and Gabriel had been the first to get aboard and had taken seats by Mr. Peregrine in the prow, they were the last to get out, by which time the boat was rocking and sliding in the surf. Darwen went first, but the boat pitched suddenly. He stumbled but Mr. Peregrine came off worse. As the old man slipped backwards, his hand reached for the prow and caught on a rusted rivet which stood proud and sharp.

"Mr. Peregrine!" Darwen shouted. "Are you OK?"

"What?" said the teacher, his face blank.

"Your hand," said Darwen.

"Let me see," said Jorge, scrambling over.

"It's fine," said Mr. Peregrine.

Jorge didn't listen, but turned the teacher's hand over. He winced, sucking the air in between his lips, and for a moment Darwen's head swam. There was a deep gash running across Mr. Peregrine's palm, deep enough that Darwen could see what looked like muscle inside, though the cut beneath the flap of skin was bloodless.

Jorge exclaimed in Spanish, then helped Mr. Peregrine up and over the side, though the water was waist-deep. He hurried Mr. Peregrine up the beach to where a cooler of supplies had been unloaded and took out a first aid kit. Darwen and Gabriel splashed after him, labouring in the surf, feeling the shingle beneath their feet sucking away with each outrushing wave. By the time the boys reached Jorge, Mr. Peregrine's hand had already been smeared with ointment and bandaged. The teacher looked calm but Jorge and Gabriel were both anxious.

"You want to go back to the camp?" asked Jorge.

"No," said the teacher. "I need to supervise the excursion."

"It must hurt," said Jorge.

"Not as much as you would think," said Mr. Peregrine, climbing carefully out of his waders and smiling, "and I'm tougher than I look."

Darwen watched them as the girls crowded round and there was something odd about the way Gabriel looked at Mr. Peregrine. The boy's eyes were hard and focused.

Mr. Peregrine, for his part, merely shrugged and smiled blithely. "See," he said. "It has already stopped bleeding. Let's not overreact. Very well," he added, turning to the gathering students, "this way, everyone."

Darwen glanced at Gabriel, but whatever he thought he had seen in the boy's face before was gone, so that he wondered if he had imagined it.

Once the other boat had arrived, a pair of rickety jeeps, a pickup truck and an ancient minibus ferried the students up through Drake Bay and into the heavily-wooded hills behind them. Darwen made the journey in the open back of the pickup, which would have been fun if he had had someone to share it with. Rik had deliberately hung back and came in the minibus with Alex.

The zip line turned out to be what Darwen called an aerial runway: a cable strung between poles down which you slid. Darwen had seen them on playgrounds and campsites, but nothing could have prepared him for the length and height of this particular specimen. There were twenty stages, some of them hundreds of meters long, designed to take them through the very canopy of the rainforest and back to the campsite. They hiked up to the starting point – a wooden platform built around a massive tree which had to be accessed by ladders – wearing helmets and a complex system of straps and carabineers.

"It's perfectly safe," said Jorge, smiling.

It didn't feel it. The first platform was a hundred feet in the air, and the cable extended out over a valley which fell sharply away. The greenery below didn't seem too distant, but Darwen knew that the leaves were the tops of trees, some of which were very tall. It was a long way to fall if something went wrong.

"Who is going to go first?" asked Jorge.

Everyone looked around, some uncertain, some clearly afraid. Darwen's eyes met Rik's and for a second he thought there would be a shared comment or joke, but Rik scowled and looked away.

"I'll go first," volunteered Darwen.

He had come all this way. He wasn't about to let Rik spoil it.

Jorge and the pickup driver checked his harness, snapped a new cable in place and told him how to control the speed of his descent.

"Put your right hand up here," instructed Jorge. "If you are going too fast, lean back and pull down on this leather part. This is your brake."

Darwen didn't see the "brake" making much difference, but he could feel everyone watching him and was determined not to show his fear.

"Have fun, Arkwright," called Nathan. "Try not to fall hundreds of feet to your messy death."

"Ready?" said Jorge, swinging him into position.

"Ready," Darwen lied.

And then he was off . . .

For a split second he thought he had come adrift, that the cable had broken and he was just falling, but the sensation passed, and he was soon arcing out over the treetops, speeding faster and faster, the drone of the pulley wheels rising in pitch as he hurtled along. Trees beside him whipped past in a flash of green, and then he was out in the blue air, looking down on the jungle canopy, swooping bird-like towards the next station, where one of the jeep drivers was waiting, braced for impact. For a moment all the tension, the problems and anxieties of the trip fell away, and Darwen was just a boy flying above the treetops and feeling the wind on his face.

He whooped with delight, and an unmistakable bird called back at him before taking flight, a bird with a beak as long and heavy as its body.

"A toucan," he exclaimed as he barrelled into the pick-up driver. "I saw a toucan!"

His fear was gone, as were all his concerns about Silbrica and Rik. He led the way, stage by exhilarating stage, and the zip line led them steadily back down towards the tent camp, so that two hours later they were trekking along a path which emerged behind the bathrooms

Darwen's uncomplicated happiness at the thrill of it all was disturbed only once, a little over halfway down, when he realised that the towering trees around him showed signs of considerable damage, as if something large had been moving through the canopy, snapping heavy branches as it went. He might not have thought much of it, except that he caught Jorge studying the damage with the same look of concern as on the night the village girl had gone missing. It wasn't over, no matter what Mr. Peregrine said. Somehow he would find those kids, bring them home again.

And now he knew how to do it.

The stone spheres could be made into a mirror with nothing more than water and his Mirroculist talents. He just had to gather some together, get away from everyone else and cross over to Silbrica. He even knew where he could find the stone balls, and just as he was trying to figure out how to get back to them, he had a stroke of luck.

It came in the form of an announcement from Mr. Iverson over lunch.

"Those who wish to stay in the camp this afternoon can do so," he said, "but we will be taking two boats out to Caño Island again, one for those who wish to do some more snorkelling, the other for any who want to return to the archaeological site."

That was it. Finally, after weeks of frustration, Darwen was going to be able to do something. He was going to Silbrica and he was sure that on the other side he would find Luis, Eduardo, Calida and the others. He didn't need Mr. Peregrine. He was going to complete his mission – his real mission – by himself.

But even as he thought this he found himself looking around for Rik and Alex. They were huddled together, talking earnestly as they sipped from straws stuck in green coconuts. Even as he watched, Alex got up and came over. "Mr. Richard Haggerty requests the pleasure of your company at the Caño Island dig site," she said.

"I'll bet that's not the way he said it," said Darwen.

"Not exactly," said Alex. "He thinks you ought to go there. See if there's anything you can learn about the pouncels."

"And you?" said Darwen, suddenly hopeful that Alex would come too. He needed a buffer between himself and Rik right now.

"He thinks I should come too," said Alex, "but I'm not gonna."

"Come on, Alex," said Darwen. "He won't even talk to me if you aren't there."

"Oh, I see," said Alex. "So you don't want me there because I'm your friend and the only person who doesn't think you are a lying snake, but because you want me to run interference for you with Rik."

"Run interference?" said Darwen.

"It's a football term," Alex snapped. "American football. You might wanna bone up on the culture you, ya know, *live in*. Anyway, what I'm saying is that I'm not going to be your translator or your nursemaid or the padding that stops you knocking each others' corners off."

"Is that another football phrase?"

"No, that's just me."

"But Alex . . ." Darwen implored.

"I have spoken," Alex announced, drawing herself up to her full height. "Do not ask me again."

"Fine," said Darwen. "Don't help."

"Oh, I'm helping," she said. "I'm helping you both to grow as people. Uncle Bob says that to me a lot. I think he got it from daytime TV. It's what he says when he knows I'm not happy with him, which is pretty much always, but this time I think it's actually on the money. Patch up your own squabbles, Darwen. You'll grow as a person."

And with that, she stalked off, not towards the tents but back to her table. She glanced quickly around and took a bowl of grilled chicken, then headed swiftly back towards the showers.

Darwen frowned. He didn't like being lectured by Alex, even when she was right. He considered going to find Rik, but decided he would yell at her instead.

He ambled up the track to the bathrooms, but there was no sign of Alex. He called her name and walked around the block twice, then followed the path into the woods, the one which led to the last stage of the zip line. He walked a few hundred yards into the forest, climbing steeply all the way, but there was still no sign of her and his anger turned into confusion. Where had she gone? He paused, and through the perpetual hum of the jungle came the sound of voices.

Or rather, the sound of *a* voice: Alex.

She was burbling in a low, musical tone, like she was talking to a baby.

The sound came from some way off the path to his left, but he couldn't see far enough through the trees to pinpoint the spot. He stepped carefully into the leaf litter, watching for signs of movement underfoot, and took a few stealthy paces. The sound of the voice went away, and then came back, nearer now. Darwen walked a little further, and as he emerged from behind a massive tree whose trunk seemed comprised of several plants which had grown into a single mass, he saw her.

She was sitting on the ground, cooing over something, and as Darwen watched, her hand reached into the bowl of chicken and dropped some of it. Something on the ground reached up and snatched at the meat, something ape-like but with the distinctive head of a large cat.

Darwen gasped, and as he did so, his weight shifted. A twig snapped underfoot and Alex's head spun round. Her eyes found him and she leapt to her feet, her face a mask of rage.

"You *followed* me?" she bellowed.

"What are you doing?" Darwen roared back. "You're feeding one of those things?"

"It's hurt, OK? It got shot and I've been looking after it. So now you know. Now you can take off, Darwen Arkwright!"

"Are you nuts?" said Darwen, closing on her. "These things are dangerous!"

"You sound like Scarlett."

"You saw what they did to the tapir."

"*They*, Darwen, plural. This is one. It's young and it's hurt."

"And what if the others come looking for it?"

"They haven't so far."

"How long have you been doing this? Were you ever going to tell us?"

"What, only you are allowed to have secrets, Mr. Mirroculist?"

"That is so not fair," said Darwen.

"I told Sarita," said Alex. "She helped me get food for it from the kitchens."

"You told *Sarita*!?" Darwen exclaimed. "Are you out of your tree? We have a mission, Alex! We're supposed to be finding the missing kids." He took a furious step towards her.

The motion spooked the pouncel, which got awkwardly to its feet and limped a few paces away, where it sat, baring its fangs and hissing.

"Don't scare it!" yelled Alex, though the creature seemed as alarmed by her voice as by his.

"That thing could take your hand off, and you're feeding it like it's a pet rabbit?" Darwen shouted. "That is so stupid."

"Stupid?" roared Alex, rising and squaring up to him as if ready to throw a punch. "You calling me stupid?"

Darwen braced himself, but before she could come at him, the pouncel took another shrinking step away.

"Wait," said Alex, taking a step towards it, but the movement only made it break into a run. Alex blundered after it, but the pouncel sped up, springing unevenly on its injured hind leg. In a moment, it was gone.

"Look what you did!" yelled Alex, rounding on Darwen, her eyes bright. "It's gone, and something will get it or someone will shoot it, and it's your fault."

"I didn't mean to!" said Darwen, "I just wanted to talk."

"Well I don't want to talk Darwen, OK? Not now, not ever. Just go away."

Twenty Five
CAÑO'S
SECRET

Darwen had never seen Alex so angry. He left her but did not know where to go. Rik was in the tent, but Rik wasn't talking to him either, and Mr. Peregrine was now, as far as Darwen was concerned, just another teacher. So he sat alone at one of the dining shelter tables which was piled with bundles of sticks and lengths of string, and looked out upon what had turned into a hot and glorious day feeling utterly miserable.

"Homesick, Arkwright?" called Nathan Cloten. He was playing darts with Chip Whittley in a recess at the back of the shelter.

"Not now, Nathan," said Darwen, wishing he'd spotted them before sitting down.

"Probably not homesick, anyway," Chip observed. "For him and Haggerty this is probably paradise. Haggerty lives in a barn with no roof, and Arkwright doesn't have a home, not a real one, do you Arkwright?"

Darwen's hands recognised the sticks for what they were before his conscious mind did. He whirled around, fluidly fitting an arrow into one of the few finished bows and aiming it first at Nathan, then at Chip.

They ducked comically, but they were both holding the darts they had been playing with. Darwen glanced at the arrow he had loaded. It was just a stick: straight, but without a tip of any kind. Their darts, on the other hand, had sharp metal points.

He put the bow down as quickly as he had snatched it up.

But if he thought that would end the matter, he was sorely mistaken. The two boys approached his table and stood looming over him. Chip snatched the bow and arrow off the table.

"Gonna shoot us, Arkwright, like some Indian savage?" asked Nathan.

"Leave me alone, Nathan," said Darwen.

"Or what?" taunted Chip. He had unscrewed the head of one of the darts and was trying to fit it to the arrow shaft.

"Fine," said Darwen, standing up. He just couldn't be bothered with this, and the students and teachers were already starting to gather in the camp below for the afternoon excursions. "You want to hang out here by yourselves? Fine by me."

He started to walk away.

"Hey," yelled Chip, "we didn't give you permission to leave!"

"Whatever," Darwen answered.

He didn't hear the creak of the bow or the thrum of its string. He didn't hear the whoosh of the arrow through the air. He didn't know Chip had shot at him till he felt the arrow's two inches of needle-sharp steel slam into his shoulder blade.

The pain was sudden and intense. He cried out and reached behind him in disbelief, half turning in the process. He saw Chip, his face a mask of calm, smiling slightly, but Nathan looked horrified. Darwen stumbled against one of the dining shelter's roof supports, conscious that the dart-tipped arrow waggled and slid out as he fell.

"Whittley!" someone bellowed.

Darwen was sprawled across a bench, but he thought the voice was Mr. Iverson's. There were more shouts and he felt hands on him.

"Get Jorge and the first aid kit," said Mr. Iverson. "Put that down, Whittley!"

"I'm fine," said Darwen, sitting up. "I just lost my balance."

He turned around and saw Naia, her face pale and scared, holding the arrow with the dart tip, its point smeared with blood.

"What do you think you're doing, Whittley?" said Mr. Iverson. "This is barbaric! You could have caused serious injury. I've never seen such stupidity from a Hillside student. At home, this would be a matter for the police."

That last phrase wiped the smirk off Chip's face. His haughty self-confidence fell away completely and he looked suddenly young and scared. "Sorry, sir," he said, his eyes cast down.

"Apologise to Mr. Arkwright," said Mr. Iverson, glaring at him.

"Sorry, Darwen," said Chip quickly. "I didn't mean to."

"It's OK," said Darwen. "It doesn't hurt that much."

This was a lie, but by the time Jorge had finished cleaning and patching it, it was barely even noticeable. "Change the band aid every few hours," said the guide, "and keep it clean. If it swells or gets red, let me know."

"Well," said Darwen, twisting his head over his shoulder, "I can't really see it."

"Mr. Haggerty," said Mr. Iverson. "You are sharing a tent with Mr. Arkwright, yes?"

Rik nodded but said nothing.

"Then you will keep an eye on his injury."

Rik's eyes met Darwen's and he nodded. Chip was looking at the floor while Miss Harvey berated him further. Everyone was staring at Chip with undisguised bitterness, and his eyes shone with tears, so that Darwen felt a little sorry for him. Even Nathan had backed away from his friend, as if he had something catching.

Darwen walked down to the beach, conscious that Rik was shadowing him, looking anxious, even a little guilty.

"I'm fine," Darwen repeated.

"When we get back from the dig, I'll take the band aid off and check it," said Rik. "We should wash it with drinking water."

"It's OK, really," said Darwen. As they walked away from the others he looked at his friend and took a breath. "There's something I need to tell you," he said. "Several things, actually. First, you'll never believe why Alex has been sneaking off to the woods. She's been looking after one of the pouncels."

"What?" exclaimed Rik, stopping in his tracks.

"It got shot and couldn't walk properly, so she's been feeding it."

"Feeding it what, her fingers?" said Rik. "Is she insane?"

"No more than usual," said Darwen.

It was terrible. They were discussing something awful, something which had left Alex hurt and furious, and they were doing it moments after Darwen had taken an arrow in the shoulder, but he couldn't help grinning. They were, after all, talking again.

"I don't know if we have to wait till sundown with these portals," Darwen was saying, "but we can use the stone spheres on Caño to cross over."

He couldn't help the tremor of excitement in his voice.

They climbed into the boat. Other than Jorge and Mr. Iverson, who were sitting all the way in the prow and out of earshot, the students were jockeying for places aboard the other boat. Snorkelling was still a lot more popular than archaeology. Darwen noticed that there was no sign of Chip or Nathan and thought, with a flash of grim amusement, that at very least they would be spending the afternoon cleaning tents. Only Gabriel joined them.

"You wouldn't prefer to go swimming?" asked Rik.

"Not today," said Gabriel, adjusting his veil. "I thought the archaeology thing sounded interesting."

Darwen wasn't convinced.

"Probably just wants to stick with us," said Rik after Gabriel was out of earshot.

"Yeah," said Darwen.

"Look," said Rik, "I'm sorry about before. I just didn't like being left out . . ."

"I should have taken you with me," said Darwen. "It was my fault. I'm an idiot."

Rik grinned at him. "Not compared to Alex," he said. "She was feeding one of those things? Seriously?"

"Seriously. And she told that girl from the village, Sarita, about it."

Rik gaped. "What happened to keeping things within the Peregrine Pact?" he exclaimed. "Who else knows?"

Darwen shrugged. "I think she wanted a secret of her own, That's why she didn't tell us. Because she felt we – well, *I* – had been holding out on her."

But before they could discuss the matter further, they saw her stomping stony-faced down the beach and into the water.

"You are coming to the island?" said Jorge.

"Apparently," said Alex.

Jorge reached for her hand and hauled her in. She avoided everyone's eyes but stared, haughtily out to sea.

"I'm glad you came," Darwen ventured.

"You think I'd let you two bond over how stupid you think I am?" she said, watching a tern skimming the waves off to the starboard.

"I guess not," said Darwen.

"So," she stated. "I hear you got shot,"

"Yes," said Darwen. "In the shoulder, look."

"Fantastic," she replied. "I hope it hurt."

There was an awkward pause.

"We good now?" said Rik.

"Sure," said Alex, finally turning to look at them. "Why wouldn't we be?"

Darwen grinned, and the others joined him.

"OK," said Rik, as the boat roared out of the bay and around the coast. "So now that we're talking again, I've got a few things to say, and most of them are about the stupidity of trying to hand-raise wild carnivores."

And they were off. Alex called Rik an unfeeling monster, and Rik said that he lived on a farm and he knew animals.

"It's not like Bambi, you know, Alex," he said. "The birds don't come and lay the table for you while the rabbits sing songs about how pretty you are. Animals act on instinct: fight or flight, kill or be killed. The pouncels are predators. I can't believe you!"

"Whatever," said Alex. Then turning to Darwen, she added,

"before he bursts into a chorus of 'Thank God I'm a Country Boy,' can we at least acknowledge that he said I was pretty."

"I did not!" yelled Rik, flushing pink. "I said the rabbits thought you were. If you were in a movie. And they were cartoons."

"I know what I heard," said Alex, smiling.

Darwen laughed and soon they joined him. It seemed like they hadn't laughed together for a very long time. It was a good feeling, good enough to mute the unease Darwen felt every time his eyes fell on Gabriel who was sitting very still, his head turned slightly towards them, as if he was listening very carefully to everything they said.

Darwen didn't know if he was becoming a better sailor or if he was just relieved to have Rik and Alex to talk to again, but the journey to Caño Island passed without the usual nausea. Rik had brought his pocket knife with the bundles of wood and string from the dining shelter, and they used the journey to catch up on their bow making. By the time they reached the island, they all had bows, though only Rik's looked like it might actually shoot, and Alex's arrows were all wonky.

"Doesn't matter," she said with a pointed look at Rik. "I won't be using it to hunt defenceless animals."

"If you did," said Rik, eying her bow critically, "they'd be quite safe. It's not straight."

"Straight!" said Alex. "Straight is overrated. Straight is stiff, inflexible, square. I'm a free spirit and my bow should match."

"So long as you don't mind putting your own eye out," said Rik.

They beached the boat. Jorge left the yellow plastic fuel cans up by the ranger station and headed up the trail to the dig site, chatting to Gabriel. From the shore they had been able to see the other boat unloading the students with their masks and snorkels into the water, but once they turned inland, they were completely alone.

As they walked through the jungle, Darwen told Alex and Rik about his realisation that the clown he had glimpsed in the mirror was Blackpool's World-Famous Laughing Man.

"How can it be?" said Rik.

"Must be one of those psychology thingies," said Alex. "Repressed memory or something."

"What?" asked Darwen.

"You know," said Alex airily. "In the movies there's always someone who saw something that they almost remember but can't quite because it was something really awful like a murder. But their unconscious mind holds on to a bit of it, and it keeps coming up, and eventually the character faces up to the terrible thing they've managed to forget, and that helps the police catch the killer and everything works out OK."

"I don't think that's it," said Darwen.

"I don't think it's anything," said Rik.

"I know I was scared of the Blackpool clown," said Darwen. "And there were all kinds of weird stories about it. Some people said it was inside the funhouse during a fire which destroyed the building but the clown was untouched by the blaze. And some people said that the laugh was actually recorded in an insane asylum. And some people . . ."

"I think that's more than enough information, thank you," said Alex.

Darwen looked up the trail. Jorge, Gabriel and Mr. Iverson were waiting for them.

"Mr. Iverson tells me you are keen archaeologists," Jorge said, smiling.

"They are," said Alex. "I'd rather be swimming with the fishies."

"We have our own club," said Rik, keen to show that he would not rather be swimming with the fishies.

"Have you found anything interesting?" asked Jorge.

Rik couldn't resist a sideways grin at Darwen.

Well, Darwen thought, *last year we found a scrobbler who had been shot two hundred years ago. That was fairly interesting.*

"Certainly, they have," said Mr. Iverson. "Rik has developed a whole theory about our school having been built on sacred Indian land."

"Really," said Jorge, his voice neutral. Gabriel was listening closely.

"Just a theory, right, Rik?" said Darwen, keen to steer the subject elsewhere. "It's not like we've found any real evidence."

"Well," said Jorge, "I hope we'll find something interesting today."

"Well, at least there won't be bottle caps out here," said Alex.

Rik frowned at her. He had often been accused of digging up nothing more than twenty-first century rubbish.

The group rounded the last bend in the path together and stuttered to a halt, staring at the site.

The central dig square was just as it had been before, except for one thing. Beside one of the larger stone spheres embedded in the ground was something new, something between a backpack and a kitchen appliance. It was studded with dials and switches and linked by a piece of hose to something with a nozzle and a trigger that looked like a flamethrower.

Darwen gasped. It was an energy weapon of the kind carried by scrobblers. He flashed a look at Rik and Alex.

"What's that?" said Mr. Iverson, stooping to it.

"Don't touch it!" exclaimed Rik, so that Mr. Iverson jumped and took a step back.

"Mr. Haggerty, you startled me!" he said.

"Sorry," said Rik. "I thought it looked . . . I don't know. Dangerous."

In fact, it didn't. As Darwen got closer he could see that the pack was blackened and the glass in its various controls was broken. He cautiously flipped a few switches, but nothing happened. It was quite dead.

"Whatever it is, it should not have been left here," said Jorge. "Maybe one of the archaeologists brought it to use on the site but . . ." he frowned, "I have never seen anything like it before."

Darwen didn't know why, but he wasn't sure he believed the guide.

"Even archaeological work should leave no trash behind," he said. "The island's environment must be preserved."

Jorge removed the tarp off the site and distributed the trowels which were stored in a box just outside the square.

Darwen took one last look at the burned-out energy weapon and found himself wondering why all the scrobbler equipment they had found in Costa Rica was clearly broken. He pictured the armoured bulldozer which seemed to have died the very moment it crossed over from Silbrica. What had Weazen said? Something about the old gates not working this time?

Burned out scrobbler equipment half in and half out of Silbrica, like they couldn't get it through the portal...

But animals like the pouncels could come. There had to be a reason.

"We work slowly," said Jorge. "I have strict orders from the excavation leader. One inch at a time. If you find anything at all, tell me."

It was hot work, made doubly so by the cramped conditions of the square. They couldn't all fit in at once, so they developed a rotation with two resting at a time. Twice Darwen thought he had found something, only to discover that it was just a perfectly normal piece of rock, and after half an hour, he began to wish the grownups would leave them to it and they could set to arranging the stone spheres into a circle...

"Huh," said Alex.

"What?" said Mr. Iverson, who was standing to the side, wiping the sweat from his face with a muddy hand.

"I hit something," she said, and tapped the tip of the trowel again to make the point. It chinked. "Stone, it looks like, but big and flat. And there are lines on it, like it's been carved. Is that good?"

The others stared at her for a moment, and then Rik was

pushing closer to see, and Jorge was calling for brushes from the box. They worked around the edges with the trowels and swept the surface of the stone slab clean until they could see the design etched into its surface.

The carving showed a swirl of lines beside what looked like a pole.

"It's an octopus," said Gabriel.

"But this," said Mr. Iverson, perplexed, indicating the vertical line, "looks like a tree. An octopus that lives in trees?"

Darwen said nothing. He stared at the carving, and when he looked up, Rik and Alex were both looking at him. He nodded fractionally.

It was the thing which had taken Luis. The Insidious Bleck.

So it too had been here long ago. The Guardians had been able to seal off Silbrica and its monsters from this place. But now they were back, they had a purpose and they had at least one "person" on their side – Scarlett Oppertune. Darwen didn't know how he was going to stop them, but his eyes slid over to the stone spheres half buried in the hard ground, and knew he was ready to try.

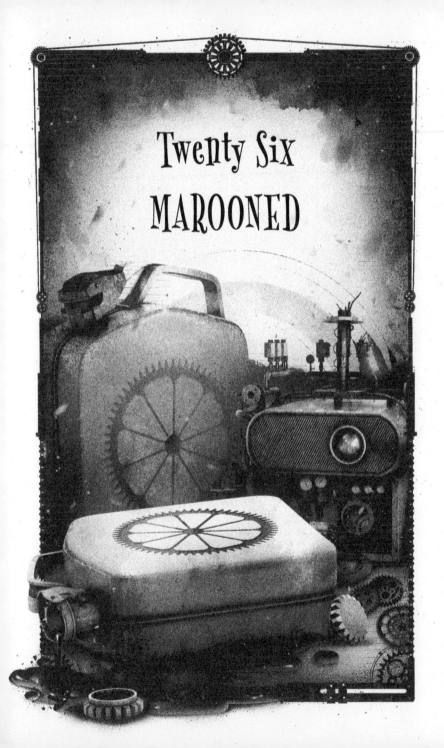

Twenty Six
MAROONED

Jorge couldn't sit still. He kept pacing around the excavated square taking pictures of the carving with a little digital camera and muttering to himself. Finally he couldn't wait any longer. "We should go back to the mainland," he said. "I need to get to a computer and consult with my colleagues."

"Your colleagues?" said Mr. Iverson.

"The archaeologists," said Jorge. "I must send these pictures to San Jose."

"I promised the students a whole afternoon of research on the island," said Mr. Iverson. "Can't it wait a few hours?"

"No," snapped Jorge. "This is important."

"So is the education of my students," said Mr. Iverson carefully.

"We'll be fine by ourselves if you want to head back," Darwen tried.

"I can't leave you here alone, even with your teacher," said Jorge. "And you can't drive the boat."

"I'll take the pictures," said Gabriel in a sudden and unexpected burst of enthusiasm. "I've had enough of archaeology anyway. I could swim across to the other boats where the others are snorkelling."

Jorge considered him and checked his watch. "The reef sharks will be starting to hunt soon, so the snorkellers will be getting ready to go."

He said this like Gabriel was merely booking a slightly earlier flight.

"Are you a strong swimmer?" asked Jorge, slipping the camera's memory stick into a zip-lock bag he had in his pocket.

"Yes," said Gabriel

Jorge hesitated, thinking, then nodded.

"OK," he said. For a moment he stood, as if still undecided, then took out a pen and wrote on a piece of paper. Gabriel read it and something came into his face, a hesitancy that might have been fear. Jorge met his eyes and nodded once before handing him the plastic bag. "Send this to my colleagues when you get back to the camp," he said. "Mr. Peregrine will know how to reach them."

Darwen was not the only one who looked surprised that Jorge had such confidence in the world studies teacher. Mr. Iverson's face was carefully blank but Alex's eyebrows were about as high as they could go. Gabriel just nodded, then set off at a run. In seconds, he had disappeared from view.

Jorge turned to find everyone looking at him. Something odd had just happened, Darwen felt sure of it, and even Mr. Iverson seemed cautious, watchful.

"Water break," Jorge said. "And snacks. But we should eat back at the ranger station. We must not contaminate the environment. Let us cover the dig site and put our tools away. There is no one on the island now but us."

Darwen felt a shiver of excitement at the idea: just the five of them on a deserted patch of jungle, ten miles out into the Pacific. It was like something out of *Treasure Island*. If only Jorge and Mr. Iverson had opted to go with Gabriel so that he could have gotten that portal working . . .

"Caño Island has been completely cut off from the rest of the peninsula," said Jorge, returning to tour-guide mode as they finished cleaning up and began the walk down to the beach, "so it has far fewer bird and animal species than on the mainland. Only one per cent of the insects which live there . . ." He stopped, seeming to forget everyone around him. He was staring at a patch of dried mud by the trail.

"What?" asked Rik. "What do you see?"

"Nothing," said Jorge, and he kicked at the earth with his boot, scuffing the dirt.

Rik gave him a hard look.

Jorge's face was expressionless, but when Mr. Iverson gave him an inquiring look, he just shrugged and smiled and moved off along the path. Darwen was about to go after the adults when Alex tugged his shirt.

"Look," she whispered.

A few feet from where Jorge had been standing there were tracks in the now-hard ground, tracks showing claws and a central talon much longer than the rest.

"You know what that means?" said Alex.

"That there are pouncels on the island," said Darwen, frowning, "and Jorge doesn't want us to know."

"And they didn't swim ten miles to get here," said Alex. "So the stone spheres back there are an active portal."

"But someone has to arrange them into a circle," said Darwen. "You don't think Jorge is working with Scarlett? They hate each other!"

"People lie, Darwen," said Alex.

Darwen hung back as she followed the others.

He had liked the guide, still did. If Jorge was working with Scarlett, if he was involved in any way with the disappearance of Luis, Eduardo, and Calida, then the world was a little less pleasant, less trustworthy, less good. But why would he be? Why would anyone be abducting children?

The thought brought a name they had barely spoken in weeks to Darwen's mind: *Greyling.*

Last time, it had been him directing Miss Murray to power his machines, and though Darwen was able to tell himself that they had not seen any direct signs of him yet – no gnashers and scrobblers, no kid-sized generators – he knew that if Greyling was somehow behind everything, behind the Insidious Bleck, things would be far worse than he imagined.

Darwen's unease deepened as he reached the beach. A strange scene was playing out there. Mr. Iverson was standing on the shore gesturing wildly with both hands towards the distant snorkellers whose boat was speeding away, with Gabriel – presumably – aboard. Jorge was kneeling beside their own boat looking serious.

Darwen broke into a run. "What's going on?" he shouted.

"Him!" yelled Rik. "It was him!"

"What are you talking about?"

"Jorge," said Rik, turning fiercely. "He did it."

"It wasn't him, Rik," said Mr. Iverson, splashing his way to the shore. "It was like this when we got here."

"Like what?" asked Darwen. "Will someone please tell me what is going on?"

Rik pointed at a patch of wet sand by the boat where Jorge was squatting. Darwen took a step towards it and was immediately overwhelmed by a familiar and powerful smell.

Petrol, or as he had gotten used to calling it over the last few months, *gasoline*.

The yellow plastic cans were cap-less and on their sides. Someone had dumped their fuel. They were stranded.

"Maybe the wind blew them over," said Mr. Iverson.

"And unscrewed the tops?" said Rik.

Jorge stood up. He met Rik's hostile gaze, then began walking down the beach towards the ranger station.

"So we're stuck here?" said Alex. "Till when? Not overnight, right? Someone will come for us before dark, yeah?"

"Mr. Iverson," called Jorge, as he walked away, "could we talk for a moment?"

Mr. Iverson, looking bewildered, hurried after him.

The students watched them go.

"It was Gabriel," said Darwen, stunned. "It had to be. That explains why he wanted to leave so quickly. But what would make him do it in the first place?"

"Because Jorge told him to," said Rik. "It's Jorge's fault, just like I've been saying it all along: we can't trust that guy."

"He expects something to happen tonight," said Darwen. It was a guess, but it felt right. "Something is going to happen and he wants to be here to see it."

"I knew we couldn't trust him," spluttered Rik.

"Rik," said Alex, in her no-nonsense voice. "Stop talking."

Rik opened his mouth to argue but she stared him down as only she could do and he turned sullenly away.

"So now what?" said Darwen. "There's no mobile phone signal out here. What about a radio?"

"Yes," said Rik, "I saw one on the shelf back there with the food supplies. It's pretty old and has a hand crank. They may be using it right now."

"Come on," said Darwen.

They ran over to the shelter and found Jorge sitting at the ancient radio. He avoided their eyes and cranked the handle vigorously, then flipped switches, crammed a battered headset on and adjusted a dial, talking. Alex listened closely, but her face showed no sign of doubt or alarm. After a few moments, he sat back and slammed the headset to the desktop, uttering a single shouted syllable which Miss Martinez was unlikely to ever teach them.

"That was a bad word," said Alex, in case they hadn't guessed. "He seems pretty upset."

"No one said he wasn't a good actor," whispered Rik.

"*Nada*," said Jorge. "Nothing. Probably no one is near the radio. They won't be till the other boat gets back. If we cannot reach them soon it will be too dark for them to come in to shore. The rocks are very dangerous and there are no lights out here."

"If they could get close to the island," said Darwen, acting as neutrally as possible to Jorge, "could we swim out to meet them?"

Jorge shook his head.

"Sharks," he said. "I will keep trying," he added, "but we should prepare to be here overnight. We should camp on the beach. It will be safer than in the rainforest."

"I thought there were no large predators on the island," said Rik, barely keeping the skepticism out of his voice.

"There are some snakes," said Jorge without looking at them directly. Darwen knew the guide was thinking about the pouncels whose tracks he had tried to hide. "Why don't you gather some wood for a fire?"

"Er . . . because it's like a hundred degrees," said Alex.

"For safety," said Jorge.

"Ah," said Alex. "Wood it is. Coming right up. Lumber. Logs. Kindling . . ."

"OK, Alex," said Rik, fishing in a box of supplies and emerging with a cigarette lighter. "We'll get the wood. Mr. Iverson can stay here with Jorge," he added, with a meaningful look at Darwen and Alex.

"What?" said Mr. Iverson, who seemed to be lost in his own thoughts. "Sure. That's fine."

As soon as they were out of earshot of the shelter Rik said, "Someone has to keep an eye on Jorge. How's Mr. I's Spanish?"

Alex waggled her hand and made a noncommittal noise: not bad, not great.

Rik raised his eyebrow.

"Good enough to tell if he's ordering Silbrican monster attacks, I guess." Alex shrugged.

"You know," said Darwen, "this is actually perfect."

"Being stranded on an island with monsters on it?" said Alex. "Yeah, it's a dream come true. No, wait. It's a *nightmare* come true."

"I mean we can activate the portal by the dig site tonight," said Darwen. "We wait for the adults to go to sleep and then we sneak up there, make a circle with the loose spheres, pour some water in – unless it rains, which it probably will – and we're in."

They looked at each other and the excitement passed through them like the electricity they were about to stimulate.

"Let's do it," said Rik.

"Agreed," said Alex, taking their hands. "But till then we let Mr. Iverson and Jorge think they're running the show. Let's get that wood."

They worked for an hour, gathering fallen timbers and branches and dragging them onto the sand where the gas had been spilled.

"Might make it easier to light at least," Rik shrugged. "And it's a good ways away from the forest. Wouldn't want to accidentally devastate the environment, would we?"

"No," said Darwen. "That's Scarlett's job, though I still don't know why."

"Maybe she doesn't need a reason," said Alex. "Maybe she just wants to destroy what other people value. Some people are like that. Ask that igornamus Chip Whittley why he killed that butterfly."

"You mean *ignoramus*," said Rik.

"I know what I mean," said Alex.

Back at the ranger station, Jorge had laid out food rations from the plastic storage bins and made coffee on a tiny propane stove. "Cream and sugar?" he asked, as he handed out chipped, enamel mugs.

"Cream?" said Alex. "We have a fridge?"

Jorge laughed, pushing one of the big Tupperware boxes. "Just the powder kind," he said. "It lasts forever." He looked out towards the ocean. "The sun is going down. Even if I reach the tent camp now on the radio, no one will come till morning. You should decide where you are going to sleep."

"What about you?" asked Darwen.

"I am not tired," said the guide, "and someone should pay attention for a while."

"Why?" said Rik.

"No reason," said Jorge, though his eyes had that evasive look again. "Just to be safe. You can take your bows."

Darwen doubted their home-made bows and arrows would be of much use if the pouncels – or worse – attacked, but since he had nothing better to offer, he just shrugged. Even Alex brought hers, though Rik gave her a *you-can't-be-serious* look.

"Don't be making fun of my bow," she said, warningly.

"Oh, it's a bow," said Rik. "I thought it was a rare one-stringed harp."

"How about I use my one-stringed harp to put an arrow in your butt?" Alex responded.

"You couldn't hit the ocean with that thing," said Rik.

"From where?" asked Alex.

"From the edge of the ocean," said Rik.

Darwen laughed.

"We'll see about that," said Alex, looking affronted. "We're going to have a little competition, you and me, Rik Haggerty."

"Let's get sorted out first," said Darwen. Then you can test whose bow is the worst."

"You mean the best," said Alex.

"I know what I mean," said Darwen, who didn't think either bow looked too impressive.

Clouds were sweeping in from the sea, promising rain, but they set up camp on the beach by the fire anyway, lugging some of the supply boxes out there to sit on. It was quieter here than the mainland, and the muted jungle buzz was without the sudden calls of birds and monkeys which they had grown used to at the camp.

"So if Gabriel marooned us here," Darwen said, thinking aloud, "because Jorge told him to, what's going on?"

"He obviously wanted to get word to his *colleagues*, whoever they really are," said Alex, "but he didn't want to leave the island. Mr. Iverson wouldn't let us go back to the mainland, so he decided to maroon us all here."

"Or he always planned for us to get stuck out on this island," said Rik. "Maybe we're about to be the first Hillsiders taken by the Insidious Bleck."

It began to rain almost as soon as they had lit the fire.

"Great," said Alex. "We'll have to sleep in the shelter."

They returned to the ranger station, cleared the wooden floor, took their shoes off, and lay there in their clothes, watching the rain by the light of the fire on the beach, waiting for the adults to fall asleep.

"This trip just keeps on getting better," said Alex. Without warning, she started to sing, rocking back and forth in time to the music.

"What are you doing?" asked Rik.

"Helps me get to sleep," she said.

"It's not doing much for me," said Rik.

"Just a few minutes," she said, "and I'll drop right off. Promise. Got any requests?"

"The Sound of Silence," Rik deadpan.

"Hilarious," said Alex. "What's that anyway, some mouldy old song your dad listens to? You need to get with the times. Try this for size."

She started warbling "Baby! Baby! Baby!" madly.

"You do this in your tent with Naia and Kahala?" Rik cut in.

"Every night," she said. "Sometimes they join in."

"And I thought sleeping in a stinky tent was bad," said Rik.

"You know whose tent is worse than yours?" whispered Alex. "Mr. P's. I had to go see him yesterday and man! I don't think he's bathed since we arrived. It's like something died in there."

"Shhh!" said Jorge suddenly. He had leapt to his feet and was standing at the back of the shelter, his lit flashlight sweeping the treeline above.

"What is it?" asked Mr. Iverson, sounding groggy.

"Everybody get to the fire!" shouted Jorge. "Quickly!"

"But it's raining!" said Alex.

"Now!" Jorge yelled.

"Is that really necessary?" said Mr. Iverson, standing and turning on the shelter's storm lantern.

The others turned to him and everyone went very still, staring with horror.

"What?" asked Mr. Iverson.

Behind the science teacher, on the very edge of the lamplight, were pairs of yellow lights.

Eyes.

"Go," said Jorge in a low voice to the students. "Get to the fire and stay there. I will bring Mr. Iverson."

"What?" said Mr. Iverson. Then he did the thing they had all been hoping he wouldn't. He turned to see what they were looking at.

Twenty Seven

THE TERROR
IN THE TREES

Mr. Iverson saw the gathering pouncels, and he panicked. He half-jumped, half-fell away from them. They reacted at once, leaping into the light, knife-like claws held out in front of them, mouths open and snarling. Mr. Iverson barely saw them. In his hurry, he stumbled, turned his ankle and fell, catching his head on the edge of the bench. The sound was sickening, a firm crack like the sound of a bat hitting a cricket ball. He lay motionless.

"Go!" roared Jorge.

Darwen, Rik and Alex ran out into the rain and down the beach towards the fire. As they ran, the shingle became sand, and all they could see in the darkness was the blazing heap of wood which roared and hissed at the rain like a volcano. Back in the station there was a crash, and Jorge's voice rang out in a wordless cry.

They heard another shout, and it seemed so much further away now that Darwen's heart sank. He didn't trust Jorge, but he liked Mr. Iverson a lot. If something bad happened to him, something he couldn't actually bring himself to imagine right now, he would never forgive himself. How many of the pouncels had there been? Five? At least that many, he thought. Maybe eight or more.

Another shout.

Darwen reached for a hefty looking tree limb stuck deep in the heart of the blaze, and pulled it out.

"What are you doing?" asked Rik.

"Going back," said Darwen.

The branch was hot in his hand, and it steamed as the rain hit it. He held it overhead and started back towards the shelter.

"Darwen, that's crazy!" shouted Rik. "There are too many of them."

Darwen didn't answer. He began to run, so that he wouldn't change his mind, looking up at the blazing branch above his head. It was still burning, but the flames were small and bluish, not nearly as impressive as he had expected them to be. He slowed. Jorge's flashlight was slashing around the ranger station like a laser. There was another crash, like overturning furniture, and the light became still.

Darwen rushed to the scene dimly but gratefully aware that Rik and Alex had brought burning brands of their own and were right at his heels.

The flashlight had rolled under the overturned table, but the lantern hanging from the roof beam was still lit. There was no sign of the pouncels. The two men were sprawled on the ground. Mr. Iverson was out cold. Jorge was crumpled in the corner, covered in blood.

Darwen ran to him instinctively and dropped to a crouch. "Jorge!" he screamed.

The guide's eyelids tightened, then opened. "I am not your enemy," he gasped between low, rasping breaths. "You have to trust me."

"Darwen!" shouted Rik.

It was a warning. Darwen turned, rising, and saw three of the pouncels, the largest he had seen, edging back into the shelter. He waved his branch at them, but the flames were virtually out. The pouncels hopped backwards as the branch scattered sparks, but then they stalked closer again.

"Go back to the fire," muttered Jorge, his eyes closing once more. "You are safer there."

"No," said Darwen. He took a step towards one of the cat-faced creatures and lunged with the branch, but it dodged, then leapt in close, claws slashing.

Darwen shrank away, but he felt a gash open along his thigh, and he cried out. Two more pouncels had joined the other three.

"Go!" shouted Jorge again. He sounded weak, but determined, and desperate though Darwen was, he knew the guide was right. They could do nothing here. He turned and fled back towards the beach.

Rik and Alex were in front of him now, and Darwen sensed their hesitation immediately. They were facing the fire, but they weren't running.

"What's the matter?" Darwen yelled, trying to see past them to the plastic storage boxes they had used as benches. "Run!"

But they didn't move, and as he took another step towards them, he saw why. Something moved between them and the sea, something quick and dangerous, silhouetted against the glow of the fire. Then another. And another. There were more pouncels on the beach. A whole pack of them.

Darwen glanced wildly to Alex and Rik. They had been cut off.

"I don't think hand-feeding them will work this time, Alex," said Rik.

"That way!" shouted Alex. "Up to the dig."

"Why?" gasped Darwen.

"Where else is there?" she replied.

She had a point. The beach wasn't safe. The shelter wasn't safe. The dig wouldn't give them any more protection, but it might buy them a little time and cover.

Alex started to run, swinging her still smoldering stick at the pouncels on the beach so that it glowed fiercely.

Out on the beach they could see the sky. Once they went up that path again, they would be in the altogether different darkness of the forest. Darwen caught a flash of movement in the darkness and he flung his stick in that direction. It flared briefly in the wind, and then landed on the beach in a shower of sparks.

They found the path, but only just. Alex's burning stick had gone out and they had no lantern. It was only due to Rik's tiny pocket flashlight that they were able to pick their way through a darkness which was almost complete. If the pouncels chose to attack now, Darwen knew they wouldn't see them till it was too late. They slowed, faltering as they traced the trail inland, but they didn't reach the dig site. A couple of hundred yards before they got there, there was a flash of lightning, and Darwen stuttered to a halt. Off to his left he had seen something in the sudden bluish white overhead, something odd which made the ground look pale. Thunder rolled overhead and then the lightning came again, and this time Darwen was looking right at it.

No more than a few yards off the path was a circle of rainwater ringed with stone spheres they hadn't noticed before. Darwen stared at it, and though the night was still warm he felt cold. He also felt with uncanny certainty that he was being watched. He turned hastily around. The others had stopped and were waiting for him.

"Turn your flashlight off," Darwen hissed.

"What is it?" Rik hissed. There was a click and the pencil-like beam of light went out.

"There's something on the path behind us," Darwen replied. He saw it only as a deeper blackness in the dark, but he knew it had not been there before. It was just the size and shape of a pouncel. One, maybe more, had tracked them.

He didn't know what to do. If only Mr. Peregrine had told him something, anything. Rik raised his hand with the tiny flashlight, aiming, but Darwen caught his wrist before he could turn it on. "That might provoke it," he said.

Rik lowered his hand and they stared into the darkness.

The lightning came again, and Darwen saw the pouncel clear as day, but it was not poised to attack. It was not even looking at them. Instead it was huddled on the ground as if terrified, and it was staring directly up into the trees.

Slowly, with a swelling sense of dread, Darwen did the same, and as the lightning flickered again, he saw it, the pale and purplish sack-like body, pulsing up there, the massive trailing tentacles, the terrible, beak like mouth with the terrifying feelers. There was no question that this was the creature carved into the ancient stone at the dig site, the thing the adults had thought was an octopus. It was suspended up there, its body the size of a car, slick under a tangle of short hair, undulating sluggishly, wrapped around a tree and hanging in the dark like a nightmare.

Darwen wasn't sure which of them had cried out. He knew it hadn't been him, because though a part of him wanted to scream, no sound would come, and he could do nothing but stand and stare in horrified silence.

The darkness was complete for five, maybe ten seconds. Darwen couldn't say for sure. But when the lightning came again the creature had moved. The sky flickered like a faulty movie projector, and the great mass of the Insidious Bleck – for that was surely what it was – was unfurling its tentacles and reaching over the path with fluid, snake-like ease. It extended its tentacles, the pale underside studded with suckers and hooks, the top side bristling with hair. When it reached the tree, it coiled one of its tentacles quickly and silently around it, and then the entire creature was hauling itself overhead, its great weight breaking off branches as it swung through the canopy. Its movement was easy and slow, so that an extraordinary possibility struck Darwen like a ray of hope in the darkness.

It hasn't seen us.

He hadn't moved a muscle since spotting it, and Darwen now found himself praying that Rik and Alex would make the same deduction. Out of the corner of his eye, however, he saw movement, a long careful loping stride which quickened suddenly. The pouncel was making a run for it.

Without pausing in its languid motion through the trees, without even clearly turning to see the pouncel at all, the Insidious Bleck dropped one long tentacle to the forest floor and snatched it up. The pouncel fought, lashing and scratching but the Bleck's tentacle had the strength and studied deliberation of an elephant's trunk. It swept the howling pouncel upwards and opened its appalling beak mouth wide to receive it.

The spell was finally broken and Darwen was able to look away at the last second. Amid the pattering rain, drops of blood fell through the leaves. Darwen couldn't think. He couldn't plan or decide what was best or smartest. The horror of the thing was too great. Without an idea in his head, without even being able to see where he was going, he ran.

Somewhere high up in the forest, a tree creaked and groaned as the monster shifted its weight suddenly. A branch snapped. Then another, and there was a new rustling in the leaves which was louder and more violent than the storm.

It was coming after him.

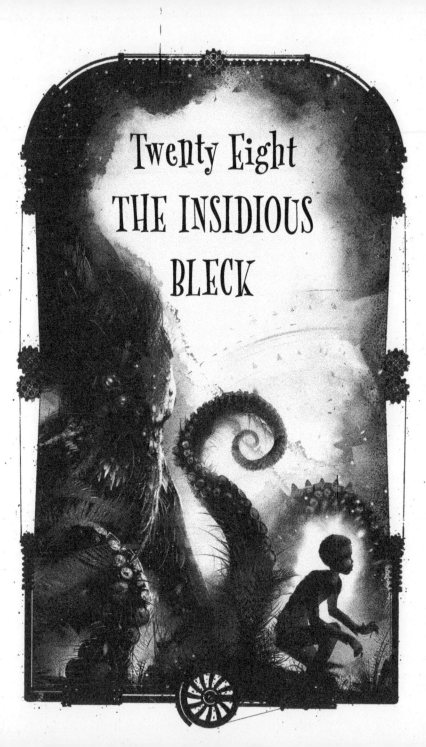

Twenty Eight

THE INSIDIOUS
BLECK

D arwen didn't even know which way he was facing. The lightning showed he was on the path, but he didn't know if he was going inland or back down to the beach. Not that it mattered. He was headed away from the creature in the treetops and his sense of the thing behind him was as good as a compass.

There was movement beside him, and even though Darwen was running, he jumped and almost stumbled. It was Rik. "It's the thing from the carving!" he gasped. "The thing which took Luis. It's going to take us too."

Darwen couldn't answer. He was sure the abomination in the trees was about to reach for him with one of those long, hairy tentacles, and then sweep him up towards that horror of a mouth. He could almost feel it inches from his skin, his hair, and the thought worked on him with a revulsion he couldn't switch off. He ran. It was all he could do.

"Where's Alex?" asked Rik, fighting to keep up.

The question punched through the smothering fog of terror and stopped Darwen cold. He didn't know. He had no idea where *he* was, let alone where Alex might be. He dropped, rolling into the leafy underbrush off the path, giving no thought to snakes and insects. He looked up. Rik was clambering awkwardly over a tree limb and squatting beside him, but beyond him, Darwen could see nothing. There were no stars, no soft street-lamp glow, no moon. Overhead, the sky was the faintest grey smear beyond the silhouettes of the trees. The wind dropped and for a second, all was perfectly still. And then the greyness seemed to shift and a blackness moved over them like a blimp drifting against the clouds.

Darwen felt its presence like a foul smell, and he shuddered before he could stop himself. Rik clamped one large, sweaty palm over Darwen's forearm, and the two boys sat motionless as the creature in the trees moved with deliberate caution above them.

It knows we're here, Darwen thought. *But not where exactly. It's waiting. Listening . . .*

His heart was racing, and he had bitten down on his lip so hard that he could taste blood in his mouth. He breathed through his nose, still as the trees themselves, and he too listened.

There had been a noise. Faint, and not up in the canopy but down on the forest floor. In the darkness Darwen had no idea how far away it had been. Ten yards? Twenty? It had been a stealthy sound. Another pouncel, perhaps. Or Alex.

Darwen turned as slowly and quietly as he could and stared into the blackness where he thought the sound had come from. Almost immediately, he heard it again. Louder now. Closer. Something coming quietly towards them across the base of the ground. Rik's grip on his arm tightened. He had heard it too.

The lightning flashed, and for a moment Darwen saw the jungle, a clutter of underbrush and tree trunks reaching up into the sky, but he saw no animal or person, nothing that might have made the noise. The darkness came again, and thunder rolled like a series of distant explosions. And beneath it, lasting a fraction longer than the thunder, something moved through the leaf litter. Not footsteps. A consistent, slithering sound . . .

The lightning came again. Darwen's first thought was that the forest had somehow grown denser, that new trees had sprouted around them. But the light lasted just long enough to see that some of what he had thought were tree trunks were purplish, and matted with short bristling hair.

The monster was trailing its tentacles from above, sweeping the ground, searching for them.

Another flicker of lightning, and Darwen had to clap a hand to his mouth. One of the great rope-like tentacles was less than a foot from his face. It hung quite still, but its tip, which bore a long, hook-like claw, writhed and pulsed like a maggot as it felt blindly for its prey. It inched towards them, and Darwen shrunk inwardly, forcing himself not to kick the vile thing away.

And then he felt it. It had brushed the fabric of his T shirt just above his shoulder. It stopped.

Darwen sat motionless and felt the tentacle grow almost thoughtfully still, and the entire world, in spite of the rain and the lightning, seemed to follow suit. For a second that felt like ten, nothing happened, and then the claw rotated a fraction, testing its hard tip against his shoulder. It pressed, then the pressure eased, and it moved more gently, almost caressing as it tried to figure out what it had found. It snaked down his chest and he felt the hard bristles brush against his cheek as it moved. He could smell it too, an old and slightly rotten smell like wet earth or mulch. It was, he thought, the aroma of the grave.

The thought was still bright and horrible in his mind when he felt the tentacle curl slightly as it moved down. It was starting to tighten. Exploration had turned into something else. It was going to take him like it had taken the others.

The realisation gave him no choice. He leapt to his feet spinning as he had seen Rik do when he was trying to break a tackle while playing football. He turned against the curl of the tentacle, rotated halfway round and broke into a run, pulling Rik after him.

Behind them, he heard the tentacle writhe, grabbing wildly at the air, breaking branches as it whirled around, searching. Then it was sucked upwards and the entire creature was on the move up in the canopy, following them.

Somehow they had to find the path. If they could get to the beach, the monster wouldn't be able to reach them from the trees. But first they had to get there. Branches whipped at their faces and arms, as they blundered through the undergrowth. One lashed the side of Darwen's neck like a scalpel, but then he was out on the wide, open beach, free of the tree limbs through which the Bleck had moved.

"This way!" shouted Rik, who seemed to have had the same idea: get to the shore, and they might be safe. He snapped on his pocket flashlight and though Darwen knew that would make them visible, he said nothing. He couldn't stand the darkness any longer and they just had to get down to the sea.

The creature seemed to sense what they were doing. Branches fell from above as it tore through the canopy, and – just when Darwen thought nothing could add to his terror – it began to scream: a deafening shriek of fury which silenced the storm and every other beast in the jungle. Darwen's skin seemed to shrink like cellophane in a candle flame, and his hair stood on end. The appalling sound lasted several seconds and Darwen felt his strength fade, as if the noise was draining the hope and courage out of him.

"Keep going," breathed Rik, lumbering into him from behind. "Don't stop."

Rik's words cleared his mind a little, and Darwen's feet began to pound the track again. Somewhere behind them they heard the groan and crack of a trunk splintering from the Bleck's weight, but they didn't pause. They ran harder than ever and suddenly, it seemed that the path, though just as windy, was sloping down.

"This is it!" shouted Rik, his flashlight waving erratically. "We're nearly there!"

Darwen found a little well of energy deep inside him, dipped into it, and accelerated along the path. They rounded one last overgrown corner and a glorious sight met their eyes. Off to the left, no more than a couple of hundred yards away, they could see the orange glow of the fire.

Rik paused, checking behind them, and his flashlight found the Bleck's pale and pulsing body up there in the treetops, its many glassy eyes staring, its tentacles spread wide, some gripping tree trunks, others poised to strike.

Darwen grabbed Rik by the back of his shirt and pulled, but the larger boy was too scared to move.

"Come on!" shouted Darwen. "Get to the fire!"

The Insidious Bleck opened its great beak-like jaws and the

mouth part feelers around it flexed hungrily.

Rik didn't move.

There was something hypnotic, snake-like about the slow unfurling of those tentacles, the way they stretched out towards them . . .

"Now!" bellowed Darwen and he kicked Rik hard in the shin.

Rik blinked, gave Darwen a startled look as if he had just woken up and then finally, started to move.

Not a moment too soon. A tentacle lashed the place where they had been.

Fortunately, they were already sprinting the final yards down to the sand. They made for the fire, vaulting over the plastic boxes of supplies, conscious as they got out from under the darkness of the trees that the rain had stopped and the clouds overhead were blowing away already. They ran on, relief washing over them with each step they took away from the trees.

"There you are!" said a voice from beside the fire. "What kept you?"

"Alex!" gasped Darwen. "Are we glad to see you!"

"I don't know," said Alex, "are you?"

"We thought . . . . you were . . . out there," Rik managed as he doubled over, breathing hard. "The thing . . ."

"The Insidious Bleck!" said Darwen. "It's back there."

Alex gazed past them, her face serious.

"Not so much *back* there," she said, "as just *there*."

No, thought Darwen. *Not here. We're safe here.*

But she was right.

Crab-like it came towards them from the treeline, half-walking, half-slithering on those awful tentacles, and on land it seemed more spider then octopus. In the firelight it looked hellish, a sprawling, throbbing horror. It was even bigger than Darwen had thought. The tentacles could have wrapped around a bus, and crushed it.

"Get your bows!" said Alex.

The idea was so preposterous that even in his terror Darwen stared at her.

"You got a better idea?" she said.

They picked up their bows and fumbled with the little stack of arrows they had made. They felt pathetically, comically inadequate.

The monster came towards them, upending the boxes so that one popped its lid and spewed its white powdery contents.

"It will be afraid of the fire," muttered Rik, feverishly.

"It's not," said Alex, as the monster clambered over the supplies.

"Well it should be," Rik answered. So saying he drew back his bow, and Darwen saw that he had set the tip of the arrow alight. He fired. The burning arrow scudded through the darkness and found one of the monster's tentacles. It bellowed in rage and its pincer-like mouth gaped at them, but it did not slow down.

"Good idea," said Alex. "Let's make it really angry."

"I wasn't aiming for it," said Rik. "I was aiming for the box! The one with no lid."

"The box?" said Darwen, not taking his eyes off the lumbering creature. "Why?"

"Just shoot it!"

Darwen didn't dare turn his back on the monster, so he thrust his arrow back in the direction of the fire and held it there without looking at it. When he put it in his bow he saw that the tip was smoldering, but was not truly alight.

Gripped with panic and feeling trapped between the beast and the flames, he fired anyway. The bow twanged absurdly and the arrow buried itself in the sand. Rik fired again, and his arrow flew up and out of sight.

The monster slid closer, raising itself over the plastic box of white powder.

"Shoot the box?" said Alex, who was sighting down her wonky bow, a burning arrow poised to fire. "Really?"

"Really!" shouted Rik.

"OK," she shrugged.

It was only feet from them now and showing no sign of slowing. Two of its tentacles were reaching for them.

"Now!" yelled Rik.

Alex fired.

What happened next took everyone by surprise. The arrow flew perfectly straight and clean, smooth as a javelin, right into the open box. The moment it made contact, there was an explosion of yellow flame considerably brighter than the fire at their backs. It roared up, engulfing the monster's body, surrounding it in a blaze so dazzling that they had to turn their eyes from it.

The Insidious Bleck roared again, but this was not anger, but a mad and desperate pain. It rocked backwards, stumbling, its underside black and scorched. The hair on its body burst into short-lived flame, and the upper parts of its tentacles looked raw and shiny. It fell back, twisting in its agony, rolling in the sand.

And then it was retreating up the beach, groaning, limping into the darkness. Moments later, it was gone.

Twenty Nine
TAKING THE INITIATIVE

"What in Krispy Kreme the heck was that?" said Alex, still kneeling like a statue, her bow extended.

"I told you," said Darwen. "It was the Insidious Bleck."

"Not that," said Alex. "The stuff in the box. What was that?"

"Non-dairy creamer," said Rik. "I saw a show about it on TV. Supposed to be highly flammable."

"Er, I'd say so," said Alex. She considered her twisted bow proudly. "Couldn't hit the ocean from the edge of the ocean, huh?"

"That shot defied the laws of physics," said Rik to Darwen.

"You can't underestimate the power of attitude," said Alex. "And style," she added. "And poise under pressure . . ."

"OK, Alex," said Rik. "It was a good shot."

"That's all I needed to hear," she said. "And I guess your science-y bit with the non-dairy creamer didn't suck either."

"We're a team," said Rik, grinning.

A team, thought Darwen, *but not the Pact.*

Mr. Peregrine had abandoned them.

"So," said Alex, "when the non-dairy-whatsit stuff went all kablooey, would you say you were right chuffed?"

"Something like that," said Rik. "We should check on Jorge," he added, gazing towards the shelter. "You think it's safe?"

"I think that octo-spider-nightmare scared off everything in a ten-mile radius," said Alex.

"Good enough," Rik declared.

The three of them set off across the beach to the ranger station. The shelter was a confusion of shattered glass, broken plastic and splintered wood. The two men were huddled in one corner, partially barricaded in with overturned tables and chairs which Rik and Darwen set to pulling away. Alex picked up Jorge's fallen flashlight and shone it as Mr. Iverson crawled out.

"Are you OK?" asked Rik.

"I'm fine," said Mr. Iverson, finding his glasses and putting them on. "Just a bit of a headache."

He didn't look fine. He looked scared and confused. But before Darwen could enquire further, Jorge emerged from the rubble and he looked worse, pale and blood spattered. Rik rummaged through a first aid box and set to dressing a particularly nasty looking gash across the man's forearm.

"It's OK," said Jorge, though he didn't resist as Rik started anointing and bandaging.

"What about you three?" said Mr. Iverson, eyeing the cut on the back of Darwen's leg. It had stopped bleeding quickly and looked much worse than it was.

"We're fine," said Darwen. "Did you see . . .?"

Jorge shot him a hard look and Darwen tried a different approach. "What did all this?" he said, gesturing vaguely at the shattered remains of the ranger station.

Everyone was watching Mr. Iverson. He rubbed the back of his head thoughtfully. "I'm not entirely sure," he said looking around him. "I assumed the storm had brought the roof in, but it doesn't look like it. I thought I saw . . ." he hesitated, shrugging, and everyone was quiet for a moment, "I'm not sure. A minor concussion, I guess. Jorge?"

"Very strong winds," said Jorge, nodding but not really looking at him. "I cut my arm on the edge of the table."

"Really?" said Mr. Iverson. It was a genuine question. The science teacher seemed thoroughly unsure of himself.

"Yes," said Jorge. "But the storm has gone now. We're safe."

Darwen found himself wondering, not for the first time, why it seemed so important to keep the truth from Mr. Iverson, who had always been kind and helpful. What difference would it make if there was one more person who knew that they were in danger from the inhabitants of another world? What possible harm could it do? It would be good to have an adult to confide in, particularly with things as they were with Mr. Peregrine . . .

But if Mr. Peregrine didn't believe him, what chance did he have of persuading Mr. Iverson, who knew nothing of Silbrica or its creatures?

No. He couldn't tell Mr. Iverson, and he didn't trust Jorge. He was on his own, as usual, or rather they were. He knew he could count on Rik and Alex. He gave them a nod to follow him.

"You're going back out there?" said Jorge, curious and concerned.

"Won't be long," said Darwen.

"Be careful," said Mr. Iverson.

"Always," said Darwen.

"Well?" said Rik, as soon as they were out of earshot of the shelter. "You think Mr. Iverson remembers more than he's saying?"

"No," said Darwen. "But listen. The monster – the Insidious Bleck – ran away."

"Well, I'm not sure about ran," said Alex. "More like limped..."

"What do you want to do?" said Rik, eyeing Darwen keenly in the last light of the dying fire.

"We should follow it," said Darwen.

"I'm sorry," said Alex. "I think I have sand in my ears. We should *what now*?"

"It's the opportunity we've been hoping for," said Darwen.

"When that creamy stuff caught fire," said Alex, "did you, you know, *inhale* any of it? Only something certainly fried your brain."

"The monster is running away, right?" Darwen insisted. "It will go through the portal to wherever Scarlett keeps it. If we follow it, we'll find Luis and the others. I know where the pool with the stones around it is."

"And if we find ourselves welcomed with open tentacle-like arms?" Alex persisted.

"You saw it," said Rik. "It's hurt and scared. It won't be waiting to attack us now."

"Oh, right," said Alex, "make me feel sorry for it!"

Darwen and Rik stared at her.

"I know," she said, holding her hands up. "It's an animal, right? It's probably just hungry."

"That's what Mr. Peregrine's been saying, but I'm not so sure," said Darwen. "It ate the pouncel right away. But us . . . It was different. Like it was trying to catch us to take us back."

"Fine," said Alex. "But I'm bringing my physics-defying bow and arrows."

"Deal," said Darwen.

Rik snapped on his flashlight.

"Lead the way," he said.

It took them only a few minutes to find the mirror pool ringed with stones, and that was moving slowly, their flashlights constantly scanning the surrounding trees for pouncels. There was no sign of life, however, and the jungle was oddly quiet after the storm. Darwen gazed at the perfectly-round depression brimming with bright rainwater, the stones around its rim arranged with mathematical precision.

"What makes you think it's still online?" said Rik. "Looks like a puddle to me."

Darwen took a step closer and leaned over to look in, dreading the sight of a beak and curled tentacles nestled within.

There was no sign of the Bleck. But there was no sign of anything else either. The water was clearly not really water, not to Darwen's eyes at least, but what it was, he couldn't say. It looked like mist, a pearly fog contained by the surface of the mirror pool in which vague, greenish lights pulsed, but beyond that . . .

"Take my hands," he said.

They did so, uncertainly. Rik's palm was hot and sweaty, Alex's cool and dry. Neither of them looked sure about this, and their lack of resolve deepened when they could see what Darwen could.

"There's nothing there," Rik cautioned. "It looks like cloud. What if it puts us in the treetops of some Silbrican jungle full of god knows what?"

"We've waited a long time for this," Darwen implored. "Alex?"

"Ready," she said.

"Rik?"

There was a moment of silence, then Rik slowly blew the air from his lungs. "Dang," he said. "OK."

"On three," said Darwen. "One. Two. Three."

They stepped into the pool.

Immediately, they found themselves on a mist-wreathed staircase, broad and fashioned from wrought iron, like the footbridge in a Victorian railway station, but huge, at least fifty feet wide, and rising – bizarrely – out of dense mist-wreathed jungle. The light had a curious greenish cast which seemed to come from the forest itself.

"Why are the stairs so wide when the portal is so small?" said Alex.

"The portal is just the stones and water on the other side," said Darwen. "They can be positioned anywhere, making the portal big as you like."

"These aren't just stairs. Look at that," said Rik, pointing to a huge lever. "They pivot, see? Pull that, and the stairs become a ramp."

"What for?" asked Alex.

"Let's find out," said Darwen.

They went down the stairs, and the metal steps rang beneath their feet as they descended into the stiff, wet fog that rose from the jungle floor. As they got lower, strange plants loomed out of the mist – thick, glossy leaves the size of elephant ears, pagoda towers of crimson flowers, bulging and pendulous amber fruit. The air was thick with the smell of damp earth and fragrances sweet and sour which hung in clouds around the vegetation. There was no breeze and the stifling heat of the jungle rose significantly as they reached the forest floor. The odd, green light seemed to emanate from the plants themselves. They throbbed as if they were taking long, slow breaths that set their leaves aglow. There was an electric hum that might have been machinery and might have been insects, and though there was no wind, Darwen could hear creeping movement all around.

"Whoa," said Alex. "This is even junglier than the place we just left."

Despite his rising unease, Darwen gave her a look. "*Junglier?*" he breathed.

"More jungle-y," she said, and then, shrugging at Rik. "More rainforest-y."

Rik barely smiled as he inched forward, leaning to avoid a massive blossom whose heavy, cream petals were etched with veins of a poisonous-looking purple. "There's a clearing," he said, moving so that the fog billowed around him.

Darwen and Alex followed, warily, and saw that he was right. Though crisscrossed with vines, the ground was open in a circle. There was nowhere else to go unless they forced their way into the seemingly impassable wall of shrubs, flowers and trees that surrounded them.

"So what do we do?" asked Alex, who was tip-toeing into the circle.

"Careful," said Rik. "There could be anything . . ."

But before he could get the warning out, something shot from the ground at Alex's feet. She leapt backwards and Darwen grabbed her arm, as a pair of vines about ten feet apart erupted from the earth and leapt straight up. It was like watching a time lapsed film of plants growing. The vines were thick, ropelike, trailing tendrils that twined and reached in the air like fingers looking for purchase. Great leaves sprouted and hung as the stems rose higher and leaned in towards each other, beginning to intertwine.

"Looks like muscadine," said Rik. "Wild grape."

"After you've dumped about a thousand gallons of Miracle Grow on it," said Alex.

"It's a gate," declared Darwen.

And as he said it, the two united vines throbbed and something coursed through them, running top to bottom, whereupon the arching space between them flickered with rippling turquoise energy that sparkled like a waterfall.

"OK," said Darwen, stepping closer so that he could feel the light from the portal flickering over his skin.

"Wait," said Alex. "I wanna try something."

And she began to pace the rest of the clearing's perimeter. As she walked, new vines burst from the ground, sped up, united and pulsed with the strange power of the gates. By the time she had rejoined them there were four new portals around the edge of the clearing.

"So which do we go through?" said Rik.

"How would Scarlett get the Bleck to . . . ," Darwen paused, stooping, then straightened up. "It's this one."

"Why that one?" asked Alex.

Darwen ran his hand down the side of one of the vines and showed them his fingers, which had come away black and greasy.

Pinched between his forefinger and thumb was a scrap of burned skin sprouting the remains of a coarse bristle. He studied the ground, following an imaginary path from the vine-gate to the great staircase. He hadn't seen it before, but by the throbbing, sickly light from this side he could make out the broken stems of plants in a clear and direct line. Something big had dragged itself straight across the clearing to the portal behind him.

"It went through here," he said.

They looked at each other, their faces ghastly in the pea-green glow.

"Ready?" said Darwen.

"I wish you'd stop asking that," said Alex. "No. We're not ready. Never will be. But we're going anyway, OK?"

"OK," echoed Darwen.

"Wait," said Rik. "Let me just check something." He stepped up close to the curtain of energy as if studying it, then being careful not to touch Darwen with any part of his body, he brought his right hand up to the portal and made contact.

There was flash of emerald-white light and Rik staggered back, shaking his fingers. His hair was standing on end and there was wisp of smoke that smelled faintly of electricity.

"That was smart," said Alex. "Time to hold hands with the Mirroculist, I think."

Rik nodded, his eyes wide. "Good call," he said.

They joined hands, and stepped through together.

It took less than a second for them each to wish they hadn't.

Thirty
THE WAREHOUSE

It was the sound that struck them first, a deafening blare of drills and hammers, the rumble of heavy machinery and the clang of metal. The smudged and brownish air was thick with the smells of welding torches, smoke and oil, and after the brightness of the energy curtain it took them a moment to see where they were.

Indoors, thought Darwen. *Not a jungle locus. Some kind of hangar or warehouse.*

He could feel stone flags beneath his feet. As he gaped through the murk, his eyes stung and ran, but he made out shapes in pools of feeble yellow light: great, iron hulks linked with girders and cables and studded with warning lamps, engines with riveted water tanks and tall funnels, and – strangest of all – a massive iron cage the size of a house, a cage whose bars flickered with electricity. Inside, huddled against the back wall, was the Insidious Bleck.

So his suspicion had been right. The Bleck was not acting alone. But it wasn't its own master either.

Darwen stared, and as his eyes grew accustomed to the dim light, he could see that the warehouse was packed with other items, even stranger than the now confined beast that Darwen had long thought was acting on its own volition, out of some kind of centuries-long imperative. There were statues in gold and gaudy colours, booths and tents for sideshows and fairground games, a dusty carousel with painted horses and mystic symbols lettered in enticing paint. It felt like an abandoned carnival or circus, but then something else caught his eye: a long black metal tube like a submarine but on caterpillar tracks like a tank. The tube had smoky windows.

Darwen didn't need to get up close to know that it contained child-sized seats and metal harnesses linked by wires to oversized batteries. It was a generator like the one he had destroyed in Moth's forest, and there would be children in it. But this one was on wheels, and was pointed right at the archway through which they had just come. That meant only one thing.

They – whoever they were – planned to bring it through.

That was why the iron steps up to the jungle portal became a ramp. Darwen looked around and saw massive bulldozers arranged like tanks and other pieces of machinery – including more generators – which they were still finishing.

And inside each one of them there would be children. Luis, Eduardo and Calida, for sure. Others too whose names he did not know, names they could only tell him after he had gotten them out.

But that was easier said than done, because the warehouse wasn't just full of machines. It was alive with man-sized figures in overalls, their heads hooded with what looked like grotesque, bronze-coloured gasmasks.

Scrobblers.

They were a good hundred yards away but there was no doubt in Darwen's mind: bigger and scarier than any he had seen before, several of them armed with huge, strange-looking weapons sprouting copper pipes and iron blast shields, but scrobblers all the same. Darwen watched them, and that was when he saw it. Right in the middle of all that weird carnival bric-a-brac, seated on a raised platform, was something that chilled Darwen's blood more than the scrobblers, more even than the terrible generator.

It was a glass case with what looked to be a dummy seated inside. The figure was dressed in clown clothes, and had orange hair and a little blue hat, but its staring eyes had a manic focus, and its gaping mouth was black, hollow, and lined with bright teeth.

"No," Darwen muttered.

"What?" Rik whispered.

"Just . . . don't look at it," said Darwen. "I have to get to that generator."

"But there are scrobblers everywhere!" hissed Alex.

"This is what we came for," said Darwen. "I have to."

And he took a step forward.

Instantly the mechanical clown kicked into sudden and horrible life. It lurched backward and forward, its movements jerky and unnatural, and as it did so the laughter started, full-voiced, but recorded, as if coming from long ago.

Whatever else it was, the clown's laughter was a species of alarm. The scrobblers straightened up, turning, roaring with muffled anger as they spotted Darwen, Rik and Alex.

One of them raised what looked like a cannon fixed by a metal arm to the harness it was wearing, pumped back a slide, and fired. There was a crack like thunder, a rush of smoke with a hot, flaming centre, and something shot towards them. For a fraction of a second Darwen thought madly of tentacles, before realising that it was, in fact, a tangle of steel cable and hooks: a net.

He dove to his right and the steel trap missed him by a hair's breadth. It hit Rik and Alex, throwing them back and springing closed around them. The web tightened and with a squeal of metal a winch mechanism on the scrobbler's back started to draw them towards it. Darwen caught a glimpse of Alex's face as they were pulled past him. Her eyes were wide with horror. Rik was crumpled, his eyes shut. He had been knocked unconscious by the impact.

Darwen sprang to his feet and ran after the metal net, not knowing what to do, but sure he had to help. Other scrobblers had focused on him now, and one of them fired another of the harpoon traps. It careened over his head and snapped back again as it exhausted the slack with a sound like a whip cracking. He ducked as it cannoned back towards the scrobbler, then ran forward again, swallowing down the terror that he was actually moving *towards* the enemy. One of the scrobblers, its red eyes just visible through the glass of its gas mask, had picked up a heavy wrench in its massive fists and was swinging it menacingly, the muscles of its greenish arms rippling.

Darwen took one more stride, then flung himself headlong onto the net. He seized the cables but was almost thrown off as it sped back towards the scrobbler like a retractable tape measure. Alex was squirming inside, but Rik was motionless and his eyes were still closed. Darwen scrambled for a release mechanism, but the tension of the cable pulling kept it shut tight.

"There's got to be some sort of quick-release catch!" shouted Alex over the cackling laughter of the clown. The scrobbler with the wrench had taken a long stride towards them.

Darwen looked wildly around. He had no more than ten seconds. Less if the one with the wrench decided to rush them rather than wait for the winch to do its work.

As the three of them were pulled closer, the net ploughed through cast-off cable and discarded tools. Darwen saw a metal implement and reached for it, without knowing for sure what it was till he had it: a crowbar, long and heavy with a spike at one end.

He swung it at the clasp which fastened the net to the cable, missed, and tried again. The point slid off the iron, but Darwen had put all his weight into the strike, and he couldn't stop it from slamming into the stone floor beneath. Sparks sprayed from the tip of the crowbar for a moment, and then, with a terrible keening sound, the net's progress stopped so abruptly that Darwen was thrown forward.

The crowbar had gone through the net and lodged in a gap between the uneven flag stones. The pitch of the winch shifted up a register, whining dangerously, and Darwen rolled round to see the scrobbler batting at the controls with its massive, clawed hands as smoke issued from one side. Whatever the creature was trying to do didn't work, because it pitched suddenly forward onto its face.

With the net stuck, the winch was pulling the scrobbler towards them!

Darwen got to his knees and fumbled for the clasp where the crowbar was jammed into the ground. There was a single, restraining bolt holding it to the net. He seized it and tried twisting the nut off the end but his sweaty fingers slid and it wouldn't move. The scrobbler on the end of the cable was getting closer, sliding on its back towards them as the one with the wrench gave chase.

Darwen gritted his teeth and tried again, sure his hands were bleeding, and suddenly the nut moved.

Darwen spun it off. Then he tugged at the bolt, ignoring the scrobblers who were almost on top of him now.

It came free in his hands and several things happened at once. The scrobbler which had been winched towards them stopped abruptly as the cable tore free, and the scrobbler with the wrench tripped heavily over its companion. In the same instant, the net sprang open, and Alex emerged with impossible speed.

Rik, however, did not move.

Darwen pulled at him, but the boy was too heavy, too tangled up in the trap.

"We have to go!" shouted Alex.

More scrobblers were coming from all over the great smoky, chamber. Dozens of them. One of them fired some version of the energy weapon Darwen had seen at Halloween, and a great jet like lightning tore across the room and slammed into the wall beside them like an artillery shell. There was a blaze of light so bright that for a moment Darwen couldn't see at all, could only feel Alex pulling at him. "Rik!" he shouted. "Wake up!"

But Rik didn't stir, and dimly, horribly, Darwen realised that Alex was right. He couldn't even let her go by herself. She needed him to open the portal.

The scrobbler with the wrench was back up and running. Others were only feet behind that one.

Wiping angry tears from his eyes, he muttered, "sorry" and

"I'll come back", and then he sprang to his feet, shooting one last desperate look at the generator he had not reached. He ran back the way they had come, snatching at Alex's hand as he did so, the clown's laughter still ringing in his ears.

They crashed through the curtain of energy which led back to the jungle clearing, and Darwen stumbled in his haste. Alex's hand slipped from his just as they came through and she tore across the circle on the other side, falling straight into one of the other vine-framed portals, despite her attempts to stop herself. Darwen saw the arch in front of her, saw the flickering wall of light and waited for her shout of pain as she bounced off.

But she made no sound. And instead of being thrown back as Rik had, she rolled right through. The flickering curtain closed behind her, and Darwen could only stare in disbelief.

What on earth . . .?

He stood up. Should he go after her or abandon her as he had abandoned Rik? The scrobblers would be following. He had no time to decide . . .

And then she was back, standing in the gateway looking astonished and scared. "Pouncels," she said. "Lots of them. Go!"

They ran along the path from the clearing and onto the wrought-iron staircase. As they reached it, they heard the crackle of a portal opening behind them and the scrobbler with the wrench came barrelling out into the green-lit jungle.

"Go!" shouted Alex again.

The scrobbler turned its terrible, gas-masked face and came after them.

Darwen ran up the stairs two at a time, reaching behind for Alex as he got to the top. She didn't wait to take his hand, however, and went straight through the portal. He followed, horror and confusion and panic fighting inside his head for predominance, and then he was out in the clammy night air of Caño Island again.

Darwen stopped, all the terrible things that had happened breaking over him.

He had failed to get Luis. And they had left Rik behind.

"Darwen!" Alex screamed.

A gas mask was coming up through the portal. For a moment Darwen could see its hateful red eyes through the glass, the green-tinged skin and yellowing tusks beneath the brass and leather, but he felt frozen, like he had left half of himself there on the other side of the mirror back in the warehouse with Rik.

"Darwen!" Alex again shrieked.

And that was all it took.

Darwen came to life again, kicking the stone spheres out of position. There was a flicker, and a pop. The scrobbler dropped out of sight, and the portal became dark, leaf-strewn earth once more.

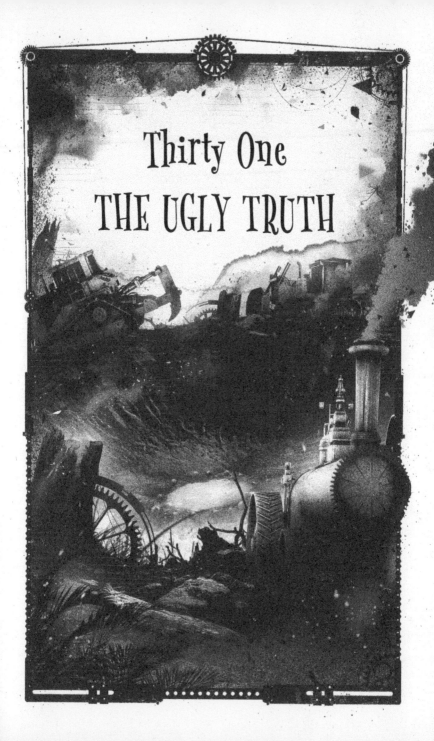

Thirty One
THE UGLY TRUTH

The boat arrived for them shortly after dawn. The official word was that Rik had gotten lost in the storm, so while Darwen and Alex were ferried back to the mainland with a stunned Mr. Iverson and a taciturn Jorge to be fed and their wounds tended, a team of three local people who knew the rainforest best, would comb the island for him. The journey back was spent in absolute silence, a silence Darwen did not break till he found Mr. Peregrine in his odd-smelling tent. "They took him," he said in a flat, hollow voice. "The scrobblers took Rik."

"Scrobblers?" said Mr. Peregrine, his teacup poised at his lips, his injured hand still bandaged. "Are you sure?"

"We saw them," said Alex, coming up behind Darwen "They nearly got us too."

"We had no choice," Darwen added, desolate but determined to explain this above all. "We had to leave him. But we're going back. We just need to figure out how . . ." He had not discussed this with Alex, but he knew he didn't need to.

She just nodded, her face defiant.

"Scrobblers?" Mr. Peregrine repeated.

"And you know who they work for," said Alex.

"Well, historically . . ." Mr. Peregrine began, but Darwen cut him off.

"Greyling," said Darwen. He said it without bitterness, without triumph, but he gave Mr. Peregrine a long, frank look, until the teacher finally sat back.

"Greyling?" said Mr. Peregrine, incredulous. "Greyling was defeated. This has nothing to do with . . ."

"It does," said Darwen. "I saw the generators. It's him."

"Did you see him?" asked Mr. Peregrine.

Darwen shook his head, but at that moment they heard people on the track to the village: two local adults and their three small children loaded with bags going down to the beach. Scarlett had bought off another family.

"That's not all," said Darwen. "Gabriel marooned us on that island on purpose. Possibly with Jorge's help. We were supposed to be taken by the Bleck."

"Whatever is taking the children is just an animal," said Mr. Peregrine, smiling. "It's not working with anyone. I realise that you have had a terrible ordeal, but . . ."

"No," said Darwen, his eyes full of fire. "You don't. You weren't there. You didn't see. That's why I'm telling you." He paused, then continued more stoically, determined to get his point across. "You were right that it's not the Bleck that's primarily responsible. For all the rumours, it appears to be what you say it is – an animal. But there's a kind of portal junction which connects several Silbrican jungle locuses, and, with Scarlett's help, Greyling is using it to send the Bleck through to kidnap children. It doesn't eat them. It takes them and they go into the generator." Darwen gave Mr. Peregrine a half second to let all of it sink in. "Once Greyling's figured out how to get machinery through the portals, they're going to bring the generators through. They will then have a power source in our world. Rik . . ." his voice fractured, and he had to clear his throat before continuing, "is probably already inside."

"And the pouncels?" asked Mr. Peregrine, his expression still guarded.

"They're irrelevant," answered Darwen automatically. "I think they're getting into our world by accident."

Mr. Peregrine stared at him for a long moment, then put his cup down and got to his feet.

"Oh, and I opened a portal," said Alex. "By myself. Not much of an upside, I'll grant you, but still. Kind of cool."

"You did what?" said Mr. Peregrine, staring at her.

"Opened a portal," said Alex. "Without touching Darwen or nothing. Fell right through it into this weird-looking jungle where about twenty pouncels were hanging out. Got the heck out of there faster than green grass through a goose."

"But how . . . ?" said Mr. Peregrine.

"Don't ask me," said Alex. "Guess the world now has two Mirroculists. Count 'em, see?"

She pointed first at Darwen and then at herself.

"Maybe it's like an upgrade," she said. "If you spend a lot of time nearly getting killed over there, they let you in and out all by your lonesome."

More than anything they had told him, more even than Rik's capture, this seemed to arrest Mr. Peregrine's attention.

Darwen was annoyed. "I'm telling you all this so you can help me when I go back," he said.

"I need to . . . ," Mr. Peregrine began, but he still seemed preoccupied, and was regarding Alex with a peculiar intensity. "I'll catch up with you later," he said, walking briskly off the platform and up towards the dining shelter.

"O . . . .K . . ." said Alex, as she watched him go. "You ever get the feeling someone's not telling us everything?"

"How about *anything*?" said Darwen.

"I can smell smoke," said Alex. "Why can I smell smoke?"

Darwen turned toward the dining shelter and saw an unwelcome figure in crisp khakis and a safari shirt on the path.

"There you are, Arkwright," said Mr. Sumners. "Lessons have begun. I suggest you bring your notebooks and pens."

Darwen stared at him. "Lessons?" he said. "Now?"

"Life at Hillside goes on," said the maths teacher.

"We're not at Hillside," said Alex. "We're in the jungle and one of our friends is missing."

"Hillside Academy," said Mr. Sumners drawing himself up, "is a state of mind. We ahhhh take it wherever we go. It is our guide, our compass and our mode of being, all of which makes this," he gestured at the trees around them, "a school, not a holiday resort. As for Mr. Haggerty, I am confident the locals will find him. It's not that large an island. Now, time for class."

He walked away, and Darwen, suddenly flooded with rage, took a step after him.

"Whoa there, tiger," said Alex, staying him with a hand. "We've got bigger fish to fry. Sumners is an insufferable loser but the chances of him strapping us into a machine that drains our life force to power his microwave are slim. Let's stay focused, yeah?"

Darwen couldn't argue with that. "We need to get ready," he said, pulling himself together. "We need a plan, and a weapon."

"I'm thinking bows and arrows plus a vat of coffee creamer aren't gonna cut it," said Alex.

"Agreed," said Darwen. "But if Mr. P has a Silbrican rocket launcher in his tent, he hasn't mentioned it."

"Judging by the smell, I'd say he's more likely to be hoarding some very old cheese," said Alex. "And even if he had a weapon, I'm not convinced he'd give it to us."

"What do you mean?"

"Well, he's not exactly helped out a lot so far, has he?"

"He's the one who brought us here in the first place," said Darwen, looking away. "His mirror showed me Luis being abducted."

"That was handy, wasn't it?"

"What do you mean…?" Darwen faltered. There was something in Alex's eyes that he hadn't seen before, soeme terrible thought that she couldn't put into words. "What?"

"Don't freak out on me, OK?" she said, her voice lowering. "But, have you considered the possibility that Mr. Peregrine isn't being honest with us?"

"He's made some mistakes," admitted Darwen.

"What if they weren't mistakes?" Alex said.

Darwen stared at her, and for a moment everything around them, the cries of birds and monkeys, the wash of the ocean, the distant chatter of students, all went away. "What are you saying?" he said.

He couldn't explain it, but something cold and terrible was welling up inside him, something worse than fear, and it brought tears to his eyes.

"We came here," said Alex, staring at the ground, "because Mr. P brought us. Then his portable portal took us to the very worst place possible and we were lucky to get back alive."

"He said it malfunctioned . . ."

"And you didn't believe him," she interrupted. "You thought it had been tampered with, that it was a trap to get us killed. What if it was? What if it was him who set it?"

Darwen turned away, his eyes swimming. "I know he's been skeptical," he said, unsure why he was trying to defend Mr. Peregrine. Alex was saying no more than he had begun to think himself. She was just pushing it further. "But he sent the oven door that took me to Weazen."

"You don't even know that for sure," she said. "It was mailed to you. The one useful thing you've been given might not have come from him. Darwen, from day one you've told him that the kids were being taken by the Insidious Bleck, and from day one he said that it didn't exist. We've seen it. You say Scarlett is controlling the Bleck and he says she's not. Turns out, she is. You say she's working for Greyling, he says she's not. I think you're right. So either he doesn't know what he's talking about, or he's lying."

Darwen stared straight ahead, refusing to accept Alex's explanation.

She continued, her voice softer this time though no less commanding. "We escaped the Bleck. If we had relied on him, we'd be dead. Again."

"So he made a mistake . . ."

"What if he didn't? What if he's working for . . .?"

"NO!" shouted Darwen again, his hands coming up to his ears as if he could blot out her challenge, stop it from giving fire to all his own smoldering doubts. "He wouldn't. He's my friend . . . My . . ."

Darwen's blood roared in his ears but he kept his fists clenched to his sides.

"He's not," said Alex. "I know you want him to be, but he's not. And you are going to have to think real hard about how much he's helping, because if you just trust him blindly . . . I don't know. I see badness ahead."

"Why would he send us into a trap?" said Darwen, quietly, as if his own voice was afraid of admitting the possibility. All of a sudden he remembered the blood he had seen on the note attached to the oven door.

"You're the Mirroculist, Darwen, remember? You are what Greyling fears most: a person who can see right into what he's doing and can come in and stop him. You are the target. Rik and I are just . . . bystanders."

"Not if you're a Mirroculist too," he replied.

"Don't think that hasn't occurred to me," she said.

"And they already have Rik," said Darwen, squeezing his eyes shut. "It's my fault. I have to . . ."

He started to walk.

"Where are you going?"

"To find Mr. Peregrine," said Darwen, not looking back.

"And do what?"

"I'm going to ask him which side he's on," said Darwen, still pressing forward.

"Oh, that's genius," said Alex, running up behind him. "Masterful spy work there. Ask him which side he's on, because if he wants us dead he's really gonna just tell you the truth."

"You have a better plan?"

"That's not a plan."

"A better idea, then," he said, turning to glower at her.

"Well, for one thing," she said, "I'm coming with you."

Darwen shrugged, and together they marched up the path towards the dining shelter. They were almost there when they realised something was going on. The quiet of the lesson had been broken by the sounds of voices and shifting benches. By the time Darwen and Alex could see properly, the students were streaming up past the washrooms and onto the trail into the jungle. There were teachers and camp workers with them, several of them running.

Darwen and Alex gave chase, conscious that the tang of woodsmoke in the air was getting stronger. The group moved on through the trees, all the way up to where the end of the zip line was fixed to the final tower. It was immediately clear what had attracted the attention, and Darwen could only stare in amazement.

A huge circle at least fifty yards across had been cleared out of the jungle. Monumental trees had been pushed over, torched in pyres around the rim and the underbrush scraped clean right down to the dirt. In the centre was a ring of stone spheres and a shallow pool. Around the edge were bright yellow bulldozers marked with the logo of Sunbelt Vacation Properties.

The babble of excitement died as soon as the students saw what had happened. The forest which had breathed and called and pulsed with life, was dead, ravaged and smoking. The silence was appalling and Darwen saw that even the teachers looked stunned and uncertain. Miss Martinez was sobbing quietly.

"Three cheers for progress!" shouted Nathan Cloten. "Hip, hip, hooray!"

Barry Fails joined in, but no one else did, and Naia Petrakis turned such a fierce look on them that they stopped, smirking.

Standing beside one of the yellow bulldozers, Mr. Peregrine and Jorge were talking earnestly. Darwen looked into the water at the edge of the circle and saw only his reflection, but there was no question that this was a portal. All that was needed was for the sun to come down, and then it would come online.

He left Alex, pushing his way through the crowd, but Jorge saw him coming.

"Stay back," Jorge ordered. "It is very dangerous here. Everyone needs to go back to the camp. Señor Delgado!" he called and the man from the village pushed his way through the crowd. He was carrying a rifle and there were other villagers with him, all armed. They stood around the circle of observers like guards, their backs to the devastation in the centre. "No one is to come in this area."

Jorge turned and started walking out of the blasted clearing, Mr. Peregrine at his side. Darwen was about to head them off when a hand caught at his elbow. It was Alex.

"What?" he said.

"It's not just this," said Alex, and her eyes were shiny. "It's worse."

"What do you mean?" Darwen asked. "What's happened?"

"Two more kids have been taken," she said. "Gabriel and Chip." Darwen stared at her.

"Are you sure?" he asked. "Gabriel? But he was working with Jorge! And Chip Whittley?"

She nodded.

Darwen marched towards Mr. Peregrine and Jorge so forcefully that both men stopped.

"What are you going to do?" he demanded. "To get them back. Rik and Gabriel. And Chip. What are you going to do?"

"I don't know what you mean . . ." Jorge began.

"Yes, you do," said Darwen. "You know all about it. So do you," he added to Mr. Peregrine, "and so does Gabriel who marooned us on the island for the Insidious Bleck."

Jorge opened his mouth to say something, but changed his mind. Instead, he looked at Mr. Peregrine, who sighed. "We should probably talk," he said.

"In the office then," said Jorge, who looked irritated. "Now get these people away from here."

As the students were corralled and led complaining back to the dining shelter, Darwen and Alex slipped into the office by the kitchen and waited. Barry Fails saw them, but he just assumed they were in trouble and made faces. Mr. Sumners saw them, but his protests were cut off by Mr. Peregrine. Mr. Iverson saw them, and his eyes tightened with puzzlement and suspicion.

Darwen and Alex ignored them all, waiting.

At last Mr. Peregrine and Jorge entered the wooden structure together and closed the door behind them. Jorge's eyes flicked to Mr. Peregrine, who just nodded.

"I am an emissary from the Guardian Council of Silbrica," said Jorge. "I was assigned to this territory a year ago and am the ranking official in matters concerning this region."

Darwen looked at Mr. Peregrine, but the old man was silent, his eyes downcast and his face sombre. Whatever they were about to be told was not good news.

"You were brought here to find tears in the fabric of the barriers between worlds," Jorge continued. "You have failed in that task and your mission is at an end. I suggest you rejoin your classmates . . ."

"What?" sputtered Darwen. "We did find them, and they're not tears, they're portals. People make them! There's one back there behind the camp!"

"That is all I am at liberty to say," said Jorge.

Mr. Peregrine coughed quietly and, when Jorge looked at him, nodded slowly once more.

"Very well," said Jorge. "The creature who calls herself Scarlett Oppertune has made an offer to the council through me. We, the camp and the villagers, are to leave this place for her development. The council has agreed to her terms."

Darwen's jaw dropped open. "You can't be serious!" he exclaimed.

"If we stay," Jorge said, "more children will be taken. The Oppertune creature has plans . . ."

"Greyling," said Darwen. "She works for Greyling."

"Greyling?" Jorge repeated, eyebrows raised. "No," he continued, shaking his head. "The situation is bad but there is no reason to think . . ."

"Scarlett is Miss Murray," said Darwen. "I'm almost sure of it. I saw Scarlett transform and inside she looks exactly like the eel-thing that came out of Miss Murray. Let's not forget that she worked for Greyling last year. That's why she has a scrobbler army and generators . . ."

"No," said Jorge, the half-smile was gone now, and the look he shot Mr. Peregrine was impatient. "You should not encourage such fantasies, Octavius," he said. "I have told you this before. We already have two real problems. Let's not invent a third."

"Two problems?" asked Alex.

"I mean that things are bad enough with this Bleck creature loose and Miss Murray's demands without imagining that Greyling himself is somehow involved."

Darwen couldn't believe what he was hearing. "You don't have two problems," he said. "You don't even have three. You have one. Scarlett and the Bleck and Greyling are working together! The Bleck creature isn't loose at all: it's in a cage, sent out specifically to take kids and bring them back for Greyling's generators."

"Nonsense," Jorge reposted. "Miss Oppertune intends to establish a place for herself here. We have decided that we cannot fight her without considerable loss, and the council feels that if a portion of the world has to be given over to her, it is better that it is a place like this rather than . . ."

"Somewhere closer to home," Alex cut in. "Somewhere with richer people in it."

"It is not an ideal situation," said Jorge. "We have to make the best of a bad predicament. You will all be going back to Hillside tomorrow anyway . . ."

"And you get what in return?" Darwen demanded.

"Scarlett will sign a treaty promising not to expand from this area," said Jorge.

Alex gave a caustic bark of laughter. "And you buy that?" she said. "Boy, you are cute, but you're dumb. This is just wrong."

"We have no reason to think . . ." Jorge began.

Darwen cut him off, his voice cold and hard as steel. "She's right," he said. "You're dumb. Scarlett wants this area because it's dotted with those stone spheres which she can use to open up portals anywhere she likes. All she has to do is collect them up, put them in whatever place she wants, whatever country she wants, add water and invade. She's going to build a base here for her master, and then he's going to go wherever he feels like going and you won't be able to stop him."

"Miss Oppertune is a businesswoman," said Jorge. "We will be able to make a fair deal with her."

"She puts children in Greyling's machines," Darwen exclaimed. "She takes them from their families and drains them, and you think you can *deal* with her?"

"You are confusing separate problems," said Jorge. "And imagining others. The Council knows nothing of these generators you speak of."

"We've seen them," Darwen insisted.

"We have only your word for that," said Jorge. He seemed slightly embarrassed to have to call Darwen a liar to his face, but clearly thought they could dance around it no longer.

There was a moment's silence.

"Mr. P?" Alex demanded. "You go along with this?"

"I serve the council, of course," observed Mr. Peregrine. "But . . ."

"Hold it," said Jorge. "You don't want to say anything else."

"Let him speak," said Darwen. "It's time he told us the truth."

Mr. Peregrine considered him and Darwen thought he saw a flash of something in his eyes that was almost a smile. A fat, black fly had settled on his cheek just below his left eye, but he didn't seem to notice. "Truth," he said, musing. "Very well. I think that you, Darwen Arkwright, do not need the Guardian Council. I think they know that and are afraid. I think that you should open the portal behind the campsite . . ."

"Now wait a minute," sputtered Jorge.

"Open the portal," Mr. Peregrine persisted, "and see for yourself."

The old man's manner was quite different. His eyes were full of a strange intensity and the flicker of a smile was now unmistakable. Still, though, his body hadn't moved a muscle and the fly on his face was still there.

"Octavius," said Jorge to Mr. Peregrine, fuming, "we have known each other a long time, but you leave me no choice. I am relieving you of your authority."

"Which was to be expected," said Mr. Peregrine, finally moving so that the fly was dislodged and flew buzzing around the office. "The Guardians never did tolerate opposing positions very well."

"Come on, Alex," said Darwen. "I guess we'll have to stop him by ourselves."

"Darwen I understand your feelings . . ." said Jorge.

"You understand nothing," said Darwen, turning on him savagely. "You believe in nothing."

"If you interfere with the Guardians' wishes," said Jorge, "we will have to stop you."

"Yeah, pretty boy?" said Alex, stepping so close to where Jorge was sitting that her face was inches from his. "Bring it on."

Thirty Two

RISKY

MOVES

Darwen and Alex had left the office full of defiance and determination. Five hours later, their plans and preparations made, that had not changed.

"You OK?" Darwen asked Alex.

"I think so."

"We have a little over an hour till sunset," said Darwen. "I think you should go."

She nodded, but still looked uncertain.

"What if I can't...?"

"You'll be fine," he said. "I trust you."

"Great," she frowned. "No pressure."

Darwen grinned and watched her leave, before setting off on his own. She was making for the houses by the football field; he was heading into the jungle again.

Though the sky over the ocean was painted with the soft blue and gold of twilight, the forest itself was getting dark fast. Since Darwen had decided that he couldn't stick to the path all the way for fear of being seen, he had to pick his way through the trees, studying the leaves at his feet for signs of movement. No one had seen a bushmaster or fer-de-lance so far, and he prayed he wouldn't be the first, particularly not out here by himself in the gathering gloom. He tried not to think about the wandering pouncels.

It took him over half an hour to complete the journey, which was odd because he knew he would soon be covering the exact same distance in a matter of seconds. At one point he had pushed a little too far north and had only caught himself when he saw the

401

trees thinning suddenly: it was the clearing. He waited, conscious of a man – Mr. Delgado, he thought – pacing the perimeter with his rifle. Again, Darwen crept west. He didn't swing back north till he knew he was well past the circle of yellow bulldozers.

How could anyone not be outraged?

Perhaps, as Rik said, they just didn't care. Hillside looked after its own, and the people who lived here – worthy though they were of the kind of study you would apply to Latin or algebra – were anything but. For the students this was a trip into a different world. It might be a kind of theme park erected for their amusement, but as a place where people lived it was no more real to them than Blackpool Pleasure Beach.

For a moment the image of the clown face came into Darwen's mind and he heard its cycling laughter, but he pushed the memory away.

Even in daylight it would be hard to navigate through this part of the jungle. To the north and east the ground rose steeply, but down here Darwen could see nothing beyond the trees surrounding him. Only when there was a gap in the canopy could he correct his course based on the metal cable high above the treetops, and as the light dropped still further he would lose even that.

He checked his watch and picked up the pace.

The woods hummed with the chirp of insects, and once Darwen spotted a brilliant yellow and black frog, bright as plastic, sitting on a leaf. He kept his distance, knowing it was poisonous. Once, he heard movement off in the undergrowth to his right and saw bushes shift as the creature – pig, coati, deer or something predatory like a mountain lion? – moved off. He was still watching for the animal when he realised he had found what he was looking for.

It was, simply, a tree. A big one that lanced up into the canopy like the mast of a ship. It was twined with ancient vines thick as Darwen's waist. These had grown into the bark as they spiralled up and at various heights on the trunk, steel cables had been bolted into place. Spikes were set into the tree all the way up: a kind of ladder.

Darwen took a long look up, wiped the sweat from his brow, and started to climb.

It was slow, precarious going and by the time he reached the planked platform, the sun was down entirely. He moved cautiously, feeling his way around, and clinging to the vast trunk. It was so dark that it hardly made a difference, but he kept his eyes focused on the tree itself, not turning outwards till he felt absolutely secure.

He was at least a hundred feet up, gazing out over the dark jungle canopy. The zip line's twined steel cable ran up to the northwest and down, back over that distant clearing with its yellow bulldozers, to the camp. From here he could barely make out the space where the trees had been cut. It seemed very far below and miles away, though he knew he would cover the distance in under a minute once he got moving.

From his backpack he fished out a harness which he had taken from the office that afternoon and stood on tiptoes to hook it over the cable. He was struggling with it when a whir of movement and a volley of sound exploded inches above his head. He jumped, lost his balance, and stumbled towards the edge of the platform, as the toucan – fortunately, that's all that it was – rocketed into the dusk. He caught himself, but the harness slipped, hung mesmerisingly on a stray branch, then fell all the way to the bottom.

Darwen swore, then checked his watch. Perhaps he would have time to climb back down . . .

Darwen barely completed the thought when a flicker, like lightning, flashed up from the forest floor in the distance behind the camp. He watched it change to a soft radiant glow, circular, in the middle of the clearing.

It was now or never. There was certainly no time to make a perilous climb back down the tree for the harness.

Fumbling with the dread of what he was about to do, Darwen unthreaded the belt from his pants and reached up. He looped the belt over the cable twice, threaded the end through the buckle, and twined what was left around his wrist. He tried a little jump to see if it would take his weight, and the belt slid a few inches down the zip line, leading Darwen to drop his feet to the platform in panic.

His hands and face were sweating. He could feel its cold trickle down his back, soaking his shirt. He felt the air beneath him stir and was reminded of just how far he had to fall, how much danger awaited him even if he succeeded.

He gritted his teeth, stepped out off the platform and into nothing.

He shot down the zip line, the wind rushing against his face, and almost immediately he could feel the leather of the belt getting hot. He tried to adjust it, but his weight was too great. He was also picking up speed.

He took his eyes off the belt, which he thought had started to smoke, and realised just how quickly he was going. Ahead and below, he could make out the clearing, lit by the soft glow of the portal. And then he saw a flash and a fraction later, heard the crack of a rifle from the trees below.

They had seen him.

He pulled his legs up, feeling the heat in the leather starting to burn his fingers, and looked down. The pool gazed up at him like an eye. He was still forty feet above it, but it had to be . . .

Now.

He untwisted the belt from his wrist, held for one last second, then let go.

He fell like a stone, pointing with his feet, hoping against hope that he would hit the target and not the ground that would surely kill him. He dropped through the darkness, heard the singing path of another bullet speeding past him and then entered the pearly glow of the portal.

There was no splash. There was only the sudden dazzling flare of energy, blinding him completely for a second, and then only chaos and pain.

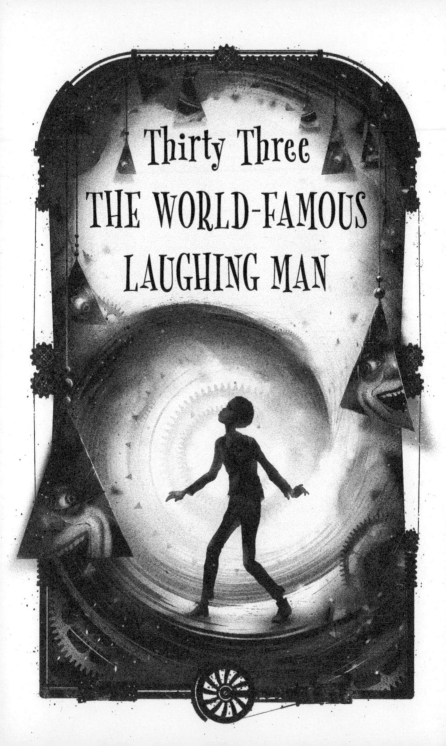

Thirty Three

THE WORLD-FAMOUS LAUGHING MAN

It took a second for Darwen to realise what had happened. He had expected the shock in his legs and knees, but the shot to his right arm and forehead took him so completely by surprise that he almost blacked out. He opened his eyes, his head swimming, but he was still moving, falling, rolling down the wrought-iron stairs from the portal into the thick greenish fog of the jungle locus. He was holding something large and padded, like an oddly-shaped leather couch that was falling with him, and it was that object that was protecting him from the hard, metal edges of the steps. He had reached the bottom before he realised that the couch was actually nothing of the kind.

It was a massive toad. Or very nearly. It was like a toad, its skin warty and brownish, its eyes huge and bulging, its mouth wide and flat, but it was also like a scrobbler. It had paws like hands with long, horny nails, and it was longer than a toad so that it might stand upright. It also wore fragments of armour and equipment.

It hit the ground with a thud, and rolled onto its back. For a moment Darwen lay on top of it, staring into the blank eyes of the appalling creature he had landed on. Then he was scrambling off, terrified and staring, but the monster didn't move, and its huge brown fists were open. The collision had knocked it out.

Darwen looked hastily round. It seemed like this was the lone guard. The jungle clearing with its vine-framed portals looked exactly as it had when he had seen it last.

Darwen's eyes returned to the prone toad-man. It was wearing what looked like pieces of stained chain mail looped across its chest and round its long, powerful limbs, and its head was half-covered by a leather helmet to which metal plates had been fastened. It wore an oversized backpack covered in dials and switches, all sparking ominously, which seemed to disappear into the creature's neck somehow. Darwen nudged the helmet with his foot and it moved enough to show that the tubes from the backpack fitted through brass valves right into the monster's throat. Darwen shuddered. With an effort he lifted one of the beast's massive muscular arms and revealed a belt holster. He peered again into its face to ensure those dreadful bulbous, eyes were still blank, then unfastened the holster's flap and drew out a kind of pistol.

It was so heavy it would take both hands to aim and fire, and it wasn't quite like any gun Darwen had ever seen before, with its brass barrel and the curious bulb of blue glass which stuck out just beside the heavy trigger.

He considered shoving it down the back of his jeans, but decided that this was a pretty good way of accidentally blowing his legs off. He held it in front of him instead, and crossed over to the portal he had entered with Alex and Rik, but left only with Alex.

He knew what was inside, knew also that if he was spotted right away he was as good as dead, gun or no gun, but he thought again of his friends, of Luis, the boy he had seen in the grip of the Bleck weeks ago, and of that awful generator which was to roll into his own world. He had no choice.

He took a deep breath and stepped through.

Things had changed since Darwen's last visit to the warehouse locus. What had been dark and smoky was now full of hard, brittle light, and the air pulsed with the swirling, wheezy music of a carnival organ. The wheeled generator had been swung around and shunted up to the very archway by a huge, armoured bulldozer covered in pipes and gears, which made the Sunbelt Vacation machines look like toys. As soon as Darwen stepped in he was up against it. This was a stroke of luck, as it meant he didn't have to try to cross the vast warehouse unseen. Before the generator had been bare and cold, black iron, but now it was roughly painted in candy-stripe red and white like a circus tent. He ducked behind one of the great sets of wheels and looked for an entrance hatch.

Lights glowed dimly along the generator's length, and Darwen guessed that the cables which trailed from it were powering everything in the warehouse even as they prepared to unhook it for the short journey fifty feet up through the portal and into the jungle clearing a world away. Darwen didn't need to look through the portholes in the side to know where that power was coming from, but he was also sure that they couldn't get it through the gate. He didn't know why, but the scrobbler machines stopped working when taken through the stone sphere portals. That was why Scarlett was using a living being like the Bleck, and it meant that he still had time.

He peered through a gap in the caterpillar tracks and saw that the rest of the great chamber was pulsing with activity. There were the awful, headless gnashers bounding about on their knuckles, dragging spools of cable and machine parts, their shark-mouths gaping across their chests like savage gashes. There were scrobblers with tools and weapons, their gasmasks slapped with bright paint so that they all had leering, rigid clown faces. There were more of the ugly toad-men, some squatting, their heads low, others making slow, grotesque hops around the machinery, their warty skin like under-filled leather sacks. They all wore the control-studded backpacks, all wired directly into their throats. All the way at the back there was the Insidious Bleck, pulsing slowly in its cage, watched warily by a handful of scrobblers with energy weapons. If any of them spotted him, he was dead. Simple as that.

Cluttering the floor were discarded sideshow booths and fun fair rides. He could see a long counter with air rifles fastened to it and a mechanical parade of rubber duck targets. There were the cup-like seats from a luminous green Waltzer studded with oversized light bulbs, red bumper cars stacked up with their rod-like antenna, and the lurid entrance sign for a ghost train, hung with fake cobweb. Above them all, its back turned toward Darwen and sitting dark, still and silent in his glass box was the World-Famous Laughing Man.

Darwen tore his eyes away and scanned the room for Greyling whom he had seen last year as a glowing, silvery man in a hooded cloak. There was no sign of him, and only one figure truly stood out: a glamorous woman in a carefully-tailored suit of shocking pink. Scarlett Oppertune. She, it seemed, was in charge.

Darwen watched her pointing and ordering, sending the gnashers and scrobblers scrambling to do her bidding, and a deep anger welled up inside him. This was all her doing, the abandoned village, the shattered jungle, the kidnapped children, and whatever her master, Greyling, planned to do once he had his base established.

Darwen had to force himself to return his focus to the generator. Before anything else happened, he had to get the children out. He had been searching for Luis for weeks, for Eduardo and Calida, and now for Rik . . .

But how?

The underside of the machine was like a great iron pipe which had been bolted together in sections. Each nut was the size of Darwen's fist. No way in there.

He crept out, keeping the hulking torpedo shape of the generator between him and the scrobbler army and its high-heeled general. He climbed onto the tracked wheels and then up onto the generator itself. There were portholes along the side, and through them a yellowish radiance streamed out. Reluctantly, Darwen looked in.

There were ten seats, eight of them already occupied. He saw Calida, Luis, and other local children whose faces he didn't recognise, all strapped in place, with metal headpieces wired into the generator's circuitry. At the far end was Chip, slumped over as if asleep, and beside him . . .

"Rik," Darwen breathed.

From here it was impossible to say how many of the children were still alive.

There was one way in: a hatch with a red-painted wheel like an air lock. Darwen set down the heavy pistol, got hold of the wheel and tried to turn it first one way, then the other, but it wouldn't move. He strained, sweating, till he thought his muscles would tear from his bones, but the wheel wouldn't budge.

He sank back, gasping, and in his exhaustion he failed to notice the pistol which had been balanced precariously on a ledge behind him. He nudged it, saw – as if in slow motion – as it wobbled and fell, swung his hand to catch it, and only succeeded in losing his balance. He slipped off the generator, hitting the ground hard, no more than a second after the pistol had clattered its way down among the valves and pipes.

And then the laughter started. It seemed to come from all around, the same cycling roar of hysteria, and over in the centre of the warehouse, Darwen could see the mechanical clown turning towards him and rocking in his chair.

They had seen him.

Darwen hurled himself to the ground as the first uneven salvo of energy weapon fire came streaking towards him. It lit the air like lightning, cannoning off the iron apparatus around him with showers of sparks. Somewhere at his back, a valve burst and steam rushed out in a hot and angry hiss.

Scarlett Oppertune spun towards him, her face a mask of fury. She bellowed her orders to the scrobblers. "Don't shoot at him, you idiots! You'll damage the equipment. Bring him to me."

As the hulking figures started their ponderous advance – joined by one of the monstrous toad-creatures, the elbows of its forelegs splayed out as it lumbered forward – Darwen made a choice.

He knew he couldn't get the generator hatch open by himself. He dropped to his knees, reaching under the pipes and dusty cables, fingers straining, searching. The nearest scrobbler was only ten yards away, and there was a gnasher loping in his shadow, its shark mouth gaping. Darwen felt something hard, snatched at it and came up with the pistol in his hands. He aimed and pulled the trigger.

For a moment, nothing happened, then Scarlett began to laugh, a low, throaty chuckle of real amusement.

The scrobbler, which had hesitated, came on again, quicker now. The toad was coming too, and much faster than Darwen had thought possible. It opened that massive horizontal slash of a mouth and Darwen suddenly knew how it would catch him.

Its tongue . . .

He stared at the gun. Maybe it had broken when it fell, or wasn't loaded or . . . wasn't turned on! There was a switch just above the trigger guard. He flicked it over and the glass bulb on the side glowed blue and steady, the whole pistol shivering in his grasp. The energy throbbed inside it and the weapon become distinctly live, hovering, shifting, as if eager to find a target. It took all Darwen's strength to keep it pointed in front of him. Once again, this time, wincing away from it as he did so, he squeezed the trigger.

The pistol leapt in his hands. What came out of the end was not like a bullet at all. Instead a stream of blue-white force shot from the end and held like a rope for as long as he held the trigger. It wasn't tight and hard like a laser, but wandered and sparked erratically, so that the scrobbler had to sprawl a good ten feet out of its line of fire to be safe. The toad-creature behind wasn't so fortunate. It strayed into the energy stream and was blown backwards off its feet. When it hit the ground, it lay motionless and smoking, its tongue lolling.

Darwen released the trigger, scared of the power he had unleashed, but confident that he had created a useful standoff. Scarlett, who wasn't laughing anymore, had retreated behind a massive Egyptian sarcophagus with a gold, death mask, and the scrobblers were lumbering into cover all around the warehouse. Only the blind gnashers seemed uncertain, stock-still and testing the charged air with their probing tongues, as the laughter of the mechanical clown rose in pitch and volume, drowning out the carnival music. Darwen had bought himself valuable seconds.

But to do what? He couldn't use the pistol to open the generator without killing everyone inside, and though the gun was still humming, it was less than it had been. He wouldn't get many more shots like that out of it. His eyes flashed desperately around the warehouse with its gleaming side shows and carousel animals. The scrobblers were starting to inch towards him again. A voice came from the great gold sarcophagus: Scarlett.

"Well, now Mr. Arkwright," she said. "We've been expecting you. So nice to see you again. Well, not really, but we must observe the pleasantries. As I recall, you made life rather difficult for me back in Atlanta when you knew me as Miss Murray. I won't be permitting anything like that tonight. So, while you have made quite an entrance, I'm afraid it won't improve the manner of your exit. But you have my attention. So let's see if we can come to some kind of agreement that might help you avoid any unpleasantness."

Darwen looked up. *Some kind of agreement?*

"I mean," she continued, "we can do it by the book: you sit there shooting till your weapon runs out of energy, and then my trusty agents gather you up and feed you into the generator or," she paused, savouring the possibility, "we can try something different."

"Like what?" Darwen shouted back, stalling.

"Okeydoke," she said, suddenly chipper, "well how about this? How about you kick your little gun over to one of my gas-masked friends, and I'll get you a milkshake – chocolate, of course – and we can have a little chat about some alternative futures."

Milkshake?

"Like I'd trust you!" Darwen shouted back. "You'd kill me as soon as you had the chance."

"Trust?" she laughed. "Who's talking about trust? I may have been a teacher but I'm also a businesswoman. I wouldn't expect you to take my offer without a decent incentive. Lay down your weapon, walk away from the generator, and we'll talk. I could certainly make it worth your while."

"Meaning what?" said Darwen.

"Meaning that the New Council might make room for the Mirroculist," she said, her voice silky now. "You've been confused, that's all. Learn to see things from our perspective and oh, Darwen! What wonders will be open to you."

New Council? Darwen thought. But that's not what he said aloud. "Wonders?" he echoed, lowering the pistol a little in his hands.

"All the marvels of Silbrica," she purred. "Not the few tame locuses your friend Mr. Peregrine has shown you, but whole worlds beyond your imagination! Stand with us and you will be able to stride between them all without so much as a thought, and with them will come power! It must be so tiresome, all your potential wasted on the petty doings of school and homework and bullies, trudging from place to place, sitting in traffic, when you could be leaping from portal to portal. How tedious it must be for you! How lonely!"

Distantly Darwen was aware of the laughter of the clown still and he remembered taking his mother's hand all those years ago at the Pleasure Beach in Blackpool.

Lonely.

"You talk about trust, but you can't trust the Old Guardians any more than you believe you can trust me," she went on. "You know that. The members of the old council were always liars and manipulators. What have they told you of their real purpose, I wonder? Not much. Enough lies and misdirection to keep their pet squint at their side, but not nearly enough of what is really going on. Because, Darwen Arkwright, if a Mirroculist like yourself could see the true picture, you would quickly snap Mr. Peregrine's leash, the rope of lies with which he keeps you tethered, and then you would really come into your own. You haven't begun to tap the kind of power you could wield. The old shopkeeper won't let you. But join us, and things could be very different.

"The Guardians will be replaced," Scarlett purred, and now she stepped out into the open again, moving to where a great, red lever stuck out from a bank of valves and dials. "I could give you a seat on the council which will take their place. And then you could have anything you wanted. With me beside you, Darwen Arkwright, and my master at our head, who could stand in your way?"

Darwen felt a rush of something unexpected, a thrill of pleasurable anticipation. Power. He had never had it. He had a gift, but to be able to use it for whatever he wanted, not having to worry about other people . . .

"She speaks the truth."

The voice seemed to come from all around. It was calm and low, distant but crystal clear and it unwound like smoke in Darwen's ears. He realised that the mechanical laughter which had been ringing through the building, had stopped. He looked up. The clown's face had changed. It was still the same figure, but what had been hard and shiny was now pliable and soft, like flesh, and the eyes, which were open now, were somehow, unmistakably, alive.

Greyling.

Darwen knew him at once, even in the clown's impossible face.

"You recognise me," said the clown. "How gratifying."

"I knew it would be you in the end," said Darwen.

"Of course you did," said Greyling. There was something of the clown in his voice, a lilting playfulness that went through Darwen like fingernails on a blackboard. "Because you are clever. Because you are talented in ways those around you cannot begin to appreciate."

"What do you want with this place?" Darwen asked.

"The place is irrelevant," said the clown, its head lolling, "or it would be without these wonderful little stone spheres. They really are remarkable, Darwen. You know what gives them their power, of course? It's not the stone itself. It's the labour that went into making them. The care. The respect. They were produced by a people without the most basic of metal tools. Do you have any idea how much work that would take? The time? The craft? The *love*? There's power there, Darwen. We had to adjust our equipment, of course, fine-tune the frequency to make them resonate in just the right way, but the real power came from the stones themselves. They hold the memory of those who made them like the tracks of tears. Emotional residue, Darwen. Potent stuff. They have only one drawback, which you have kindly sidestepped for me."

Darwen frowned. "I haven't done anything for you."

"Actually," said Greyling. "You have. As you know, those wonderful little stone spheres can be used to open portals, but as you have probably begun to realise, anything to do with Silbrica – especially the power bound to its portals – is tied to thought, to intention. If it wasn't, I would never have been able to get so much energy out of a few children's books and toys last year. The people who made the stone balls knew nothing of machinery, Darwen, and their respect for – even love of – the jungle and all that lived in it was almost boundless. Again, there's power there, and it lingers, but it's a particular kind of power and it doesn't suit all things. Imagine my disappointment when I found that my wonderful machines all died as they tried to cross through the gates! It was very frustrating to have to rely on living creatures like the Bleck to do my work for me."

"So you can't bring the generator through after all!" said Darwen, practically shouting. "You've lost."

"You misunderstand me," said Greyling. "I cannot open the stone sphere portals for my beautiful and terrible machines. Only the Mirroculist can do that, because the Mirroculist masters the portal from whichever side he is on, while my powers are limited to Silbrica only." He paused, like a magician savouring the moment before the magical reveal, and Darwen felt a swelling sense of dread. "That is why I brought you here," Greyling continued. "So that you could do for me the one thing I could not: open a nice wide gateway for my scrobblers and their equipment, including of course, their generators. I am immensely grateful."

Darwen stared at him, his confusion turning to dismay. His gaze flashed over the scrobblers, the armoured bulldozers and the generators which sat as if waiting biding their time, and the horrified realiszation finally hit him. He knew what they had been waiting for. He remembered the zip line, his long slow fall through the portal . . .

No.

"Thanks to your spectacular entrance tonight," the clown continued, "I can now pronounce this portal open to whatever I want to send through it!"

As he spoke, Scarlett threw the great, red lever beside her and there was a hiss of static. Darwen turned back towards the sound and saw that the arch was now flooded with a blue radiance that came from beyond the portal.

"My lords, ladies and gentlemen," Greyling sang out, like he was introducing a circus act, "thanks to our most honoured guest, the world-famous Mirroculist, Darwen Arkwright, the invasion of the human world has begun!"

Thirty Four

CHOICES

arwen stared at the portal, overwhelmed by a sense of despair so crushing that he could not speak. Everything he had done had been in vain. All his courage, his determination – it had been for nothing. He had thought he was a hero, a saviour, but all the time Greyling had been toying with him, luring him, so that he would do the one thing Greyling could not do for himself.

He had failed. Worse, he had handed victory to the enemy.

"I had hoped," Greyling continued, "that you would have helped willingly, knowingly, rather than by stumbling accidentally as you have, and I still believe that we might be partners in greatness. With a Mirroculist of your talent at my side, what could we not achieve?"

There was a pause, and Scarlett's eyes flicked between them, watchful.

Then the clown Greyling smiled. "Darwen," he said, "you have already opened my portal for me. Would you care to have done it as my friend, or as my enemy? We may not have such an opportunity again, Darwen Arkwright. Join me."

"Why do you look like that?" asked Darwen.

Greyling seemed to hesitate.

"You know things about me," said Darwen, answering his own question. "About my past. You can change the way people see you and you tapped into my memories somehow, looking for something that would make you feel . . . familiar, comforting. Something that would associate you with happy times in my life. But I think Alex was right. There's something in my head that's trying to send me a message. I don't know why but when you chose the way you would appear to me, you got it wrong. I remembered Blackpool," he said, thinking it through, "because going to the illuminations had reminded me of going there with my parents. You found the right place, the right moment, but you chose something I always hated, something that scared me, and you know what I think? I think that somehow, *I did that*. Without knowing, without even sensing you were doing it, some part of me made you choose the wrong image so that when the time came for me to choose, I would recognise you for what you are. And now, that time has come and I've made my choice."

Darwen stood up. He took a long, steadying breath, raised the pistol in two hands, and fired, clamping the trigger down, emptying the weapon.

The energy stream sent the strange fairground shadows leaping as if the carousel horses had come to life and the clown had grown twenty feet. Then there was a fizz, a pop, and the gun died in Darwen's hands.

"Missed," said Scarlett, smiling her toothy politician's smile. "And now it's all empty."

She leapt towards him, something of the eel-creature's speed in her uncanny approach, and in moments she was close enough to touch. Instinctively he reached for her face, clamping his hand to her mouth and holding on. It had worked once before . . .

But she did not wince away in pain as she had at Halloween, and when he released her, the smile was back. "You didn't think we'd try again till we had found a way around that little weakness, did you?" she said, silkily. "Ironic, isn't it? You have opened the portal for us, and none of your little friends will be able to come and help you. Not without the Mirroculist to hold their hands. You are going to regret not being a better shot, little boy."

"Who says I missed?" said Darwen, recovering his defiance. "I wasn't aiming at you."

She smiled, thinking this was a ruse, but then she heard the scrobblers streaming out of the shadows. She caught their panic and turned.

The cage door was still smoking where Darwen had hit the lock. It hung open. And in great undulating waves of its sinewy tentacles, the Insidious Bleck was coming out.

Darwen wasn't sure, but he thought it looked angry.

It moved with extraordinary speed, pulling itself from the wreckage of the cage and crawling on the elbows of its tentacles across the factory floor. It tossed aside a pair of scrobblers and a gnasher, one of which had tried to stick it with some kind of spear wired to the pack on the scrobbler's back: a cattle prod. The scrobbler was down, but the prod was still sparking as if jammed in the on position. Scarlett had bolted into the cover of the fairground clutter, but the monster seemed uninterested in her. It was making for the portal, trying to get out.

Darwen ran towards it. Diving towards the prone scrobbler, he rolled into a crouch with the cattle prod pointed up at the Bleck. The cable reaching to the scrobbler's pack gave him just enough room to lunge once and find the underside of one of those bristle-covered tentacles. There was a sound like fish going into a deep fryer, and the Bleck screamed, shrinking away. Darwen waited to make sure it had seen him, then ran, hard and fast as he could, back towards the generator. Again, he dove, sliding into the dust beneath the machine, drawing his legs up tight as the Bleck came after him.

If it was patient, he thought, it would seek him out with its tentacles, probing till it found him, and then it would drag him out and lift him up to that awful beak. But it wasn't patient. It was furious. It had been kept penned for weeks, perhaps months, pushed and prodded and caged by creatures of malice and greed, and it was now blind with rage.

Which was what Darwen wanted.

The Bleck caught the generator in its immense tentacles and lifted the entire thing off him. In the sudden light, Darwen saw its furious eyes and, dimly, heard Scarlett scream with anger as it cast the generator aside. There was a crash that shook the warehouse and a series of popping explosions.

The room was filled with a terrible, high-pitched shrieking. It was the clown, Greyling, raging as he lurched back and forth in his chair.

A tentacle caught Darwen like a massive python and snatched him up into the air. His legs kicked, but his arms were bound fast to his sides. He could do nothing. He smelled the monster's breath and saw the pulsing feelers around the mouth reaching for him as the great, razor-sharp beak opened.

Then there was a flash and the Bleck quivered. Its eyes widened, then dimmed. It collapsed and Darwen found himself rolling free. Another flash. Scarlett Oppertune had taken one of the scrobbler's energy weapons and fired it directly into the Bleck's fleshy underside. Her face was a mask of fury and hatred. She shot again, and the monster twitched. Then again, and again, until the weapon would fire no more.

For a moment Darwen thought Scarlett had saved him on purpose, but one look at her told him that was not true. She had just been angry, furious with the creature which had finally refused to do her bidding. She still wanted him dead.

Scarlett turned to the generator, which was lying on its side, its rivets popped and its seams broken open, before her gaze again found Darwen. All the style and polish was gone from her face now, it was so twisted with bitterness and savagery. She aimed the weapon at Darwen and tried the trigger again, but it merely clicked. "Kill him!" she shouted at the dazed scrobblers. "Now!"

But as she gave the order, something remarkable happened.

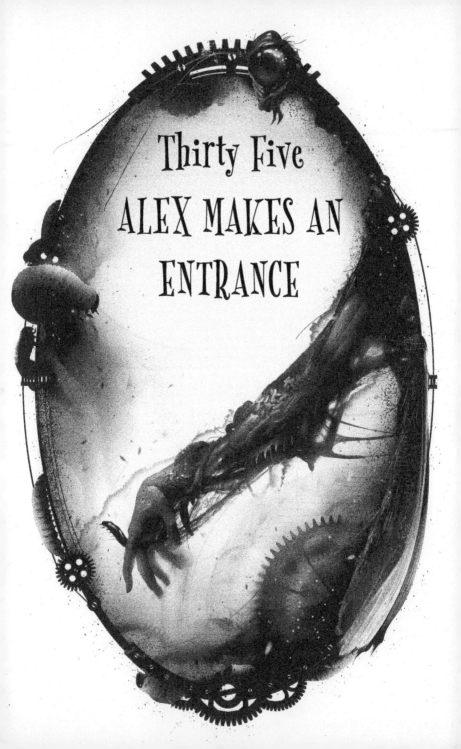

Thirty Five

ALEX MAKES AN ENTRANCE

Alex had just stepped through the portal.

"Hey Darwen," she said. "How's it going?"

"Been better," said Darwen.

"Two Mirroculists!" exclaimed Scarlett, her blue eyes narrowing with disbelief. "How can there be two Mirroculists?"

"Must be one of those Buy One Get One Free deals," answered Alex. "Your lucky day. Not so lucky for Señor Delgado and his pals. They were on their way to help out here and really didn't see me coming."

"Rik and the others are in there," said Darwen, pointing at the ruptured generator. "Get them out."

"Oh, I don't think so," said Scarlett with a nasty grin. "It's time you learned some manners, young lady. You might have somehow slipped past those half-wit humans but you are in my world now and that means . . ."

But before she finished her remark her voice trailed off. She shaded her eyes and peered past Darwen towards the flickering portal.

"Oh," said Alex, who was stretching one hand back into the shimmering curtain of light. "You thought I came by myself? You really have to stop underestimating us."

Scarlett reached into her dainty purse and came up with a pistol, small but quite lethal. She raised it to shoot and something hurtled past Darwen's head, hit Scarlett hard in the face and sent her sprawling. At first Darwen thought it was one of the stone spheres but then it bounced. Darwen had known that sound all his life.

A football.

He turned, and there was Felippe, Sarita, and Calida's mother. Last of all came Mr. Peregrine.

Darwen stared at the teacher, almost overwhelmed by a relief so sharp it brought tears to his eyes. Mr. Peregrine met his eyes and nodded once, smiling. Darwen nodded back, then he pointed at the generator and shouted, "get them out of there!"

Scarlett was getting to her feet, but her unintended header had left her face warped and torn, and as she tried to adjust it, it ripped further. With a shout of frustration she opened her mouth wide, and the great eel-creature spilled slickly out, leaving the Scarlett suit crumpled on the ground.

"Do you have any idea how hard it is to grow those things?" she spat, turning on Darwen. The voice was slightly slurred, as if the eel's lips and tongue couldn't form the words properly, but the hard eyes were still Scarlett's. "You will pay for it with your sorry, pathetic little lives. Scrobblers!" she roared. "Once and for all. Wipe. Them. Out."

Darwen looked around. The scrobblers which had scattered during the attack of the Bleck were reforming and checking their weapons. Two of the hulking toad-things were hopping slowly forward, their immense mouths gaping. To his right, Mrs. Delgado was pulling the dazed and pale children from the wreckage of the generator. Rik and Chip were there, and Gabriel was unsteadily carrying the boy who Darwen had seen taken by the Bleck all those weeks ago: Luis. Gabriel was gazing into the boy's still face, his face tear-streaked and suddenly, Darwen understood.

They were brothers.

That story Alex had told him about how Luis had a brother named Eduardo who had searched for him till he had collapsed of exhaustion was about Gabriel all along! But he hadn't been abducted by the Bleck. Somehow he had met Jorge, and the Guardians had put him to work.

But even as the truth registered, Darwen realised that there was one more tiny form in the generator, the first boy to have been taken, and one no one was trying to get him out. He was already dead. But then, so were they all or would be very soon. The scrobbler army was sighting their weapons on the humans.

"Get down!" Darwen yelled, running towards them.

They turned as if in a dream, looking for cover just as the first shots came. One of the toads shot its tongue at them and Darwen was horrified to see the thing extend at least twenty feet. It struck the side of the generator and stuck there, slamming the metal pod with a surge of energy. In that moment a new threat presented itself: the toads could direct the power from their backpacks through their bodies.

The children and their would-be rescuers cowered behind the shattered generator as the scrobblers poured shot after deafening shot at them, and the machinery around crackled and exploded. Darwen hunkered down, scanning the anxious faces around him. Rik was rubbing his face as if trying to wake himself up, but there was no sign of Alex.

"What is going on?" said Chip, vaguely. All his usual cockiness was gone and he looked young and frightened. "Who are those men with the . . . faces?"

"I'll tell you later," said Darwen. "Just keep your head down."

It didn't seem like they – the humans – had any choices, and the scrobblers knew it. While one or two fired occasionally to keep them pinned down, the others were coming closer, some of them switching to wrenches and crowbars as they came.

Rik was clenching and unclenching his fists as he tried to shake off the drowsiness of the generator. "If we can get over there," he said, "we might make it to the portal."

"Where?" said Mr. Peregrine, moving in the direction Rik had indicated.

"There!" shouted Rik. "I think I can make it. Get out of the way, and I'll draw their fire."

But before either of them could move, the boy Darwen was used to calling Gabriel stepped forward. He had something in his hand, a water bottle without a cap, and as Rik gaped he jerked it in Mr. Peregrine's direction splashing the teacher across the face.

"That wasn't very nice," said Mr. Peregrine in an odd voice, his bandaged hand to his cheek.

"Get out of the way," Rik began, but then Mr. Peregrine took his hand away from his face and everyone stared. Where the water had hit him his skin was falling away, dissolving, and beneath it all was black and shiny.

"Well, now," said Mr. Peregrine, with a strange, lopsided smile that seemed to split his face. "It seems the cat is out of the bag."

He pulled the bandage from his hand and two of the fingers came with it, the flesh melting where it had gotten wet. The long, bloodless cut across his palm looked pale and greenish now and the wound was wriggling with maggots which scattered and fell as something long and black poked out and through. The rod-like limb was slick, and ended in a cruel, hooked claw which sliced the wound wide from the inside. First the hand, then the whole arm peeled back, the insides pale, sickly and glistening like meat left out of the fridge.

"No!" gasped Rik.

Mr. Peregrine twisted sideways, using his good hand to grasp the splitting flesh which now reached his shoulder. He tore it back, peeling his chest open so that the thing inside could clamber out in a thicket of shiny black limbs. As the insect form stepped out of the ruined flesh suit, it shook its head and what was left of Mr. Peregrine slipped to the ground. In its place were composite eyes and a black and gaping insect mouth.

Darwen stared at the old man's deflated body on the ground and for a moment, he could not breathe. It wasn't horror. It was despair. Tears sprang to his eyes and all strength drained from him so that he swayed as if about to collapse.

Not Mr. Peregrine. Not Mr. Peregrine.

But even in his shock and misery Darwen forced himself to look into the monstrous insect eyes, and he knew them.

Mr. Jenkins.

"Remember me?" said the insect in a harsh, brittle voice which stretched its dripping mouthparts. "I have looked forward to this."

And as Rik shrieked, the insect creature sprang at Darwen.

The others screamed, spilling out into the open as they fought to get away from the creature, out to where the scrobblers were waiting.

Darwen kicked and punched but the Jenkins creature was too strong for him. It slammed him to the ground, its weight on his chest and its awful face inches from his throat. Its mouth parts moved and its maw clicked open and closed in excitement.

Then it shuddered and rolled off, dislodged by a firm kick to its head. Rik. Darwen scrabbled to his feet. He staggered back and into something hard: one of the tank-bulldozers.

There was a ladder fitted to one side. Darwen swung himself up and started throwing switches and pulling levers. A scrobbler fired at him, but the shot ricocheted off the armoured plate just as the engine came roaring to life. If he could buy the others a minute, less, they might get out. He shoved another lever and the great tracked juggernaut lurched forward.

The scrobblers scattered again. There was no steering wheel, just a pair of levers. Darwen pushed hard on the left one and the bulldozer slewed to the side, crates exploding into splinters under its massive tracks. Scarlett was shouting and pointing, but even as Darwen shrunk low in his seat to avoid another flashing energy shot, he saw his target. The hideous, lurching clown loomed over him, its face set, its mouth moving in commands he couldn't hear over the bellow of the engine. Darwen slammed both levers, and the bulldozer surged forward.

The clown turned to him at the last moment, the smooth amusement replaced with a deep, malicious hatred.

It screamed once, and then the great plough of the bulldozer crashed through the glass case and into its body. The head kicked backwards, the body buckled and fell beneath the machine's deadly treads, and all was ground to powder.

Darwen saw the moment Greyling left. One moment the clown's eyes were alive and full of wrath and the next, they were just painted glass again. The leader of the New Council was gone.

Darwen grabbed the levers to send the bulldozer at the nearest group of scrobblers, turning to find the Jenkins insect on top of the bulldozer and poised to strike. He tried to dodge, but the insect claw caught him on the shoulder, and as he slumped backwards his shirt snagged on one of the levers. The machine leapt suddenly to the left and then locked itself in a slow, dizzying spin. A toad tongue shot through the air. Darwen leaned back as it missed his head by inches, but he felt the surge of electricity as it struck the bulldozer. The engine died in a puff of black smoke. Then he was being lifted bodily by those long, impossibly strong insect legs, and Mr. Jenkins dropped him heavily to the warehouse floor.

Wordlessly the scrobbler troops corralled the captives, the children shrinking from the blank stare of the bloated toads. Darwen looked hopelessly up. There was no way out.

The Scarlett eel glared at the shattered remains of the clown.

"You haven't killed him," she hissed, pivoting on her tail and gaping at him between words so her pointed teeth showed like rows of knives. "But you will be punished anyway."

"What are you going to do?" snapped Darwen with all the defiance he could muster. "Kill me?"

"Of course," she said. "Last."

Darwen looked wildly around. His eyes found Rik, but he still couldn't see Alex. She must have been hit.

Well, he thought. *At least she was spared this.*

A strange silence had descended on the warehouse. Distantly there were the snaps and fizzes of broken machinery, but no one spoke, and even Mrs. Delgado's tears were silent. The scrobblers raised their weapons, gazing blankly through their masks, but even they did not bellow or snarl. Everyone knew. This would be an execution, not a battle.

One more moment of stillness and then . . . an electronic hiss from the portal.

There was Alex, standing half in, half out, silhouetted in the flickering light, holding the gateway open for . . . who?

Not *who*? What?

Darwen caught the movement which was quick, and stealthy, and animal.

No, he thought. *It couldn't be.*

Scarlett turned, puzzled, and for a second the scrobblers just stood there.

And then in a blur of fur and claws, they came: the pouncels from the jungle locus, led by one which was slightly smaller than the others and which moved with a limp. They streaked in, and the scrobblers fell back, firing, shrieking and bellowing as the pouncels flew at them. One of the toads shot out its tongue and caught a pouncel, zapping it lifeless before it pulled it into its sickening mouth.

But then something like a rocket struck the toad and it went down in a blaze of light and smoke.

Someone had come with the pouncels, and he was shooting back. It was Weazen – he was alive! – and he was picking off the enemy like a tiny otter-sized sharpshooter, blasting openings for the boiling mass of pouncels which dragged the scrobblers and gnashers down in a wild, animal frenzy.

The thing which had been Scarlett Oppertune snapped its jaws, throwing the pouncels off, but there were too many of them and they were too fast. Her hard, little eyes found Darwen. She reached towards him, imploring, desperate, and without thinking he took a step towards her, extending his hand. She snatched at it, caught his fingers in her teeth, and held on, even as the pouncels pulled her backwards. She didn't bite down, just gripped like she was holding on to a lifeline. Darwen felt Rik grab his free arm so that he wouldn't be sucked into the pouncels' snapping fury, and saw realisation flash through Scarlett's animal face; for her, it was over.

Her jaws relaxed a little and Darwen felt her slipping away, but then her grip tightened again, her bright eyes snapped wide open and, with her last ounce of strength, she pulled herself close enough to whisper into his face, releasing his hand as she spoke. "If you ever find him, ask him how he knew your name."

And then she was yanked backwards and the pouncels fell on her.

For a second, Darwen stood where he was, stunned, dimly aware that Rik was dragging him back and away. Weazen sent a barrage of covering fire over their heads, and Darwen shrank back, Scarlett's words rolling around in his head.

Alex had stayed where she was and Darwen, barely daring to glance back to the fight, led the children with Mrs. Delgado back to the portal and out. He paused only to see the Jenkins insect which had been chasing them being sucked backwards into the surging throng of pouncels, where it fell, shrieking, and vanished.

Darwen hesitated, his eyes flashing around the great chamber, searching.

"Time to go, Darwen Arkwright," said Weazen, who appeared next to him, his blaster at the ready. "He's not here."

"I can't leave him!" said Darwen. Tears suddenly burned hot in his eyes and he shouted at the top of his lungs, "Mr. Peregrine! Mr. Peregrine, where are you?"

He took a step into the warehouse but Weazen caught his arm with one tiny but powerful claw. "It's not safe," he said. "The whole place is going to go up," he said, pulling at Darwen so he had to stoop to look the little creature in his pale, masked face. "He's not here."

Darwen's eyes fell on a painted hand – the last shattered remnant of the laughing clown – and then, as one of the pieces of equipment wired to the generator exploded with a burst of orange flame, he let Weazen pull him back towards the portal and out into his own world.

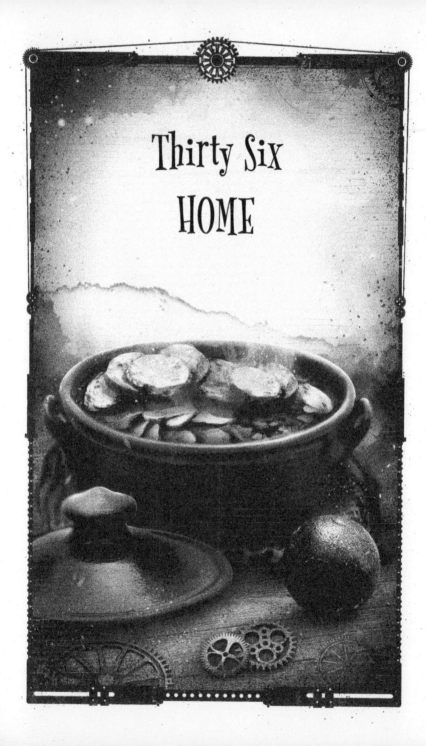

Thirty Six
HOME

"How much does Chip remember?" asked Alex as she watched Rik and Darwen pack.

"Don't know," said Rik. "He's not talking; not to me, anyway. Looks kind of spooked."

"Like he's a butterfly that got hit with a book?" asked Alex.

"Kind of," said Rik.

"Good," said Alex. "Do you know how he finished up there in the first place?"

"The thing that called itself Mr. Peregrine took him," said Rik. "Whittley must have seen some stuff, but he was pretty out of it. We all were. In the generator you sort of lose track of who you are. I wouldn't be surprised if Chip's a bit hazy on what actually happened."

"Probably good," said Alex. "Though no one is going to be hazy about us going home without Mr. P."

There was a long silence.

"You think he's . . .?" Alex began.

"No," Darwen cut in. "Scarlett – Miss Murray – said something about talking to him if I found him. I don't know how those flesh suit things work, but I don't think they are the bodies of the people they look like."

"So you think they're, like, cloned from living tissue or something?" Rik asked.

"I don't know," said Darwen.

"Like they keep the real person alive and grow the suit – or whatever it is – from the person . . ."

"I don't know."

"You think that's why the fake Mr. P smelled weird and didn't want to get wet?"

"Rik," said Darwen, giving him a hard look. "I really don't know."

"Rik is right, more or less," said a voice. They turned to find Jorge watching them cautiously.

"You," said Alex.

"Darwen," said Jorge, ignoring her tone. "Rik. Alex. I've come to thank you. What you did last night was extremely . . . brave, and er . . . courageous."

Darwen nodded, but he didn't speak.

"The Guardian Council wishes to honour you," Jorge began, but Darwen cut him off.

"The Guardians told me to stay out of it," he said. "I acted against their orders."

"That's true," said Jorge, looking uncomfortable, "but given the outcome – your success – they are prepared to overlook the manner of your behaviour."

"Is that right?" said Darwen quietly, smiling.

"How nice of them," said Alex, whose face was stern.

"This honour," said Rik, "not some kind of cash prize, is it?"

Before Jorge could respond, Darwen spoke. "I won't be taking any of their honours," he said. "In fact, I don't think that the Guardian council and I are going to be on speaking terms from here on."

Jorge's face clouded. "What do you mean? You are their Mirroculist. You work on their instructions."

"Yeah?" said Darwen. "I'm not sure I like the kind of instructions I've been getting. I was told that the Guardians wanted to make a deal with Greyling. I was told to abandon the people who live here, the rainforest itself, even my friends. Now, I don't always know what the right thing to do is, but I know that some things are worth fighting for, and I never abandon my friends. So unless there's something else you have to say, you can be on your way."

For a moment it looked like Jorge was going to argue, but then he nodded simply, his face set. He half-turned to leave, but stopped himself. "We think Mr. Peregrine is still alive," he said. "He seems to have been taken by Greyling two months ago in preparation for . . . everything. He knows a great deal which the enemy might find useful. Rescuing him will be a priority for the Guardians. Whether you choose to work with the council on this is, of course, your decision."

He walked away, and the three students watched him go.

"He sent me the oven door," said Darwen.

"Mr. Peregrine?" said Alex.

"The real Mr. Peregrine," said Darwen, "not the Jenkins-suit-thing. It may have been the last thing he did before they took him. We have to get him back."

"Well duh!" said Alex. "We're the Peregrine Pact, remember? Of course we're going to rescue him."

"With or without the council's help?" asked Rik.

"Not sure yet," said Darwen. "What have the students been told?"

"Melissa Young said that Mr. Peregrine had to go home early," said Rik. "Family emergency."

Darwen sighed. He had been morose all morning and it wasn't just because they were heading back to regular classes and a comparatively cold, Atlantan winter. His mind was full of questions, some of them so unsettling that he wasn't sure he wanted to know the answers.

"Look at him," said Alex to Rik, "like his goldfish died. You should be celebrating, man. You know what we pulled off last night? We stopped Greyling! We saved the jungle . . ."

"Rainforest," inserted Rik.

"You do that one more time," snapped Alex, "and I'll slap you till you squeal. Hand to God." She turned back to Darwen. "You listening? We turned the pouncels on Scarlett Murray, or whatever we call her eel-headed self, and we saved a bunch of kids."

"Not all of them," said Darwen.

"No," Alex agreed. "Not all of them."

They had not been able to remove that one small body from the generator before the whole place had come down around their ears.

"You can't always save everyone, Darwen," said Alex. "That's not how it works."

"How what works?"

"Life," she said. "The world. You do what you can. You try your best. You move on. A lot of people owe you their lives, Darwen Arkwright. I won't let you beat yourself up because you aren't Superman. You should be . . ."

"Right chuffed?" Darwen supplied.

"Exactly," said Alex. "Oh, and guess what?"

"What?" said Rik.

"Sarita told me that now that Scarlett's development plans have fallen through some of the families are going to move back."

"I'm surprised you involved the local kids," said Darwen. "I thought you would keep it within the Peregrine Pact."

Alex shrugged. "It was their fight too," she said. "In some ways, more than ours."

"What do they say about what happened?" asked Darwen.

"They're sort of rolling with it," Alex said, frowning. "It's weird. It's like, they didn't know about the portals and stuff but they aren't exactly surprised to find they were there, and that there were monsters coming through. I don't think they'll be bringing in the big city reporters or anything. They'll just get on with their lives. Speaking of which," she added, turning to Rik, "you said they didn't have anything beyond the rainforest and their past: the shattered remnants of a once-noble history, remember?"

"So?" said Rik.

"So it's not true," she said. "They have each other. They have family, which means more to them than anything. They showed that last night."

Darwen nodded.

Family. He felt the word like a warm spot in a cold bed, and for a moment he was jealous of them.

"Anyway," said Rik, "if the reporters do come there's nothing for them to see. The scrobbler engines never made it through.

The portals don't work anymore. Whatever got destroyed in the warehouse last night, it messed up the gates. Even the circle of stones under the zip line closed up right after we came out of it."

"You know what this means," said Darwen, softly.

"What?" said Rik.

"It might be just us. Rescuing Mr. Peregrine, protecting Silbrica, defending our world against Greyling's invasion. We might have to do all of it by ourselves, without the Guardians' help, possibly even . . ."

His voice trailed off.

"Against them?" said Alex. "Not sure I like the sound of that."

"No," said Rik. "That would not be good."

Alex raised her eyebrows at the understatement.

"Hi Chip," said Rik, cutting her off.

The tall, good-looking boy was walking down from the dining shelter with his bags. He slowed and his eyes narrowed as he saw them. He looked uncertain, suspicious.

"So," said Rik breezily. "Interesting trip, huh?"

Chip Whittley just stood there, looking at them. "Last night," he stammered. "That place. Where . . .? What . . .?"

Darwen tensed.

Fortunately, the previous night wasn't the only thing on Chip's – rather meager – mind. Chip looked at them, then turned and stared at the ocean. At last, his gaze fell on Alex, then dropped to the ground. "Listen," he said, his voice low. "About that butterfly . . ." The words dried up and he stood rigid, his fists clenched, eyes staring at a tiny hermit crab in the grass.

"What about it?" said Alex.

Chip looked up and Darwen was amazed to see that his eyes shone with unshed tears but at the same moment, there were sounds of people coming down the path. Nathan and Barry, with Genevieve and Melissa at their heels.

Panic crossed Chip's face.

"What's going on here?" said Nathan. "Saying goodbye to the jungle creatures, Chip?"

Chip blinked, and for the briefest moment Darwen thought he saw a spasm of anguish in the boy's face before it set into its usual haughty confidence. "Something like that," he said, turning back to Nathan. "Come on. I want to get a good place in the boat."

Together, they walked down to the beach leaving Darwen, Rik and Alex by the tent.

"So close," said Alex. "For a second there, he was nearly human. Ah well."

"After what he went through," Rik exclaimed, "how can he just go back to being . . . like himself?"

"Easier this way," said Alex. "And besides, now I can go back to hating him. The trip has brought me clarity."

"That's not all you got out of this trip," said Rik grudgingly. "You're a Mirroculist too. I still can't see through the mirrors, let alone open them, but you two . . ."

"Maybe it's just here," said Alex, shrugging. "Maybe something about those stones rubbed off on me. We'll have to test it when we get back. If all I can see through Darwen's oven door is Aunt Honoria's apple pie, then I guess I'm not a real Mirroculist after all."

"You're just saying that so I won't feel left out," said Rik.

"Partly," said Alex. "And partly because I like saying 'apple pie.' Red beans and rice is all well and groovygood, but I'm ready for some down home cooking."

"You won't get it from Aunt Honoria," said Darwen, shouldering his backpack. "She doesn't cook."

"You think the pouncels got out before the place blew?" asked Alex.

"Weazen said most of them made it," said Darwen. "I take it the leader was the one you looked after?"

"And you said they were just animals," said Alex. "There's no *just* about it. Smart, they were, and loyal. More than some people. Like Sasha. You reckon the Bleck knew what it was doing when it destroyed the generator?"

"I thought it was just mad," said Darwen, "but maybe there was more to it."

"And this Weazen character," said Rik, "he's a feisty little weasel, isn't he?"

"I wouldn't call him that if I were you," said Darwen.

"You think we'll see him again?" asked Rik.

"Definitely," said Alex. "We have to find Mr. P. We'll need whatever friends we still have."

Darwen nodded. It could not be a coincidence that he had not been able to reach Moth. Greyling must have sealed her locus so he couldn't learn anything about what was happening from her. He would need to find a way in. "You think Weazen and the dellfeys will stand with us if it means going against the Guardians?" he asked.

"You really don't get loyalty, do you, Darwen?" said Alex. "Of course they'll stand with us. If you had a dog, you'd know."

Rik was gazing along the shore path towards the village. People were coming. Mrs. Delgado, holding her daughter's hand and some of the village children. Sarita was with them and Felippe with his sister, Calida. Behind them were two boys, one they had called Gabriel – Eduardo – and his brother, Luis.

"We have come to say goodbye," said Sarita. "And thank you."

Mrs. Delgado stepped forward and took Darwen's hand. Into it she pressed a small stone sphere about the size of a tennis ball.

"What?" he said. "I can't take this. I appreciate it and everything, but it belongs to you. To your people."

As the woman continued to press it, nodding and smiling, Sarita spoke up. "It is not ancient," she said. "Some of the villagers still make the stone balls to mark special places. They make them the old way. It takes a very long time. She wants you to have it."

Darwen gazed at it. It was heavy and perfectly round.

"Thank you," he said. "It is beautiful."

Alex jabbered in Spanish and the children laughed.

"What?" asked Rik and Darwen together.

"I was just thanking Felippe for that shot to Scarlett's head. I think it would have scored from the halfway line."

Darwen and Rik shook Felippe's hand.

"Too bad we never got to have a rematch," said Darwen.

"Yes," said Felippe. He added something in Spanish and the kids laughed again.

"He said they went easy on you the first time," said Alex.

Gabriel – Eduardo – stepped forward and offered Darwen his hand. "Can we speak in private?" he asked. He seemed older now, more confident and direct now that he had his true identity back.

Darwen flushed, then nodded. "Sure," he said.

Darwen and the two brothers walked down to the beach in silence. A scarlet macaw flew up from one of the palm trees calling, and Darwen found that such things still amazed him.

"I am sorry that I did not trust you," said the boy formerly known as Gabriel. "Jorge told me that you might be dangerous, that you might not follow the Guardians' wishes, and that I should hide who he was from you." Eduardo paused, glancing down at his feet in shame. "I spied on you. I spilled the gasoline from the boat because he wanted to see what would come through the portals after dark. He wanted to see if you were right about Bleck and if there was evidence of Greyling. He didn't want to tell you about it, but needed you there to open the portal if it appeared." He inhaled, his breath catching in his throat.. "I did not know how much danger I had put you in. I am sorry."

"It's OK," said Darwen. Then a realisation struck. "You wore that veil so that the local kids wouldn't recognise you, didn't you?"

Eduardo grinned and nodded, peeking at Luis for approval.

"I'll bet you had a lot of explaining to do last night," said Darwen.

"Not as much as you would think," said Eduardo. "They are just happy that we are back. When the creature disguised as Mr. Peregrine gave you the portal, I recognised it, and I knew where it would take you to because I had been there. It was a place in Silbrica which Jorge used to communicate with the Guardians.

It would have exposed him. I reset the device. I think that made it open up in the last place it was used. Since Mr. Peregrine was one of those flesh-suit things, that probably put you in danger too."

Darwen thought back to their nightmarish experience in the Jenkins house, but found himself shrugging. "It's OK," he said. "I would have probably just ended up in front of Greyling sooner. That's what that fake Mr. Peregrine would have wanted."

Eduardo shook his head in ostensible agreement, and Darwen searched his face. "Tell me about how you became involved with the Guardians."

"Everything I did," said Eduardo, giving Darwen a level, piercing look, "I did to find my brother. I should have joined you, but I did not know that then. The Guardians came to me when I was lost, when the search for Luis had deprived me of my ability to think. They used me, but I had to trust them, because losing my brother was like losing a part of myself. It made me alone. You understand?"

Darwen nodded and looked down. He understood all too well.

Luis spoke up. "Thank you," he said. Simply.

He looked embarrassed, unsure of himself, and it struck Darwen as strange that this was the first time they had spoken.

"I remembered your face," said the boy, "from when the monster took me. When I was awake in the machine, when I could remember who I was, I thought of your face and I thought you would come for me. I knew my brother would search for me too, so I had two . . ." he sought for the word, then spoke quickly in Spanish.

Eduardo smiled and, clearly wishing he didn't have to say it, completed his brother's thought. "Heroes," he said.

"Heroes," Luis agreed.

Darwen smiled and – as much to change the subject as anything else – turned back to Eduardo. "Why were you with Chip?" he asked.

"The thing which said it was Mr. Peregrine was suspicious of me because I was always watching you and talking to Jorge," said Eduardo. "I think it knew who I was. It said it wanted to show me something, something about the village children who had been taken. I didn't trust him but I had to see, so I took someone with me. I thought that if one of the Hillside students went missing, then you would go looking for him. It was . . . a mistake."

"Why Chip?"

Eduardo flushed, ashamed of himself. "Because I thought that whoever went with me might never get out," he said. He looked down and was about to say more when Alex yelled from the camp.

"They're leaving!" she called.

The three boys nodded, relieved to rejoin the others.

"We will meet again, Darwen Arkwright," said the boy they had called Gabriel. "I am sure of it."

"I'd like that," said Darwen.

They shook hands and said good bye. Alex hugged everyone, then waved expansively as they walked back along the shore.

Darwen slipped the stone sphere into his backpack and said, "OK. Is that everything?"

"Looks like," said Rik. "I guess they'll leave Mr. P's stuff here."

"I for one am not touching it," said Alex. "And stop calling him Mr. P."

"You'd rather I called him Mr. Jenkins?" said Rik.

"How about Swamp Thing?" said Alex. "Swampy for short. It suits his smell."

"Those people suits they wear," said Rik, "you think they have to fill them out with struts and wires and stuff like you do when you stuff an animal?"

"When you *what*?" said Alex, giving him her beadiest stare.

"I have an uncle who's an amateur taxidermist. He had this raccoon that he hit with his truck one night . . ."

"Fascinating though this story is sure to be," Alex interjected, "I don't need more details about the insides of animals and the exploits of your hillbilly family."

"Who are you calling hillbillies?" Rik exclaimed.

And they were off, a squabble that lasted all the way to the boat, then back round the cove to the main village and halfway back to the airstrip.

Darwen gazed out of the jeep window as they forded a brown river, watching something that might have been a log and might have been a crocodile, and he grinned to himself. It had been an amazing trip, but he was ready for . . .

Home?

Well, Atlanta. The smile stayed on his lips, but faded from his eyes. He couldn't keep thinking of his aunt's apartment like it was a hotel in some place he was visiting for a while. England was part of his past. He may never return now and if he did, it would be as a different person. Because it wasn't just that he no longer had family there that would make any trip to Lancashire strange. He had changed. He knew it. What he had done last night would have been completely beyond him only a few months ago. Losing his parents and coming to America had torn him apart, but he had grown, strengthened in the process. His parents, he felt sure, would be proud of him.

He just wished they could see.

"Look Dad, what I can do," he thought. "Look mum. It looks like a mirror but I can go through it. I can fight monsters too. I even wiped the smile off that chuffin' clown from Blackpool."

He wiped his eyes, grinning, and as he pictured the mayhem of those final moments in the warehouse, Scarlett's parting words came back to him.

"Ask him how he knew your name."

For a moment he had thought she meant Greyling but that wasn't right. Last night he had been thinking about rescuing Mr. Peregrine and had found himself remembering their first meeting in his shop just after Darwen had arrived in Atlanta. They had been talking about the shopkeeper's old clock which said only if it was day or night and was accurate up to about twenty seconds. Darwen had said that he was sure that was good enough but the shopkeeper had turned that odd look of his on him and said, "Never be sure about such things. A lot can happen in twenty seconds, Mr. Arkwright."

But Darwen had not told him his name.

It had struck him as odd at the time but he had forgotten

the moment entirely until last night. He was sure that was what Scarlett had meant, but how had she known about it and why did she think it significant? And what did it mean that Alex had, at least for the time being, become what everyone said was impossible: a *second* Mirroculist? He didn't know why he put those two questions together, but in his gut he knew they were connected, that if he could find out more about what it was to be a squint, he would be able to answer both. When he found the real Mr. Peregrine – and he *would* find him – he would have a lot of questions for the old shopkeeper.

That would have to wait. For now there was the weary journey, which seemed a lot less exciting in this direction, and then getting home and getting clean – properly clean – for the first time in a week, and getting truly dry, and sleeping in his own bed . . .

He smiled again. It might not be home exactly, not yet, but there was a lot to be said for his aunt's Atlantan apartment.

"Now that I'm a Mirroculist," said Alex, "I think I should write a book about it. One day, when I'm famous for saving the world, people will want to know all about my first experience as a squint. I will call it *Alexandra O'Connor and her Mirroculist Mission*."

"What about us?" said Rik.

"You're not a squint," said Alex.

"Thanks. What about Darwen then?"

"*Darwen Arkwright and the Mirroculist Mission*?" said Alex derisively. "That's terrible. Darwen is a ridiculous name. Sorry, but it is. No one is called Darwen. You have to give the reading public something they can relate to."

"I wonder why I can't open the portals," said Rik.

"Maybe it's a race thing," said Alex.

"What?"

"Hey, I'm just saying. I'm black. Darwen is half-black."

"Mixed race," said Darwen.

"Why would race have anything to do with it?" said Rik.

"Maybe because the white folks have enough power already, so we get this," said Alex.

"Right," said Rik, rolling his eyes. "Because you and Chip Whittley are really living on the poverty line."

They reached Hartsfield-Jackson Airport in Atlanta in the late-afternoon and were met by Alex's mom and her baby sister, Kaitlin. They had been delegated to pick up Darwen and Rik, whose father would be coming to collect him from Aunt Honoria's place later. They were all going there.

They said their goodbyes to the other students, then found their way to Mrs. O'Connor's car in the frigid car park, all the while telling her tales of what they had been doing in the jungle and all the things they had seen. Well, some of them. They left out anything to do with Silbrica but that didn't seem to make their adventures any less exciting. Mrs. O'Connor hugged Alex to her at each mention of snakes and spiders and poison dart frogs, punctuating each new detail with a cry of "Oh, my lord!"

They drove through Atlanta's traffic-jammed streets and Darwen was surprised to find the massive city's tower blocks and motorways familiar, even comforting, after his spell in the jungle.

At their apartment building, Darwen, Rik and Alex lugged the bags into the lift under the watchful eye of Mrs. O'Connor and Kaitlin, and rode up to the seventeenth floor. As they got higher, Darwen felt an unease like embarrassment or anxiety, swelling like the pressure in his ears. In many ways, his aunt was still a stranger to him. He didn't want everyone watching his reunion with her. By the time he had dragged his bag out onto their floor, he was feeling distinctly uncomfortable and was beginning to wish Rik and Alex had gone straight home.

But as he reached their apartment door, something remarkable happened. Darwen was muttering vaguely that his aunt didn't normally have company over, when he stopped short, sniffing the air.

It couldn't be.

It was a warm, rich smell of potato and onion cooked slowly with stewing beef, a hearty smell that took him right back into his best, most cherished memories.

Lancashire hotpot.

The door opened before he could knock, and there was aunt Honoria, smiling and a little teary, and wearing – for the first time Darwen had ever seen – an apron which was dusted with flour. She folded him into her arms and, forgetting the others entirely, Darwen embraced her.

"Welcome home," she said.

Acknowledgements

Special thanks to Professor John Hoopes and
Anne Egitto for fielding questions about the archaeology
of Costa Rica and the stone spheres. Thanks also to
my agent Stacey Glick, my editor, Debbie Williams, my
illustrator Manuel Šumberac, designer Becky Chilcott
and all at UCLan publishing, especially MA Publishing
students Abigail Hodge and Amy-Louise Carr. Finally,
thanks to my family who keep me grounded in this
world while helping me invent others.

About the Author

A. J. HARTLEY is the award-winning *New York Times* bestselling author of 20 novels for children, adults and young adults in a variety of genres.

Born and raised in Preston, Lancashire, he lives now with his wife and son in the United States where he is the Robinson Professor of Shakespeare at the University of North Carolina, Charlotte. He is also an Honorary Fellow of the University of Central Lancashire.

You can learn more than you can ever possibly want to know about him at
www.ajhartley.net

About the Illustrator

MANUEL ŠUMBAREC was born in 1988 in Pula, Croatia. He obtained a Masters in Animation and New Media from the Academy of Fine Arts in Zagreb. He is a member of the Filmmakers Association of Croatia.

Manuel works in the fields of animation and illustration to produce animated films, music videos, children's books and book covers. He creates his illustrations using digital techniques combined with traditional media.

He has received numerous awards for his work including an Excellent Prize at the Japan Illustrators' Association Awards and the prestigious Grigor Vitez Award for Best Illustration.

To find out more, visit
www.manuelsumberac.com

Find out what happens to Darwen
next in his third adventure

THE MIRRORS
SHATTERED

Coming 2020!